MAN-KZIN WARS XV

MAN-KZIN WARS XV

Hal Colebatch

Martin L. Shoemaker

Jason Fregeau

Jessica Q. Fox

Brendan DuBois

Brad R. Torgersen

CREATED BY

LARRY NIVEN

BAEN

A Baen Books Original

Baen Publishing Enterprises
P.O. Box 1403
Riverdale, NY 10471
www.baen.com

ISBN: 978-1-4814-8377-3

Cover art by Stephen Hickman

First printing, February 2019

Distributed by Simon & Schuster
1230 Avenue of the Americas
New York, NY 10020

Printed in the United States of America

10 9 8 7 6 5 4 3 2 1

❧ CONTENTS ❧

MAN-KZIN WARS XV

SALES PITCH

by Hal Colebatch

🐾 SALES PITCH 🐾

THE TRADING POST was located on the satellite of a remote dwarf star.

It was well defended with a Jotok garrison. That was a condition which those who the humans would one day call Puppeteers had imposed when it had been built several centuries before.

No Puppeteer had actually set foot there since the garrison was installed. Automatic defenses destroyed any dust or debris—or anything but a recognized and licenced Jotok ship—that drew near.

Although the two races had been trading with one another for centuries, communication had been remote and exclusively electronic.

No Jotok was known to have ever seen a Puppeteer, nor even an accurate image of one of them.

Some thoughtful Jotoki—a few were still interested in such things—had speculated about their appearance, and a variety of theories and guesses had been made.

On the whole, however, the Jotok were content with a steady trade and predictable profits.

At the trading post the puppeteers presented themselves via holograms, they themselves remaining aboard their ship, hanging in space with engines idling some distance off.

The time-lapse in conversations suggested to the Jotok that the Puppeteer ship was at least a few light-minutes away, but this could not be proved—the delay might have been simply to create that impression: If the puppeteers had FTL (one of many things they were reticent about), it might be much further.

Drones counterfeited the signatures of its engines further to forestall the curious.

Several centuries of peaceful and profitable communication since the Puppeteers had allowed the Jotok first to discover them, or rather their holograms, had smoothed relationships. The Puppeteers, however, still did not believe in taking chances.

The hologram images of "themselves" which the Puppeteers projected in their conferences were somewhat edited, but, being an ethical species, they allowed the Jotok to be aware of this. What they really looked like, the Jotok were free to speculate.

It was not that the Puppeteers, however many heads and limbs they had, would necessarily appear strange to the Jotoki—themselves five-armed colonial animals whose adult entities could deploy the considerable resources of five linked brains—but the Puppeteers believed the less personal information anyone had about them, the better.

Their viewing screen showed a Jotok-like figure, but both parties knew without openly saying so that this was probably an artifact.

And, after all, to the Jotok it did not matter exactly what the Puppeteers looked like, or even what they thought, so long as they were convinced that they were an ethical species and honest trading partners.

The Jotok had gradually developed the great virtue of traders: attention to business and disregard for inessentials.

They still had some scientific curiosity but it tended to be directed to strictly practical ends, such as improving their gravity-planer space drives. It was enough that each race knew the other to be trustworthy. Puppeteers' extreme caution had come to be regarded by the Jotoki as a foible.

"You may be interested to know that we are branching into employment agency work," the Puppeteer spokesperson told his Jotok opposite number, Jarmalternovgot (a fragment of their name being derived from each of their entities).

The Jotok waved two of their arms politely. "Indeed? We are surprised you would be interested in anything of such a small scale."

"But this is no small scale. Indeed I am surprised no one in all the planets has thought of it before. We act as an employment agency for races, a broker for races' talents. Indeed, I hope you may, in due course, wish to employ our services in this regard."

"Say on." Jarmalternovgot found they were quite relaxed in the presence of the Puppeteer's image, though they guessed the Puppeteer was analyzing their actions minutely. They did not know that centuries before, when the trading post was being built, the Puppeteers had installed a mild narcotic into its life-system's atmosphere as an aid to that very relaxation. It made trade negotiations easier.

"We know of eighteen races located more-or-less in our vicinity of the spiral arm—that is to say, near enough for STL travel between their planets not to take a prohibitively long time—that have become sapient.

"Some, we know, have had your help in lifting themselves to various levels of science and technology. Except for yourselves, they, of course, all remain unaware of our own existence.

"Six of these have achieved space travel, although not to our own degree of effectiveness. Yours is the greatest of these, with the best drives and a true interstellar trade empire. We like and trust you because we know you have done this peacefully, or very largely so— we were observing you long before our respective races first made contact.

"Most of the spacefaring races," it continued, "have established, or tried to establish, colonies on worlds or planetoids near them."

"Yes, we know of these. Our own trade empire is, as you are aware, quite extensive." Jarmalternovgot wondered between themselves why the Puppeteer was telling them things that were already common knowledge.

"However, virtually no colony world is ideal for its colonizers," the Puppeteer went on. "Some sapients are able to colonize many worlds with the aid of machinery, and with what may be a great expenditure of capital and resources, which I am sure you would rather see them invest in immediately profitable trading."

The Jotoks' attention increased. The Puppeteer was one of the very few non-Jotok beings who could read Jotok body language and noted it.

"However, so often a new world turns out for the colonists to be too hot, too cold, too wet, too dry, too heavy, too light. Life is possible, of course, or there would not be a colony at all, but until some accommodation is made with the new conditions, life for the colonists is often distinctly uncomfortable. Huge amounts of money are often thrown away.

"Sometimes it turns out no adjustment is possible, the difficulties are too great, and the colony dies, with or without the colonizers being evacuated.

"I might again say here that we deeply admire your own race's successful colonizing efforts and also what you have done to lift so many primitive worlds from backwardness and barbarism."

"Obviously successful merchants need wealthy customers," Jarmalternovgot replied. "Yet some of our philosophers have called attention to the fact that the work our people do in raising backward worlds may be seen as indistinguishable from altruism."

"And sometimes your raising of primitive races is done at great cost. Remember the massacre of your people at Qua Effertsion when you tried to outlaw slavery and the sacrifice of intelligent prisoners there? It is something for which we honor you." The Puppeteer's voice was full of warmth, admiration and regret.

"We remember. We did not know you took such an interest in us. But there were other massacres on a dozen other worlds when our policies of spreading peace and prosperity conflicted with primitive taboos."

"Quite. Civilization in the galaxy owes your people a debt which it would be hard to repay.

"But to return to the matter of failed colonies. We and agents of ours have discovered the remains of more than a hundred such failed colonies attempted by various races. From your point of view the markets of a hundred worlds are lost, not to mention potential sources of raw materials which you need.

"The colonies were often undertaken in the first place because the colony worlds were mineral rich—so rich that in some cases that fact blinded the colonizers' judgment as to their real viability.

"Yet when we have examined the history of the various failed colonies, we have come to conclude that another race, with different abilities—different tolerances to gravity, radiation levels, atmospheric composition, native proteins, different norms of heat and cold, and so forth—in many instances might well have colonized them successfully and lived pleasant and affluent lives, or at least altered them to conform with the original discoverers' needs.

"You see how this gave us the idea of an employment agency? Certain races are willing to pay well to have others, better adapted for their colony world, to live on it, tame its extremes, remove hostile life-forms, and eventually perhaps alter it for their tastes. There is nothing small in the financial returns for us, I assure you. Well, that is one aspect of it. There are others. We trade, it might be said, in talents. We have established as a fact that some races are lucky, and that fact can be put to various uses. And we do not fear competition."

That last was certainly something for the Jotok to file away in their brains. If they did not fear competition, they must have a very good reason indeed for not fearing it. A rare hint tending to confirm something which the Jotok Trade Council had long suspected: The Puppeteers possessed a faster-than-light drive. *Well, at least we know about it, now*, they thought.

"That is very interesting, but why tell us? We have no use for such a service. We find needs and supply them. Our technology is the envy of many races. But customers with no needs are as useless to us as customers too poor to buy."

"I might mention," replied the Puppeteer, "that such services and race-talents include military security. That is a line we have been developing recently. Every developed race, surely, has its rogues and outlaws. We have heard reports of piracy in some sections of space... Of course you can defend your own."

"Of course," said the Jotok shortly. Traders as they were, Jotok security was good. Whatever their real feelings, it would have been the most elementary of errors to betray interest at this stage. In any case their brains were quarreling among themselves.

The Puppeteer continued: "But with due respect to your security forces, are such pirates worth the lives of a single Jotoki entity? For every pirate shot fired from a clumsy musket on some backward world five of your brains may die!

"Your lasers and plasma cannon may make short work of spears and gunpowder, even of chemical rockets, yet a shower of spears can destroy the Jotoki technicians setting up a trading post or even a laser point in some wilderness.

"You now can pay others to take risks for you.

"It would make both economic and social sense for others to do the military work. You are wealthy enough to afford it. It's been done in the past, in the history of several worlds, and no one is the worse for it."

Jarmalternovgot considered the matter with all their brains. "There is perhaps something in what you say," they admitted at length. "We encounter primitive and hostile races sometimes, and we sadly have seen our youngsters die before their time, sometimes when they have just joined and are little more than tadpoles. But of course we would need to place such a matter before the full Trade Council."

"I know a world that might supply such a security force," the Puppeteer told them. "An all-round force deployable in many situations. The inhabitants have mostly an iron-age culture, but owing to subtle interventions of our own, some of the more advanced have discovered gunpowder. In fact we have given them a little push in the direction of, eventually, rocketry. Their world has two large moons and several small ones, which will give them something to aim at.

"I think they would fit in well with the technicalities of your trade empire, given a little coaching."

"From what you say, I take it they are fighters?"

"You might say that."

"Then why should we not fear *them*?" A slightly odd question to put to the most cowardly race known. Puppeteers feared *everything*. They were also, however, capable of a certain cold-blooded objectivity. And they had, Jarmalternovgot reflected, built up an empire whose power and extent none of the races they dealt with could even guess at. They must be doing some things right.

"Your technology will always allow you to retain "—the Puppeteer was about to say "the upper hoof" but realized such a metaphor would be both meaningless and perhaps revealing to Jotoki—"a sure advantage."

"May I see one?"

"Certainly." The holo of the pseudo-Jotok disappeared and a new one took its place. The Jotoki backed hastily away, holo or not.

"I think you will agree that it looks capable enough." No one could have told anything different about the synthesized voice, for example that it was being heavily edited to hide the Puppeteer's own terror.

The Puppeteer also omitted to mention that the figure was barely half-size and the fangs and claws had been reduced even further.

"What are they called?"

"Kzin. Means 'Hero.'"

"How would we recruit them?"

"We can perhaps help with advice there. We have much experience in dealing with alien races without showing ourselves. You know it is only because of the exceptional level of trust that we have in you that we have shown ourselves to you to the extent that we have. But you may be sure we have, over a long period of time, evolved protocols for dealing with such situations."

"The negotiations were successful?" The Hindmost Puppeteer asked his negotiator.

"I believe the Jotoki will come to see the value of alien security guards. Expensive pirate activity has increased in several of their sectors, as you are aware."

"And as I directed. It is unfortunate for them."

Had the Puppeteer been capable of pity, it would have felt it for the Jotoki and their fellows then. A benevolent race, even if their trade empire was beginning to impact on the Puppeteers' own. Their loss would be felt in much of the galaxy.

Further, though the Puppeteers had, centuries ago, directed the Jotokis' research and development in the direction of gravity control, a technology which did not compete with the Puppeteers' FTL drive, but which they could make use of in certain areas, some Jotoki scientists had recently embarked on experiments which might eventually lead them to an FTL drive of their own.

Further, some were starting to suspect their science had been deliberately directed away from the possibility of FTL. Whether or not they suspected the Puppeteers of this manipulation yet was uncertain but it was inevitable that, if this suspicion gained ground, it would inevitably fix on the Puppeteers. They were the only species the Jotok knew with science in advance of their own.

It would be easy enough, since that suspicion was planted, to guess why the Puppeteers had interfered with Jotok scientific advancement: FTL would be seen as for what it was, a jealously guarded secret and monopoly.

It was time for the Jotok to go.

Inhibitions could be engineered into the Kzin which, once they had taken over the Jotokis' technology, would activate against further research and development along such lines. If, despite this, they still looked like becoming a threat, they could be taken care of before that threat developed.

More importantly, their trading on often-dangerous worlds meant the Jotoki had kept up good weapons, though with no great enthusiasm for their use, certainly not on a large scale. Like all the other spacefaring races, centuries of peace and prosperity had civilized them too much for that.

Give these barbaric Kzin access to the Jotoki's gravity drives and arsenals, and the next step would have been taken in the Puppeteers' plan: raise the Kzin to technological power—something that they would never achieve on their own—and then raise another race to fight them.

Given no competition, their own arrogance and savagery would develop into fatal handicaps. As a purely warrior race the Kzin, unchallenged, would have certain limitations. Meeting a clever and adaptable foe would broaden and strengthen them. The result, given Puppeteer manipulation, should be, eventually, a race or races capable of handling anything short of the Puppeteers themselves.

The Outsiders, the strange deep-space beings with whom the Puppeteers sometimes traded, had dropped hints of some approaching menace, either from the galactic core, or from further up the spiral arm. In either event, the Puppeteers would have a race or races to meet it without risking their own necks.

"What if these Kzin become a threat to *us*?"

"Your caution is exemplary as ever, Hindmost, but I do not believe such a danger could develop. We will control the situation with our usual indirect methods, and should they become even a potential danger to us, we shall have long-range warning. We can drop their fleet and their homeworld into its own sun."

The Puppeteers had much advanced science, but it was in defensive weaponry, the result of centuries of research, that they excelled. They could move worlds if necessary, expensive though it was, and their spacecraft were invulnerable to everything but antimatter.

"And the second race, the element that mixes with them to make the iron into steel?"

"I have them picked out. They are much less advanced than these Kzin but full of promise. Omnivores, so they should be at least as easy to control. Their brains are comparable to the Kzin, or can be made so by a few subtle interventions.

"They have one oversized moon hanging in their sky at night, which will give them also something to aim at initially, and their system has a belt of mineral-rich asteroids, many of which could be made habitable with work—sufficient incentives to get them into space."

"Their next nearest star—a double or triple system—also has an asteroid belt and a habitable planet, very similar to their own, and will also in due course be a tempting target, but with no intelligent life such as would provide serious competition once they got there.

"They are far enough away from the Kzin for us to reasonably expect that they will have the art of space travel developed somewhat beyond the elementary stage by the time we bring them together."

"And if they never go into space? Or never find the Kzin?"

"Then, sooner or later, the Kzin will find them. They will become the Kzin's slaves and prey, and we will find other ways of controlling them."

"Will they have weapons as good as the Jotoki?"

"Their space travel will be nudged in the direction of reaction drives. I expect them to become quite proficient with those. The Kzin will have something obviously superior in the gravity planer and I think will not proceed with development of reaction drives. But the potential of reaction drives as weapons can be realized very quickly."

"And are they warlike *enough*? Will their warrior instincts survive them developing the degree of co-operation necessary for space flight?"

"Oh, yes. I think they are warlike enough. That I can safely say."

SINGER-OF-TRUTH

by Martin L. Shoemaker

🐾 SINGER-OF-TRUTH 🐾

WHEN COLONEL TOWNE entered her office, Captain Billings rose and saluted.

Towne didn't seem intimidated as she returned the salute. "At ease, captain." Billings relaxed. Standing at attention always worried him that he might come across as aggressive and large, a bad trait in his business. "You're the new head doc?"

"Yes, I am, colonel," Billings said, raising his voice to be heard over the intermittent snarling from a wall speaker, "though the official title is Strategic Psychoanalyst."

"Too many syllables," Towne said. "Head doc is quicker."

Billings found himself liking the colonel. She wasn't just military, she thought for herself. He answered, "Yes, colonel, reporting as ordered."

"Welcome to D0G-7," Towne said. That was the codename for this shabby rock on the fringe of the front: a supply depot, a transfer center, and a field hospital. And now also a POW camp.

"Thank you, colonel," Billings said, "I'd like to get started right away. Specifically I'd like to know what's up with that . . ." He pointed at the wall speaker. "That . . ."

Colonel Towne raised an eyebrow. "Caterwauling?"

Billings grinned in response; but then he dropped the grin. "I forgot," he said. "No grinning around kzinti."

"Not a good idea here. They take grinning as a threat."

"I know, colonel. If I'm going to produce actionable psychoanalysis,

15

I need to win their respect, understand their feelings, and get them to open up."

"Good luck with that," Towne said. "I hope you have better luck with it than Captain Sanchez had."

"Sanchez?" Billings asked.

"The head doc before you."

"Ah," Billings said. "Did Sanchez rotate back home?"

"No. She grinned."

Inside the secure zone, Towne led the way to a security door, where she scanned her badge and pressed her face to an ident mask. A green light appeared over the mask, and the door opened, closing behind her after she walked through.

Billings scanned his badge and pressed his face against the mask. The light lit, and Billings stepped through the door.

"Right this way," Towne said.

Billings saw medical bays with examination tables and instruments. "This is your infirmary. Is the kzin ill?"

"Here he is," Towne said. "You'll see for yourself."

This bay door was closed, with yet another ident mask for access. Towne pressed her face to the mask; and this time, a screen next to it lit up. A face appeared, a man in augmented armor. "Colonel Towne," the man said.

"Yes," she answered. "And also Captain Billings."

"Captain Billings, sir," the guard said, "please identify, sir." Billings pressed his face to the mask, the door slid open, and Towne led Billings into the exam bay. A second guard stood by the exam table; and past him, Billings saw the kzin strapped to the table. He had interviewed many kzinti during his training; but this one . . . Scars . . . Burns . . . So much hair torn out, Billings wasn't sure of its true color.

"What have you done to this kzin?" Billings demanded. Despite his years of psych counseling, some of his old fighting rage came out.

But Towne shook her head. "It wasn't us, captain," she said. "It was them. The kzinti."

"Them?" Billings turned back to the giant, cat-like creature. He was smaller than the average kzin. That was a hazard in a culture driven by status (or *strakh* as they called it). His fur had been shaved in places, revealing stitches.

"We barely got him out alive," Towne said. "The guards had to shock the entire block this time—"

"This time?" Billings asked.

"It was the third attack on him. They really hate him."

"And why?"

"You're the head doc. You tell me."

"What's his title?" Billings asked. Kzinti did not have full Names until they earned them. Any kzin less than an officer rank had only a title; and even most officers had only half-names, indicating that they did not have breeding status.

Towne answered, "He hasn't been very talkative, although sometimes he breaks out in that noise. The others called him simply Exile. He did something to get on the outs with them. That's why he's still in here: next time they might kill him."

The door guard snorted. Colonel Towne turned on him. "You have something to say, Miller?" she asked.

"Colonel, nothing," the guard answered.

"Out with it, Miller." The colonel glared at him.

Miller hesitated. Finally he said, "Colonel, with respect: if they kill him, that will be one less cat in the galaxy."

Billings shook his head at the atavism. Once the psychists—his predecessors—had found ways to train hostility out of the human species. That had almost gotten humanity killed when the kzinti had arrived and launched an immediate war. In the generation since, society had tried to roll back the psychists' changes, to recreate an aggressive sense of self-defense and territoriality. There was constant debate both in government and in psychoanalytics about the right level of aggression; and Billings was never sure on any given day whether they had too gone too far or not enough.

And that was from personal experience. In his youth, Billings had been a fighter, constantly in trouble in the rough neighborhood where he had grown up. Had it not been for the right psychotherapist, Dr. Tanner, he might have ended up dead in the streets—or maybe on the battlefield, slaughtered by kzinti. Instead, he had been so impressed by Tanner that he had followed in his footsteps.

Billings didn't know enough to evaluate this guard. Had the man fought the kzinti? Had he lost companions to them?

Towne, however, was not so forgiving. "Miller, summon your relief. We'll talk later about your attitude towards prisoners."

Billings looked back to the kzin. "Why's he strapped down?"

Colonel Towne explained, "Whenever a prisoner in the infirmary isn't behind a barrier, it must be strapped down."

"Even when he's as badly injured as this?"

"Don't let him fool you," Towne said. "I've seen a kzin with an arm and a foot cut off take out two troopers."

"But this . . ." Billings stared into the kzin's eyes. It looked terrified. Billings crouched near its head, and he spoke in the Hero's Tongue. "Are you well?" The kzin stared at Billings but did not answer. "Do you understand me?"

The kzin closed his eyes. Just then the door chimed, and Colonel Towne went to the security panel. "Miller," she said, "your relief is here. Report to Briggs for punishment duty." Another guard came in, Miller went out, and the door closed behind him.

The kzin stared at the second guard. Its breathing slowed, and it relaxed. Billings realized that it had been tense, ready to fight back, even in the straps. "Did the other guard hurt you?" Billings asked.

Still the kzin said nothing. Maybe if Billings addressed him directly. "Exile, did—"

"My title is not Exile," the kzin interrupted in its own language.

Billings was careful not to show a response. "I am corrected," he said. "Kzin, tell me your title, so that I may address you properly."

The kzin's ears unfurled slightly, a sign that Billings read as interest. "My commander addressed me as Singer-of-Truth."

"Your commander?"

"Yes," the kzin said. "Kchee-Commander. He is dead."

Towne came over to Billings and the kzin. "You spit and yowl well, captain," she said.

Billings shook his head. "I'm still learning," he said in English. "I'll have to gargle tonight, but I'm getting better."

Billings turned back to the kzin and returned to the Hero's Tongue. "Singer-of-Truth . . ." he said. And then a thought occurred. "Earlier, were you singing?"

"I was," the kzin answered. "Until that other one, the Miller . . ."

Billings was surprised by the name. The kzin was a good listener. "Miller did something to you?"

"He made barbaric noises," Singer answered. "And he struck me with fists in those metal gloves. Many times, until I stopped."

"That was wrong," Billings said.

At that, the kzin showed his teeth. "I am Singer-of-Truth! I do not lie."

"No," Billings said, "you were not wrong. He was." He stood, switching to English. "Captain, the kzin reports that Miller beat him into silence."

Colonel Towne turned to the second guard. "Is this true?"

The man swallowed. "Yes, colonel."

"Why didn't you report it, Rayburn? Never mind. Summon your relief. You can go join Miller in my waiting room." Towne turned to Billings. "Tell the prisoner that these men will be punished. Extend my assurance that this will not happen again."

"Yes, colonel." Billings crouched back down by the kzin, snarling, "My commander extends her apologies."

At that, Singer's ears unfurled. "I am uncaste," he said. "Commanders do not apologize to uncaste."

"Human commanders do," Billings replied. "When they have not followed their rules."

"Commanders *make* rules," Singer said.

"We have higher commanders who make these rules," Billings said. "And a good commander ensures that they are followed."

"Humans," Singer said. "Always a mystery. Tell your commander that were I not strapped down, I would bow in proper deference to her generosity. Even if she is female."

Billings turned back to the Colonel. "He says thank you."

"That's an awful lot of yowl for thank you," Towne said.

"I summarized," Billings said with a grin.

Suddenly the kzin spasmed in its restraints, and Billings realized his mistake. He dropped the grin. "Calm, Singer-of-Truth," he said. "No threat was intended."

"The Miller . . ." Singer said. "He threatened often."

Billings answered, "Miller and the other, Rayburn, shall be punished for how they treated you."

"No! I beg the commander not do that to me."

"To you?" Billings asked.

"If they are punished because of me," Singer said, "they will find me. They will probably kill me, strapped down like this."

Billings was sure now that he saw fear in the kzin's eyes. "Do not worry," he said, "I will not allow that to happen."

"*You* will not?" Singer asked. "Are you a sub-commander?"

"I . . . am responsible for your safety."

"Uncaste have no safety. I live at the will of my commander."

Billings looked at the older bruises and cuts. "He did this?"

The kzin's eyes narrowed. "No, he is dead. Killed in the prison. The lesser castes killed him and ate his heart for his failure in battle."

Billings winced. He knew kzin pack dynamics was complicated, but this was new. "But they let you live?"

The kzin closed his eyes. "I am uncaste, the lowest of slaves. I have no *strakh*, so I can have no failures. The losses on the field of battle were not mine. So they let me live, so that I can serve the new commander once he is established."

"But they did this." Billings gestured at the injuries.

"No," Singer said. "That came later. They did not like my singing any more than did Miller."

Billings was intrigued. This might be an insight into kzin thinking. "Singer-of-Truth, would you sing the songs for me?"

Singer's eyes opened wide. "I am uncaste. You do not ask an uncaste. Especially my commander does not ask."

"Your commander?"

"Kchee-Commander is dead," Singer said. "You claim responsibility for my safety. Until someone arrives with a better claim, you are my commander."

"Very well, Singer-of-Truth. Sing to me."

So the kzin sang. Now Billings could make out the words, and a rhythm as well. It would never be popular in human space, but this was music of a sort. And the words . . .

"Gather and hear my song, kzinti heroes. I am Singer-of-Truth, and my songs never lie. But it will be difficult, my song, as you learn of the human heroes.

"They came from far stars, treading the space, the territory that was ours. They came without fear. Without knowing what fear was. And without knowing how to fight. Yet here they are, these Heroic Humans.

"They drew the first blood, with weapons they knew not they had. And though kzinti struck back, they have not relented, these Heroic Humans.

"In but one generation, their slaves became heroes, and fight like kzinti, but better. More victories theirs, more worlds we lose, more ground that is ours. For such is the way when kzinti heroes face our first worthy rivals, these Heroic Humans.

"Come kzinti all, heroes and halfcaste and slaves, to learn this new song. A new sun has risen, a new day red with battle, and the field is not to be ours. Always has it been: *strakh* goes to the victor, so know you their names: These Heroic Humans."

Billings replayed the song from his data pad. He understood now why the other kzinti had attacked Singer: the song was akin to sacrilege to a kzin mind.

Yet to Singer, it was Truth. Singer had an artistic sense of pride in the truth of his work. Billings was convinced of the kzin's intelligence. Singer had to know how the other kzinti would react; yet he had sung the song anyway. The kzinti might not respect that, but Billings did. The brave truth-teller had a long tradition in human cultural history.

Billings was still going over his notes of the day when his phone buzzed. "Captain Billings," he said.

"Captain," a young male voice said from the phone, "this is Lieutenant Handel from Colonel Roth's office. The Colonel has asked me to find out why you haven't checked in yet."

"I signed in this morning, in Colonel Towne's office."

"Oh," Handel said. "That's a problem. I wouldn't say that to Colonel Roth. He expects you in his office immediately. I suggest you have an explanation by the time you get here."

As Billings approached the hospital admin building, a guard stepped forward to block his path. Billings presented his identification badge, but the man shook his head. "I'm sorry, we don't honor that ID here, sir. Please present your travel papers, and then step aside for identity scanning." So Billings went through a full scan again, right down to a check for cyber implants. Only then did the guard open the door.

A young lieutenant met them as they entered. "Captain Billings,

Lieutenant Handel. The Colonel will see you. Now, sir." He led Billings through the outer office and into Roth's.

Handel saluted the colonel behind the desk. "Colonel Roth, Captain Billings, as you ordered."

Billings matched the salute. Roth, a balding bear of a man, did not look up from his computer as he answered, "Dismissed, Handel."

"Captain Billings," Roth said, "my sources tell me that you reported to Towne today."

Billings sensed that Roth was big on protocol: the neatness of the office, his perfectly maintained uniform, and his own bearing all told Billings that the place was *military*. So he held the salute, waiting for it to be acknowledged. "Yes, Colonel, that's where the transport dropped me off."

"Is that an excuse?" Roth asked.

"No, Colonel, just the facts."

At that, Roth looked up, but he still did not return the salute. Billings sensed that there was a dominance game going on, and he would play it out.

"The facts," Roth said, "are that you are a psychoanalyst. Medical personnel serve in the hospital, where I am the commander. You report to me. Is that understood, captain?"

"Colonel," Billings answered, "request permission to drop my salute so that I may show you my transfer orders."

Roth returned the salute, and Billings dropped his, then reached into his pocket and pulled out a transfer chit. "Colonel, I am assigned as a strategic psychoanalyst. I'm not on hospital staff, and I'm not here to treat patients."

"You'll damn well treat patients if I tell you to," Roth said. "Lord knows we have plenty of neurotics out here!"

Billings saw one of the neurotics right before his eyes, but it would be injudicious to say so. "I'll do what I can, colonel. But my direct report is to Strategic Operations, and my operational report is to Colonel Towne. No disrespect intended, colonel, but I have my orders."

"Towne?" Roth dropped the chit into his computer and looked at the screen. "Damn! This isn't what I requested at all. I wanted a therapist for the unit, not another Speaker-to-Cats."

Billings sensed that the colonel really was concerned, so it was time to be conciliatory. "Colonel, may I speak frankly?"

Roth pointed at his office doors. "When those doors are closed, I insist upon it. Tell me what I need to know . . . *especially* if I won't like it." The Colonel smiled, closed-mouthed, and Billings's respect for him grew.

"Colonel," Billings said, "if you have concerns about psychological stress in your unit, then I'll find some time to help . . . as my duties permit."

Roth inclined his head slightly. "I'll be grateful." He rose from behind his desk. "We've gotten off on the wrong foot, captain. Let's put that behind us. Let me show you around the hospital."

Roth led Billings into the hospital proper, starting with the emergency ward. He showed off their equipment, which was good for a field hospital. He also introduced Billings to staff who were sitting around talking, save for two handling a patient.

When Roth saw the patient, he said, "Let me see his chart." A nurse handed him a tablet. "Another training injury, I see. When this man's out of treatment, have him report to me for remedial instruction." Roth led Billings out of the room.

"Training injury?" Billings asked.

"The man let himself get too close to an unsecured prisoner," Roth replied. "We put that down as a training injury, since clearly his training has been defective."

"But then your reports—"

"—aren't worth the electrons they're printed on."

"But why falsify the reports?"

"They're not falsified," Roth said, "they're . . . interpreted."

"Call it what you will, they're false. Why?"

"Captain," Roth said, "I'm a doctor. I am sick of all the bloodshed in this goddamned war. We need people like you to help us find peace somehow. What we *don't* need are more reports to inflame passions that are already near a boil. If humanity engages in wholesale slaughter of the kzinti, well . . . I don't see how that makes us the superior species, just superior butchers. So I paint things in the most positive light, to give peacemakers like you a chance to find a less bloody solution."

Briggs nodded. He sympathized with Roth, and he realized that the man was overcompensating: his strict military demeanor was a big contrast from the humanitarian side he had just revealed. "I understand, colonel," he said.

"That's good," Roth said. "We'll get along just fine."

By the end of the tour, Billings saw his mission in a much more personal light. He had done residency in a rehab clinic on Earth. The most common neurosis had been psychological rejection of transplant limbs. Here . . . Paranoia. Claustrophobia. Phobias of all kinds. And of course, radical ailurophobia.

And more. Obsessive-compulsive disorder. Oppositional defiant disorder. Anger, fear, rebellion . . . Behaviors that had been all but unknown on Earth for centuries were everywhere he turned on D0G-7. He could fill an academic journal here.

But this wasn't academic, it was life or death. For these soldiers, and possibly for humanity as well. Billings was gaining a new respect for the goals of the psychists, if not their methods and results. With troubled minds like these, even if humanity survived the kzinti, would it survive itself?

By the end of the tour, Billings still had not answered two important questions: where was his office? And where were his quarters? He called Lieutenant Handel.

"I'm sorry," the lieutenant said, "I don't have that in my paperwork. That's up to the quartermaster." He gave Billings instructions that led across the parade ground, a big circular lawn in the center of D0G-7. The prison, hospital, and depot were arranged equally around the circle.

When Billings got to the depot, the gate guard glanced at his hospital badge and lifted the gate for him. Billings crossed through and followed a stone walk to the depot admin building.

Another guard stood outside, this time stepping forward to challenge billings. "State your business here, captain."

"I'm here to get my assignments for office and quarters."

"I see. Well, that office is closed for the night. Come back in the morning."

"In the morning? Where do I sleep tonight?"

"Well . . ." The guard smiled. "I have a friend in the office. She might be able to process your order, but that'll take time away from other valuable work. She'd need a reason for that."

"My being without a bunk is the reason."

"No," the guard said. "I mean a financial reason."

Billings felt slow. This had been a long day. The guard was asking for a bribe, for himself and the unnamed friend.

Billings didn't want to get into a conflict. He eyed the guard carefully, and he did a quick estimate. Knowing the man's approximate pay grade, Billings estimated what an hour of the guard's time was worth, and then he doubled that to cover the friend. He forwarded those credits to the man's comp.

From the way the man's eyes lit up, Billings knew that he had overestimated. The signs were obvious to Billings: the upturn in the man's grin, the widened eyes, the quickening of breath. Billings would have to recalibrate his scale of graft on D0G-7. He didn't want to be seen as an easy mark. The guard opened the door, and Billings walked through to the quartermaster's office.

The first thing Billings saw was a counter, and beyond it a bullpen full of unoccupied desks. A woman stood behind the counter, a short, dusky-skinned corporal with a bored look on her face. "Captain Billings?" she said.

"Yes," he answered. "I'm here for my room assignments."

"You know, you're after-hours," she said. "You're cutting into my personal time. I *like* my personal time."

"I'm sorry, Corporal . . ." Billings checked her ID. "Nitay. I thought the door guard had cleared that up."

Nitay shook her head. "He cleared up *his* time," she said. "Doesn't do a thing for mine."

Now Billings felt like an easy mark; but what could he do? It's not like he could tell Colonel Kane that his soldiers wouldn't stay bribed. So he forwarded another payment to Nitay's account, roughly two-thirds of what he had already paid.

Nitay looked at her new credit balance, and she sighed. "All right," she said, "I'll see what I have open. We've got some spaces reserved for visiting dignitaries. Let me see . . . It looks like I can get you an office on the north side of Depot Town. And a bunk in visiting quarters on the south side."

"A bunk?" Billings said.

"It's all I have," she answered. "At least what I've been able to find so far . . ." The pause stretched out, and Billings realized that she was holding out for more money.

"I was really hoping something in the hospital," he said. "Or maybe the detention compound."

"Are you sure?" Nitay asked. She looked up at him and smiled broadly. "A big guy like you could have a lot of fun in Depot Town."

Billings studied Nitay's face to assess what her interest might be; but she was unreadable. "No, I really think it's best if I'm in the compound. Is there any way . . .?" He pushed more credits to her account.

"Well," Nitay said, "I suppose it could be argued that you're a visiting dignitary . . . Here." She handed him a pad showing a virtual tour of a combination quarters and office. "I think I can make this available," she continued. "Of course, if a general or a UN rep shows up, I'll have to bump you."

"I understand," Billings said. "Where's this located?"

Nitay tapped the pad, and a map zoomed in on the POW compound. "Right here, just off officer country in the camp."

"Perfect!" Billings said. "Thank you, corporal, that will do nicely. I've had a long day, I can't wait to hit the sack."

"All right," Nitay said, tapping some keys on her console. "It's done. You can hit the sack. And if you want some company . . ."

This time, Billings had no trouble making out her intentions. He smiled as he answered, "That sounds . . . pleasant, corporal, but I really do need my sleep."

Billings woke the next day, startled to find himself in new, strange quarters. He hadn't slept well, his dreams troubled by the events of the day before. He had to remind himself: he had a mission here, and it didn't involve resolving the psychological dynamics of D0G-7.

But he really wasn't sure. Maybe those dynamics were part of the problem. He went into his office. The situational psychoses he observed concerned him: Towne with her nervous worry over the prisoners, Roth with his fears for the wounded, and Kane with his little fiefdom. Strategic Ops may have missed a key point in his mission: it wasn't enough to persuade kzinti to offer surrender; they would have to persuade humans to accept it as well. Was the situation on D0G-7 ordinary? Was it repeating at many bases across human space? Were the neuroses a product of the stress? Or something more basic, a product of unleashing humanity's aggression?

But in the meantime, there was one more faction Billings needed to talk with, the most important faction for his mission: kzinti. For that, he would have to go out into the yard. And that meant he would need muscle.

The yard was a large force-fenced area to the northeast of the prison. A healthy kzin needed to spend much of the day outdoors, with open sky above. They sublimated that urge during space travel, but it was always there. Kzinti became violent toward each other when confined to barracks. Singer-of-Truth wasn't the only one to be attacked while in captivity.

So Billings stood in the training center, learning the rules for entering the yard. The instructor, Sergeant Cole, showed him how to strap on excursion armor and how to walk about in it. Cole also checked Billings's accuracy with a side arm, and frowned when he saw the results. "Captain," he said, "I don't think you could hit a sleeping kzin."

"I wasn't hired for my marksmanship, sergeant." The fights of Billings's youth had been unarmed, mostly. He'd never learned to shoot, and had scored poorly in training.

"Captain. On a battlefield, you wouldn't last two minutes even as big as you are, I'm sorry to say."

Billings looked down at the sleek metal shell that encased him. It was fluorescent green, so that you couldn't miss it in the brush. It made him stand a good five centimeters taller, and he felt larger in all dimensions. Yet at the same time, servos within made him feel almost graceful inside it. "Two minutes?" Cole nodded. "And how will I do in the compound?"

"Five minutes, captain," Cole said. "I'll have to come with you, and another escort as well."

"Sergeant, I need the kzinti to open up to me. To trust me. Bringing my own enforcer squad is no way to accomplish that."

"Neither is dying, captain," Cole said. "I'm responsible for your safety. You have your mission, and I have mine."

Billings conceded to Cole. Sergeant North suited up as well, and the three of them went into the compound.

"Look over there," Cole said. "Those buildings detached from our compound are the barracks. There are tunnels to them from our buildings. That gives us a controlled access route. We used to lock the tunnel doors, but now the colonel says to give the cats free reign. They can be anywhere out here, so watch your step. And watch for any alert on your heads-up."

North added, "Captain, if you see an alert, I recommend fetal position. It's undignified, but in that position, these suits are like tanks. The suit'll sense your defensive maneuver, and it'll pull together into a shell even kzin muscles can't pull apart. If you were better with a gun . . ."

"I'm not," Billings replied, "but I think I can turtle."

The reddish native brush was not exactly trees. It had broad canopies, like the leaves of trees, but no large trunks. Instead it had stalks, like giant bamboo; and the canopy was a broadening of the stalks near the top.

As the trio approached one thicket of stalks, Cole held up his hand for them to stop. "North . . ." he said quietly.

"On it," North replied, and he turned to look behind them, scanning with eyes and sensors.

Cole kept his eyes focused on the thicket. "Prisoner, come out and identify yourself."

Billings's heads-up sensors picked out movement, and his thermal sensors lit up. A fuzzy outline appeared as a kzin stepped out from behind the stalks.

"I . . . Guard-scout," the kzin said.

Cole shook his head. "North, what do you see?"

North answered, "Two more watching from behind blinds."

"That's against regulations," Cole said to the kzin.

The kzin answered simply, "I Guard-Scout."

"Damn," Cole said. "Some of them speak English, most of them don't. And it's hard to tell which is which."

"Sergeant," Billings said, "let me talk to him." He turned to the kzin. "I see you," he said in the Hero's Tongue. "I am Captain Ted Billings of the human military."

"I see you," the kzin answered. I am "Scout-of-Guards, servant of Kzaii-Commander."

Billings glanced over at Cole. "Scout-of-Guards, these are my guards. They are concerned that your companions have violated regulations. It is not permitted to build blinds. And your pride-mates should not hide behind them."

Scout-of-Guards waved toward the blinds, and the other two kzinti came out. "We do not answer to human regulations," he said. "We answer to Kzaii-Commander."

Billings frowned. Frowning was safe in front of kzinti. Scout's behavior didn't seem like simple defiance, more like a reasoned position. "Scout-of-Guards," Billings said, "you understand that prisoners are supposed to follow regulations?"

"We understand that uncaste and lower officers must obey the commander, and that Kzaii-Commander has ordered us to prepare for battle with Hrung-Captain."

"Hrung-Captain?" Billings asked.

"A rebel who seeks to rule this compound. We do not hide from humans, but from renegades. That is why I have this post: when guards come, I can assure them that we are not hunting . . . *them*."

"So you wanted to get caught?"

"If I didn't, you would not have caught me."

Billings kept his eyes on Scout as he switched to English. "They're expecting an attack from other kzinti. We're not their targets, but we could get caught up in something ugly. Keep your eyes open." He switched back to the Hero's Tongue. "Scout-of-Guards, take me to Kzaii-Commander. I will speak with him."

The kzin turned and gestured to follow him. "Gentlemen," Billings said in English, "we're off to meet the Kzaii-Commander."

The guards followed Billings, North scanning behind as Cole scanned ahead. The track through the brush was difficult for Billings to pick out. He'd grown up in the massive urban district of Greater Rapids, and his only experience with wilderness had been well-groomed parks. But Scout had little difficulty finding the track, and he pointed out places for Billings to avoid obstacles. The going was slow, but steady.

When the attack happened, it was so fast that Billings almost missed it. Scout snarled "Down!" as he dove to his left, behind a cluster of stalks. At the same instant, a large blur of orange and white fur flew through the space where Scout had stood. Another blur rushed toward Billings, and he remembered his promise to Cole: he dropped into a turtle crouch. The joints of his armor stiffened, and the shell expanded.

Suit sensors indicated a pitched battle around him: snarls in the

Hero's Tongue, cries of pain, and sounds of Cole's and North's high-powered pulse guns blasting several times.

And just that quickly, it was over. "Captain Billings," Cole said over the comm, "you can relax."

"No, I can't," Billings answered. "You never told me how to unturtle."

Cole laughed. "Just say your identity code to the suit, sir, and then 'Unlock.'"

Billings did, and his suit returned to normal mode. He straightened up and looked around. Two kzinti lay on the ground, their striped fur marred by burns. "Are they . . ."

"Yes, sir," North said. "Two less cats to worry about."

North's cynical tone bothered Billings, but he'd analyze that later. He switched to the Hero's Tongue. "Scout-of-Guards?"

Scout appeared from behind the stalks. His claws were still extended, but he drew them in when he looked at Cole and the man's rifle. His arms and his left shoulder bore fresh scars from other claws. His mouth dripped red with blood. "I prevail," Scout answered. "Hrung-Captain's slave will not bother us again."

"Damn it!" Billings swore in English. Then he hissed, "Scout-of-Guards, if you kzinti keep this up, we will have no one left to guard."

"Discipline must be maintained," Scout answered. "Even the lowest uncaste know that."

Billings thought. "Even Singer-of-Truth?"

Scout's eyes grew narrow, and his lips parted, showing the blood. "I do not speak of exiles." He turned back to the trail.

Eventually Billings saw a clearing ahead. Scout held up a hand to stop the humans, and then he growled to unseen listeners. "Scout-of-Guards reports to Kzaii-Commander with human Captain Ted Billings, who would speak with the commander."

From somewhere unseen, a voice answered, "Scout-of-Guards, your charges must wait. We are consulting with Kzaii-Commander."

Billings answered, "We will wait." He spoke in the Hero's Tongue. He didn't want Kzaii-Commander to think that Billings was keeping secrets from them.

Soon the voice spoke again. "Kzaii-Commander would speak with Captain Ted Billings. Bring him and his slaves forward."

Scout led them into the clearing, where a large kzin with black and reddish stripes sat upon a pallet of stalks. Around the pallet stood five kzinti, poised and ready for trouble.

Scout led forward, and he crouched down at the pallet, bowing his head. "As you requested, Kzaii-Commander. The humans."

Kzaii-Commander looked at the spots of blood and the claw marks on Scout's arms. "There was a fight?"

"Yes, Kzaii-Commander," Scout said. "Some of Hrung-Captain's slaves. With the help of these humans, we slew them all."

Kzaii-Commander looked at his paw, flexing his claws out and back in. "Such a waste of good warriors," he said.

"I agree, Kzaii-Commander," Billings said.

The kzin looked up at Billings. "You are Captain Ted Billings? It is you who badly speaks the Hero's Tongue?"

"Yes," Billings answered. "I can attest that Scout-of-Guards reacted swiftly, evading an ambush while warning me away."

The commander turned back to Scout. "I would expect no less," he said. "It is as I ordered: no human is to be harmed . . . unless at my command, of course. The human guards, with their temporary advantage in armor and weapons—" He glared at Cole and North "—wreak terrible vengeance for any assault upon a human. The cost in heroes is higher than we can bear. We will attack when I think conditions merit, not before."

Billings didn't know whether to be terrified or amused. Kzaii-Commander's blunt reply about some future attack wasn't boasting, that was just the way kzinti thought. It wasn't even that different from human soldiers: they had drilled into them that if taken prisoner, their first responsibility was to escape. Humans were just more discreet about it.

But the kzinti . . . "And Hrung-Captain disagrees with your position?" he asked.

Kzaii-Commander answered, "Hrung-Captain wants to continue the fight until one side or the other is dead. He thinks that biding our time here in your prison is a sign of weakness. He says he can feel his *strakh* draining away.

"And so he challenged me," Kzaii-Commander continued. "He styles himself Hrung-Commander! He has gathered kzinti who share his mad plan, and made camp elsewhere in this compound."

"So he thinks to escape?" Billings asked. "Or to revolt against the guards?"

"No, human," Kzaii-Commander answered. "First he seeks to defeat me, humiliate me, and finally eat my heart. Just as I ate the heart of Kchee-Commander after the defeat of our unit by the human forces. I called him out, I told him he had no *strakh*, and I attacked. The battle was short; and at the end, I stood over his bloodied body, his heart on my claws."

Billings shook his head. "But if you're worried about losing kzinti, why would you kill one of your own?"

"Because he was weak," the commander answered. "Defeated. Had lost all *strakh*. It was right that I should command, but no kzinti would follow me if I had not proven myself worthy."

Billings frowned inwardly. Everything Kzaii-Commander said made sense according to kzin psychology, but Billings was still learning to think that way. And until he did, he couldn't possibly succeed in his mission. Kzinti wouldn't surrender to each other, how could he expect them to surrender to humans?

"Kzaii-Commander," Billings said, "does Hrung-Captain have to die to satisfy your *strakh*?"

"I do not need his death," the commander replied, "just his obedience. But that would cost him too much *strakh*."

Billings reached to scratch his head, then realized that was ridiculous in the excursion armor. "So you deposed Kchee-Commander because he lost *strakh* by losing to humans in battle."

"Yes."

"And Hrung-Captain has challenged your own *strakh*, even though it was you who slew Kchee-Commander."

"A number of us banded together. The commander had his loyal officers. Deposing him was more than any one kzin could do."

"And Hrung-Captain . . . He was one of your accomplices?"

"Yes, he was. But then he was supposed to submit to me!"

Billings was getting a clearer picture. "Help me further, Kzaii-Commander. On Kzin, would you expect Hrung-Captain to submit to you? Would you kill him if he did not?"

"There are rules," the commander said. "The high castes do not want our forces depleted of heroes we may need in battle. When there is a dispute over *strakh*, the Patriarch or his advisors determine the settlement. One remains, while the other is exiled to a new territory where he may prove his *strakh* anew."

"Exiled?" Billings asked. "Like Singer-of-Truth?"

Kzaii-Commander opened his lips partly, showing his teeth. "There is none by that title. Do not speak of him again. The exile is fortunate to live."

Billings filed that away. Singer was a sore subject. He almost apologized, but that was a sign of weakness among kzinti.

And then Billings had a thought. "Kzaii-Commander, you have not killed me. Why is that?"

Again the commander showed his teeth. "If you wish, I can oblige." But then he looked away. "It is not easy, Captain Ted Billings, to be a prisoner. I would kill you if I could, for the *strakh* that I would earn. But kzinti are not foolish. The reprisals would be horrible. You humans, fully armed and armored, versus those kzinti who remain in this prison? We would have glorious deaths, but we would have no survivors. It would not serve the purposes of the Patriarch."

Billings nodded. "So you acknowledge that we humans are in a position of superior authority here." Billings chose his words carefully. Superior authority, not superiority. He wanted the kzin thinking about chain of command, not *strakh*.

Kzaii-Commander glared at Billings. "I will not use those words. But you are not wrong."

"And Kzaii-Commander," Billings continued, "I have the highest *strakh* of any human on this planet."

"A boastful claim," the commander answered. "Why should I believe it?"

"Do you speak the human tongue?"

"Enough," the commander said.

Billings looked aside at Cole, and he said in English, "Sergeant, did you try to keep me from entering this compound?"

Billings was pleased that Cole did not miss a beat before answering. "Yes, Captain, I did."

"And did I obey you?"

"No, you did not."

In passable English, Kzaii-Commander responded, "I can read human ranks, Captain Ted billings. You outrank the one called Cole by several levels in your hierarchy."

Billings nodded. "I do. Sergeant Cole, why did you try to keep me out?"

"Orders from Colonel Towne, captain," Cole replied. "She told me to talk you out of it."

"Did she also tell you that she had already ordered me not to go in? And that I had chosen to ignore her order?"

"Yes, she did, captain."

Billings turned back to Kzaii-Commander. "You know the rank of a colonel compared to a captain?"

"Yes," the commander answered, "two ranks higher. But she is a female!"

Before Billings could respond, Cole said, "Commander, that doesn't matter to her. Doesn't matter in our forces at all. Colonel Towne is one tough hero, sir."

"With plenty of *strakh*?" Billings asked.

Cole answered, "I'm still not sure I understand *strakh*, Captain, but yes. I would say she is full of *strakh*."

Billings returned to the Hero's Tongue. "Humans have many kinds of *strakh*. Some comes from our place in the hierarchy, but some comes with our mission, delegated to us by our commanders. I answer to what you might call the Patriarch's Council. They have given me a mission that gives me more *strakh* than Colonel Towne or anyone else on this planet. In the pursuit of my mission, I do what I choose."

Kzaii-Commander thought on this. "This is a strange, complicated concept," he said. "How do you know whom you may order and to whom you must submit?"

"Mastering those rules can take a lifetime," Billings said.

"But I speak truth: I am in charge of your fate. I could declare that discussion with you is pointless, and every kzin here would be put to death." It was an exaggeration, Billings thought, but not without truth. If he reported that surrender was not a possibility, then there were those in Strategic Ops who would argue for eliminating the kzinti as a threat, once and for all.

"But I do not do this," Billings continued. "I do not give up hope for my mission. But there are lesser punishments I could deal out. I could have you bound. I could have you beaten." He never would, but . . . "And I could have you . . . exiled."

Kzaii-Commander half rose; but just that quickly, Cole's rifle raised. "Be calm," Billings said, waving the kzin to sit back down. "I did not say I *would*, only that I *could*."

"So you claim the privileges of Patriarch's Council," Kzaii-Commander answered.

"I do. And as such, I command you to teach me. Is there another alternative to death or exile?"

"Sometimes . . ." the commander said. "Sometimes there is not a question of *strakh*, of who was right or wrong. There is only a question of equitable division of what was earned by many."

"Is this not a question of equitable division?"

"No!" the commander snarled. "I planned the removal of Kchee-Commander. I have the right to command here."

"You have the right to command *here* . . ." Billings said. He pulled out his pad and pulled up a map of the compound. He traced a ravine that cut through it, and then he pointed at the territory on the other side of it. "But what about *there*?"

Captain Billings found himself back in the quartermaster's office. Once again, Nitay waited on him.

Colonel Towne had reluctantly agreed to the partition plan, but she had raised a practical objection: the camp had no more force towers with which to construct a fence between the territories. Without a fence, border conflicts between the two kzin factions were inevitable.

So Billings decided to talk to Colonel Kane about requisitioning towers. "Look," he said to Nitay, pointing at his pad, "the manifest says there are towers in storage."

Nitay pointed back at her own tablet. "And my inventory says there aren't any."

"But that has to be wrong," Billings said. "These manifests were checked both at the source and at delivery. Sixty force towers don't just disappear."

"Are you questioning Colonel Kane's inventory?"

"No, but . . . Can I speak to the colonel? Maybe there's something you've overlooked."

"The Colonel's not in," she said.

"Not in? But I came early this time." Billings waved at all the desks, filled with workers.

Nitay look and nodded. "Yes, we're open now, but that doesn't mean the colonel's in. He has business elsewhere."

"Elsewhere? Where is there to go? Where could he be?"

Nitay leaned over the counter, and she gestured for Billings to lean in as well. "Look," she whispered, "I like you. It doesn't do to get on Colonel Kane's bad side. He can make things difficult for you, and you don't have enough money to buy your way out of that. I wouldn't question the inventory."

Billings chewed over the warning. "This is important," he said. "I have to talk to the colonel. Where can I find him?"

"Well," Nitay said, "it's heading towards lunch. You'll probably find him at the motor pool."

"The motor pool?"

"I told you," she said, "we have fun in Depot Town."

The motor pool was surprisingly hard to find. It seemed like half the crates on D0G-7 had been arranged as walls to block it in. As he got closer, Billings heard a dull rumble that soon resolved into many shouting voices.

Billings turned a corner between the crates, and he found his way blocked by a portable barricade with two guards behind it. "You have business here, Captain?" the female guard asked.

"I've . . . come to see Colonel Kane," Billings said.

"Colonel Kane is not expecting visitors."

"I know," Billings said, "but this is important."

"Important?" the guard said.

Billings sighed. He was learning how things worked in Depot Town. He pushed some credits to the guard's account, and she let him through. As she pulled the barricade back in place behind him, Billings asked, "And where do I find the colonel?"

"Just keep going," she answered. "You can't miss him."

Billings turned the corner, and the noise became a wall of sound: shouts and jeers, with an occasional heavy thud. Ahead of him was a large crowd, craning to see past each other.

Billings couldn't see through the crowd. Then he looked behind himself, and he saw that crates had been rearranged as seating. They were half-full of cheering onlookers, but there was room for Billings. He made his way up until he could see over the crowd, and then he turned around.

In a clearing, stanchions with ropes marked off a square. Two soldiers fought, bareknuckle boxing. Both men were bruised. The shorter man's cheek was split. The other had a line of blood running from the corner of his mouth.

Billings didn't need to wonder whether Colonel Kane knew what was going on in his base. On the far edge of the ring, he saw a raised dais, with a big office chair on top of it. And the man sitting in that chair could only be Colonel Kane.

Billings worked his way back down to the ground level and then squeezed around the edge of the crowd. He'd gone maybe fifteen meters when the crowd suddenly grew quiet, and he heard the thud of a body hitting the ground. The crowd went wild with cheers and boos. This continued for over a minute as Billings worked his way around; but then suddenly the crowd packed in on him, and he was pushed up against the wall. Soon he saw why: the crowd parted to let two strong troopers come through, carrying the unconscious form of the taller boxer.

As the men passed, Billings quickly crossed the gap they left behind. No one looked as he made his way to the dais; but when he got there, a guard put a hand on his chest. "Where you going, captain?"

"I need to see Colonel Kane."

"I heard that rumor," the man said. "My orders are nobody disturbs the colonel when he's enjoying a good fight."

Billings looked back through the crowd. "It doesn't look like there's a fight right now."

"Ah, officers," the man said. "Think you're so smart."

"Look," Billings said, "I need to see the colonel. How much will it cost me?"

"You don't have that much," the man said. "For the right price, I can ask."

And so it was that a much poorer Billings stood at the dais next to Colonel Kane. Depot Town was expensive: in two days, Billings had burned through his credit allotment for the week.

Kane was a short, thin officer with a prominent nose and a menacing look in his eyes. Those eyes glanced quickly about, completing his raptor-like appearance. Billings imagined the man swooping down on unsuspecting prey . . . though from the way things ran in Depot town, the man was probably after the prey's wallet.

"I'm told you have business with me," the colonel said.

Billings could see how this was going to go. Colonel Kane had his own little empire here on D0G-7, and he expected you to bow down and kiss his ring to get anything done. "Colonel," Billings said, "I need to talk you about force towers."

Kane looked up. "You need force towers?"

"Yes," Billings said, "I need to set up a—"

Kane held up a hand. "No explanation necessary, captain. You need force towers, and somewhere here . . ." Kane looked around at all the crates. ". . . I may just have some. For the right price."

"Colonel," Billings said, "you have sixty of them, and they're military property. The military needs them."

Kane laughed, showing a wide set of teeth that would've likely gotten him killed back in the compound. "Where there's need, there's price, my boy," Kane said.

"Colonel, you're not doing anything with them."

"No," Kane answered, "but if these towers are valuable to you, that makes them valuable to me."

"Colonel, we need them to stop the kzinti from slaughtering each other."

"Ah . . ." Kane said. "An appeal to my humanitarian side . . . Don't waste your breath. The way I see it, the cats are all gonna end up dead anyway. It's them or us. I don't care if they do the job or we do. Hell, it's a better bargain for us if they do."

Billings found himself really disliking Kane. That feeling was clouding his objectivity, which only added to his annoyance. He took a deep breath and tried again. "All right, colonel, what's it going to take to get those towers?"

Kane looked him up and down. "You don't have that much," the colonel said. "I know your pay scale."

"No," Billings said, "I mean what's it going to take? Who do I have to get in Strategic Ops to order you to release them?"

Again Kane laughed. "Strategic Ops doesn't give a shit about my little operation. This is a little backwater of the big war, and they just want it to run smoothly. I keep it smooth. Greased, even. Plus I've got friends at ops who are greased."

That shocked Billings. Humanity's future was at stake, and yet someone in Ops was willing to take bribes?

But at the same time, he saw Kane's point. Ops wanted to keep the war machine running and the kzinti at bay. They needed troops at bases like this, and lots of them. Maybe it made sense to tolerate a few "overhead" charges to keep the base running.

He looked around. "You have a sweet set up here, colonel."

Kane answered, "What a delightful line! Straight out of an old tough guy film. That's always the prelude to a threat, isn't it? What? You're going to have me inspected? Inspectors are cheap to buy off. Really, what threat can you offer?"

Billings knew his answer, but it depended on his judgment of Kane's lackeys. How loyal were they? Only one way to find out. Billings opened his pad. "This is strategic Psychoanalyst Captain Ted Billings. Report on Colonel Seth Kane. I see signs of severe stress, near the breaking point. I may recommend immediate psychological discharge and rotation back to Earth."

Kane's mouth gaped. "You wouldn't."

"It'd be a shame to give all this up, colonel." Billings looked at the men who hovered close beside him. "I wouldn't try it, gentlemen. Anything that happens will be picked up and recorded. You don't want assaulting an officer on your records."

Kane stared at Billings and then waved his men away. "You wouldn't dare."

"In an instant," Billings said, "but I'd rather not. I'd rather find a way that we can all get along on this planet. Surely there must be some way to see clear to release those towers. It's not like you've invested any actual money in them . . ."

"No," Kane said, "but there's a principle here. I can't have people see me as some sort of . . . charity . . ."

"Then perhaps some sort of token payment . . ."

Kane frowned. "Let me think on that." Then his eyes lit up. "I know what I'd like to see."

"Oh?"

Kane pointed toward a new boxing match in the makeshift ring. "I'd like to see a couple of cats in there."

"You want to see kzinti fighting?"

"No," Kane said. "I want to see humans fighting kzinti."

"That's ridiculous!" Billings said. "kzinti are too big. No human would have a chance in a fair fight."

"Who said anything about a fair fight?" Kane said. He grinned; and for the first time, Billings saw a grin the way kzinti saw it. It was predatory, humorless. A threat.

"Not a chance, colonel," Billings replied. "If that's your price, then no deal. Think of something else."

"Oh, I will," the colonel said, the grin fading away quickly. "Come by and see me tomorrow morning in my office. We can discuss this privately. I'll name my price then."

There was nothing more that Billings could do about the partition that day, so he turned his mind to his side project: Singer-of-Truth. He navigated the multiple scans to get to the prison ward, only to find out that Singer was no longer there.

"Where's the prisoner?" he asked the nearest guard.

"Sir, he was transferred out."

"Transferred? To where?"

"Sir, you'd have to check with Colonel Towne."

Billings punched up Briggs on the comm. "Lieutenant, I need to speak to the colonel right away."

Billings saw stress in Briggs's eyes. "Sir, she had no choice in the matter, sir. She got orders from Strategic Ops, sir. Somehow they heard a rumor that she was giving special treatment to a prisoner, that made her look bad. Sir, she had to transfer the prisoner back to the compound, sir."

"Shit!" As Billings ran towards the compound access, he wondered how that rumor had gotten to Strategic Ops. Roth couldn't be that vindictive, could he? Or was Kane flexing his muscle to show Billings what he could do?

Billings got to the compound just in time to see North firing as a squad retreated back to the entrance. They pulled a repulsor sled with them. Singer's bloodied body lay upon it.

They didn't bother with straps to hold Singer down as Colonel Roth performed surgery. The kzin was heavily sedated, and too injured to be a threat even if he were conscious.

Roth and three assistants performed the surgery, while Towne and Billings watched on a monitor. In a ritual older than human spaceflight, Roth asked for instruments and uttered commands, and his team functioned as extra hands and eyes for him. This was a rare sight in the era of auto docs and transplant limbs, but D0G-7 didn't have any kzin auto docs.

Finally, Roth stepped back from the table and pulled off his surgical mask. "If there's a more idiotic way to learn kzin anatomy," he said, "I can't imagine what it is." He looked at the monitor. "But I think he'll live, colonel. For an uncaste, he sure is one tough kzin, surviving this twice."

From the bitter tone in Roth's voice, Billings knew the man had had nothing to do with turning Singer out into the compound. And the distraught look on Towne's face said it hadn't been her, either. That eliminated two of the three obvious suspects, Billings thought; but it didn't have to be anyone obvious. There were damn few humans here who had any sympathy for kzinti.

Towne said, "All right, can we strap him down now?"

"Great balls, woman!" Roth answered. "He's unconscious. Can't you leave him be?"

"You just said it, colonel," Towne answered. "We still don't know a lot about kzin physiology. Unless you can guarantee me how long he'll be out, I need him strapped. Now."

"All right," Roth said. "Let my team get out of here. We should've brought him to the hospital. We're better equipped."

"But your security wouldn't be up to holding a kzin," Towne answered as Roth exited the ward room. Then she nodded to the guards. "Strap him down." And then in a softer voice, "But be careful of the sutures and the IVs. He's been through enough."

"Colonel," Billings said. Roth and Towne both looked at him. "Colonel Towne, can I stay with the patient?"

Town studied his face. "What about your mission, captain?"

"This is part of that mission, colonel," Billings said. "I want to be here when Singer wakes up."

Singer slept more than four hours, giving Billings plenty of time to go over his notes on the forces at play on D0G-7. Most of them were aboveboard, easily identified: Kane's greed, Roth's compassion, Towne's concern, Towne and Roth's rivalry, Kzaii and Hrung's rivalry, and seemingly everyone's contempt for Singer—and maybe for Billings himself. He didn't seem to be scoring a lot of points with anybody.

Then there were more general forces: discontent, boredom, greed, and hatred for the enemy. These were subject to different analytical techniques. A group had more inertia and was easier to predict than an individual; but when a group turned, it could turn quickly and catch you up in a sudden shift.

Billings was still trying to identify plausible goals for the different parties in his analysis, when Singer started to cough. Alarms chimed. Billings looked at the kzin just his eyes opened. "Captain Ted Billings," Singer said in the Hero's Tongue.

"It's good to hear your voice, Singer-of-Truth."

"Captain Ted Billings," Singer repeated, "it is not proper for my commander to speak that way to me. I am beneath your concern."

"Proper for humans and proper for kzinti are not the same."

"I begin to understand that," Singer agreed, "but it is a complicated truth. I am still studying it."

"Studying it?" Billings asked.

"Yes," Singer replied. "To sing the truth, I must know it. That means I must understand it. And there are many sorts of truth. Do not humans know this as well?"

"I think so," Billings answered. "But I want to be sure. Tell me of your different kinds of truth."

"There are many," Singer said. "First is truth as measured. Facts that any uncaste can measure with accuracy."

"Understood," Billings said.

"Then there are complex facts which can still be measured. These require special skill to determine. Such as the speed at which light passes from prey to hunter. This is a constant which may be measured by those of the technician caste."

Billings nodded. He hadn't expected a science lecture.

Singer continued, "And then there is truth of *strakh*. Truth which is only true because all agree on it. If all disagreed, it would no longer be true. *Strakh* itself is one of these, of course. If the hero fails, but no one knows that, he loses no *strakh* . . . at least not if he can conceal his shame."

"So *strakh* is truth, but only as perceived by others," Billings said.

"Yes. There are many such social truths which change over time. The best size of a pride, for example, varies depending on how rich the world is on which the pride lives. When food is scarce, large prides are considered an insult to other kzinti."

Billings nodded, and Singer continued, "And there is the truth that is personal. What one kzinti knows, even if no one else does. In his heart, he knows it to be true. But others may reject it, especially if it runs counter to a social truth."

"And that is the nature of your ballads?" Billings asked. "That is what got you into trouble?"

"Yes, Captain Ted Billings. I have seen the truth: humans will win this war as they won so many other battles before. It is in your nature to change the rules until you find rules that work to your advantage. It is in our nature to cling to traditions. True innovation is rare. Humans found your own way into space. We had to take spaceflight from our conquerors."

"But we didn't invent hyperspace," Billings said.

"I know," Singer said. "We have similarities. But still . . . You adapt in ways we cannot. And that will be our defeat."

"And that is why the kzinti attacked you again?"

"No, not this time," Singer said. "Your Colonel Towne advised me to use a human word, discretion. She said it was . . ."

"The better part of valor," Billings completed the quote. "But then which faction attacked you? Kzaii-Commander or Hrung-Captain? And why?"

"It was both," Singer said. "First Kzaii-Commander; and then when I fled his territory, Hrung-Commander. By then I was so weak, I could flee no more. Had your guards not rescued me, Hrung-Commander would be eating my heart right now."

"But what did you do to upset both of them?" Billings asked.

Singer stared straight into Billings's face. "Each asked me to give him my loyalty as his slave," Singer said. "I had to tell each the truth: I am already slave to Captain Ted Billings."

The next morning, Billings arrived early for his meeting with Kane. The quartermaster staff pointedly ignored him, including Nitay. Billings saw how this was going to play out. He didn't sit, because that would make it easier to ignore him. He wouldn't surrender this dominance game without a fight.

At last a buzz came from Nitay's console, and she looked up at Billings. "Go on in." Just three words, in a resentful tone. So much for fun in Depot Town . . .

Billings walked into the colonel's office. The man slouched behind his desk, leaning back, with a plate of fried eggs in his lap. He looked up. "Close the door." And he looked back down at his eggs. Billings closed the door, then turned back and offered a salute. When Kane didn't look up, Billings lowered his hand.

Kane kept eating. This was another part of the dominance game: he would make Billings wait until he was ready, and ignore him until then. Billings almost laughed, it was so obvious.

Finally, Kane put away the last of the eggs, and he set the plate on a pile of dishes beside his desk. Then he looked up. "Captain, what am I going to do with you?"

"You're going to give me my force towers."

Kane gave a low chuckle. "Do you really think your little threat is going to work on me?"

"It already has, colonel. That's why we're here now. You know that one word from me could put an end to all of this."

"If I let you send that word . . ."

"Is that a threat, colonel?" Billings reached for his comm.

Kane waved a hand. "Don't bother, your signal is blocked in here. I prefer no unexpected audiences for my discussions."

"I can always file it later," Billings said. "There's nothing you can do to stop me."

"Oh, I could stop you . . . permanently . . . If I spread the right money in the right places, you'd have an accident."

Billings wasn't intimidated. He'd made sure that Towne and Roth knew where he was and who he was meeting with. "That would bring on the investigation, colonel. I've made sure of that. And that would end your little operation just as surely as the psych report. So let's stop playing games. You're going to give me the towers, we're just haggling over the price. We're reasonable men, we can work something out, but I *will* have those towers."

Again Kane gave his evil grin. "You're quite the fighter, aren't you, captain? Big, strapping young man like yourself . . . I'll bet you been in a lot of fights."

Billings flushed. "I'm a doctor," he said. "A psychoanalyst. I fight with words, not with fists."

"But you've fought in the past, haven't you?" Billings blinked. Kane had done his research. "You embarrassed me, captain, in front of my loyal men. That's going to cost you more than the towers."

"What? You want an apology? Call them in, I'll apologize."

"No," Kane said, "that would be too easy. I need something a little more public, more humiliating . . . And more profitable. Captain, you're going to fight in my ring."

"What? That little guy?"

That got a laugh from Kane. "Diego? Lord, no, the man's half kzin! Against an amateur like you . . . He would tear your heart out and eat it. No, you're going to fight Mullins. The big guy."

"Not exactly my weight class."

"We only have two weight classes, captain: winners and losers." Kane stared into Billings's eyes. "And you're going to be one of the winners."

"What?"

"I've already started the rumors," Kane said. "The doctor out from Earth has challenged Mountain Mullins in the ring. Bets are running against you nearly five to one. So when, three minutes in, you land a lucky punch on his jaw, the crowd will erupt. When you follow up with a couple of body blows, bringing him to his knees . . . Well you won't be popular, because a lot of people will lose a lot of money when you finish him off."

"You think Mullins will throw the fight?"

"Mullins does what I tell him to. Let me worry about that. But that's the deal, captain, take it or leave it: you get into the ring, let me turn a tidy profit, or no towers."

Billings considered it, and then finally he nodded. This would let Colonel Kane save face, and the man needed a face-saving gesture. If Billings pushed him too far, the colonel might actually follow through on his threats. So Billings would give him this, for the sake of the mission.

But then he thought . . . "Three minutes in, you say?"

"Ah," the Colonel said with the evil grin on his face. "For the first two minutes . . . you're gonna hurt."

Billings barely made it back to his office before his comm buzzed again. "Captain Billings," he said.

Colonel Towne answered. "Billings, we have a . . . situation in the compound. We need you here."

🐾 🐾 🐾

When Billings was armored up, North let him into the enclosure. Cole stood inside, standing guard with a squad of other troops in front of Colonel Towne. Before them stood two groups of kzinti, just out of leaping distance from each other. At the front of the northern group was Hrung-Commander, and in front of the other was Kzaii-Commander. They both watched expectantly, their eyes showing readiness. To pounce, or to talk? There was only one way to find out. "What's up, Colonel?"

Towne turned to Billings. "They said the partition was off if they couldn't speak to you. They wouldn't say about what, and no one else would do."

"All right," Billings said, "I'll talk to them." He stepped in front of the crowd of guards, feet firmly planted, arms wide, hands on hips. He wanted to come across as ready and unafraid.

Then he addressed the kzinti in the Hero's Tongue. "Brave heroes, you asked to speak with me."

"No," Kzaii said, "we demanded to speak to. And you came."

Hrung snarled. "No, *she* demanded. A female. And you came, like a whimpering kit."

"She did not summon me," Billings replied. "And you did not. My mission summoned me. *Strakh* demanded, not you."

The kzinti paused, and Billings resisted the urge to smile. He had just challenged them as surely as with a grin, but with the politest of words . . . Well, polite for the Hero's Tongue.

When neither kzin answered, Billings continued. "Speak up! I am commander of this planet, and you will answer me."

At that, Kzaii chuckled. "You claim to have high *strakh* here, but we have not seen you earn it. Prove to us your *strakh*."

Billings shook his head. "I do not prove to lower castes. I command."

"Yet that is not what the winds tell us," Hrung answered. "We hear that tomorrow, you will fight to prove your command."

Damn! How had word traveled so quickly? That couldn't be an accident. Kane was behind it, screwing with Billings's mission.

"That is a human matter," Billings said. "No concern of yours."

"It is a *strakh* matter," Kzaii replied. "Do you have something to hide, commander?"

"No."

"Then we must see this battle." The kzin bared its teeth. "You will show us who has the *strakh* on this planet."

Billings wasn't sure where to turn. Towne was touchy and cautious because somebody had ratted her out. And Roth was a fine surgeon, but Billings wasn't ready to trust him yet. And neither colonel could be unaware of how Kane ran his depot, could they? Were they in on the take? Did he have some leverage over them?

But Billings had an old trick up his sleeve: often in helping someone else with their problems, he'd get new perspective on his own. So he visited the only creature on D0G-7 who might be beneath the notice of Kane: Singer-of-Truth.

Billings scanned into the wardroom, and the guard nodded. "Captain Billings," she said, "please state your purpose here."

"Patient therapy session," Billings answered. "*Private* therapy session. I need to ask you to leave, corporal."

"No can do, captain," the guard answered. "Regulations. I can't leave you alone with the prisoner."

"He's strapped down . . ."

"I have my orders, captain." Billings looked over at Singer, who was looking back at him. Then he turned back to the guard, and in the Hero's Tongue, he uttered the foulest insult he could think of. A sharp hiss of air intake from Singer told him just how foul the insult had been.

But the guard didn't blink. If she'd understood the insult, she was one hell of an actor. Billings returned to English. "All right, corporal. But at least give us some distance, will you?"

"I'll be over by the door," she answered.

Billings pulled up a chair next to the kzin. "Singer-of-Truth, you look better."

"I *am* better, Commander Ted billings. If you remove the straps, I'm ready to serve you."

"Higher orders require the straps remain," Billings answered. "I seek authorization to remove them, but it will take time."

"So my commander has a commander, and more commanders above. Always is it so. Even the Patriarch is not truly free, for he may be deposed if he loses *strakh*."

"Yes, I must answer to a commander. Does that cost me *strakh* to kzinti eyes?" Billings asked.

"Not if the commander is worthy," Singer answered. "To follow one whom other kzinti would follow is merely good judgment."

Billings thought over that. Who did he follow? He answered to Strategic Ops, but that didn't give him immunity from the orders of Towne or Roth. Or even Kane, for that matter. At the moment, Kane was as much his commander as anyone.

Billings changed his tack. "Singer-of-Truth . . . Why truth?"

"I would gain no *strakh* as Singer-of-Falsehood," Singer answered. "Who values lies?"

"But cannot a lie provide *strakh*? Can it not let you conceal and mislead so others will do what you want? What about the hunter who stalks downwind, and who hides behind blinds?"

"That is not falsehood," Singer answered. "That is tactics. You limit what your opponent knows."

"And what about knowledge? If the kzinti know of a new weapon, do they share that with humans, because that is truth?"

"Hardly," Singer answered. "Just because you know the truth, does not mean you must share it with everyone."

"Yet you feel compelled to share your new ballads?"

"Because I think not knowing this truth, not understanding it, shall be the death of the kzinti."

That was when Billings realized . . . "You're a hero."

"I am a Singer-of-Truth. I'm not a hero. I do not fight."

"A hero is not one who fights," Billings answered. "A hero is one who is willing to fight, willing to die for what he believes is important. Not for *strakh*. *Strakh* is just a public truth of what the hero has accomplished. But the hero is not in what the public sees, it is in the private truth that the hero knows."

"Commander Ted Billings, you are also a Singer-of-Truth! Many live their whole lives without understanding what you said."

"Thank you, Singer-of-Truth. And I understand more. I say again: you are a hero. You would teach the kzinti your truth, even if you die in the attempt."

Singer lowered his eyelids. "When I was tested, I chose to live. I did not stand by the truth. Now I am . . . exiled."

Billings couldn't agree. Yes, Singer had faltered at the end; but before that he had risked his life for the truth. This kzin did not believe that good could come from falsehood.

And what did Billings believe? Was a thrown fight a small price, a tiny falsehood in the service of his mission? This wasn't about abstract principles, it was about the survival of the kzin race! Or maybe the human race, or maybe both.

"No," Billings said. "I appoint you as Singer-of-Truth, and I expect you to live up to that. Answer me: if one does a dishonorable thing and no one sees it, does one lose *strakh*?"

A human officer might have asked why Billings changed the subject. But Singer was a kzin, uncaste. He did not question. "If the kzin is a true hero, he will admit his crime to his pride. He will accept discommendation, even if it costs him *strakh*. A higher *strakh* is at stake. And if he should not, the truth will gnaw at his heart. He might deceive others, but not himself. His pride will smell shame. In the end, he will falter, and fall."

"You believe this?" Billings asked.

"It is true of kzinti," Singer said. "Is it true of humans?"

Billings was too smart to believe that. Humans could be incredibly self-deceptive. But was it true of him?

This kzinti who called himself his slave set a mighty high bar for Billings to clear. Billings knew: he must find a way for the truth to come out. For him, and for Singer.

"Your problem, Singer-of-Truth, is not your Truth. Your problem is in how you tell it. Have you ever heard of satire?"

Billings was glad to learn that Towne knew about the boxing. That made his request to her easier. But still she called him insults he hadn't heard since his days as a street fighter. He just calmly let her vent; and when she was done, he made his request again, and then explained his reasons. He wasn't sure if he convinced her, or if he simply wore her out. But she agreed.

So it was that when Billings reached the motor pool, a hush fell over the crowd when they saw his guests: Hrung, Kzaii, and Singer-of-Truth. Plus a squad of guards to keep an eye on the kzinti. Towne had been adamant about that.

A wall of bodies blocked their entrance, topped by a wall of faces:

many curious, most hostile, and a few disgusted. They shouted, but Billings just stood calmly. The tumult built, and Billings began to fear that the guards would have to protect the kzinti from the humans, not the other way around.

But then an air horn sounded, and Kane's voice came over the PA system. "Let them through."

With that, the crowd gave way, creating a road to the makeshift ring and beyond, up to Colonel Kane's dais. Billings did not rush. He waited until the path was completely clear, and then he nodded at the kzinti and the guards. At a measured pace, he led them forward. When they stood before the raised platform, Billings said simply, "Good afternoon, colonel."

Kane smiled. Without looking, Billings knew that the kzinti commanders tensed for a fight. They couldn't help their instincts. But as Billings was learning, kzinti were more than their instincts. And so he said in the Hero's Tongue, "He's unworthy." He glanced sideways, and the kzinti relaxed.

Then Billings turned back to Kane, and the colonel said, "I thought you couldn't bring me cats for the ring."

"They're not for the ring," Billings said in English. "They're my guests, and I expect them to be treated with respect." Billings smiled at Kane, and there was no mirth in it at all. It was a threat that would make any kzin proud.

Kane's left eyebrow twitched, and Billings almost shouted in triumph. The colonel was worried. His sources hadn't told him about this turn. That little bit of uncertainty gave Billings all the confidence he needed to pull this plan off.

But Kane wasn't ready to give in. "Captain, you know the regulations: pusillanimous conduct in the face of the enemy is a court-martial affair. You really want to take that risk?"

"Colonel," Billings answered, "I know how this game is played: none of us were ever here."

"And the guards?" Kane asked.

"They're not guards," Billings said. "They're my entourage. Now are we going to talk, or are we going to have a fight?"

"Fight, of course," Kane said. "Any time you're ready."

"Hold it!" Billings said. "I need accommodations for my guests. Find them some large seats. Ringside, of course."

Kane nodded, and sturdy seats were dragged out. Hrung and Kzaii took theirs, but Singer remained standing.

"Something wrong with his chair?" Kane asked.

"No," Billings said, "but I have a special assignment for Singer-of-Truth, with help from Sergeant Cole. They're going to be my ring announcers, in English and in the Hero's Tongue."

"Ring announcers?"

"Come, colonel," Billings said, "is this place amateur hour? You need announcers. I'll even provide my own megaphone."

Kane sighed. "Your conditions are beginning to bore me, captain. Do what you like, but get started." With that, Kane leaned back in his chair and stared expectantly.

Billings stripped off his warm-up jacket and pants, leaving him in shorts, sneakers, and a white muscle shirt. He heard a rumble from the other side of the ring as the crowd parted to let Mullins through. The man stood a head above the rest. Mullins grinned, and the kzinti snarled. Billings turned to them. "That is a challenge, but it's a challenge for *me*."

Kzaii said, "Captain Ted Billings, if he eats your heart, I shall challenge him as commander."

"Kzaii, if he eats my heart, be my guest."

Billings stepped into makeshift ring, and he held out his hands to Mullins. "I don't see any referee," he said. "Do we wait for a bell, or—"

Mullins lunged, landing his big, hammy right fist on Billings's jaw. Billings had enough warning to pull back, blunting much of the impact—and still, his head rang.

After seeing the previous fight, Billings knew he really had no chance against Mullins. He could dodge for a time, but not forever. Mullins's better reach made it nearly impossible for Billings to land a blow without the element of surprise.

Or, of course, instructions from Kane. Three minutes in.

Then over the crowd Billings heard Singer from ringside:

"And so began Billings versus the Mountain. A deceitful blow, without notice that the battle had begun. When Man meets Mountain, always the Mountain must win. Man struggles to stand, while the Mountain abides."

Billings wasn't nimble enough, and Mullins jabbed his left into

Billings's ribs. Billings gasped while barely deflecting a right jab that smashed his own fist against his cheek.

"The Mountain ignores the Man. He is nothing to it. A pebble to an avalanche."

Another left jab, this one a glancing blow off Billings's shoulder, and half his arm went numb. He let the man get too close, he couldn't—Out of nowhere, Mullins's right smashed into Billings's temple. Billings fell.

"The Man plummets down. The Mountain looms over him."

"Get up," Mullins hissed, just barely audible over the crowd. "You've got more beating to come."

And slowly . . . Ribs aching, arm numb, head throbbing . . . Billings rose to his feet. The crowd roared for blood. Billings's blood.

"What fool is the Man? The Mountain has no mercy. The Man fell. The Man will fall again. The Man will always fall."

Mullins had backed away, playing with Billings. Now he came charging back; but despite his pain, Billings dodged aside and managed to land one solid right into the man's solar plexus. Mullins gasped for air.

"And still he gets up. Still he fights. The Mountain cannot lose, but the Man cannot give up. He does not know how."

More from surprise than from the punch, Mullins hesitated. Billings went in with more jabs; but Mullins deflected them, and Billings's fists landed in the man's ribs. They might as well have struck an armored transport.

But at the same time, Billings aimed a roundhouse at Mullins's jaw. The man grinned as he jerked his head back away from the blow . . . And Billings connected with his larynx.

"How could it be? A Man cannot hurt a Mountain!"

"Billings!" Kane's voice rose above the crowd.

Involuntarily, Billings looked up at the fight clock. One minute, forty seconds. The fight had to last into the third minute for Kane to make his money.

Not that there was a risk of Billings ending it early. That glance had been all the distraction that Mullins needed. With his right hand still raised against his throat, the man lumbered forward, jabbing with his left. Then when he got close, his right smashed down upon Billings's head. Billings's world spun.

"The Man might strike the Mountain, but the Mountain must break the Man."

Billings staggered away, arms flailing in front of him in an ineffective defense. Mullins laughed as he gave chase.

But then the clock chimed the start of the third minute, and Mullins slowed with a gagging sound. Whether acting, or whether Billings had done some real damage, Billings couldn't tell; but this gave him time to recover his wits and to put up a better guard. And this time, when Mullins came in, the man faltered. His blows were just a bit slower, less powerful, and Billings was able to block them.

Mullins got closer, crouched down for effect, and winked at Billings. He dropped his left guard a few inches, giving Billings his opening. Billings wound back with his right and swung for all he was worth, straight at Mullins's jaw. This time, Mullins did not back away.

And at the last instant, Billings pulled back. And Mullins fell anyway.

"And the Mountain flinched! The Man felled the Mountain without a touch! By *strakh* alone he prevails!"

From the ground, Mullins looked up, anger and confusion in his eyes. He got back to his feet, and he charged straight at Billings with no attempt at defense. Again Billings let fly with his most powerful blow; but at the last instant, again Billings pulled back, this time dancing away so there could be no doubt that he hadn't touched Mullins. And again, Mullins fell, as if tripping over his feet.

"Again the Mountain flinches! The Man does not touch the Mountain, yet the Mountain dare not touch the Man. It has its *orders!*"

The crowd roared in anger. This time Mullins got up with murder in his eye. Billings stepped away again, and this time . . . This time, he remembered Singer, ready to die for the truth. Chin up, arms wide, Billings stood waiting for the deadly blow.

"Mullins!" Kane shouted. And the mountain stopped, confused, and looked at his commander.

Enraged, Kane rose from the dais and rushed toward the ring. "Billings! What are you doing?"

Billings grinned. "I'm giving the people what they want. Their money's worth. Or should I say, your money's worth."

Kane's guards had formed a cordon around them, guns raised at the crowd. The spectators pressed forward as close as they dared, shouting threats at Kane and the guards.

"You're finished, colonel," Billings shouted over the tumult. "I refuse to win. You're going to have to pay off every bet and more: everyone on D0G-7 now knows you rigged this." Billings looked at Singer. "The dishonor you did in private is now public. You have no *strakh* here. If I were you, I'd take that psych discharge, so I can get you out of here with your skin intact. These people are ready to eat your heart."

Singer added one more line, with Cole translating: "And even in losing, the Man wins. This Heroic Human."

At that, Kane snapped. He rushed at Billings, arms outstretched. But while Billings was no match for Mullins, he was more than capable of handling the scrawny little colonel. A quick punch to the jaw and a box to the ear, and Kane went down.

Before Kane's guards could react, Billings's entourage had their rifles out, pointed at the men. "You'll drop those guns and walk away now," Cole said.

As one, the two kzinti commanders stood behind Cole and bared their fangs at the guards. "Do not threaten Commander Ted Billings," Kzaii said in English.

Hrung snarled a kzin insult in the Hero's Tongue: "I wonder how you taste." The guards didn't appear to understand, but they dropped their weapons.

Billings grabbed the megaphone from Cole, and he called out to the crowd. "It's done! Return to your stations. Colonel Kane is finished here. All accounts will be settled after a thorough audit. Now get out here!" There was more grumbling, but Cole turned his rifle on the fight clock, shattering it with a pulse. Billings added, "Now!"

This wouldn't be the end of it, Billings knew that. Oh, he had accomplished his immediate goals. Hrung and Kzaii understood now that he was not a commander to be taken lightly. Now perhaps Singer would be safe under his protection. And maybe he'd learned a secret to kzinti surrender: be a bigger hero, and get them to acknowledge his *strakh*.

But as for the humans here . . . There were going to be long-standing resentments. Kane loyalists would want to strike back.

Gamblers who felt cheated would lash out. Billings would bet there would be dozens of fights before the day was done, and some of the hostility would take a long time to work out.

It looked like the D0G-7 therapist had a lot of work ahead.

THE THIRD KZIN

by Jason Fregeau

☙ CHAPTER 1 ☙

ONE YEAR after liberation music played in Munchen, upbeat melodies with a resounding sadness. Musicians with old instruments from the old world—mandolins, dulcimers, zithers—performed to knots of people on corners and across the stoops of the formerly grand strassen. Along the blocks, empty stores overwhelmed the open few. The once-lively city seemed cast in black-and-white, like an ancient 2-D movie. Even the spindly trees, caught in the long Wunderland fall, dropped colorless leaves from graying trunks along the mottled paving stones.

Curbside at the Munchen spaceport, Martin Cheshire squinted against the early morning light, searching the faces in the ground cars humming by. He felt lightheaded from the trip: Sol to Alpha Centauri via hyperspace, a long layover in the stinking caverns of Tiamat awaiting approval to proceed down-well, then a turbulent planetfall. His feet, clumsy in the .61 gravity, planted in a loose, overshot way, as he stretched and bent, hunting for his friend.

Soon he would see Lim, a happiness well worth any discomfort. Years—and light-years—had separated them. Cheshire grinned as he imagined their meeting: the handshake, the hug, and the invariable, "Hello, old friend."

He startled at a cracked voice near his elbow: "Herr Cheshire?"

"Yes?" Cheshire looked down, past the top of the man's brittle hair to a set of watery green eyes.

"My name is Kirkland, Vilt Kirkland." The man's face, pinched and angled like his body, revealed long decades. "I've come to fetch you. I'm afraid there's been a terrible accident."

"Accident?" The light gravity suddenly felt heavy.

"Yes, but I'm afraid there's not much time. I shall explain on the way to the cemetery."

"Cemetery!"

"Yes, yes, this way." The little man grabbed Cheshire's duffel and proceeded down the walk.

Cheshire balked. "Look, what's going on?"

The little man did not stop, calling over his shoulder, "No time, no time."

Angry and confused, Cheshire glowered, but followed his duffel into a battered ground car parked not far down the strasse. "Lim Welson was supposed to meet me."

"Yes, terrible, terrible." Kirkland engaged the auto-drive. "Our friend is dead, I'm sorry to tell you. We're on the way to his reclamation."

Cheshire blinked at Kirkland. Lim's smile, full of promise and adventure, flashed then disappeared. He fluttered a hand to eyes and pinched tears from the corners. "How'd it happen?"

"Terrible, terrible accident." Kirkland took a raspy breath. "None of us saw it coming. We were right in front of his apartment, just leaving for the brewery. One moment he was fine and the next he couldn't breathe. His throat closed completely. We did all we could— it was just him and me and Herr Langbroek-Kikkert, and we did all we could—but we just couldn't get any air into him. Even the paramedics couldn't help and, well, by the time we got him to the hospital, well . . . Just terrible!"

"But, what happened? Why did he stop breathing?"

Kirkland hunched his shoulders and leaned toward Cheshire. "Peanuts," he whispered. "Some sort of peanut allergy."

Cheshire flinched, disgusted by the man's oily smell. "But, that's impossible."

"Impossible?" Kirkland took a deep interest in the car's instruments. "Why do you say, 'impossible,' Herr Cheshire?"

"He loved peanuts. He was always eating them. How could he suddenly grow allergic?"

The little man slid away and crossed his arms. "I am not a doctor. All I know is what I saw. It was a shock to us all."

The ground car hummed along the strassen, avoiding pedestrians, carts, and potholes. Kirkland ran a finger along the dash and grimaced at the coat of black dust. "You knew our Lim well?"

"We grew up together—school, dating, air cars—all the usual stuff." Tears burned his eyes again, but he blinked them away. A friendship of twenty years to be buried on a strange planet, killed by peanuts, of all things.

"A sad time, a sad time." Kirkland attempted a greasy smile. "Be assured, Lim was most concerned about you. He and I were talking about you just before . . . before the incident. He would not want you to . . . suffer at his . . . loss."

"Thank you, Mr. Kirkland." Cheshire's voice trembled with harsh control. "His death just doesn't seem to make sense."

The car rolled through an arched gateway and up a drive to a sullen single-story building set in a rolling, walled-off park. A mix of Wunderland and Earth trees, slender in the lower gravity, dotted the shallow hills and dales. Remembrance stones, stark white among the withered leaves, were scattered among the trees. Cheshire and Kirkland entered the utilitarian building, decorated with shabby antiques and musty tapestries.

From the back, Cheshire scanned the room, shocked at the rows of empty chairs. A chipped wooden coffin, for show only and oft reused, occupied the far end. A fat man—the fattest man Cheshire had ever seen—lounged at the back. Next to him, an old black man ran a limber hand through his shocking white hair. He touched the fat man's arm to call his attention to Cheshire. At the front, a young man sat with studied indifference, both hands clasped around a knee. And directly before the coffin stood a tall woman, veiled and cloaked in mourning. Her shoulders shook.

At the coffin, a young priest finished the committal service and held out a silver bowl of earth to the woman. She shook her head, turned resolutely, and walked blindly past. The priest offered the bowl to the young man near the front, who took it with a nod and proceeded to sprinkle a bit of the earth over a funnel set into the foot of the battered coffin. The priest offered the bowl to the fat man and his black partner, but they stood and turned away.

Cheshire refused to believe as he walked, numb and slow, between the rows of white folding chairs. *Where is everyone? Why is no one here?* A single photo perched on the coffin: Welson—dapper, hair wavy brown, smile indulgently askance.

Kirkland followed, ignoring the fat man and his partner as they studied Cheshire.

"Can I see him?" Cheshire asked the priest. He ran a hand along the chipped wood. "I haven't seen him in a long time."

"I don't think that's a good idea, eh?" said the young man who had sat at the front. Lanky, with the strange off-center beard of a Herrenmann, he spoke with an affected Wunderlander's accent.

"This is our friend, Antoon Langbroek-Kikkert." Kirkland touched the young man's shoulder. "He was there, with us, when Lim, when—"

"His whole face was swollen and, frankly, by the time we got him to hospital, his color . . . well, his face had turned this color, eh?" Langbroek-Kikkert ran a thumb and finger along the lapel of his plum suit coat. "It's not a face you'll want to remember him by."

Cheshire felt sick. *These are Lim's friends?* The priest offered him the silver bowl, and he sprinkled a sad bit of earth into the worn funnel. The priest then offered the bowl to Kirkland, who scattered some grains and thrust the bowl back.

"What now?" Grief centered in Cheshire's chest, drawing his thoughts into repeating circles.

"After you leave, his body will be reclaimed," said the priest. "If you like, for a small fee, the cemetery will erect a remembrance stone. I could bless it if you like." He added, "For a small fee."

"No, I meant, what do I do now?" Cheshire locked bewildered eyes with Langbroek-Kikkert. "Lim sent for me—he even paid for the trip. I was going to work for him, but what now?"

The Herrenmann gave a tight smile and returned Cheshire's gaze. "We shall see, eh?"

"Yes, yes, we shall see, we shall see." Kirkland patted Cheshire's arm. "Perhaps you'd like to return to Sol?"

"A perfect idea." Langbroek-Kikkert lifted an accusing chin. "I'm afraid there's not much left of Wunderland to see, eh? Not after you flatlanders got through with it."

"What?" Cheshire stepped back, surprised by the young man's anger.

"Settle, Antoon. It was the UNSN's fault, not Herr Cheshire here."
Kirkland locked up Cheshire's arm in his and whispered, "I'm afraid
you'll get a bit of that around here, but no matter, no matter."

"I don't understa—"

"Come along. We'll get you a room in the Shrader while you wait
for your flight home. Don't you think that's a good idea, Antoon?"
Kirkland did not wait for an answer, but tugged Cheshire halfway
down the aisle. Langbroek-Kikkert followed close behind. Cheshire
resisted, then wrested his arm from the cracked man's grip.

"I think I'll fend for myself." He raised flat hands against
Kirkland's attempts to reattach. "Thank you anyway."

"No, we insist, eh?" Langbroek-Kikkert made his own grab.
"Come with us."

Cheshire backpedaled, but before he could reach the door the
bulk of the fat man stopped him. "You could come with us," the man
said. "We have a car and can drop you anywhere."

Cheshire glanced at Langbroek-Kikkert and Kirkland, who had
retreated to a wary distance. He looked into the face of the fat man—
sparkling green eyes set deep above his round cheeks—and to the
craggy black man smiling by his side.

"Buford Early and damn glad to meet you!" The black man fished
in his rumpled suit jacket and produced three cheroots. "Smoke?"

"No. No, thank you." Cheshire wanted to close his eyes, to blink
away the bewilderment. *Who are these people?*

The fat man shrugged and plucked two of the cheroots from
Early's fingers. Early grinned and stuck the remaining stick into the
side of his mouth. "What's your name, son?"

"Marty Cheshire." He peered down the aisle at Kirkland and
Langbroek-Kikkert, who were engaged in agitated whispers and
quick glares, and made a choice. "I think I'll take you up on that ride."

"Excellent! Hyek-ek, ah!" The fat man's laugh rolled through his
body. "Right this way."

The party of three ambled out the building, the fat man in a
waddling lead.

"I need my bag." Cheshire detoured to Kirkland's unlocked car.
Early stopped to light his cheroot, but Cheshire noticed him assess
the exit for threats. *Lim, what have you gotten me into?*

Cheshire joined the other two at a dented ground car. His door ground closed and sealed with a halfhearted sigh. "You could do with a body shop or two in this town."

"Indeed, yes, we could do with a great many things these days." The fat man held out a massive hand. "Schreibman."

Cheshire shook his hand. "Good to meet you." He settled into his seat as Schreibman set the auto-drive in motion. "I have to apologize. I just arrived from Sol, found out my friend is dead from peanuts—of all things—and now his so-called friends want to send me packing. I just . . . I just don't know what's going on."

"Sounds like a bitch of day, all right," said Early. "Perhaps you'd like a drink?"

Finally, some small sign of friendship. "I'd like that, yes."

"What do you think, Dolf?" Early asked Schreibman. "Harold's?"

"Everyone meets at Harold's. Hyek, hyek!"

Cheshire watched out the windows as the car hummed down the strassen. Toward the center of town, the traffic picked up. They passed the occasional cart pulled by thin kzinti, giant orange tigers striped with black. Masters now employed by former slaves, they hauled produce carts, bread carts, clothes carts; junkmen, dairymen, tradesmen. A householder called from a window for a cart to stop, and the ground car idled behind. The cart-man, a baker, picked two loaves of bread and met the householder on her stoop. His great paws idle on the worn wooden crossbar, the scrawny kzin stood, looking neither right nor left nor down—just distant, to a lost horizon.

"I've never seen a kzin before," Cheshire said. "I never understood how big they are."

"Nine feet and near a quarter ton," said Early. "Though that one's looking rather poorly."

Cheshire noted missing patches of fur with raw skin beneath. The alien's bat-like ears trembled, and his hairless rattail hung without expression. Taken by a sudden itch, the kzin licked at a forearm, gnawed the skin, and licked again. As the itch subsided the kzin worked his mouth, rolled his pink tongue around sharp yellow teeth, and spat a wad of orange/black fur to the cobblestones.

"What's wrong with him?"

"Nothing a strakkaker wouldn't fix," Schreibman said. "*Verdammt* ratcats."

"A vitamin deficiency." Early smiled around his cigar. "Something in their diet disagrees with them."

"Hyek-yek! Hyek-yek!" Schreibman's ill-humor had passed.

The baker returned from the stoop and mounted the cart. A word passed, and the kzin strained into the crossbar. The cart rumbled down the strasse and, as the ground car passed, Cheshire stared at the felinoid. Cracked footpads left bloody prints along the stones—fresh blood mixed with track-upon-track of purple blood-prints that snaked along the gutter.

"We're here," Schreibman said. "And just in time. I'm about to melt away to nothing."

A luminous holosign floated above a reinforced door: *HAROLD'S TERRAN BAR: A WORLD ON ITS OWN*, with *humans only* just below. And scratched on the brickwork, *no collabos!!!!*

Cheshire parted the beaded curtain of the vestibule and entered a bar empty of customers. The morning smell of stale smoke and rancid beer permeated the rooms. At the musicomp, a lithe Asian woman lounged, reviewing scores. Schreibman held up three fat fingers to a pasty-faced bartender, who rolled her eyes but worked the beer taps.

"What brings you to Wunderland?" Early asked after they had pushed their way around a small cafe table.

"My friend, Lim Wel—but you know him. You were at his funeral."

"Oh, yes, we knew him." Early exchanged a look with Schreibman. "Was Wilhelm Crenvins a friend of yours, too?"

"No, never heard of him. Who is he?"

Without a word, the bartender delivered three beers. Cheshire smiled at her, but she rolled her eyes again and returned to sulk behind the bar.

"No one. Just curious." Early sipped his beer. "You were about to tell us what brought you to Wunderland."

"Lim sent for me, asked me to come from Sol to join him. He said he needed my expertise, whatever that means, and he sent me a ticket on a hyperspace liner."

"A hyperspace liner!" Early shook his head. "God damn. I remember when we had a hard time getting those junkers to even start. Now the bastards are takin' fares like taxis."

"What do you do?" asked Schreibman.

"I'm a lawyer." He smiled with a shy pride.

Schreibman tapped the side of his glass and snorted.

"But I'm not a bad guy," Cheshire said with a desperate humor. "Hyek!"

Early dropped a restraining hand on the fat man's arm. "You must be one goddamn good lawyer to warrant a hyperspace fare. What kind of law?"

"Well, nothing in particular. I just passed the bar when Lim asked me to join him, so I haven't had any practice."

"How long did you know Lim?" asked Schreibman.

"We grew up together. He . . . he was my best friend for the longest time." Cheshire's face softened as he remembered. "He had this way . . . somehow, he knew how to find adventure. One time—we were just in grade school—we cut class to go the shops nearby. 'Let's go exploring,' he said and—pop!—there he went, right into the basement of some building. We rooted around for a good hour or so. I don't remember if we found anything, but then the cops showed up."

"What happened?" Early sipped his beer.

"Oh, I got caught. Lim mumbled about telling them it was a school project or some such rot. And it didn't go well, as you might expect. Oh, the dressing down I got from my moms . . ."

"And Welson . . . I mean Lim—what happened to him?" Early asked.

"When I went to talk to the cops he disappeared. I don't think they even saw him."

"You two go way back, then," Schreibman said. "He could trust you. Maybe that's why he needed you."

"Trust is one goddamn powerful tool," Early said. "Armies march on loyalty."

"Armies?" Cheshire asked.

"He's better off now, if you ask me," said Schreibman. "And a lot of other folks as well."

Cheshire cocked his head. "It sounds like maybe you didn't like him."

"Purely a professional opinion," Schreibman said. "I'm sure he was a marvelous fellow. What he did, of course, is another matter entirely." The fat man shook his head. "He was the worst of the worst."

"Do you know what your friend did for a living, Mr. Cheshire?" Early asked.

"Not exactly. He said something about the food industry. I assume he needed help with imports of food from Sol."

"Black market," said Schreibman. "You name it, he was into it. But his latest project, well, that just stunk to *hoch Himmel*."

Cheshire straightened. "I'm beginning to not like your attitude, friend. Who the hell are you guys, anyway?"

"We've been investigating Herr Welson for some time now," Schreibman said. "This is General Buford Early of the UNSN, and I'm Detective Dolf Schreibman of the Munchen Polizei."

Cheshire slapped his palms on the tabletop. "What's this been, some sort of interrogation?" He stood. An angry heat hardened in his cheeks, his brow. "What right have you to trick me like this?"

"Please calm down, Herr Cheshire." Schreibman tried a genial smile, but his small eyes ruined the attempt.

"My friend is dead, his so-called friends practically kidnap me, and two cops pump me for information—what the Finagle is wrong with this planet?"

"Sit down, Mr. Cheshire." Early smoothed the tabletop with his hand. "You're making an unnecessary scene. If you take your seat, we'll try to explain as best we can."

"No, thank you. I'm quite done with explanations for today. Thanks for the beer, fat man. I didn't touch it, so help yourself, not that you need it."

Early and Schreibman watched Cheshire's back as he stormed out. The two officers exchanged glances.

"I suppose we should put a tail on him," said Early.

"That would be for the best. Since it's still my city and still my planet, we'll use my people."

"Of course."

Schreibman sighed. "We're short handed as usual, so I'll have to take tonight's shift." He finished his beer and picked up Cheshire's. "It's hormonal. I have major faults in my leptin genetics."

"You have major faults, all right."

"Nothing an extra-large autodoc couldn't fix. Lie to me again how we'll soon get them from Sol."

❧ CHAPTER 2 ❧

THE KZIN LABELED "Gopher" used his ample time to think. Mostly he thought about the monkeys around him—their strange habits, their honorless deeds, their impenetrable contradictions. Chuut-Riit, the last kzin governor of the planet, had lectured about the worth of monkeys—he even used that unpronounceable word, "human," instead of the typical, "*kz'eerkt*."

"Study them," the Most Honored had said, his visage broadcast across the world and into the Alpha Centauri system. "They are our tomorrow. For we are Heroes—Heroes of ancient bloodlines stretched across the galaxy, from Home to *Ka'ashi*. And, as Heroes, we do not cringe when confronted with mysteries, when burdened by the unknown. You, and you alone, have been chosen by the Fanged God to share a planet with a great challenge, perhaps the greatest since Chaz-Ritt brought the Jotoki magic of technology to our claws."

And here the Ritt's words conveyed the light touch of a sharp tooth: "For you are not just Heroes of the Patriarchy, destined to bring honor to yourselves, your houses, and your kind. You are not just warriors, duty bound to follow orders without hesitation. And you are not just kzin. You are more than all of that combined. You are *wunderkzin*."

Gopher shifted on the sturdy table he'd converted into a traditional *fooch*. Only months after his lecture, the great Chuut-Riit was shred by the claws of his starving kits, and the nascent Fifth Fleet tore itself apart. And the *kz'eerkt—human—*forces arrived from their

68

home world. Gopher flared his nostrils in frustration. If the Fanged God meant for kzinti to be challenged, why did he include disgrace and dishonor? Why did he require humiliation?

"Herr ratcat! Time to earn your keep," the monkey named Vilt Kirkland said in halting Heroes' Tongue. He poked around a doorway and tossed a satchel onto the floor before the *fooch*. "If you please, deliver to Rhinehold Strasse. *Verstehst du*?"

"Urr." Gopher unwound and yawned in disdain as he clipped the satchel to his webbed vest. Kirkland retreated.

In the street, Gopher paused to sniff the scents of Munchen. Sewage and brackish shallows tainted the wind flowing from the distant Donau River. Closer by, in the brewery, fermenting grain shed rot and decay into the air, permeating the buildings and even the iron-gray sky. Gopher shuffed, clearing his nostrils, and began an easy lope.

Wunderkzin. The name tasted strange, like a divergent scent on a long hunt. Or like the edge of an unexplored forest. And where did duty lie in that name? Where was the honor?

Honor died the day of—that *kz'eerkt* word—*surrender*. Gopher relived that day, his last day named "Recruit," as he passed the brick rubble of smashed buildings.

"Into the tall grass." Prakk-Captain had often said the words—a teaching—but this time he meant it literally. He snared Recruit's tactical harness, flung him into the weeds, and dropped prone. Beyond the grassland and a thick concrete barrier, a UNSN technical hovered into view, flanked by soldiers floating in gravity belts.

"There are but a paw's worth, sir." Recruit checked the charge on his beam rifle. "I'll take the flyers. You take the crew."

Prakk-Captain waggled an ear mirthfully. "We die today, but not for a pawful." He nodded to a rise just behind the technical and flared his nostrils. "Scent. Use all your senses. They're guarding a monkey encampment—perhaps a command center. Why kill a pawful when we could kill eights-upon-eights?"

"First Sergeant always said to take the opportunity presented, sir."

"First Sergeant died honorably." Prakk-Captain checked the charge on his weapon. "But he died on the first day, along with his entire command. How many eights have you and I killed since?"

"One plus two, sir." Recruit glanced at the trophy ears on his commander's belt. He touched his *w'tsai*, the kzin ceremonial dagger gifted from his Sire. Soon he would have his first. Soon.

"And with the Fanged God's indulgence, we will kill twice that by the day's end. This way." Prakk-Captain shoved away in a belly-crawl that curved toward the concrete wall. Recruit twitched his tail in irritation, but followed. Prakk-Captain had kept them alive and fighting. And he had a partial name, a conferment of honor, which required not just obedience, but also respect.

They made the wall and crouched in its sheltering angle. In the far distance, across the field and beyond the littered asphalt, the spaceport's control tower burned like a ruined candle. UNSN vehicles and personnel swarmed the support buildings and hangars. Prakk-Captain peered at his devastated command. "We will make the monkeys pay."

Recruit raked his claws across his muzzle in a passionate salute. "Command me!"

The older kzin scented the air. "What do you smell?"

"Cordite. Burned bodies, wood, and melted plastics, sir."

"Closer. What's over the wall?"

Recruit fleered. "The monkey technical with two inside, seven fliers surround, sir."

"Good. And what does the monkey scent tell you?"

The young kzin flicked his tail in sudden realization. "Boredom. Fatigue. A . . . a . . . tired joy? Sir?"

Prakk-Captain waggled his whiskers in thought. "Just so. A very strange scent for troops in battle." His tail flicked in consternation. "To them the war is over."

"Let us teach them otherwise, sir!"

"This way." Prakk-Captain hugged the wall as they worked away from the technical. At an abandoned security gate, he peeked low, listened, and scented the wind. "A road leads around the hill, away from the technical and toward the encampment. All seems clear. There are vehicle barriers for cover, but we will be exposed until we reach them. Stay low and remember—we lurk in the grass. We hunt. The time will come for us to scream and leap, but we will choose that time."

Prakk-Captain slipped through the gate, fast and low. Recruit counted an eight and followed. The asphalt and green-orange grass and smoky sky swirled past. His back hit the thick concrete, and he scrunched against the old kzin, who sniffed the air.

"They saw us. They come."

Recruit disciplined himself not to peek, but followed Prakk-Captain's instruction about using his senses. The hum of the technical waxed, and the monkey scents appeared in the wind. He reached with hunting-sense—a hazy telepathy evolved to find prey. "They fear us, sir!"

"They fear death. All monkeys have that fear—it's a near constant in their lives. Have you not felt it before?"

"No, sir. My sire used the unclean beasts as farm slaves, far from the main estate. I rarely met monkeys—only during hunts."

"I envy you." Prakk-Captain's tail undulated in regret. "You have lived the old life, away from these *kz'eerkt*. Sometimes I fear we have been tainted."

"Like lurking in the tall grass, sir?"

"Yes, perhaps." Prakk-Captain growled, low and comforting. "But soon, for us, that will be over. When I signal, you fire upon the fliers, and I will take the crew. If any lives, we scream and leap."

"Sir!" He restrained himself, but only just.

A sound drifted to them, an amplified monkey voice. Prakk-Captain stiffened.

"What is it, sir?"

"Do you not speak Interworld?"

"No, sir."

"The monkey says that hostilities have ceased. He invites us to break cover without harm."

"A monkey trick, sir!"

"Perhaps." The old kzin whipped his tail in anger. "He says it is the order of Hroth-Staff Officer!"

"Lies!" Anger echoed through Recruit—anger at the days of lurking in the tall grass, at the steady defeats dealt by mere monkeys, and at this mindless *kz'eerkt* ploy. He spun to face the wall and bobbed up. The technical lay at a safe distance, its escorts landed behind cover. He spent eight rounds, which only ablated the vehicle's armor.

"You gave away our position!" Prakk-Captain cuffed Recruit on the shoulder, claws extended just enough to draw thin lines of blood. "You move only when ordered!"

Behind the cramped cover, Recruit ritually cowered as best he could. On the other side of the concrete, the technical ticked as it brought its main gun to bear.

"Stand to." Prakk-Captain shoved Recruit against the concrete. "You have the proper hot-blood of a young kzin. But you must learn to cool it with your head, not overheat it with your liver."

"Sir." Shame at his dishonor tempered his anger.

The old kzin's whiskers quivered in thought. "An order must be obeyed, but is an order relayed by a monkey to be obeyed?" He opened a paw. "Assume the monkey does not lie. That means all is lost. Yet honor requires us to be prideful, even in defeat. Honor requires us to give our lives for the Patriarchy, to die honorably in battle."

"Command me!" To regain honor, he would follow any order to the letter.

"We have lost surprise, but the monkeys fear for their lives. That is advantage enough. We—" A voice drifted to them. Prakk-Captain waggled his ears in laughter. "They repeat this supposed order and add insults."

"Insults, sir?"

"Insults are the fangs and claws of the weak. They want to provoke us into further attack. They, too, seek honor." His tail undulated in thought. "They fear, but they conquer it." He pondered a moment longer, then waggled his ears. "There are two sure things in this universe: death and the ability of monkeys to confound."

Recruit waggled his ears, sharing the laugh.

"On my order, we—"

A concussion grenade skittered at their feet. Prakk-Captain reached, fumbled, and grabbed the sphere. He launched into the protection of the wall, his arm a lever to toss the grenade up and over. A *pop*, and the old kzin spun into a heavy crouch, the bloody rags of his left arm cradled in his right.

Recruit fired a suppressing volley, then crouched by his commander. From his tactical vest he pulled a dark plastic pouch, which he punched hard and tore open. Prakk-Captain shoved the remnants of his arm into the pouch and sighed as medical foam swaddled the seared flesh and bone. He grinned at Recruit, ropes of saliva punctuating his anger.

"I will cover fire. You break to the next barrier. Then the next. Work your way below the crown of the hill and get a grenade under that vehicle."

"Sir!"

Prakk-Captain heaved to the wall, his blast rifle at rest on his ruined arm, and sent two accurate shots into the cabin of the technical.

Recruit broke cover in a crouched run and skidded behind the second barrier. He paused to assess the enemy's positions based upon return fire, but there was none. The main gun of the technical remained poised, but unfired. He dropped below the barrier, puzzled by the monkey silence.

Prakk-Captain called and pointed. A civilian aircar circled above, then dropped to the field between them and the monkeys. The half figure of Hroarh-Captain, his lower torso long-ago replaced by a hover platform, exited the car. A stocky UNSN officer accompanied him. The two waved, an order to the combatants to emerge and converge. Prakk-Captain and Recruit met at the car, saluted the senior officer, and stood at attention.

"At ease." Emotion whipped Hroarh-Captain's whiskers, a poor substitute for his tail. "Where is the rest of your command?"

"Honorably dead, sir."

"Just so." Hroarh-Captain tensed. His whiskers quivered in disgust. "My last order is to inform all remaining kzinti of Patriarchy's 'surrender.'" He used Interworld, since no such kzin word existed. "By order of Hroth-Staff Officer, all Patriarch Forces are dissolved. This is Staff Colonel Cumpston, who has charge of kzin affairs."

"You will not be mistreated," said the UNSN officer in perfect Heroes' Tongue. "You are under joint UNSN–Free Wunderland jurisdiction."

"Hroarh-Captain, I obey your orders!" Prakk-Captain, at stiff attention, trembled with uncertainty.

"I am no longer in command." He held his half frame ridged on the floating platform. "There are no longer any forces to command. I can only communicate to you the final counsel of Hroth-Staff

Officer to all kzinti: you are not permitted to die heroically. Trust that the Patriarchy will some day return and, until you can further that day, a dead Hero is of no use to the Riit."

Prakk-Captain sagged. The words ripped deeper than the concussion grenade that had taken his arm.

"My . . . my honor."

"Attention!" Hroarh-Captain roared.

Prakk-Captain snapped to, then sagged again. Recruit feared the old kzin would break discipline and drop his beam rifle. He thought to catch his captain under his good arm, but honor required he remain at attention.

Hroarh-Captain growled in Imperative Tense, "We have taken oaths, and our Honor is in obedience to orders."

"Yes, sir." A scent of grief punctuated the old kzin's words.

"The human will give you coordinates. Report to them."

"Yes, sir." Quiet, near inaudible.

"You are a professional, a former officer of the Patriarchy, and a Hero with a partial name. Act in accordance with your station!" Hroarh-Captain spun his platform to return to the car. The UNSN officer stood before Prakk-Captain, who seemed blind and deaf. Eventually the officer broke protocol, handed the coordinates to Recruit, and returned to the car.

The former kzin soldiers watched the aircar lift, hover, and slide away.

Prakk-Captain dropped his rifle and crumpled into the grass. "'Act in accordance with your station,'" he muttered. "How? If I cannot die honorably for the Patriarch, what action is left?" His eyes widened, deep violet in pain. "Where is the honor in obeying a dishonorable order?"

☙ CHAPTER 3 ☙

CHESHIRE lifted his duffel from Schreibman's car and proceeded down the block. Consulting his infocomp, he decided to see where Lim used to live, a vigorous walk away. The light gravity added a spring to his step that he did not feel. The primary sun, Alpha, blinked through chinks in the iron clouds, but shed little warmth.

The door to Lim's building was propped open, as was the door to his apartment. A willowy woman, her back to the entrance, hummed as she danced a slow sway. Her thick chestnut hair, long at the back but cut short at the sides in a belter's crest, rippled highlights in the dappled light from the window.

He knocked, two tentative taps. "Hello?"

She froze and glowered at him over her shoulder. "Yes?"

"I'm a friend of Lim's." After his morning he felt abashed, expecting the worst.

"Isn't everyone?" She swung round and drew her arms akimbo. "What do you want?"

"Lim sent for me. From Sol. Maybe he told you about me?" He stepped into the apartment. "I'm Martin Cheshire."

She narrowed her eyes for a moment then, smile radiant, reached for his hand. She moved with the economic grace of a rock-jack from the asteroid belt. "Of course, Mr. Cheshire. Lim told me so much about you. Welcome! Welcome!"

She pulled him from the door and guided him to a chair, which he accepted with relief. The apartment, though one room, was enormous and tall ceilinged. Dark cherry trim with elaborate carvings offset the smooth cream walls and the warm oak floors. Areas of the apartment—sitting, kitchen, bed—were tastefully screened from the central living area. Floor-to-ceiling windows, framed with sumptuous curtains, looked out on the strasse below.

"Quite a place."

"Lim loved his luxuries." Her confident smile relaxed him—a welcome change in this bitch of a day.

"'If it's not worth buying, it's not worth having.'"

Her smile faded. "Perhaps. But with Lim, some things bought weren't worth having."

"I don't follow . . ." Again uncertain, he gripped the chair arms. *Did everyone on this planet hate Lim?*

"Oh, never mind." She frowned at him. "I'm afraid I have some bad news, Mr. Cheshire."

"Yes, I know." He blinked, willing himself not to tear. "I was at the funeral."

She started. "My apologies. I'm afraid I was hardly in a frame of mind to notice anything."

"That was you, wearing the veil?"

"Lim and I were lovers."

He felt the ancient, jealous twinge—the old wish to have Lim all to himself. He sighed and suppressed the feeling. Yet again.

She watched her hands, quiet in her lap, then looked up and smiled. She was radiant in the late morning light. "You knew him well?"

"We grew up together."

"Tell me about him." She seemed eager, a passion to know more.

Cheshire understood that passion and gazed at the distant ceiling in warm remembrance. "He was always the guy everyone was hungry to know. I felt lucky to be his friend. He could walk into a room—a party, say—and know everyone by name by the end of the evening. And he used that—boy, did he use that. I remember once, at university, he fell in with a records' clerk in the academic office. 'Well, old friend,' he said to me. 'No more studying this semester. It's all in the bag.' And damn if he wasn't right—straight A's for him without a lick of work. Good thing none of the professors got wind, but Lim was always lucky like that."

"That poor woman. She must have felt quite used."

"Man. But it turned out okay. Lim sent him in my direction, and we got along like a habitat on fire." Cheshire grew pensive. "He seemed to do that a lot—Lim, I mean. He sent his former flames my way. Ah, but who am I to complain? Always the best for Lim, so being his friend had its benefits."

"Like picking up his leftovers?"

Her tone brought him up sharp. "What is it with people around here? A man's dead, and all folks can do is bad-mouth him."

She demurred, dropping her gaze to her lap. "I'm sorry, Mr. Cheshire. The occupation was hard on us. It taught us to be hard on each other . . . and on ourselves."

"I'm sorry." He passed a hand across his face. "I can't imagine what it was like to live under the kzin, much less grow up with them."

"I was lucky I suppose. I grew up in the Swarm where we had a bit more freedom."

"The Swarm? You mean the Serpent Swarm? Like Sol's asteroid belt?"

"Exactly. Spread among the rocks, we were a bit harder for the pussies to control."

"What brought you to Munchen?" He asked to be polite, but suddenly realized he wished to know more about her. About Lim's lover.

She drew a controlled breath. "Have you ever heard of the UNSN *Yamamoto*?"

"Earth's counterattack against the kzin here on Wunderland?"

"What an . . . antiseptic way to put it. About two years ago the *Yamamoto* entered our system traveling at near the speed of light. It dropped iron shots at 'strategic assets' in the Swarm and on the planet. The shots weren't bombs—they didn't have to be. Traveling at .99c they had megatons of kinetic energy and vaporized whatever they hit."

He saw her pain. "Your family?"

She nodded. "They were on Bessemer, a processing asteroid. I was on Tiamat, trying to secure supplies."

"I'm sorry." *A planet of sadness and loss.*

"Thank you, Mr. Cheshire, but there's more. You see, at the time of the attack, Munchen was packed with refugees from the hinterlands—forced labor for the kzin factories. When the shots hit, they threw dust and smoke high into the atmosphere, cutting sunlight for months. It killed crops planet-wide. And even before the food shortages, medical care and sanitation were barbaric— pre-twenty-second-century standards."

Her liquid brandy eyes tracked motes of dust in the weak sunlight. "When the crowds pressed together to celebrate liberation, no one foresaw the pandemic—'Kzin Flu,' they called it. Some say it was a bioweapon set by the kzinti in retaliation, but I don't believe it. For six months the carts carrying the dead outnumbered all the others. Remember, we didn't have autodocs—we hardly had any medicine at all. And I can't say I understand it, but I heard that our dependence on autodocs had weakened the population's immune system—our blood and guts just didn't have the old immunities built up."

She sat forward and locked eyes. "It killed thousands. Slowly. It would have been more merciful if the *Yamamoto* had dropped a shot directly center city."

"I'm sorry," he mumbled and looked away. After a moment he glanced back. She stared, watching the parades of the dead.

He thought to touch a gentle finger to her knee, but rejected it as too forward. Instead, he said, "You still haven't explained how you ended up here. Or with Lim."

The parades dissolved. She snapped her fingers and bounced out of the chair. "I've been a neglectful host, Mr. Cheshire. Can I offer you something—Tea? Beer? I can set the water boiling while I tell you the grand story of Lim and Maddie."

"I'll try a beer and . . . what did you say? 'Maddie'?"

"Oh, I'm so sorry." She grasped his hand with a warm grace. "I haven't introduced myself. I'm Maddelena Valli. My friends call me Maddie, the rest call me Mad!"

🐾 CHAPTER 4 🐾

BACK FROM THE RHINEHOLD Strasse delivery, Gopher rode the gravity lift to the brewery's fifth floor office. In the reception area, the monkey—the *human*—named Vilt Kirkland glanced up from the infocomp on his desk. Gopher detached the satchel, and the monkey took it from his paw without flinch or hesitation. Gopher approved—too many monkeys showed too much fear when dealing with Heroes.

The monkey rifled the contents: flat plant matter covered with writing. Gopher peered at the papers with an unaccustomed curiosity. In a world of instant point-to-point communication, why these monkeys would use such a flimsy physical medium left Gopher in a track without scent.

"Payday for you," Kirkland said in halting Heroes' Tongue. Gopher tensed—the mangling of the kzin language by a foul monkey used to mean immediate death. Gopher's tail flicked in frustration as he willed himself calm. *Immediate death—in better times. In better times.*

The monkey rubbed his oily hands together. He opened a drawer, cracked an ancient strongbox, and consulted one of the papers from the satchel. "Three hundred krona a week, correct?"

"Yes." Gopher's tail twitched in disgust at the monkey's zeal over shiny tokens.

"Minus thirty-two in . . . taxes." The monkey eyed Gopher. "You're still paying for your webbing vest?"

"It was to be paid off after three periods. That was five periods ago."

79

"Are you sure? It says here you're still paying. Do you have anything in writing to show you paid it off?"

"You have given me no such writing."

"Then I have to go by what it says here." Kirkland smiled, but with lips sealed. The kzin took bared teeth as a challenge to fight. "You agree, rules are rules, don't you?"

"I consent that is the case."

"Good then!" The monkey nodded relief, a hint of glee in his eyes. "Minus fifteen for the webbing, which leaves two fifty-three. Now, your kind works in base eight, correct?"

Gopher flexed his four-digit paws. "Yes. Base eight."

"So, converting two fifty-three to base eight . . ." Kirkland worked the infocomp. "We owe you one hundred seventy krona." He kept his eyes fixed on the screen and held his breath. Gopher rumbled deep in his chest.

"Do not try to trick me, monkey." The kzin leaned forward and whipped his tail in vexation. The small office filled with orange hackles and the threat-scent of ginger "The conversion math is easy and needs nothing but the quick mind of a Hero. The amount is one seventy-one."

The greasy monkey breathed a ragged sigh. Then rallied his anger. "*Verdammt*, be easy!" He counted krona from the strongbox. "There. One hundred seventy-one krona. One lousy coin. A mistake I make, *ja*? Are we set then?"

Gopher lowered his hackles and said with disdain, "You are to tell me where to go."

The monkey covered his mouth to hide his teeth, bared in a nervous laugh. "Tell you where to go. . . . Tell you where to go. . . ." The monkey rocked in his mirth. "I could tell you where to go."

"Yes, please." Gopher whipped his tail, revolted by the monkey's incomprehensible humor.

The monkey coughed and hid his whole face in his hands. His body shuddered. Finally he gasped, "Go home. No more work for today. Just go home."

Gopher rumbled assent and left the office.

Still chuckling, Kirkland dipped into the strong-box and pocketed 129 krona.

🐾 🐾 🐾

As he loped back to his apartment, Gopher puzzled over the strange math used by the monkeys for their money. An amount in base ten should be paid in base ten, but the monkeys insisted in paying in base eight. Yet the same monkeys demanded payment in base ten. The kzin system—debts of honor—while never simple, would at least balance out. There was no honor in the monkey money.

Prakk-Invalid stirred on his *fooch* when Gopher stooped into the dark basement apartment. The usual smells assaulted: mold on the stone behind the rotting wallboards; stale urine from the shabby recycler; iron and salt from the improvised autokitchen. And Prakk-Invalid. Gopher sniffed.

"Monkey beer." Not an accusation, not an admonition; a simple statement of fact.

"Just a little." Prakk-Invalid's eyes glowed violet with pain. "Enough to keep the tremors from. . . ." He rumbled into silence. He licked the stub of his missing left forearm.

"You stink. Worse than a wet *kz'eerkt* on a hot day."

Prakk-Invalid bared his bloody teeth and growled. "Your mother whelped *sthondat* excrement. Come closer, and I'll wipe away her dishonor."

Gopher slid his claws in and out, then waggled his ears in amusement. "A Hero once taught me that insults are the fangs and claws of the weak. Have you eaten today?" He turned to the autokitchen as Prakk-Invalid collapsed into himself in despair.

"Not as such." The old kzin shook his dirty mane to soothe himself. "Nothing smells right."

"No," Gopher agreed. The autokitchen—ripped from a kzin ship—never worked right. And ship's food, the bare minimum for sustenance during long years in space, tasted of carrion and offal.

"Do you remember our first hunt together?" Gopher dialed two meals. "In the park?"

Prakk-Invalid paused to fold an ear in a chuckle. "That monkey who refused to run."

"Yes! Two eights of his monkey brothers run past, seeking shelter in the forest like proper prey. And he sits. Sits!"

"His back to us." Prakk-Invalid slashed the air with a paw. "Do you think he thought, if he could not see us, we could not see him?"

"I would put nothing beyond the thoughts of these monkeys." Gopher pulled two warm slabs of raw "meat" from the autokitchen and tossed one to his former officer. He settled himself on his own *fooch* and licked some blood from the bottom of the ration before it could drip. "He chanted something in their foul language. What did he say?"

"Some monkey prayer. I understood only a very little: 'valley of death' or some such. Inspiring for a monkey, I suppose, but nothing for a Hero."

"A Hero would face death, claws and fangs ready."

"A scream and a leap, a scream and a leap." Prakk-Invalid stared. The slab dripped from his paw onto his brittle fur.

"The blood . . ." Gopher said. Prakk-Invalid started, then licked at the slab. "The blood from his neck."

"A lovely stream. I never knew a single blow could sever a monkey head from his neck. We nearly missed the rest of the hunt."

"His head made a marvelous *sklernak* ball—until you broke it open."

"I stepped on it." Prakk-Invalid furled his ears in laughter and shred a chunk of his slab. "It parted at the nose cavity in perfect symmetry. The monkeys have thick heads—but only when it comes to thinking!"

Gopher furled his ears and flicked his tail in bemusement as he watched his old officer chew, swallow, and rend another bite. He would stay with the old kzin, distract him from his drink. Maybe later that night, when Prakk-Invalid slept, Gopher might find and smash the stash of monkey beer. Then, tomorrow perhaps, a kzin could once again be a Hero.

☙ CHAPTER 5 ☙

MAD BOUNCED behind the screen to the kitchen. After a tink of glass and the pop of containers, she appeared with two amber mugs with respectable heads.

"Lim brews this." She sipped. "He calls it a native pale ale. I call it delicious."

Cheshire sipped. "It's very good." He frowned. "It tastes a little like eggs."

"Doesn't it, though." She leaned toward him, an invitation to conspiracy. "I tease him about it all the time. Do you know what he says?"

"No." He leaned, too, sharing the conspiracy.

"He says, 'Maddie, it's a pregnant beer, full of possibilities. Mark my words, Maddie, good things will be born from this beer.'"

He chuckled. "That bastard. Everything was a speech."

She sat back, settling into her story. "So, I was in Tiamat, and you know what a hellhole it is."

"I was there a week and it felt like a year."

"I spent a year and it felt like a lifetime. Everyone related to me dead—Ma, Da, Narrlah and her kits. Rock-jacks take care of their own, but there are limits when you're stuck in an overcrowded ball of iron ruled by the pussies and their bastard collabos. I didn't starve, and I didn't beg, and I didn't have to whore myself out, so I still have that bit of self-respect."

"What did you do?" Her beautiful stillness fascinated him. *Lim sure knows how to pick them.*

She shrugged. "What everyone else was doing: buying and selling on the black market. And with the collapse of the pussy occupation, the market became, well . . . grayer."

"What did you sell?"

She settled hot brandy eyes into his. "Vengeance."

He looked away and hid his unease with a sip of beer. "What kind of vengeance?"

"All kinds. The market blossomed after the pussies lost control. Collabos, family feuds, political assassinations. I daresay I made quite a name for myself in that hunk of iron."

He blinked in disbelief. "Wasn't it dangerous?"

"I loved it. My da used to say, 'A rock-jack either learns to hold his breath or how to breathe vacuum.' Without a family to worry about—reprisals, you know—I was pretty much untouchable. Of course I had my limits: no children and no *yakuza*. But beyond that, fair game."

"Excuse me. *Yakuza*?"

"Japanese syndicate. Probably the last bastion of honorable humanity in that rock. At least, in my opinion. Everyone else was corrupt. But what do you expect after fifty years of occupation?"

Cheshire shifted uneasily, but decided to be blunt. "I expect you're seeing things as an orphaned rock-jack injected into harsh times."

She pinned his eyes, but he smiled and said, "Let me guess. You've killed men for less?"

She laughed, high and sweet. "Oh, Mr. Cheshire. It's a business, not a vendetta."

"How professional of you." He tilted his head in contrition. "But I guess I am being provocative. Please forgive me. I've never met an assassin—at least none that I know of."

She laughed again, and he smiled at her, relieved by her humor.

"So, how did you meet Lim?" he asked.

"I had a contract to kill him."

His face locked into a wooden smile; her sweetness now frightened him. *Did she murder Lim?* He decided not to ask and managed a gruff, "Oh?"

"It was the usual: secret client, payment in mixed ores, method to my discretion. Strange, though. He hadn't been in that rock more than a day. I had to wonder who he pissed off so quickly."

"Doesn't sound like Lim." He took a guarded sip of beer.

"Probably someone followed him from Sol. Or someone knew him from Sol." She shrugged. "No matter. I might wonder, but I didn't ask questions. I watched him for two full days and saw nothing special. No bodyguards, no extra security on his quarters, no attempt to vary his schedule. I decided to wait for him in his bedroom. I might be observed coming and going, but there'd be nothing to link me directly."

"How did you plan to do it?" *Peanut allergy, perhaps?*

Her face went blank. "I enjoy working with my hands." When he didn't react, she pouted. "You're a tough crowd, Mr. Cheshire."

He shrugged. "I'm a friend of Lim's. You learn to expect the unexpected." He reassured himself with a touch to his duffel. He could be out the open door in less than a second. "What happened?"

"I stood about an hour just inside the door to his bedroom. I disabled all the lights but one, so when he flipped the switch it'd shine direct in his eyes. I heard him enter the apartment, alone as usual, and klutz around in the kitchen for a time. I wasn't sure of his night habits—I thought he might watch some tri-d for a while—but pretty quick he was at the bedroom door."

"And?" He covered his tension with another sip.

"And he said, 'I'm glad you're finally here. The wait has been tedious.' He was backlit by the lights in the living area, and I could tell he was just speaking blindly into the dark of the bedroom. But he knew I was there. Somewhere." She leaned toward him, another conspiratorial invitation. "To tell the truth, I'd never been so scared during a job. Oh, I've been discovered and chased and even pinned a time or two, but I always knew why, knew where I'd screwed up. That . . ." She shivered. "That was uncanny."

He declined the invitation and did not lean toward her. "What did you do?" He hoped he sounded nonchalant.

"I focused on my breath and assessed the situation. He was alone. His hands were empty. He knew I was around, but not my location. But he was prepared for me. Evaluate: fulfill the contract now or retreat and try again later?"

Cheshire squinted in thought. "Neither. At that moment, there's insufficient information. Perhaps he's just making a lucky guess and will walk away. Or perhaps he'll switch on the light, blind himself, and give you an advantage. But at that moment, sit tight."

"Very good! Have you ever thought of assassination as a career path?" She sipped her beer. "What is it that you do, Mr. Cheshire?"

He shifted in his seat, discomfited by the non sequitur. "I'm an attorney, though I only just passed the bar on Earth. I haven't had much practice."

"I suppose I could make the boorish comparison between lawyers and paid assassins."

"Of course, but I think you're anything but boorish. So, you're standing next to the man you're contracted to kill . . ."

"And he turned away, stood with his back to the door for a moment and said, 'The only way out is through the living area, so you have to reveal yourself sooner or later. When you do, there'll be a drink waiting. Nothing else. Except for some conversation, if you're interested.' And he walked away. I heard him in the kitchen. Ice in glasses. Poured liquid. A settling onto the couch facing the door."

"So, he offered his assassin a drink. Sounds like Lim. What did you do?"

"I waited. Perhaps an hour, likely more. Eventually, I heard him stand. He said, 'Your ice has melted. I'll freshen this up for you.' I waited for kitchen sounds and quick-peeked around the lower part of the door. He was in the kitchen, back to me, but too far to get to without exposure. And the exit door was just beyond him."

"You were trapped. So, more waiting?"

"Nope. I chose a chair, and I was in it before he turned with a glass in each hand. I swear, he smiled at me as if I'd been there all along. 'Which glass would you like?' he asked. 'Left,' I said. 'Your left or my left?' 'Whichever left isn't poisoned,' I said. And the rest is history. We murdered each other in bed that night, and I followed him down-well a week later."

"I love a happy ending."

She lay her head back against the chair and gazed out the window. Her eyes brightened with tears, and she pressed fingers to her lips.

"There are no happy endings in Munchen," she whispered. "Lim is dead."

☙ CHAPTER 6 ☙

RESTLESSNESS took Prakk-Invalid in the late afternoon, a bad sign. Kzin soldiers, often faced with interminable waiting between battles, trained in ways to occupy the time. Gopher daydreamed, though the viscera of those dreams—heroic victory in a fierce fight; recognition and a name; grants of land and kzinretti—echoed distant and empty. What chance for legend lay in carrying satchels for monkeys, to monkeys, across a monkey city?

His ragged friend swung his legs off his *fooch* and grimaced as the cracked pads of his feet scuffed the floor. Prakk-Invalid rubbed the sparse fur on his belly with the stump of his arm and wet his nose with his dish-towel tongue.

"I smell something." His violet eyes, bloodshot and rheumy, scanned the room.

"The monkey beer is made from cattle feed. You smell like a grass-eater."

Prank-Invalid's hairless tail lashed in annoyance. "My one good arm is all that's needed to separate your insolent tongue from your arrogant throat."

Gopher fleered, but remained sprawled on his *fooch*. "My arrogant throat gags at your insolent smell."

The old kzin furled his ears, and a dangerous ginger scent wafted through the small space. Gopher grinned in defiance, but stayed ensconced. For a moment they quivered in a stiff tableau: two despondent kzinti in a dank cellar room on an abandoned block of a damaged city.

Prakk-Invalid waggled his ears in delighted surprise. "You test me!"

"'Lie in the tall grass until you are ready—leap no sooner.' I wondered if you remembered."

"'Si-Riit tested his teacher and did not find him wanting.'"

"I never thought you a scholar."

The old kzin preened his whiskers. "A good soldier learns many things."

Gopher hooked his tail with a claw and inspected the tip. "I learn, but nothing seems of importance—not these days, with the fleet destroyed and the monkeys in charge. When I was Recruit and you were Prakk-Captain, I understood what was important: honor, discipline, training. Now, what remains? I discipline myself to hope for the Patriarchy's return, and I train daily in the carrying of sacks for monkeys." He lightly drew a claw across his bare tail to leave a purple hairline of blood. "And what of honor? Where is the honor in this existence?"

Prakk-Invalid rumbled, but someone pounded on the apartment door. "Your honor knocks?" He waggled his ears. "Enter!"

Landlord Irfreed Jahn-Johsep swung open the door, but remained in the hall. He rubbed his lopsided face fur—an unfortunate maroon that clashed with the short burgundy fur around his ears—and scrunched his long, thin nose at the smell in the room. He spoke the hiss-and-spit of the Heroes' Tongue: "A good day to you, honored Heroes."

"Use slave patois," Prakk-Invalid snapped. Jahn-Johsep cocked his head and said—in Equal's Tense—"A Hero's expectations are always to be considered, but in these days expectations cannot always be met."

Ears furled, the old kzin sheathed and unsheathed his claws. "One day you will pay for your insolence."

"Perhaps. But today you pay your rent."

Claws sheathed, Prakk-Invalid turned his back on the monkey, who ignored the insult.

"Four hundred krona," the landlord said. Gopher stirred from his *fooch*, dug in a pouch on his harness, and extracted a pawful of coins and bills, which he dropped into the human's cupped hands. The monkey assayed the funds and frowned. "You are short forty-seven krona."

Gopher waived a paw in dismissal. "We have no other monkey money."

"I thought today was your payday."

Gopher's tail twitched in irritation. "You have all I received and more."

"You told me that you get three hundred krona a week. What happened to the rest?"

Gopher tweaked his tail, a kzinti shrug. "Taxes. Conversion from base ten to base eight. Payment for this web vest. Today's pay was one hundred seventy-one krona. The monkey even tried to withhold one krona, which I slashed without mercy." He swiped the air with a single claw. "Money is never simple with you . . . *humans*."

Jahn-Johsep whitened. "You slashed someone?"

The kzin waggled his ears in a dry laugh. "No, but perhaps I should have."

The landlord tugged his face fur and shook his head. "Honored Hero, I have warned you time and again that this base-eight conversion is a trick—a monkey trick—to cheat you. And yet you allow these *proles* to dishonor you and the worth of your work."

"I care not. There is no worth in delivering monkey bags, and there is no honor in monkey money."

"Except you need money—monkey money—to pay the monkey rent." The landlord ran a hand through his head fur. "You work at the brewery, *ja*? I will talk to them."

Prakk-Invalid growled over his shoulder, "You will do no such thing."

"Honored Hero, you know of my history—my long cooperation and assistance during the occupation. Your disdain for all things human would have been proper and honorable before the arrival of the UNSN Armada, but we are in a different world now. You still have my admiration, and I beg you to let me serve you—and me! Let me talk to these men."

"You only seek your share of the monkey money."

"Without which you will have no apartment, no food . . ." The landlord sniffed. "And no beer. I seek money, yes, but only to keep you off the strassen. Or have you forgotten the extermination squads roaming the city?"

Prakk-Invalid rounded, his ears flattened. Ginger scent wafted through the doorway.

The monkey took a cautious step back. "I'm trying to help."

"Leave now." Gopher aligned shoulder to shoulder with his old captain.

"You owe forty-seven more krona. Let me help."

Gopher unsheathed a single claw and slashed the air. The landlord ran. Gopher shut the door.

Prakk-Invalid waggled his ears in laughter. "I told you I smelled something."

🐾 CHAPTER 7 🐾

CHESHIRE WATCHED MAD WEEP and wished he could do the same, but strong feeling seemed too distant. Instead he felt numb. And a restless wish to do something. Lim was dead; bright adventure had thickened to gray iron.

Mad sipped her drink and composed herself. "You must excuse me, Mr. Cheshire."

"Not at all . . . Not at all . . ." he muttered. "It's all so senseless."

"He was coming to my apartment." She sniffed and smiled at him. "His friend, Kirkland, said they were talking about me when . . . when . . ."

He stiffened. "That's odd. Kirkland said they were talking about me when it happened."

"Perhaps Mr. Kirkland was just trying to be kind."

"Perhaps. But he also said they were headed to the brewery."

A knock startled them. A crooked man dressed in smeared coveralls peered from the apartment doorway. "Excuse me, Fraulein Valli. I am to be locking up soon."

"Of course, Herr Nietschul. Mr. Cheshire, this is Herr Nietschul, the building's porter."

"Porter?" Cheshire stood to shake the man's calloused hand.

"I watch the building. Repairs, cleaning, such."

"Ah, a superintendent."

"Yes, yes, a superintendent." Nietschul widened his eyes. "You are also from Sol?"

"Just arrived. I'm a friend of Lim Welson's." He felt a twinge of apprehension. *Everyone else had dumped on Lim. What bad things would Nietschul say?*

"Oh, I am very sorry, very sorry. He was a fine man. Friendly. And vigorous, so very vigorous. A shame what happened."

"Yes, it's hard to believe." A flicker of anger kindled at the unfairness.

Nietschul lifted his chin. "I saw it, you know. I was cleaning the windows in the apartment next door."

Mad stood close to Cheshire. He felt she might lean on him.

"They said it was quick." She quivered. "Was it? Was it quick?"

"*Ja*, it was quick. I heard him and his friends—Langbroek-Kikkert and . . . what is his name?"

"Kirkland?"

"Yes, Herr Kirkland leave. They were whispering—usually loudly they talk, but this day they whispered. I hear the front door close and then, a few moments later, Herr Kirkland said, 'We've got him. Get out of here!' I looked out the window, down to the street. I could not see much with them so close to the building, but I saw the three of them huddled around the body. They—"

Cheshire interrupted. "Wait. 'The three of them'? I understood it was only Kirkland and this Langbroek fellow. There was a third?"

"Yes, yes, a third. Not a man—a kzin. Kirkland said something—that kzin snarling—and the kzin ran off. Herr Kirkland began yelling, 'Help.' I called paramedics and went down, but it was too late. Herr Welson was, well, unrecognizable. His face—bloated and purple. So terrible." He made a little bow to Mad. "I'm sorry, Fraulein. It is a very sad business."

"Thank you, Herr Nietschul."

"You saw a kzin with them?" The story sounded incredible. "What did the police say when you told them?"

The porter puffed his cheeks. "Polizei? There were no polizei, just paramedics. Why would polizei be interested in an illness?"

"You didn't think it was important to tell someone?" Cheshire drew himself tall with indignation. "This was a man's life."

The porter flung a hand in disgust and turned away. "I didn't want trouble then, and I don't want trouble now. Fraulein Valli, your friend, he is not welcome here. Please, I have to lock up."

"Yes, Herr Nietschul. Please, Mr. Cheshire, he's not at fault here."

"I suppose." Cheshire wiped a discouraged hand across his face. "Let's get out of here."

On the street, carts, cart-men, and kzin huddled in lunchtime bunches along the strassen. The clouds had broken further, and the sun painted the gray cobblestones with its brightness. A wet smell from the Donau mingled with the dusts of the street. Mad took up Cheshire's arm in hers. "Where to now, Mr. Cheshire? Do you have a place to stay?"

"No, not yet." He ran the strap from his duffel over his shoulder. "It just doesn't add up."

"You can put your things in my apartment. In fact, you can stay there, too. I have a spare room and—no objections!" She laughed, bright and musical. "I promise not to kill you."

He returned her smile. "If I'm lucky, perhaps you'll 'murder' me instead?" With her arm locked in his, he had to look up to see into her cheerful eyes. He felt his fear of her melt away.

"Luck may have nothing to do with it." She blinked and searched the sky. "I might not want to be alone tonight." She pulled on his arm. "This way."

They walked along the gray strassen, the sun lighting their way. At the corner a semicircular knot listened to a zither player perched halfway up a stoop. His bony hands attempted a jaunty tune. From time to time he searched the faces of the listeners—looked but never found. His sadly played tune followed them down the street.

"What doesn't add up, Mr. Cheshire?"

"What? Oh. These stories about Lim's death. Did you ever see him eat peanuts?"

"Of course. He eats them all the time, especially when he's thinking. He likes to say, 'My great weaknesses are peanuts and pretty faces.'"

"Exactly. But he supposedly died from a peanut allergy. And this kzin—where did he come from? Did Kirkland mention a kzin to you?"

"No. Does it matter?"

"The cops seemed to think Lim was mixed up in something pretty bad. And now—"

"The cops?"

"They picked me up at the funeral. Tried to be all buddy-buddy with me."

"Schreibman?"

"You know him?"

She kicked a small stone and, when they reached it, kicked it again. "Detective Schreibman has it out for Lim."

"He's the one who told me Lim was mixed up in something." The stone lay in Cheshire's path. He kicked it, but it shanked over the curb. "Was he? Was Lim mixed up in something?"

"Of course Lim's mixed up in something. We all are. Haven't you been listening? It's how we survive."

"What was it?" Something bad. Always something bad. *Why do you get mixed up in these things, Lim?*

"I don't know. I never asked—force of habit I guess—and he never told me. He has the brewery and that's legitimate. But there could be other things."

Cheshire shook his head. "Kirkland's story has holes. Not big ones, but enough to make me wonder. Maybe that 'something' Lim was mixed in killed him. You're the assassin. What if someone wanted to murder Lim, but make it look like an accident? Maybe it wasn't a peanut allergy. Isn't there stuff that'll kill in the same way?"

She pursed her lips and frowned. "I think we need to visit Mr. Kirkland."

They strolled across a boulevard, interrupted by a single ground car, and drew abreast of a rusty iron fence edging a small park. Through a stone gate and down a white gravel path, a group of school children sprawled before a tall booth topped with a miniature stage. A faded banner announced "PUNCH and JUDY," with "Professor Hottentotten" lettered beneath. The children squealed as Punch— big nosed and dressed in faded pastels—beat a battered kzin puppet with a slapstick.

Mad and Cheshire purchased hand-meals from a nearby vendor. They crunched along the white gravel. The laughter and catcalls of the children drifted into the ghostly trees.

"I can't imagine growing up under the kzin," Cheshire said.

"I can't imagine growing up without them."

"What do you mean?" He stole a glance and felt the old, odd pride of having a pretty girl on his arm.

She shrugged. "Fifty years is a long time—over three generations. Maybe you fear them and what they do. Maybe you hate them for ruling you. But after awhile, they're just there, like a force of nature. So you get up in the morning, and maybe you go to work, but more often than not, you just scrounge for food or money or medicine. You do what you need to get through." She set her lips in a grim smile. "You live your life with an everyday bravery."

He could see the slave pain in her eyes. "And now?"

She lifted her chin to the bright sky. "Now we're free."

"Are they still a force of nature?"

She pondered. "In a way, yes. At first I thought we should've wiped them out. Why do we need quarter-ton cats with bad tempers roaming around? But then I saw them pulling the carts and carrying the bodies and doing the thousand things we told them to, and I realized it's a way to heal. The kzin are so much a part of us. If we killed them off, we'd be lost. We'd lose part of who we were when we were slaves."

"Retribution? You get to treat them like slaves?"

She shook her head, her face harsh. "No. I know some—a lot—who want that. Or to wipe them from the system. I still don't know why the UNSN stopped—they could've exterminated every last one of them. But they didn't. So now we have to deal with them. But not as slaves. We can't do to them what they did to us. We have to be better."

"Why?" He hoped he just sounded curious, but Mad skid to a stop, dropped his arm, and pinned him with hot brandy eyes.

"Because we're not kzin. We're human. And that has to mean something, something better than slash and kill and maim. Some people want to revive the hunting parks—you know, the ones used by the pussies to hunt humans? Except humans would hunt kzinti instead." She took a steadying breath. "We can never be stronger or more fierce. We'll lose if we try to become like them. So we have to be better. Do you see?"

Cheshire pondered. "We'll lose if we try to become like they are. We have to be stronger in other ways. We have to be clever."

"Exactly." She locked his elbow in hers again, and they proceeded down the path. "Whether we like it or not, they're a part of this world. Somehow we have to learn to live with them."

"But, how?" The question intrigued him.

She shrugged. "It's a big planet. We don't have to kill them, but we don't have to live around them, either."

"Segregation?" He gave a rueful smile. "Who would pull your bread carts?"

"Oh, we'd find something. If the UNSN would let us build the things we need instead of arming the Hyperdrive Armada, there'd be plenty of alternatives."

"That force liberated your system."

"That *clever* force." She laughed, her vehemence dropping away. "Oh, Mr. Cheshire. We're just two small people who'll never make a difference. We could argue until the gagrumphers came home, but that won't change a thing. Shall we concentrate on the task at hand?"

He barked a laugh, nonplussed by her mercurial change in mood. She was right, of course. He patted her hand in the crook of his elbow. "You're good company, Maddie."

"Thank you, Mr. Cheshire. I enjoy your company as well." The warm light from Alpha danced in her eyes. Up ahead, a broken stone gate marked the end of the park.

She pursed her lips, and a frown chased back into her face. "I tried to talk with Lim about this, about how we needed to live with the kzinti, but he wouldn't have any of it. 'Burn the ratcats,' he said. 'Burn them to the ground and scatter the ashes in orbit as a warning to their vermin kind.' He talked a lot about what the pussies had done to Sol."

"He lost his father and an older brother during the third invasion. Torch riders."

"He told me. Courageous, attacking an enemy with only your rocket exhaust. He wanted to be brave, like them, but he'd say, 'I've got to do more, Maddie. A ship or two—what difference does that make? I want to strike hard at the very souls of these bastards. I don't want to bloody their noses—I want to rip off their limbs and give them a mirror so they can watch themselves bleed to death.'"

Cheshire laughed. "Lim sure could talk."

Beyond the park, they rounded a corner, and Mad caught up

sharp. A ragged assembly of police ground cars clogged the street in front of her building. "What the Finagle?"

A black policewoman, round faced and full of bustle, stood at the top of the stoop. "I can't let you enter."

"I live here."

"Maddelena Valli?"

"Yes."

"Please go up."

Another policeman, muscles poured into a uniform, stood at the entrance to the apartment. Through the open door, a bustle of officers tossed the room—pictures, clothes, cushions, towels, dishes, cutlery, foodstuffs were picked up, examined, and thrown into piles. Detective Schreibman appeared in the doorway.

"You again," Cheshire said as he flung a hand at the fat man.

"What's going on here?" Mad's tone sounded low and dangerous.

"Ah, Herr Cheshire," Schreibman said. "You do run with an interesting crowd."

"What is going on here?" she asked again.

"Routine investigation of an anonymous tip."

"Do you have a warrant?" Cheshire asked.

Schreibman lifted an eyebrow. "Ah yes, the lawyer. Earning your keep already?" He produced a folded paper from his pocket and thrust it to Mad, who eyed the writing, then handed it to Cheshire.

"'Criminal conspiracy'? Conspiracy to do what?" Cheshire asked.

"I can't divulge details of an active investigation."

"But you have to have a crime to commit conspiracy. What's the crime?"

"I can't divulge details of an active investigation."

Cheshire slapped the paper. "This would never hold up in court."

"Properly signed by a magistrate." Schreibman let a smile crack his full-moon face. "Everything in *ordnung*."

"Hardly."

"In any case, Fraulein Valli, please come with us." Schreibman snapped fat fingers, and the policeman at the door slid up to Mad to clutch her upper arm.

Cheshire scowled. "You're arresting her? On what charge?"

"Fraulein's transit documents from Tiamat to Wunderland are not in order."

"Oh? Show me the arrest warrant."

Schreibman shifted uncomfortably, but his voice betrayed no hesitation. "We have evidence that the Fraulein is planet-side illegally. No warrant is necessary."

"Well, I'm afraid it is, buddy-boy. You know as well as I do that you have to get a warrant from the Tiamat Legation before you can arrest a citizen of the Swarm for anything except a violent crime. It seems bastards like you were trumping up charges against Swarmers, so you lost your discretion to arrest at will. Oh, and that's been the law for over seventy years." To Mad he said, "I guess I am earning my keep today."

Schreibman glowered, but nodded to the policeman, who released Mad's arm. "You're only postponing the inevitable, Herr Cheshire. I'll have a warrant by tomorrow morning."

"One day at a time."

"In the meantime, Fraulein, your apartment is sealed. Any objections, Herr Cheshire?"

Cheshire pondered, but shook his head.

"If you'll excuse me." Schreibman made a thick bow and disappeared into the apartment. The policeman stood in the open door and studied them with hard eyes.

"Damn," Cheshire said.

☙ CHAPTER 8 ☙

PRAKK-INVALID lay very still. Tiny Jotoki—sentient starfish with five arms—crawled at the corner of the ceiling and the wall. More advanced in the shadows on the floor. They meant to drop on him— or climb the legs of the *fooch*—and wriggle under his fur. He began to pant; ropes of drool hung down shattered lips.

Gopher unbent from where he napped and studied his friend.

The ragged kzin jolted upright. He felt them! They were on him already! He swept his paw along his legs, but the Jotoki dropped from the ceiling onto his shoulders. Onto his head! They squirmed to his ears—into his ears!—and piped complicated harmonic tunes with their five mouths.

Gopher leaped to Prakk-Invalid and grasped the ruined kzin's face between his paws. "Be still, and tell me the problem."

"They sing!" he wailed. He tried to grab Gopher's arm with his missing hand and swiped at the aliens with his other. "The Jotoki sing!"

"There are no Jotoki. There is no singing."

The old captain froze. He stared unseeing into Gopher's eyes. "They sing of monkey honor filling the galaxy. They sing . . . they sing of Heroes, gone from the galaxy—gone for so long that even the dust of their memory is forgotten." His eyes widened. "The Jotoki rejoice."

"There are no Jotoki." Gopher swung onto the *fooch* and wrapped his arms around Prakk-Invalid. "You dream—that is all." He attempted to groom him, but hunks of brittle fur came away with each rough lick. The old kzin began to purr, ragged and halting.

Gopher rocked him, just a little.

This is not the monkey beer.

He frowned at a vague memory, hunted its scent, then hummed a long-forgotten tune. He felt his friend relax.

"Mama," Prakk-Invalid said.

"Hush."

"Mama, I hurt."

"Be brave, little one."

"I will. I promise."

Gopher rocked and considered options. Neither the monkey paramedics nor the monkey hospital would help a kzin. He remembered a Hero once spoke of a kzin hospice far north of the old city, but would they help a kzin who was not dying? Gopher froze. *Was Prakk-Captain dying?*

"I must carry you," he said. "It is a long way. You must be strong for . . . for Mama."

The old kzin waggled his whiskers. "I will."

Gopher slid off the *fooch*, pulled him to the edge, and turned his back. "Put your arms around my neck."

His arms secure, Gopher wrapped Prakk-Invalid's legs around his torso and took his friend's mass onto his back. He weighed nothing, only bones through melted flesh.

By late afternoon, the iron-gray sky of the morning had broken into brilliant blue. Gopher traversed the tired blocks until they found Lange Strasse, a straight boulevard that served the northern suburbs. He fell into a steady, long-distance lope, his friend bobbing across his back. A smattering of tired monkeys—early releasees from the factory complexes north of the city—jolted aside as the nine-foot orange pair loomed.

Gopher felt Prakk-Invalid's head swing up, and a clear voice asked, "Where are we going?"

"North."

The old kzin studied the answer, but asked nothing more. Instead he said, "I have been hunting the question of *kz'eerkt*—I mean, human—honor."

Gopher slowed for a moment. *Was Prakk-Invalid recovering?* Yet he'd seen wounded rally, only to falter soon after. He resumed his determined pace and asked, "What have you scented?"

"There are two types of honor—"

"More than two."

"Do not interrupt. In this hunt, there are two: personal and public. The personal consists of the character traits of a good soldier of the Patriarch—obedient to orders, competent in performance, prideful in spirit. All these feed personal honor."

The northern factories now lined the strasse. Gopher dodged through a great flow of astonished workers. "And the public honor?"

"That is the honor conferred by others."

"A name? Land? Rank?" Gopher's greater height allowed him to pick paths through the crowds.

"Those are but the trappings. Public honor is the respect conferred by others. It is the step-aside, the straight-tailed salute . . ." He wheezed in a hollow fit. He spit and lay a dribbling muzzle against Gopher's shoulder. "I am tired."

"Public honor," Gopher prompted. The crowds of alarmed monkeys were thinning.

The old kzin bounced in silence. Finally he said, "Public honor is a name whispered even after death. A kzin gone, but not forgotten."

"And what does that have to do with the monkeys?"

"On this planet, in these circumstances, we must win public honor not just from our kind, but from the monkeys as well. It is the logical extension of the Ritt's teachings. Now that we are among them—alone among them—we must win their respect. We must learn their ways, including the ways of their money, and defend our honor in all our dealings. We must learn to count. Your claw—" His breath bubbled against Gopher's back. "Your claw . . . against the human . . . one krona. We must do that more."

The factories gave way to ancient wood buildings. The Hero had said, "Follow the stench." Gopher sampled the air and traced a faint smell of suffering and death. He swung to the east. "We are nearly there."

"Good. The Jotoki are close behind. I hear them singing."

An unmarked building reeked. A pair of glass and steel doors ground open as they approached. In the lobby, a monkey in a UNSN uniform sprang from behind a desk. "This way," he said in perfect Heroes' Tongue and pushed through a tall set of double doors into a kzin infirmary.

At parade rest, Gopher stood a stony watch as a silver-furred kzin scanned Prakk-Invalid's twisting form. The doctor demanded a medical history, which Gopher provided as best he could. After several shots, an IV, and a respirator, Prakk-Invalid appeared to rest easy.

"Will he recover?" Gopher asked.

The doctor twitched uncertain whiskers. "Likely not, though there is no predicting for certain."

Gopher knew, but he asked anyway. "What caused this?"

"The monkey beer. I think there are certain . . ." The doctor whipped his tail. "Certain aspects that can bring injury."

"How long might he live?"

"He likely will expire shortly, but if he lives the night, he might recover."

Honor required a death-watch. "I will stay."

The doctor flattened his ears in anger. "I am dishonored to say the humans prohibit healthy kzinti from remaining in this facility. I am ordered to enforce this rule. You cannot stay."

Gopher bared his teeth and growled long and low. His paw crept to the *w'tsai* on his web vest.

The doctor slid a paw to his *w'tsai* and growled in return. "I have many ears. Do not test me."

The UNSN monkey appeared in the doorway, a military stunner in his hand. "Is assistance needed?"

Gopher continued a low, offset rumble while he pondered. Honor required a fight. Yet, he would fall immediately to the stunner and be dumped outside the building. *What would Prakk-Captain do?*

He covered his teeth. "I will go." His paw retreated from his *w'tsai*.

The doctor relaxed and flicked his tail in studied acknowledgment. "I will send word should he live."

Gopher followed the UNSN monkey to the reception area and pushed out the anemic doors. On the strasse, before the dilapidated and stinking infirmary, he blinked up at the terrible blue sky.

Prakk-Captain. He could not yet bring himself to whisper his name.

☙ CHAPTER 9 ☙

On the strasse in front of Mad's apartment, Cheshire asked, "What now?"

"That fat shit." Mad shivered with the effort to restrain herself. "That fat shit."

Cheshire stepped back and held the duffel at his knees, between him and Mad. He wondered whether being in the company of an assassin with the nickname, "Mad," might be a Bad Idea.

She threw back her head and screamed at her apartment window, "You! Fat! Shit!" The policewoman took a concerned step down the stoop. Mad closed her eyes, gulped a breath, and let it go in slow suspiration. She blinked, her eyes damp and shining, and smiled at him.

"I guess we find a hotel," she said. "I have—wait, what if they froze my bank accounts? Damn it, we need to find an infocomp."

"I have an infocomp."

"A personal infocomp?"

He nodded and slid his sleeve up. She cradled his wrist with both hands while she gazed at the watch-sized box. "Does everyone in Sol have one?"

"Just about." He felt an unjust pride.

"We have so much catching up to do."

As feared, her accounts were frozen.

"I have money," he said. "And we can fight Schreibman."

Her mouth pressed in a grim line, and she shook her head. "No.

The fat shit is right. Lim finagled my transit documents so I could accompany him down-well. Otherwise, I'd still be waiting."

"Well, he's got to get a warrant. And then he has to find you. In the meantime, we'll figure a way to fight it. It's just the law—there are always arguments to be made."

"How did you know that thing about warrants for Swarm citizens?"

"Lim wanted me to help him with his legal matters, so I read up on Wunderland law while in transit."

She gave him a sad smile. "I've known you only a few hours, and I already owe you. I can see why Lim likes you."

He held her eyes for a moment, then blushed and looked at the prideful blue sky. The clouds had disappeared, and a faint Beta, the second sun of Alpha Centauri, peeked at them from above a rooftop. He bounced the duffel with playful knees. "Hotel first, or Kirkland?"

"Kirkland."

"I'm never going to get rid of this bag, am I?"

"Why don't you just drop it?"

"It's all I've got." He gave the bag a happy squeeze. "They don't let you pack much, so I brought what was important. Not just clothes—history, you know? Even the bag—it used to be Lim's." He smoothed a hand over the embroidered initials, LOW. He laughed. "It's been with me across four light-years. Relatively speaking, that's nearly forever."

"How sentimental, Mr. Cheshire."

"Guilty as charged." He hugged the bag. "It might be all I have left of Lim."

They called Kirkland, who at first begged off meeting, but a voice in the background—imperious and sharp—caused him to swallow his reluctance. An hour later, they entered the wrought-iron gates of the Lebensraum Brewing Company, a compound of buildings on the banks of the Donau River. Long stone buildings, clean washed and labeled with well-lettered wood signs, clustered around the central five-story brewhouse. A plump guard in a spotless uniform accompanied them to the front office, where they enquired after Herr Kirkland. A lanky woman, handsome but studious in an old-fashioned pair of glasses, frowned at them.

"Herr Kirkland is in the tower office."

"He's expecting us." Cheshire smiled his warm, charm-the-bureaucrat smile. "I'm Lim Welson's friend, Martin Cheshire. And this is Maddelena Valli."

"A moment." After hushed conversation over her desk infocomp, she said with a nod to the guard, "Kenkel will escort you up."

The interior of the brewhouse hummed with hustle. Smells of grain—dusty or wet or toasted—wafted throughout. A well-ordered dance of kzin gravity sledges, staffed by uniformed humans, shifted hops and malted barley from the kilns in the outer courtyard to hungry hoppers ranked along the walls. Long, geometrical spans of pipes shot at strange angles to unseen destinations far above. Five enormous copper kettles marched in unison down the center of the building, flanked by lesser steel fermentation tanks. And through it all, blurred belts of bottles droned like ancient airplanes on their way to drop dangerous loads on the unsuspecting.

The guard escorted them to a kzin gravity plate pressed into service as an elevator. They rose past the pipes, structural girders, and steel catwalks to a mesh landing bordered by pipe railing. The guard unlocked a single rope, ushered them from the grav-plate onto the landing, and snapped the rope into place. The grav-plate sunk from view, back to the ground, five floors below.

The guard escorted them through a thick door, which closed out the factory noise. Kirkland, greasy and dark, fidgeted behind a receptionist's desk, which protected a carved set of double doors to an inner office. Kirkland rose and clasped their hands with a damp, dead-fish shake. He tried to smile, but only leered as he said, "Welcome! Welcome! So nice to see you again, Herr Cheshire, Fraulein. Please, have a seat."

The desk infocomp beeped. Kirkland glanced at the machine— the display had been turned so only he could see—and said, "Can I offer you anything? A drink, perhaps? Food?" With wan smiles, Mad and Cheshire shook their heads.

"No? Well, don't be afraid to speak up if you change minds, *ja*?" Kirkland settled into the receptionist's chair. "What might I do for you?"

"Could you tell us again about . . . about Lim's passing?" Mad held her back rigid as she sat at the edge of a supple leather armchair.

"Lim's passing?" Kirkland gazed at the fabric of his chair's arm, which he stroked like a pet. "Truly unfortunate. But what could I add?"

"Please, just tell it again." Her Swarmer stillness belied the turmoil beneath.

"Well, umm," he glanced at the infocomp. "I met Lim at his apartment. We were heading to the brewery, umm . . ." He glanced at her, but avoided her eyes. "After we were to meet you at your apartment, Fraulein." He measured the texture of the chair arm. "Lim mentioned your arrival, Herr Cheshire, and I . . . I . . . I said he should introduce Herr Cheshire to you, Fraulein." Kirkland pulled a gray square of fabric from a jacket pocket, wiped his forehead and dried each finger of each hand. "So, you see, as I said, we were talking about you—both of you—just before the incident."

"And?" Cheshire hoped he hid his own turmoil. *You're a bad liar, Mr. Kirkland.*

"We were just leaving the building when Lim became silent. I looked at him, and already . . ." Kirkland gave a shaky sigh. "And already his face was big. So big. And a ghastly shade of purple. His eyes . . ." Kirkland shuddered. "His eyes pleaded. He could not talk, but how those eyes pleaded. I will never forget."

The infocomp beeped, and Kirkland glanced at the screen. Abashed, he straightened in his chair and folded his hands on the desk. "I helped him to the ground and loosened his collar. Then I called out for help, which someone must have heard, since the paramedics showed up soon after. But it was to no avail."

Cheshire narrowed his eyes. "You said it was an allergy attack. How do you know it was peanuts?"

Kirkland seemed relieved. "The coroner, that was his finding. You met him, Herr Cheshire, at the funeral."

"What? That man with the funny beard?"

"Yes." Kirkland fidgeted, then finally added, "A business acquaintance of mine. Of ours."

"Why was no one else at the funeral?" Mad's hands lay deadly still in her lap. "Where were Lim's other 'business acquaintances'?" She leaned, an imperceptible closing of the distance between her and Kirkland, a small threat louder than a shout. "Why weren't our friends invited?"

Kirkland roused himself. "Fraulein Valli, I appreciate the

strain—we all feel his loss. But I do not mean to become the focus of . . . of . . ." The infocomp beeped, and Kirkland repeated the words he read with relief. "Of indelicate questions."

Cheshire began to slide a comforting hand to Mad's knee, but thought better of it. "I have an 'indelicate question' for you, Mr. Kirkland. When Lim had his allergy attack, in front of his building, what was the kzin doing there?"

"What was a kzin doing there?" Kirkland settled back into his chair. "What kzin, Herr Cheshire?"

"The kzin who was with you and Lim. The kzin who you talked to, who ran away before the paramedics arrived."

"What an extraordinary claim." Kirkland began to rise, but the beep of the infocomp replaced him in his seat. "What makes you say that, Herr Cheshire?"

"The porter was washing windows and saw it."

"Oh. And what else did he say he saw?"

"Just that. You talked to the kzin, and he ran away. Then you began yelling for help."

The infocomp beeped. Kirkland glanced at the screen and gave a nervous cough. "Of course, of course. The kzin. He was just passing by and asked whether he could help. Well, you know Herr Welson's prejudices toward the kzin—you especially, Fraulein." From his chair, he bowed slightly toward her. "I thought it best to turn him down, so he ran off." Kirkland wrinkled his nose. "A simple explanation. Nothing dramatic, Herr Cheshire."

Mad glared at Kirkland. Cheshire pulled his lower lip. "Yes, a simple explanation." He caught her eye and raised his eyebrows. "I think we're done here. What do you think, Maddie?"

She began to protest, but Kirkland jumped from his chair and rounded the desk. "So good to see you both again." He shook their hands with newfound warmth. "I'm glad I could clear up your concerns. You see it was all just a tragedy, just a tragedy."

"Indeed," Cheshire said and hefted his duffel. Beyond the outer door, the sounds of the brewery hammered at them. "Quite an operation you have here."

Kirkland stood in the doorway, reluctant to follow them onto the mesh landing. "Largest private employer in Munchen," Kirkland said with a genuine smile. "We run around the clock."

"Lim owned the brewery?"

"With his partners, yes."

"Was there a will, Mr. Kirkland?"

"A will?" Kirkland glanced over his shoulder at the unavailable infocomp. "I am not sure, Herr Cheshire. Would a will make a difference?"

"Beats me. I don't know anything about Wunderland law—I was just asking."

"Of course, of course. I assume you will be heading back to Sol immediately?"

"Yes, I suppose. Without Lim, I'm afraid I'm a little lost."

"Indeed. As are we all." Kirkland bowed. "Fraulein Valli. Herr Cheshire. Kenkel will show you out."

On the strasse outside the brewery gate, Cheshire offered his elbow to Mad. "Let's get out of here."

They hurried down random cobblestone streets until they found themselves on a worn dirt path in a treeless park along the banks of the Donau. Alpha waned and hinted at sunset. A damp breeze crossed the river with wafts of muck and tides.

"I think we can talk here," Cheshire said.

"That was worthless."

He felt her shiver, and he patted her hand. "Don't despair." He smiled grimly. "Or do. I'm pretty sure Lim's partners killed him. Under Wunderland law, if there's no will, a partner's share automatically vests with the remaining partners. So there's your motive. And that coroner—he was there when Lim died. I bet if we searched the public records, we'd find he's a partner in the brewery, along with Kirkland and a bunch of other lowlifes."

"But why kill Lim?"

Cheshire shrugged. "He got in over his head—at least, that's what the cops seem to think. You said that to survive around here you've got to get mixed up in questionable things. So Lim comes from Sol— no friends, no family—and uses his money to start a business with some less-than-desirable characters. The business takes off. Why keep the flatlander around?" *Oh Lim, your adventures finally killed you.*

She gave a pensive nod. "That story about the kzin. No pussy would offer help to a human. He was there for a reason."

"Did you see the way Kirkland was eyeing the infocomp? Someone was watching us and feeding him lines."

She squeezed his arm. "I just hope they were satisfied with his performance."

The concern in her voice caught him short. "What do you mean?"

"I mean . . ." She leaned close and whispered. "I mean we're being followed."

☙ CHAPTER 10 ☙

GOPHER HUNKERED onto all fours and ran. South. First through rough-patched asphalt streets serving shamed wooden shacks, portions fallen open to the Wunderland weather. Then along concrete roadways lined with angular steel buildings, the ways crowded with chattering monkeys intent on their business. Finally, into the maze of strassen of Old Munchen with its familiar cobblestones and ghost row houses. His paws echoed in a rhythmic slap that seeped deep into his empty mind.

He skidded to a stop, stood erect, and fleered as he sniffed surroundings. The river rolled deep and slow five blocks east. A thicket of monkeys—migrating north and south, to and from work—thronged Lange Strasse seven blocks to the west. And ten blocks southeast, the brewery shed its burned-grain stink into the city proper. He shuffed to clear his nose and continued at a slow walk toward home.

Home. Without Prakk-Invalid. No more concern to fill his days; no more cajoling the old kzin to eat; no more missing monkey money from the pouch on his harness, spent on monkey beer. No more payment on an endless debt of honor.

He passed a manret with a careless child following behind. The child pointed at Gopher and cried, loud and alarmed, in the senseless monkey tongue. The manret pounced on the child, slapped it with her clawless hand and shoved it along. The child cried, loud again, and met with another slap. Gopher grinned at them, a gesture without anger. The manret collected the child into her arms and hurried away.

He continued his slow walk and pondered the manret's suitable conditioning of the young monkey. A kzinret would do the same—his mother would have done the same. Perhaps monkeys and kzinti shared some common thread of honor, woven into the upbringing of the young. How else to explain the monkey victory over the Patriarchy?

He wondered what the young monkey had said.

At a corner a group of monkeys surrounded a young male lying flat on his back on the cobblestone street. Blood seeped from gashed flesh through shred clothes—a kzin paw had slashed across his back and down his side. A monkey cried at Gopher's appearance; he and four others fled down an alley.

The remaining monkeys stood aside as Gopher approached. One monkey chattered at him—a question? An explanation? Gopher gave a loud chuff and said nothing. Another monkey flung an empty hand at him, chattered, then flung his hands toward where the four had disappeared. Gopher twitched his whiskers with disinterest. The monkeys chattered, and several stooped to grab the arms and legs of the prostrate human. Gopher chuffed again and moved on.

Monkey chatter. Gopher swung to watch as they carried away the bleeding man. "Learn to count," Prakk-Invalid had said. What was the monkey word for *one*? To learn to count, he had to learn the monkey chatter.

"Interworld," he said, the word strangled by awkward lips, a pallet stiffened by the proper Heroes' Tongue. From the procession, a monkey peered back.

"Interworld," Gopher said to him—loud, better pronounced. The monkey hurried away.

Two blocks south, he nearly stumbled over a monkey who sat on the walk, his back against a granite plinth.

"Honored Hero, could you spare some change for a fellow warrior?" The monkey spoke in passable Heroes' Tongue. He wore a fouled UNSN jumpsuit, the insignia of the space corps on the shoulder. On his sleeve, a layer of pips signified Heroes killed in action.

Gopher touched a pouch and remembered the landlord. "I have no . . . money." He withheld the *monkey*, an awkward omission.

"Times are hard for soldiers, human and Hero alike." The monkey wrinkled his face. "Do you have the sickness?"

Gopher surveyed himself—Prakk-Invalid's fluids matted the fur on his shoulders and upper arms. "No." He licked clean a bicep.

The monkey drew up his knees and said something in Interworld.

"I speak the Heroes' Tongue," Gopher said. After a hesitation, "I wish to learn Interworld."

"Good luck with that." The monkey yawned, careful to cover his teeth with a clawless hand. "Though I've met some Heroes who speak it well."

"How do I learn?"

The monkey moved his shoulders in some meaningful way. "I don't know." He hugged his knees, laid a stubbled cheek on an arm, and peered up. "Another time, another place, we would have fought."

"We would have brought honor to each other."

The monkey moved his head up and down. "Times are hard on warriors when there is no war."

"Perhaps there are other ways to earn honor?"

On the filthy sidewalk, along the gray cobblestone strasse, the monkey closed his eyes. "Honor is given or taken. Honor cannot be earned."

Gopher rumbled and whipped his tail in agreement. "Do you have a name?"

"Jonah Matthieson. Have you been given a name?"

"I am known as Gopher." He swallowed shame at repeating the monkey word.

The monkey moved his head up and down. "A label." He closed his eyes again. "You deserve a better label."

"It is what I do."

"You have given me no coin, but you have given me attention, which is the only other thing a beggar can hope for." He smiled, his lips a thin line. "I will give you a better label." He unfolded his legs and sat up straight. "I give you the man label *Seeker*. You seek to learn Interworld."

"Seeker." The Interworld word felt familiar, a hiss across lips.

"Yes, good." The monkey bobbed his head.

"Seeker of Interworld."

"Yes," the monkey said in the Heroes' Tongue and repeated in Interworld, "Yes."

Seeker curled his ears in pleasure. "Yes," he said in Interworld.

The monkey scrunched his face. In Heroes' Tongue he said, "I'll give you one more thing: a warning. There is an extermination squad around here, so go with awareness. They leaped on a Hero not long ago. Fortunately for the Hero—and unfortunately for them—they took a casualty. So keep to the tall grass." He hugged his knees and said in Interworld, "Carefully."

Seeker of Interworld repeated the meaningless sound. "Carefully."

"Yes," the monkey soldier said in Interworld.

"I thank you, Jonah Matthieson."

❧ CHAPTER 11 ❧

"FOLLOWED?" Cheshire blinked but didn't turn his head. "Where?"

"Behind us. She's on a bench pretending to stare at the river."

"How long?" He suppressed a hint of panic. *Lim's killers.*

Mad shook her head. "I only spotted her when we entered the park. There's not enough cover, so she stood out. For all I know she's been with us since Lim's apartment."

They sped up. To sneak a peek, Mad threw back her head and laughed. "She's on the move."

He knew, but asked anyway, "Who would follow us?"

"Who do you think?"

"But why?" The panic tried to rise again.

"I'll ask her."

He dropped his duffel and grabbed the hand on his elbow. "No! We don't want to provoke them."

"They are provoking me."

"Right now they're hoping they answered all our questions and we'll go away. If we confront them—Lim's murderers—what do you think they'll do?"

"You should be worried about what I'll do."

"Believe me, I am."

She grinned and picked up the duffel. Up ahead, the park ended in riprap, and the path hooked toward a battered stone archway.

"What now, Mr. Cheshire?"

"Do Swarmers know how to run?"

"Try me."

At the park entrance they strolled past the arch. Cheshire glanced at the figure not far behind before the stone blocked the view. Without a word they began to run.

His feet chattered on the cobblestones. The light gravity flung each stride impossibly far. He stumbled; she caught his arm.

"Take this." She draped the duffel's strap across his shoulder. "It'll give you mass."

Behind them the woman—a dark shape against the green of the Donau—exited the park in a hurry. When she saw their distance, she began to run.

"Left!" They entered a narrow alley of greasy brick. The weight of the duffel gave purchase to his steps, but threw off his balance. She strode ahead.

"I can't keep up."

"This way!" At a four-way intersection of alleys, she hooked another left. The rhythmic slap of the pursuer's feet echoed off the brickwork.

Mad slowed and grabbed his arm. "Move, flatlander!"

He doubled his effort and kept up. They reached a strasse and hooked left again.

"Maybe - we - should - split - up." His breath came ragged in the thin Wunderland air.

"If - you - want," she panted back. "If she - follows me - you know - what - I'll do."

"Never - mind."

At the corner they were back on the street with the park gate. She tugged him behind the edge of the building.

"Break," she wheezed. She peeked low around the corner. "She - just - came - out - the - alley."

"Let's - go."

They pounded down the street. Just past the alley, he tugged her into a recessed doorway. They rattled the locked handle on a stout wood door. Mad set to run again.

"Wait," he panted. "Maybe - we'll - get - lucky."

She peeked around the edge of the recess. "She's standing - at the alley. She's looking - at the - park gate. She's . . . oops!" Mad ducked back. "I don't think - she saw me."

She snuck a peek. "Finagle! She's walking this way."

"Run?"

"I'm done running." Mad's frame flexed. She seemed to liquefy then harden into supple steel.

"Please don't." He didn't know what to fear more: their pursuer or Mad's violence.

She grinned. "Give me another option."

On the strasse a ground car stopped and honked. The passenger door opened, and Buford Early leaned from the driver's seat. "Get the hell in here!"

They piled in, and Early accelerated. Far behind, the woman threw up her hands in exasperation. Early chuckled.

"That was lucky." Cheshire settled into his seat, relieved to set the duffel at his feet.

"Luck had nothing to do with it." Mad scowled at Early. "You were following us."

"Good goddamn thing, too." Early set the controls to automatic and faced them. "You do get around, Mr. Cheshire."

"I'm beginning to think that everyone on this planet has nothing better to do than give me a hard time."

"Buford Early, ma'am."

"Maddelena Valli."

"Good to meet you. I'm sorry about your boyfriend."

"You knew Lim?" She gave the rumpled black man a hopeful smile.

"I knew of him. I never had the pleasure of a meeting."

Cheshire pointed a dismissive hand. "Early here was one of the cops at Lim's funeral."

"Oh."

"Come now, Miss Valli. Not all cops are bad, just as not all assassins are bad."

"Who are you?" she asked with proper wariness.

"He's with the UNSN," Cheshire said. "He's an admiral or something."

"General, my boy. General."

"Where are you taking us?" Cheshire began to regret getting into the car.

"I have something you both need to see."

🐾   🐾   🐾

The ground car drove them through the gray streets, the cobbles humming under the tires. Near a newer section of the city, the streets smoothed into concrete, and the buildings twisted into modern shapes. Parades of kzin sledges slowed their travel, and determined human workers hurried on the sidewalks.

"What is this area?" Cheshire asked with mild curiosity, surprised at the change from the old city.

"Industrial park. Built by the ratcats to help arm their Fifth Fleet, but now it's being used to arm the Hyperdrive Armada. The whole economy of Wunderland is tooled for war."

"Just like under the pussies," Mad said.

Early raised an eyebrow. He pulled three cheroots from his jacket and repocketed two at their refusal. He lit and puffed toward a vent. "Give it time. We've got resources pouring in from Sol, as well as from the other colonies. Opportunities are opening up. Lim Welson was an example of that—capital seeking new markets. Mr. Cheshire, you're also an example of that. In a galaxy at war, why do you think we allow civilian hyperspace transports? Wunderland needs money and material. But most of all, it needs people."

"Flatlanders?" Mad crossed her arms. "Cows and sheep."

Early grinned. "Was Welson a cow or a sheep?"

She glowered and said nothing. The streets changed again—potholed asphalt bordered by ancient wood barracks. The ground car turned into a drive and parked in a lot.

"What is this place?" Cheshire asked over the roof of the car. A weathered portico covered part of a circular drive. A pair of glass-and-steel doors ground opened as they approached.

"Hospice." Early crushed his cheroot underfoot. "Kzin hospice."

Beyond the double doors, Early nodded to a receptionist dressed in UNSN fatigues. The soldier saluted and said, "Grassak-Medic is waiting at the nurse's station, sir."

They proceeded through another set of double doors. A stench clutched at them, sliding deep fingers of funk into their mouths and noses.

"What's that smell?" Cheshire asked.

"Death," Early said.

🐾   🐾   🐾

At the nurse's station a kzin, his orange and black coat streaked with silver, greeted them in passable Interworld. "Salutations, General Buford Early."

"Hello, Grassak-Medic. These are my friends, Maddelena Valli and Martin Cheshire."

The kzin rumbled and waved his tail in greeting.

"He says, 'hello,'" said Early. "Our friend here was a doctor on staff with the household of Chuut-Riit."

Mad nodded, and Cheshire said, "I am honored that you are the first kzin whom I have met face to face. Your distinguished presence brings distinction to our meeting."

Early guffawed, but the kzin flicked his tail in approval. "The recognition of the privilege of being the first to so meet is a tribute." The kzin turned to Early and chuckled his ears. "You could take a lesson in manners from Martin Cheshire."

"You're not the first to complain about my manners, doc."

"Martin Cheshire, where did you learn formal kzin greetings?"

"I'm from Sol. The trip gave me time to study up."

"Then perhaps you studied the Kzin Question?" Grassak-Medic's whiskers trembled with interest.

"No, I've not heard of that. What is it?"

Early cocked his head and pursed his lips. "I'd love to hear a flatlander's take on our little problem."

The kzin undulated his tail in puzzlement, but ignored Early's comment. "What should be done with the kzinti who remain on Wunderland. One option would be extermination—quick, easy, and the least problematic . . ." The kzin twitched his ears in amusement. "If you humans believe your losses would be acceptable."

"And the other option?" Cheshire wondered at the felinoid's noble confidence. *I'm talking politics with a ratcat.*

"On the other paw, there is integration. Humans and kzinti living together."

"Or segregation," Mad said. "They live their lives, we live ours." She shuddered. "We were their slaves—why would we want to live with them?"

"We have segregation now," said Grassak-Medic. "In Munchen, no more than two kzinti can live in the same city block. No kzin is allowed a bank account. No kzin can seek legal remedies against a human. We have no representation in the Provisional Government. Would you say, Maddelena Valli, that the kzinti are being allowed to live their lives?"

Early wagged a finger. "Some would say you bastards lost, so tough whiskers."

Grassak-Medic again undulated his tail in puzzlement. "General Buford Early, conversation with you is always a lesson in human vernacular."

"I'll take that as a compliment."

"Indeed." Grassak-Medic waived a dismissive paw. "I understand you argue on behalf of your devil-god, since you have expressed to me your belief in integration. Whether we lost and whether the Patriarchy will return are irrelevancies. What must be addressed is the here and now. If you will not exterminate us, then we must live together."

"I've only been down-well a few hours, but I've seen what we—we humans—think about kzinti. Isn't that what you need to change? How do you propose doing that?"

"Not just myself," Grassak-Medic said. "Others, human and kzin, think the same way. Change must come from those in power and, unless you humans are willing to subjugate yourself once more . . ." His ears twitched. "Then the change must come from the humans in power."

"The Provisional Government," said Mad. "Good luck."

"Indeed." Grassak-Medic's tail flicked with agitation. "General Buford Early brought you here to see something, and I'd like to show it to you. This way."

He stooped through another set of double doors. The stench thickened as they entered a long medical ward. On either side *foochesth* lined the walls, occupied by ragged kzinti—curled in tight balls, sprawled as limp starfish, slung in weak lumps. Rough skin oozed purple blood. Hunks of orange and black fur swirled off the beds and floated across the floor, stirred by the passing of an occasional caregiver. A low rumble of purring filled the ward and blended with whimpers for water or the Fanged God or death.

"This . . ." Grassak-Medic's Interworld faltered. "This is what segregation accomplishes."

Cheshire felt acid vomit in his throat. "What happened to them?"

"Vitamin deficiency," Early said. "Not enough biotin."

"Didn't you say that before? What causes it?"

"Too much avidin in their diet."

"The alcohol does not help." Grassak-Medic slipped next to a prostrate kzin, the stump of his left arm thrown over his eyes. A respirator ticked. The doctor detached a medical scanner from his belt.

"Alcohol?" Cheshire felt a chill of realization. *Lim's brewery.*

"On the kzin homeworld there is no beer," Early said without humor. "The kzinti are drinking beer, and the beer has avidin in it— a protein that attaches to biotin. Without sufficient biotin, the kzinti get sick."

"Rashes, hair loss, and paresthesia, to start." Grassak-Medic pressed a claw to the medical scanner. "Later comes anemia, lethargy, and myalgias."

"Paresthesia? Myalgias?" asked Mad.

"That feeling like pins and needles," said Early. "Myalgias. That's, um . . ."

"Muscle pains." The kzin closed the medical scanner. "Finally, anorexia, hallucinations, and death." He removed the respirator and smoothed the whiskers on the kzin's muzzle. "This Hero is dead."

"The kzinti are drinking themselves to death?" Cheshire asked.

"In essence, yes." The doctor's lips twitched in anger.

"Why don't you stop it?"

"Now we splinter the bone and get to the marrow," said Grassak-Medic. "General Buford Early, you must do something soon."

"Doc, I would if I could, but I only work here."

The kzin narrowed his eyes and absently unsheathed a claw. "You jest while Heroes die."

"I mean no disrespect. I'm working on a solution, but I hope you understand, it's not something I can do instantly or easily." Early placed an avuncular hand on Cheshire's shoulder. "I think we've seen enough. Let's get out of this stink." To the kzin he said, "Thank you, doc. I'll see my friends out and be back in a moment. I have something to discuss with you."

"Of course, General Buford Early. There was much honor in meeting you, Martin Cheshire and Maddelena Valli, though these circumstances proffer no tribute."

"Uh, nice meeting you." Cheshire could find nothing more to say. "Thank you."

In the parking lot, Cheshire stopped at the hood of the car. Anger sparked deep within him. "Why did you show us this?"

"I wanted you to see what your friend was doing."

"You're saying Lim's responsible?" Mad asked.

"More than responsible. He's not just brewing beer—he's adding avidin to the beer. We think it's on purpose, to deplete biotin from the kzinti who drink it."

Cheshire ran a desperate hand through his hair. "Are you saying that Lim was trying to poison people?"

"Not people, my boy, kzinti. And making a pretty pfennig in the process."

"Am I going to end up like that?" Mad shuddered. "I drink it all the time."

"The effect on humans is minor," Early said. "Kzin physiology is particularly vulnerable."

"But why are the kzinti drinking it, if it makes them sick?" she asked. "The pussies are anything but stupid."

"They are the remnants of an ancient empire that never, ever lost in battle. The kzinti remaining on Wunderland could not even die honorably. Why do humans drink to excess? Because life is good? Actually, I think it's a pretty hopeful sign."

"A hopeful sign? How can this be a hopeful sign?"

"It's a sign that kzin psychology is not that different from human. If a Kzin will drink himself to death because he feels like a loser, then maybe some of the mind tricks we've developed to help ourselves will work on them."

Mad folded her arms about herself and measured the sky with a dispirited glance. "So, Lim was trying to kill the kzinti on Wunderland."

"Perhaps. But not all of them are on the sauce—just a core group in Munchen, though Lebensraum is beginning to export to Tiamat."

"Tigertown?"

"Yah." Early hawked then spit on the asphalt. "That stink is still in my nose."

"Why don't you stop them—Lebensraum, I mean." Cheshire felt anger and despair, but wished he could feel nothing.

"Ah, politics," Early said. "My favorite. You see, outside the UNSN factories, the Lebensraum brewery is the largest employer in Munchen. And the largest taxpayer. We tried to have the Provisional Government prohibit the addition of avidin to the beer, but your friend Lim claimed it was an old Earth recipe and that any 'tinkering' by the government would ruin his business. He even threatened to close shop and return to Sol, so the politicians folded."

"And that's it? There's nothing else to be done?" *Lim, what have you done?*

"Well, our fat friend is trying to get evidence that the avidin is being added to the beer intentionally to harm the kzinti. He rolled an assistant brewmaster by the name of Crenvins, who was going to testify, but he disappeared the day before Welson died. Our theory is that when Welson's partners found out about Crenvins, they plugged all the leaks they could find, including your friend."

"Schreibman?" Cheshire asked. "He didn't seem too fond of the kzinti. Why would he want to help them?"

"It's not about helping the kzinti. It's about keeping them from finding out humans are deliberately poisoning them. Can you imagine their reaction when they figure it out? Schreibman doesn't want to help the kitties—he wants to avoid more war."

Cheshire scuffed the pavement with his shoe. Mad, arms akimbo, challenged Early. "There's more to this than you're telling. Why bring us here? To make us ashamed of Lim? That's hardly a reason."

Early pulled a cheroot from his pocket. "I have to get rid of this stink." He lit the cigar and puffed into the sky. "I'm telling you this because I've been tracking you, Cheshire. There's a pin just under the left armpit of your jacket that sends audio and GPS—that's it. I'll take it, thank you. I know exactly what you've been up to, and I think you needed to know what a dangerous game you've gotten yourselves into. I'm hoping that now you've seen the truth—that your friend's death was not that big of a loss—you'll let it go."

Early pointed with the cigar. "Go home, Mr. Cheshire. I've arranged for a shuttle back to Tiamat and a liner trip back to Sol. Go home and put up a shingle, or whatever you ambulance chasers do these days. Tell your friends and family about your adventures on Wunderland. Live your life and forget about us. We don't need lawyers here—we need people who can do actual work." He shifted his cigar to Mad. "As for you, young lady, I understand there's some trouble with your transit documents. If you're willing to work for us—nothing your skills can't handle—we could see that the problem disappears."

"Transit documents . . ." She grew murderously still. "It was you," she whispered. "You told them to inspect my documents. You bastard."

Cheshire stepped between Mad and Early, his arms wide, and murmured, "No, no." Her angry body trembled against his.

Cheshire said over his shoulder to Early, "I think you know our answer."

She stepped back, her eyes locked on Early, who shrugged.

"Suit yourself." He leaned into the ground car and programmed a destination. "The car will take you to the Shrader Hotel. I have to talk to the doc."

Cheshire and Mad slipped into the car. Early leaned in. "Go home, Mr. Cheshire. And Miss Valli, do please think about my offer." He closed the door before the swearing became too intense.

Early finished his cigar, grinding the dog end under his heel. As he entered the lobby of the hospice, his personal infocomp vibrated a pattern.

"Hello, Detective."

"General Early. I hope I am not interrupting."

"Not all. What can I do you out of?"

"So quaint, your expressions." Schreibman coughed, short and dry. "I had a tail on Herr Cheshire, but she lost him."

"That's too bad."

"She reports he and Maddelena Valli got into a ground car—a ground car registered to the UNSN. Would you happen to know the whereabouts of Herr Cheshire?"

"Well, Detective, no. I do not know the exact current whereabouts of Mr. Cheshire." Early grinned. "But, if I'm any judge of character, he and Miss Valli will be at the brewery tonight, some time after dark."

"Indeed." Schreibman sounded chagrined. "It is my misfortune to have assigned myself as their shadow tonight. I assume they'll be attempting the fifth-floor office?"

"Seems likely."

"And there is to be some climbing?"

"I wouldn't doubt it."

"Then I have a favor to ask."

🐾 CHAPTER 12 🐾

ALPHA, in late afternoon repose, played hunt-and-pounce between the weathered chimneys of empty row houses. Deep shadows hugged the stones, waiting to grow long as the cold light ebbed. In the alleys, Seeker of Interworld caught scents of curiosity and hunger from small nocturnal mammals as they woke for the evening.

The words of Jonah Matthieson chased their tails as Seeker sought their meaning. *Honor cannot be earned.* Certainly true—in a crude, malformed way. *Honor is given or taken.* True, depending upon the honor. His nose twitched as he scented a truth: The monkeys . . . the *humans* had a single word for honor. Perhaps, to them, context changed the word, added meanings beyond those that the single word could convey. So, *zzr'ssta*—the honor in obeying an order to the letter—was distinguishable from *zzr'sstir*—the honor in obeying the intent of an order—only in the context used.

He stopped short. *Honor depends upon success.* A Hero could obey an order to the letter, but find dishonor in failure. Only success conferred honor—perhaps that is what the . . . human meant. Indeed, the old tales showed that only success matters: the tale of Chaz-Ritt, who ventured from his pride circle to wrest technology from the Jotoki, or the tale of Warlord Chmee at the Pillars. Even the acts of Prakk-Captain, who earned *zzr'sstir* and his name when he controlled instinct and took captives. These kzinti, named Heroes all, took an action—a successful action—that brought them their honor. No kzin ever earned lands or kits or a name by *zzr'ssta* alone.

His tail twitched in vexation. *Why wasn't I taught this?* Instead he was taught to obey orders, that there is *zzr'ssta* in an order obeyed. Another realization leapt from the tall grass: *How else could discipline be kept?* A squad of Heroes, each intent on taking honor, would accomplish nothing.

His tail undulated in slow understanding. He was no longer a squad member or even a soldier. He was *wunderkzin*, set . . . free? . . .in an alien savanna. If he wanted honor, he had to find a way to take it.

The skin of his back twitched, irritated by Prakk-Invalid's drying ooze. He paused at a vacant lot, a square with bunched orange and green weeds, and clawed away litter to reveal cleansing sand. He unhitched the web vest and gave an enormous sigh as he threw his back into a happy slide. His spine twisted with sharp, automatic lunges, and his paws flapped in the air. He half-rolled, dug claws into the dirt, and shoved with joy. Then he flipped and shoved clean the other side. With a rumble, he closed his eyes and felt his fur and flesh warm the sand.

A monkey cry woke him. Instinct froze him. He drew a slow inhalation of scents. Sour odors from four monkeys surrounded him, confirmed by scuffs of feet in the lot's litter. He peeked. Alpha had long since set, and the dark form of a monkey rippled against a gray brick background. Seeker perceived a steel bar in his hands.

A monkey spoke, and tentative steps crunched closer. Seeker let his hackles rise and felt the thrill of ginger scent fill his soul. Combat. How he had longed for combat. He almost screamed and leaped on the dark form before his eyes, but Prakk-Captain's training guided him as he lunged to his feet in a defensive crouch.

The monkeys gasped and retreated a few steps. Seeker assessed the weapons of his assailants: a length of chain, a bat used in monkey sport, and—held in the steady grip of the fourth—a police stunner. If he had followed instinct and attacked the first monkey, the fourth monkey would have stunned him senseless. *Honor on your teachings, Prakk-Captain.*

He wondered why they had not stunned him where he lay, but when were monkey reasons ever to be understood? He maneuvered so a monkey always stood in the line of fire from the stunner. He lurked, though he quivered with the desire to scream and leap.

The monkeys circled. He sensed hesitation and smelled fear. They exchanged short calls—Instructions? Taunts? Plans?—but kept a double arm's length away. He slid with short, random steps to keep them unbalanced.

"I *ch'rowled* your mother," one said in halting Heroes' Tongue. Seeker pictured a diminutive monkey male with its tiny member as it attempted to mount—and pleasure—the enormous mound of a kzinret in heat. His ears curled in laughter.

The monkey with the chain rewarded his distraction with a strike from behind. The links seared across his shoulders as they pinched fur from flesh. Seeker roared and feinted toward the monkey. The stunner hummed. Aimed in anticipation, it missed.

Mostly missed. His left paw withered with a limp tingle. He dug the claws of his left foot into the dirt and, with a scream, leaped to the right. The shadow monkey with the gun crumpled under his bulk.

The three remaining monkeys danced with a chattering hysteria as they feinted just out of reach. Seeker stood his ground, one foot on the back of the prostrate assailant. The stunner lay within his reach, but he ignored the puny weapon.

He roared a challenge. The monkeys broke and ran. Their footsteps clattered into the dark, their sour scents diminishing.

The monkey under his foot groaned and struggled for purchase in the littered sand. Seeker stepped off and onto the stunner, which he ground into the dirt. The monkey flopped to his back, his gasps punctuated with wounded whimpers.

Seeker stood over the monkey. The honor of combat required him to finish the foe, to send him as an offering to the Fanged God, to take his ears to wear on his belt. Yet, he was no longer a soldier, no longer a kzin of the old world—he was *wunderkzin*. What did honor require now? He could not wear the ears—their freshness would alert and alarm the monkeys. And the Fanged God might not accept such a puny offering. Prakk-Captain had taken prisoners, but Seeker could not do so, since no Kzin authority remained.

The monkey's gasps lightened. Seeker flexed his left paw as feeling returned. The web vest lay where he had tossed it, and he fastened it around his frame. The monkey's wounded whimpers grew to a steady cry as he cupped shadow hands over his face, featureless in the dark.

"Seeker of Interworld." The only human words he knew sounded strange. The monkey gasped, held a stiff silence, then flipped onto his stomach and attempted to crawl. Seeker stood on the monkey's leg.

"Seeker of Interworld."

The monkey bat at his foot, grabbing fur to pull himself free. Seeker peered with interest at the attempts. The monkey . . . the *human* continued to fight, continued in the face of overwhelming odds to escape. Just as a Hero would. Surely the honor of humans and the honor of kzinti were similar as well. Surely the human knew—expected—the honor due a warrior.

Seeker stooped and with a single claw severed the arteries in the human's neck. The human screamed, short and sharp. His body continued to fight, quivering in the dirt. The thin human fingers in Seeker's fur pulled with hideous strength in the finality of death.

Seeker listened to the night and scented the air. They were alone. The smell of the human's blood in the sand brought not just memories of the hunts, but also sparked his hunger. For uncounted months he had tasted only the reconstituted leavings of the autokitchen—a real meal had been out of his grasp for too long.

With a sigh, he bent to the human and began to feed.

❦ CHAPTER 13 ❦

"WELL, THAT'S IT THEN." Cheshire kicked the duffel at his feet. "Such a long way for such a short visit." He glanced askance at Mad. "At least there'll be time to 'murder' each other, if you're still interested."

"Quitter." She lounged, Swarmer-still in her seat. "I don't do quitters."

"Well, what do you suggest?" He found he feared her displeasure more than her anger.

"I suggest we bring these bastards down."

"Which bastards? There seems so many."

"Lim's partners. That fat pig and Early need evidence that they're adding avidin to the beer intentionally to hurt the pussies. So we get it for them. The partners go to jail, and we get some revenge for Lim."

"Jail? There's no law against poisoning a kzin."

"That can't be true."

"The law has little to do with what's true. Or with what's right. Or moral." Cheshire felt professorial. So far, the only lawyers he'd met were the teachers at his law school. "The law tells us what we can't do, and society tells the law what to restrict. Right now, society tells the law it's okay to kill kzinti."

"Perhaps in certain circumstances—" She glowered at Cheshire. "Never mind. I'm not a lawyer. I'll leave that to you." She smiled, and Cheshire wondered whether she meant him to be dazzled by or fearful of her mood changes.

She squinted, measuring him. "You said that, in the law, there are always arguments. They have to be breaking some law."

Cheshire grimaced as he pondered. "There are purity laws, but that might depend whether the avidin is natural or synthetic. And maybe if the additive were harmful to some people, though that would require experts and epidemiology. I guess there's always the catch-all laws: threat to public safety, breach of the peace. I don't know—I've only read the law. I never practiced."

"Maybe it doesn't matter. Maybe if we expose them, the Provisional Government will make it illegal. We'll have hurt them, and that's what counts."

"Assuming at the end of the story, we live happily ever after, how do you propose we get there?"

"Simple. That office, the one where we saw Kirkland? I'll bet there's all sorts of info in that inner office. We break in, steal the data, and toss it to Early. You go back to Sol a hero, and maybe I get to stay on Wunderland." She added, "Without working for that prick."

"'Simple.'" Cheshire studied his memory of the brewery layout. "Five floors up through a factory full of workers. Two sets of locked double doors. What about alarms? What about guards?"

"I said 'simple,' not easy or safe." She slid a languid hand down his arm. "Are you in?"

"If we're caught, they'll never find our bodies."

"Are you in?"

He grinned. "Of course."

She reprogrammed the car. "This will leave us a couple blocks away."

"Away from the brewery?" He realized she'd had a plan all along— and part of that plan was his saying yes.

"You'll see."

The ground car entered the old city just as the setting Alpha lit the sky with terrific bands of salmon, umber, and vermillion. Even after two years, the dust kicked up from the *Yamamoto*'s "shots" floated high in the thin atmosphere and reflected the sunlight in a beautiful reminder of a day of death and destruction.

The car pulled to the curb. He popped a leg out the door and said over his shoulder, "Should I leave my bag in the car?"

"If you do, you'll never see it again."

"Dammit." He hefted the duffel onto his shoulder. "I'm getting sick of this thing."

She marched them two blocks to a storefront, one of a surprising set open along the strasse.

"Business district," she said. "Dependent upon the brewery."

The windows of the shop displayed various uniforms. Inside, the shop smelled of warm cloth and fresh synthetics.

"*Guten abend*," called a tall man with a lopsided beard dyed an improbable blond. "May I help you?"

Mad gushed. "We just got jobs at the brewery. Can you believe it? I never expected they'd hire my brother and me, but there you go."

"Your *bruder*." The proprietor eyed the slender belter and the thick flatlander.

"We need uniforms," she said. "We have cash, if that's a problem."

The proprietor's active ears gave warmth to his face. "Of course, of course. Right this way."

Some time later, they exited the shop, their new uniforms stashed in Cheshire's duffel.

"Now we need some IDs. This way." Mad locked up his elbow and guided him several blocks. A familiar holosign floated: *HAROLD'S TERRAN BAR*. A large black man with Maori scars on his cheeks sat guard at the hefty door. A fat man—Cheshire thought for a moment it was Schreibman—pushed past them, out the beaded curtain inside the door. A mixed crowd—many of them in UNSN and Free Wunderlander uniforms—pressed three deep against the bar. On the dance floor, uniforms tussled among gaudy civilians, dancing to the musicomp's Meddlehoffer beat. In a far booth, two despondent kzinti huddled behind a privacy screen, which only dampened their hiss and spit as they talked.

She tugged Cheshire past the doorway and into an eddy of humanity at the edge of the bar. She scanned the tables and brightened when she caught sight of two men and an elegant woman at a central table. She slipped through the crowd, and he followed, his duffel in a bulky hug.

"Hello, Maddie." The woman's soft blonde hair was cut like Mad's swarmer crest. They touched cheeks. "So good to see you."

"And you, Ingrid. It's been too long."

"I'm so sorry about Lim." The two men murmured concurrence. "How are you holding up?"

"His funeral was today. It's . . . it's like a bad dream." Mad blinked back tears, but smiled. "I'd like you to meet my friend, Martin Cheshire. He's just in from Sol. Mr. Cheshire, this is Ingrid Schotter-Yarthkin, Claude Montferrat-Palme, and Harold Yarthkin-Schotmann."

Cheshire shook hands all round, wondering if they'd been friends with Lim. "Those names are quite a mouthful."

"Harold owns the place," Mad said.

Cheshire gazed around the bar and gave what he hoped was an appreciative smile. "This is the most life I've seen yet. Everywhere else is just dead."

"Thanks to the UNSN." Harold glowered. "I'd ask you to sit, but there are no seats left." He pushed an empty chair farther under the table.

"You'll have to excuse my husband," said Ingrid. "Sometimes he has the manners of a four-year-old."

"No offense taken." Cheshire hugged his duffel tighter. "Maddie . . ."

"Right," she said. "Claude, I need a favor."

♟ CHAPTER 14 ♟

WITHOUT PRAKK-INVALID, the apartment expanded to a crowded emptiness. Ensconced on his *fooch*, Seeker groomed blood—kzin and human—from his fur. He twisted and stretched into impossible angles to rasp his dish-towel tongue across orange and black tufts. At the end, only the litter-mate spot remained—an unreachable line between the shoulder blades, traditionally groomed by mothers, kzinretti and, rarely, friends. He finished the spot with Prakk-Invalid's long-handled brush.

And lay quiet. The telltales of the autokitchen lit the darkness. No sounds burrowed through the stone walls, and only the occasional crick of settling wood assured him his ears worked. Though his belly felt full, sleep evaded him.

If Prakk-Invalid lived, he should know by late morning. He imagined a weak-but-recovering captain, cradled by a hospice *fooch*, his ears curled in pleasured greeting, but forced the false hope from his mind.

His mission no longer included the old kzin. He was Seeker of Interworld. Where to start? Would he have to continue as a gopher? Or would his pursuit of the human language—his learning to count—earn the money for rent and for food? Could it bring riches? Seeker's whiskers twitched in anticipation. Was he the first Seeker of Interworld? Were there others? As the first, he could lay claim to vast territories—not of land, but of knowledge. Could he exact tithes from those Heroes who wished to enter his territories?

He unlimbered from the *fooch* and paced the floor. If he were not the first, would he have to tithe? No, he would fight. A Hero's challenge, just as in the old tales. He had nothing to lose and everything to gain. *I will take honor.*

Excitement quivered through his soul. He must do something, but the way evaded him. No scent; no spoor; no track. With restless endeavor, he bat at the cushions on Prakk-Invalid's *fooch*. The old kzin was dead. His possessions were forfeit. He gathered the cushions and dumped them on his *fooch*. He must make more room. The old kzin's bed disintegrated under an assault of muscle and claw, and he shoved the gathered pieces through the door into the darkened hallway. He paused over the refuse and sniffed the air.

Prakk-Invalid had disguised his scent, but the disguise gave away that which he hid. Seeker followed a trail—a disruption in the old building's dust—up an ancient wood stairway, which groaned under his weight. Six floors, and the nonpath led to a ruptured doorway. A room had burst open, hit by a stray beam or shell, and an outer wall had fallen away. A rickety *fooch* faced the opening and, in the darkness over Munchen, the lights of the spaceport winked beyond the black Donau.

He lay on the *fooch* and blinked at the sight. The spaceport lit, and a ruby laser line drew skyward, a shuttle balanced on its ablative tip. Prakk-Invalid must have spent his empty hours ruminating over his former command.

A sour smell seeped into Seeker's attention. He stretched to look beneath the couch and, with a claw, dragged an aluminum beer keg onto his lap. It felt full. He studied the bung hole and ran an experimental claw around its seal. He bent to search under the *fooch* and discovered an old gagrumpher bone, hollow, with one end worked into an intricate flange. With a push and a turn, the bone fit the keg.

He spit the first bitter swig through the open wall and into the night. *Who would drink this* sthondat *piss?* Yet, beyond the disgusting plant matter and the alarming fizz, he tasted—something. He mouthed a sample, held the brew on his tongue, and drew a bolt of air through his nose. Something beyond the bitter, beyond the grain, seeped into his sinuses—a pleasant burn, a tickle of alcohol. Once, he had sampled tuna ice cream and brandy—a favorite among the named officers—and its memory warmed him. Perhaps the taste was worth it?

With kzin courage he up-ended the keg and drank long and deep. He belched, and shuddered at the secondary taste. Yet a warmth grew within him, coursed from his paws through his arms and into his chest. He wet his nose and drew breath; the warmth filled his lungs and a vaporous pleasure expanded up and into his mind. With a sigh he pulled another long draft.

The monkeys—the *humans*—must know where he could learn Interworld. After all, it was their language, and they were in charge of everything. Yet the only humans he knew—who knew him—were at the brewery. He drew deep from the keg and belched long and loud. Perhaps the brewery humans would help, would see the honor in helping the first Seeker of Interworld. And if they didn't see, they could be persuaded.

He finished another draft. The keg sloshed, far less than half full. He curled his ears in laughter as he pictured the greasy Vilt Kirkland bent in subservience as he agreed to help Seeker in his mission. And return the money he had taken. Seeker tried to account for what he was owed: the "taxes" and the web-vest "payments" and the base eight to base ten conversions—or was it base ten to base eight? The figures swam and folded and refused to stay fixed.

No matter. He emptied the keg, disappointed it was so soon done. The monkeys would pay him back—pay him more—to see him through his important quest. Important to human and *wunderkzin* alike. He was Seeker of Interworld, and his mission would regain the glory due all kzin. His destiny lay along a path no other had sought, no other had even thought to seek, and he would travel that path straight and true.

He rose from the *fooch* and stood proud. He swayed. He stepped, but stumbled against the door frame. The shadows mocked him as the spaceport lights swam in a shifting wave. He breathed deep and ordered his mind, commanded his reflexes to obey. His destiny lay on this path, and the first stop was the brewery. He proceeded with a confident stagger down the stairs and into the Munchen night.

☙ CHAPTER 15 ☙

SEVERAL HOURS, a meal, and a couple akvavits later, Mad and Cheshire changed into their uniforms in the bar's back office. Harold insisted on sitting guard in his high-back chair and reluctantly turned away at the crucial moment.

The badges procured by Montferrat-Palme appeared real. Cheshire flicked his picture in the plastic. "Won't they check our biometrics against their employee records?"

Harold issued a cold smile. "Flatlanders. We're not so obsessed with security here. In this system, we let people breathe."

"You also let them brew poisoned beer."

"No one's forcing the ratcats to drink it." Harold dragged on his cigarette. "We all have our poisons. And it's not up to the government to tell us what we can or cannot do to ourselves."

"It's not the alcohol—we explained that. It's the additive that's killing kzinti. Shouldn't the government keep them from putting cyanide in cigarettes?"

"Let the market decide. I'd smoke the cigarettes without the cyanide."

"And if all the cigarettes had cyanide?"

Harold rolled his eyes. "If flatlanders like you were in charge, I'd take the cyanide straight."

From behind, Mad curled long fingers on Cheshire's shoulders. "If you boys are quite done." She turned him and inspected the lay of his uniform. "Sharp."

"Thanks. You, too."

"Get a room," Harold said. "Somewhere else."

Cheshire hefted his duffel. "Can I leave this here?"

Harold dragged his cigarette and screwed it out in an ashtray. "No."

On the strasse, the last long light of Alpha had faded. Ancient gas lamps cast a warm glow across the empty street corners, and vague stars winked between the rooftops. The faint red of Proxima, the runt third star of the system, declared itself between the naked branches of a spindly tree.

"Can I ask you something?" Cheshire glanced at the glints in Mad's hair.

"You can ask, but I'll probably lie."

"Well, that's honest."

"Not really. Even if I answer truthfully I can always say it was a lie later."

Cheshire blinked. "Wow. Did you ever teach law school?"

"Is that your question?"

"No." He pursed his lips and wondered whether his question were brave or foolish. "Something you said when we first met. You said that Lim bought things he didn't think were worth having."

"More like, he buys the best, but doesn't always want it after he has it."

"Something like that." He weighed the silence as they walked. "Were you talking about you?" He felt her inspiration, deep, steady.

"Yes." The word exploded with her breath. "Yes, I was talking about me. During the last week or so, he seemed distant. He said he was 'just distracted,' but we've all heard that before. What you told me—about that records' clerk and how Lim just moved on—seemed to resonate." She smiled, but her lip quivered. "Mr. Cheshire, are you sure he wanted you for your law background—or did he want you to catch . . . someone . . . on the rebound for him?"

"All he said was 'I need you.' When I asked him for what, he said, 'Oh, you know, old friend, the law and such.' He never mentioned you." He gave her a grim smile. "Would my catching you on the rebound be so bad?"

She blinked with wounded eyes, but smiled back. "I would be in expert hands, after all."

"Only the best." Again he weighed the silence. "Can I ask you one more thing?"

"If you must."

"Will you stop calling me Mr. Cheshire and call me Marty?"

She squeezed his elbow. "Very well, Marty."

At the employee gate of the brewery, Cheshire suppressed a worry that the guard from the morning, Kenkel, would be on duty, but a bored young woman glanced at their badges. She frowned at the duffel.

"What's in the bag?"

"Um, clothes."

"Why do you bring clothes?"

Mad lifted the duffel from his shoulder. "Herr Kenkel asked us to bring it." She zipped it open, and the guard poked at the contents.

"Herr Kenkel has good taste." The guard shrugged and zipped the duffel closed. "Report to the brewmaster's office—down that way and turn left."

They hustled along the busy avenue, turned left and continued past the office to the shadows of the brewery tower.

"What now?" Cheshire asked as he peered up the sheer brickwork.

She paced the edge of the building and studied approaches. Around the corner she nodded at the zigzag of a fire escape. "Boost me up."

Cheshire crouched and cupped his hands. Light in the low gravity, Mad flew to the lower rungs of a retracted escape ladder, which rattled to the ground. Cheshire slung his duffel over his shoulder and clambered after her. They drew the rumbling ladder back up.

"Hope no one heard that."

They held a few moments, but no one seemed to have noticed. They mounted the ancient iron steps, the stairway trembling and shedding rust. At each floor, they peered into the grimy access windows. On the catwalks, the uniformed workers took no notice.

At the fifth floor the escape stopped at a long landing before a wide set of modern windows. Inside, a dim light hinted at an exquisite office, though an unmade cot spoiled the appointments.

Mad swiped a finger across the glass. "Clean." She inspected the casement. "New, too." She tapped the material. "I don't think we're getting in this way."

"What now?"

"Up."

Cheshire placed his back against the window, crouched, and cupped his hands. Mad floated to the edge of the roof. She leaned out with a hand, and Cheshire scrambled up.

The inner-office skylight, also with new and modern windows, gave off a serene glow. Across the river, the lights of the spaceport winked in the cold night air, and a chill breeze nudged at their uniforms. They proceeded with quiet steps across the roof to another skylight—old, grimy windows—and peered down at the mesh landing in front of the outer-office door. She produced a knife— Cheshire startled at its sudden glint—and worked the glazing around a lower pane. She lifted the loose pane, set it on the roof, and leaned through to unlock the wide sash.

They dropped to the landing and scurried to the wall of the office. Nothing happened. Cheshire blew a sigh. "You can pick locks?"

She glowered. "Can I pick locks? Watch me."

She reached for the door handle, but grabbed air as the door opened. She stepped back in surprise. A man—dapper, hair wavy brown, smile indulgently askance—cocked his head at them.

"Lim." She panted two deep breaths. "Lim!" She flung her arms wide and lunged to hug him. Lim raised a hand, a gleam of metal in his fingers, and she crumpled to the landing.

"Maddie!" Cheshire knelt and felt for a heartbeat.

"Hello, old friend," Lim said.

"Why?" Cheshire found a pulse. "Lim!"

"Police stunner." He shrugged and pocketed the weapon. "She'll be out for a while. I'm sorry about that, but it's better this way."

Cheshire stood in mute confusion. *You're alive!* He wanted to hug his old friend, but the still form of Mad lay between them. Finally, he managed, "We thought you were dead."

Lim's face lit with an indulgent smile. "Yes, sorry about that, too. But circumstances required subterfuge. The police were getting too close for comfort. Time was needed, and faking my death seemed the best method to obtain it. I would have let you in on the secret, but it was best to keep those in the know to a minimum."

"Will she be all right?" He felt like sobbing, but held himself hard. *Lim, what are you doing?*

"From the stunner? Oh, yes. Just a wicked headache." A pensive frown shadowed his brow. "If she were to wake up." He dipped into a pocket and sighed. "By any chance, did you bring peanuts with you from Sol? No? Pity. I should have asked you to bring some. The ones they grow around here, well . . . just don't taste right."

Cheshire felt chilled. "What do you mean, 'If she were to wake up'?"

Lim pursed his lips as he gazed down at Mad. "Now that she knows I'm alive, she's a liability. I had hoped the police would take my hint about her travel documents, but here she is." He squinted in thought at the doorway of the reception area. "Perhaps this fleabag could be of assistance in that regard—if I could just get it to understand."

Cheshire startled. Through the door, in the reception area, Seeker of Interworld swayed.

Lim nodded at the kzin. "The damn thing doesn't understand Interworld, and I'll be damned if I can speak that kitty spit."

"I don't understand." Cheshire's confused hands grasped at the strap of the duffel.

"Death by kzin. Happens all the time around here: a man smiles at a kit and the ratcat daddy loses control. Someone swindles a ratcat and forgets to duck. Or a young 'Hero' pines for the days of the hunt and—*bam*—five persons in the park are dead. Easy murders, public murders, with the ratcat culprits quickly disposed of."

Lim cocked his head at Cheshire. "And you, old friend. Are you a liability?" He glided past and peered over the railing. "Even in this gravity, five stories is a long way down."

Cheshire pulled the duffel from his shoulder. He backed until his spine scraped against the wall of the reception area.

Lim studied his old friend. He dipped into his empty pocket and shrugged when the habit came up empty. "Look at us." He leaned easy against the rail. "There's no need for this drama. After all, I asked you to come here—a long journey on vague promises—and here you are. The least I could do is tell you about the job I'm offering. Won't you consider it, old friend?"

Seeker, abandoned in the reception area, stooped through the doorway and joined the humans on the mesh landing. He gazed at them with bleary red eyes.

"I was at your funeral this morning." Cheshire gave the kzin a wary glance and stared at the ghost of his friend. "Who did we bury?"

"*Whom* is what you want there. Whom did we bury?" Lim sighed. "Poor old Crenvins. I told him we would take care of him, but that fat constable had something on him."

"So, he became a liability." *Please. Stop. Please, Lim.*

"I'm afraid so. Amazing the poisons chemists come up with—and I employ the best, old friend. A little bit of this, a little bit of that, and before you know it—puff—major anaphylactic shock. Poor Kirkland. Watching Crenvins bloat freaked him out."

"That's the kind of business you're running?" A thrill of resentment ran up Cheshire's spine. *What have you become?*

"Oh yes. These are the colonies, not the merry old land of Sol. Catch as catch can and such out here. And look down." Lim peered over the railing. "See those workers down there? They look like ants, don't they? Well, just like ants, they need someone to tell them what to do, to guide them. There's tremendous opportunity here, old friend, just tremendous—if you're willing to take it." He stepped away from the railing and reached out a hand. "You could be rich, Marty. I know you—we grew up together. Remember? We used to ask each other, 'What would you do if you were rich?' Well, here's the opportunity."

Cheshire shook his head, all hope of adventure gone. "But how long would it last? You're poisoning your best customers."

"You know about that? Kirkland said you left the funeral with those cops." Lim shrugged. "No matter. I trust you, Marty. That's why I asked you to come, why I paid your fare. I know I can trust you if you make the commitment. Will you consider my offer? Please?"

"What happens when the kzinti figure out humans are deliberately making them sick? You can't kill them all, not this way. And when they find out—"

"Oh, I fully intend for them to find out. Not quite yet—we need to make penetration into Tigertown on Tiamat. But when we get enough of them sick, that's when we tell them we're responsible."

"You're going to tell the kzinti you're poisoning them?"

"Do you think I plan to poison all the bastards? Not likely, old friend. I want to make them mad at us—so mad, they start a guerrilla war, or at least try to. Then maybe we'll exterminate them, but that doesn't matter, either. The big payoff will be when the ratcat fleet comes back to this system—have no doubt about it, they'll be back—and find out we deliberately and systematically poisoned their brothers."

"They'll take revenge."

"Exactly. We need to be at war. Think about it, Marty. We've been fighting the ratcats for sixty-odd years, and through all the murder and terror and bloodshed, we produced Strather and Carmody, the stasis field, transfer booths, and the hyperdrive. Wondrous things." Lim swept a hand at the felinoid. "And prior to the kzin? We had three hundred years of brotherly love and democracy. The Long Peace. What did we produce?" He shot Cheshire a sardonic smile. "The organ banks."

Cheshire caught movement in the skylight above Lim's head. Schreibman's face bobbed like a small moon and was gone. Cheshire hefted the strap of the duffel in both hands and held it at his knees. "What about Maddie?"

Lim pursed his lips and frowned. "I'd let you pick her up, just like old times, but she's trouble. Surely you can tell that, even after just a day? She's not exactly a kzin lover, but I'm positive she wouldn't approve of what I'm doing. And she'd do something about it." He blinked in realization. "That's why you're here, isn't it. Are you working with the cops? Rooting out some evidence for them?"

Cheshire gripped the duffel strap with indignant hands. "No. We thought you were murdered by your partners, and we thought the best revenge would be to expose their secrets."

"Her idea?"

Cheshire stiffened. "Our idea."

Lim nodded at Mad's limp form. "I believe you see the danger in having her around. Don't worry—it won't be like Crenvins—I'll make sure of that. Perhaps this big bastard would like a meal. How about it?" Lim raised his voice in a futile attempt to communicate with the kzin. "Are you hungry, you big bastard? Do you want some meat?"

In response, Seeker huffed a fetid, inebriated breath and said, "Seeker of Interworld." When neither human responded, he sighed and settled into grooming a small patch on his arm.

Lim shrugged and gave a rueful nod at the kzin. "That's all I can get out of the bastard."

Schreibman appeared again in the skylight above Lim. He pointed to the kzin, then to himself. He pointed to Cheshire, then to Lim. As if stretching his neck, Cheshire nodded in subtle agreement.

"I'm not going to let you hurt Maddie." Cheshire hoped he sounded bold, but knew he didn't.

"I don't think you appreciate the severity of the situation." Lim planted himself before Seeker. "Food!" He pointed at Mad. "Food!"

Seeker's whiskers twitched with interest. "Food," the kzin repeated, the Interworld slurred and broken.

"Goddamnit!" Lim bared his teeth and chomped with exaggeration. "Eat!"

Seeker roared at the challenge. His paw lunged to his *w'tsai*.

Schreibman plunged through the skylight, one hand extended, the other on the control of his UNSN gravity belt. He mashed a shoulder into the kzin's back. Mass and momentum drove Seeker over the railing.

Cheshire swung the duffel like a hammer and caught Lim across the hips. Lim spun, hands outflung, and somersaulted over the rope guard for the gravity-plate elevator. The duffel, finally free, whirled out of sight.

As Seeker toppled, he snarled and sunk claws into Schreibman's thighs. The fat man screamed, and the two struggled in midair. The gravity belt whined in emergency overload, then failed. In the slow-motion gravity of Wunderland, the two fell five stories to the factory floor.

Cheshire dashed to the bent railing. Far below, dots of workers surrounded two still masses. A scrum of police, summoned as backup by Schreibman, barged through the main doors.

"A little help?" Lim called.

Cheshire drifted to the rope guard for the elevator. Lim dangled over the five-story drop, one hand locked onto the line.

Lim gasped, "Really, I could use a little help." Except for the hand clamped on the rope, his arm appeared lifeless. "I think I pulled out my shoulder. I can't seem . . . to get enough . . . purchase."

Cheshire squatted, his hands on his knees. "That really seems unfortunate." The adrenalin, Mad's limp form, and his friend's return from the dead vibrated through him in a sudden anger. *Who the hell are you?*

"Yes, I'm in an unfortunate spot, old friend. Do be a pal and haul me up." Lim's eyes locked onto Cheshire's. "Please?"

"I don't know. You seem to have become a . . . liability." Cheshire glanced past Lim at the elevator far below. *Is this loyalty? Is this friendship?*

"Oh, well now—"

"And you know what happens to those who become liabilities." Behind Cheshire, Mad moaned.

"I could make it worth your while."

Cheshire settled his hand onto Lim's. "I think this is all the worthwhile I need." He bent Lim's thumb away from the rope.

Below, a knot of police crowded onto the gravity lift.

Lim stared up in horror. "Marty, please don't!"

"This is for Mad." Cheshire bent Lim's small finger. When Lim tried to wriggle it back, Cheshire gave it a vicious twist, and Lim squealed in pain.

Cheshire grinned. "That was for Crenvins."

Lim whimpered. Cheshire gazed at his former friend. "But you know what?" he asked. Lim answered with pleading eyes.

"But you know what?" Cheshire demanded.

"No, what?"

"This is for me." Cheshire clenched the remaining fingers and twisted them off the rope. Lim gasped, too shocked to scream. The low gravity started its slow but inexorable work. Lim fell—and stopped, caught in the arms of the police officers riding up the lift.

🐾 **CHAPTER 16** 🐾

"COME IN, COME IN." Early ushered Mad and Cheshire into the hospital suite. The morning light from Alpha melted over the chrome, plastic, and linen of the sterile confines. In the bed, Schreibman stirred, his fat hands and face the only flesh showing from his swaddle of bandages and casts.

"Good morning! Are we finally awake?" Early asked with an accustomed sarcasm.

Schreibman croaked, then managed to say, "How long?"

"About a week. How do you feel?"

"Like *scheisse* on a hot plate."

"That good? Well, look who I brought."

"Fraulein. Herr Cheshire." The fat man's face animated. "I am glad to see you well."

"Thanks to you." Cheshire grasped Schreibman's hand. "Do you remember what happened?"

"I remember . . . I remember claws in my legs. *Verdammt!*" He winced as he flexed his thighs. "And I remember a long fall. A long fall, with a ratcat to break it at the bottom. *Gott in Himmel!* If he had fallen on me instead . . ."

"Unlucky for him," Early said. "But he'll live."

Schreibman blinked at the ceiling tiles. "Fraulein Valli."

"Yes, Detective?"

"My apologies."

"No need. It seems the transition documents have been sorted, and my bank accounts are unfrozen. Though my apartment is still a shambles."

"You understand now? The beer and the biotin and the kzin? Your boyfriend, Herr Welson?"

"Of course."

"The beer?" Schreibman asked. "What of the brewery?"

Early opened a hand at Cheshire and Mad. "Based on their testimony, the police got a search warrant and found what we needed. They shut down operations, though the new owners are restarting production tomorrow—without the avidin, of course. Oh, and surprise! The Provisional Government, in its infinite wisdom, passed a law against killing kzin. They're also, um . . . exploring— yah, that's a good word—exploring what to do next."

"And what of Herr Welson?"

"They found evidence that he and his partners poisoned poor Crenvins," Early said. "We expect an indictment any day. In the meantime, he's being held without bail. Flight risk, you know. Can't have him hightailing it back to Sol."

"Good, good." The fat man sunk into his bed. "I am tired."

"You look tired," Mad said.

He smiled. "*Danke*, Fraulein. No one wants a good illness to go unnoticed."

"We'll leave you now." Cheshire squeezed his hand. "Again, thank you."

Early leaned against the window to spy a glimpse of the couple on the street below. They exited the hospital, Mad's hand in the crook of Cheshire's elbow. She stopped and twirled, met him face to face, and kissed him in slow appreciation. Early raised his eyebrows and chuckled. "I'm not the only one who has plans for that boy."

"I would ask if your plans are good or bad," Schreibman said. "But I'm not sure they're ever good."

"He doesn't know it yet, but he's going to be defending that kzin at trial."

"Trial? A kzin in a Wunderland court?"

"Yah. It's just what this world needs: a show trial. I've got a mind to rub some human noses in the shit they've been spreading around.

This planet needs some good, old-fashioned embarrassment, and I think that boy's just the man to do it."

"On what charges?"

"He helped in the murder of Crenvins."

Schreibman blinked at the ceiling. "How would that work? Wouldn't a kzin need a jury of his peers?"

"Beats me. They'll have to figure it out. And in the process, figure out what other rights to give the bastards." He rubbed warmth into his hands. "Unless I miss my mark, that kzin's trial is going to change this world."

Schreibman sighed. "I am tired."

"Hang in there, young fella."

"Lie to me again about the oversize autodoc on its way from Sol."

Early grinned and grasped the fat man's hand. "Ah, but it is. It is."

Schreibman shoved out his chin. "You lie."

"Nope. Scheduled to arrive in this very hospital by the end of the week."

Schreibman crushed Early's fingers and blinked tears. "I could be thin again?"

"Yah." Early winced and extricated his hand. "Just as soon as it's done fixing that damn kzin."

EXCITEMENT

by Hal Colebatch and Jessica Q. Fox

❧ EXCITEMENT ❧

2438 AD, Wunderland

IT STARTED with a mysterious phone call from someone whose voice I didn't recognize. The caller ID was switched off, so that didn't tell me anything. But I could tell the voice of a kzin aristocrat without any trouble, although there were plenty of those around.

He told me what my name was, and I agreed, and he said he had a proposition for a paying job. With the Recession, FTL pilots don't get many jobs on Wunderland at the moment, so I was definitely interested. But puzzled as to why it wasn't a company interviewing me. If it was an individual, he had to have an awful lot of money, space travel doesn't come cheap. And we made an appointment to meet in an out-of-the-way place in the country that was hard to get to. I took an aircar to the coordinates he gave me, and it was miles out in the sticks, with only grass and trees for company. I was slightly nervous to tell the truth; it looked as though it might be illegal, and if it was I would knock it back, because I don't do illegal, the chances of getting away with it aren't good and if you're caught that's the end of the job market. And if I knocked it back, they (whoever *they* were) might well feel that killing me was the simplest solution to maintaining their guilty secret. So I packed a blaster and practiced doing quick draws before I went. Even so, my heart was in my mouth as I got out of the aircar.

The kzin aristocrat was already there and waiting, his own aircar standing there, with an impressive crest on the side, although he had kept out of sight until it was clear there was nobody with me. The moment he stepped into view, I recognized him. And relaxed a little, because people like him don't go around killing to preserve their secrets. It was the leader of all the kzin on Wunderland, Vaemar-Riit. I'd seen him on the videocasts, and he was now a politician, though a relatively junior one. In fact he was the only kzin in politics, unless you counted a poor kzinret that the liberals had gotten for a safe seat, not realizing how dumb most kzinretti are, and hoping, I suppose, to get some kzin crazy enough to vote for her. Fat chance.

"Vaemar-Riit," I said. "It is an honor to meet you, sir. But I am puzzled by the meeting place. And curious about the nature of the job you have for me."

"That I can understand," he said with an ear flip. "But this must remain secret until we are in space. And you will be taking me under sealed orders, nobody must know our destination until it is too late to prevent us. There are many who would think me mad to do what I propose."

I wondered what it could be. Obviously I wasn't going to be told yet. "But I have to file a flight plan," I protested.

"Then you must lie about it," he said calmly. "One ought not to lie in general, it damages the soul, but there is a special dispensation in the case of bureaucratic busybodies. Lying to them is a public duty. Those humans who matter—Guthlac, Cumpston, Dimity and the Rykermanns—are aware of my project and support it."

I swallowed. He would know the chances that this would get my pilot's license withdrawn. He would have more-than-despised me for mentioning it, but I knew he would weigh my fee accordingly. Vaemar-Riit's sense of honor was a byword.

"I think that I will be able to ensure that you have no further trouble when we return, assuming that we do. I have confidential letters from several highly placed humans who understand the importance of this business. It is only fair to warn you that there is an element of excitement involved. Naturally, you will find that attractive, but you need to be told about it."

Excitement. A human being would quite likely have said "suicidal danger," I thought. But Vaemar was definitely not a human, although he had mixed with them from infancy. Both species were brought up together in many parts of Wunderland these days, so we could get to know each other's ways.

"How long will we be away from Wunderland, assuming we survive?" I asked. "And will there be other passengers? I need to know how much to charge you for the flight."

About six months, he thought, and no, it would be just the two of us. That was going to cost a fortune, but when I told him, he shrugged as humans do, only more so, and offered me double. He was rich enough. There are several Kzin on Wunderland pining for a bit of excitement, and he had them collecting gold and precious stones in the back country, with tigrepards and lesslocks to offer a bit of stimulating company and keep their claws sharp and their ear rings respectably full.

"Why me?" I asked him.

"Because you are a good pilot, and also hold a seventh dan grade in synth. I shall need to do some training on the way there, and you may be able to assist. I expect to be involved in mortal combat. Probably more than once. I shall need to be in good shape to survive."

There was another consideration of course, but that would be too obvious to mention. I accepted there and then. It looked a crazy thing to do, but starship pilots are well known to be mad as thoats on wengle-weed, and I guess I'm as mad as any.

I rented a ship, paid a hefty deposit out of the money Vaemar had given me, filed plans for We Made It, and said I was going alone to pick up a passenger. Which wouldn't account for the provisions I had to lay in, but the people who supervise these things are lazy and little disposed to do much checking. Or maybe they thought I was going to bring back somebody very hungry. One good thing about Wunderlanders, compared to what I've heard about Earth, is that they tend to keep minding other people's business to a minimum. Early in the peace there was a statue put up to John James Cowperthwaite.

We were scheduled to take off at midnight, and I was waiting for my passenger from half an hour before. He got there at quarter to the witching hour, and we went in and sealed the ship. It was small and fast, I was hoping to cut down on the transit time to wherever the hell it was; not, I was pretty sure, We Made It.

"Head north of the ecliptic," he told me.

"I was going to do that anyway," I explained. "We're on the list as headed for We Made It, and you aren't officially here, so don't make any sound when I'm talking to flight control. Anyway, it won't matter all that much until we're a couple of light-hours out, and they'll lose interest in us by then."

"As you see fit. That destination will suit very well, initially. I think that I shall be missed before we get one light-hour out; I had to let my mate Karan know something of my intentions. She is intelligent, so she will not let the news out too soon. But there are servants, and they are sometimes inquisitive. So we may have to confess our sins before leaving the system."

"I'd rather like to know the nature of the sins myself," I told him.

"As soon as we are headed into deep space, I shall tell all," he said in his deep, rumbling voice, with the flick of the ear that said he was amused.

I lifted off at midnight, to the millisecond, with my passenger sitting beside me in the copilot's seat. Ground formalities were minimal, so I didn't have to tell any new lies. Ten minutes later we were headed out of the system, well north of the ecliptic, which always gives me a warm feeling, because the plane of the system has more random junk in it than is good for spacecraft. It's kind of embarrassing if you hit a lump of it. Also, not infrequently, fatal. We don't do Hohmann orbits, they're for the craft that stay within system, so if we hit anything there's rather likely to be a considerable velocity difference, and if there's much mass associated with it, we go up in a brief flash. And nobody wants to be dead, still less embarrassed.

"Are we in deep enough space for you to tell me where we're going?" I asked him, once I had set the computer to doing all the work.

"Yes, I think you need to know. We are going to the Patriarchy, to Kzin-home. I need to talk with the Patriarch."

I looked at him feeling somewhat stunned. I was going to be earning all that money, that was for sure. If we didn't get blasted out of space quite casually once we got into the Kzin system, we'd be bailed up for close investigation and probably executed as spies or traitors.

"Do you mind telling me *why*?" I asked.

"It is a long tale," he said.

"You know something of my story," he began. "My Sire, Chuut-Riit, had a gift of inspiring loyalty—among some humans as well as Kzin. He was killed and I was his oldest surviving male kitten, though barely weaned. His successor, old Tratt-Admiral, was devoted to Sire's memory. Instead of killing me to secure his own line, he adopted me. Then he was killed in the civil war.

"Then the humans landed from the Hyperdrive Armada. In the fighting a human with a crippled arm found me wandering and gave me to another kzin who recognized from the red fur on my chest that I was of the Riit Clan.

"He in turn gave me into the care of Rarrgh-Sergeant, now my seneschal and verderer, my step-sire and my most trusted servant.

"When, on surrender day, I was a bewildered, mewling, hiccupping kitten, he asked me my name. 'Vaemar' I told him. 'Vaemar-*Riit*!' he corrected me, tapping that red fur. He had no power to give Names, let alone confirm me as Royalty, yet that reminder of my heritage steadied me. He fled with me into wooded country to the north-east, beyond the Höhe Kalkstein, and we hunted and built up a little money doing jobs for human farmers. There were other humans, too, who became friendly with us, perhaps for reasons of their own. One taught me *chesss*. When I discovered that Dimity Carmody, a super-genius, was the only one who could give me a hard game, I realized I was a genius, too. You know I do not say that as a boast. I enrolled at München University and studied a number of human subjects.

"I came to realize the humans were grooming me to lead the kzinti of *Ka'ashi*—of Wunderland. They and Rarrgh saw to it that I did not grow up in the ease and luxury which has spoilt so many young nobles and heirs.

"I also began to wonder not *who*, but *what*, I was: Riit who was not really Riit, Kzin, perhaps, who was not really Kzin.

"Even if one is born into the Riit Clan as I am, one's name as Riit can only be given by the Patriarch or his Viceroy. Mine had been given me by an old sergeant to stop my infant squalling.

"Kzins's whole culture and history has ingrained in us the

knowledge that other races are slaves and prey, or at best worthy enemies. Yet I know that my Sire was fond of his executive secretary, the human Henrietta, and was guided by her advice, and that she wept at his death. And I have humans that I count as... friends. Rarrgh, too, I know. Let man or kzin harm, or even insult, General Leonie Rykermann in Rarrgh's presence, and they would not survive to tell of it.

"Close contact with humans has made me that contradiction in terms, an introspective Kzin. The question gnaws. Am I a traitor? A *kollaborator*? A *kwizzling*? There are Kzin who have called me those things, though generally"—he gestured to the impressive collection of the dried ears on his ear-ring —"not more than once."

"But you see my position. I am Vaemar-Riit only on Wunderland. And therefore I wish to establish my status with the Patriarch. To do this I must talk to him. No doubt he will see difficulties."

I could imagine. The Patriarch would very likely see him as a traitor to the Kzin species and have him executed, probably rather painfully. It was madly quixotic in a way. Yet I had to admire his direct way of handling affairs; certainly nobody, man or kzin, would think him a coward.

"I see," I told him.

"You do not wish to withdraw from the venture now you are fully informed?" he asked me, his eyes level.

"Of course not," I told him. "I took the job under sealed orders." I was slightly miffed that he would think I might try to pull out.

"I have had some hypnotic restrictions on what I can think about in order to ensure that I do not give away any information about our FTL technology. The kzin do not have it yet, and it might be as well to be prepared for a telepathic probe. I am concerned that you might give away some of the details of the FTL drive."

"You don't need to worry," I told him. "I mean, for centuries, Earth and Kzin-home had plenty of people who used computers and cell phones. If some had been captured by some local tribe and tortured to reveal how they worked, how much good would it have done the torturers? Well, I know how to *fly* an FTL spaceship, but I have no more idea of how they work than a human child or kzin kit playing games on a computer or cell phone. In fact nobody knows how they work. No single person. The knowledge is distributed over thousands of people. But we might have a problem, in principle, if they get some top-flight physicists and engineers and try to inspect the drive."

"Yes, I was reassured that I could divulge only a small amount of the theory at worst. Which is a long way from actually building a drive. Still, better not to let them get anything helpful. But how do you propose to make sure that nobody gets to inspect the drive?" he asked me, genuinely curious.

"It's sealed away. *I* can't get at it. I don't have the tools to get at it. It can only be inspected by engineers with the right password. Otherwise it will self-destruct. And make, I should say, a very, very big bang. We just have to convince them of that small fact."

"That should be easy enough. You merely have to explain the facts to them, and they will undoubtedly use a telepath to confirm that you believe it. Then either they accept it as truth or they do not. In the latter case, they will surely take the ship somewhere well away from Kzin-home before they try to open it. And if it is true, then there will be no more ship."

There would be no more us, either, I suspected. And even if we survived, and Vaemar got everything he wanted from the Patriarch, it would be a long, long time before we got back to Wunderland without an FTL ship to bring us back. Altogether, the whole enterprise struck me as mildly insane. Still, it wasn't going to be boring.

Except it was, of course. I mean, all space travel is. There you are in a tin can, and nothing happening, so you have time to study for your next lot of exams and practice martial arts by fighting robots made of hyperbaryonic matter, also known as fuzz. This is probably why the story has got around that all spacers are mad as thoats on wengle-weed; those who badly need the company of others to convince themselves that they actually exist were certainly going to go off their heads. Spacers, you can be sure, are people who like their own company. Lots of it.

We had gotten over a light-hour away when we received a call from Wunderland. They wanted to know if there was any sign of Vaemar on board. He heard the request for information and said nothing.

"Do you want me to answer?" I asked him. "And if I answer, do I tell the truth or count it as an enquiry from a bureaucrat?"

"Whichever you think best," Vaemar said comfortably. "They can hardly force us to return now."

"Best to just ignore it. If we had deviated from our flight plan by a few seconds of arc, they wouldn't have been able to get a message to us anyway. It has to be beamed pretty tightly at this distance. So we didn't hear it. I'll have to clean up the ship's log a bit, but that would only matter if we got back intact. Which I have to say, does not strike me as a high probability."

"It is impossible to get any sensible subjective probability for it," he said comfortably. "I have decided to go with zero point five. After all, there are only two possibilities, either we return safely or we don't."

I was pretty sure there was a fallacy in that, somewhere.

Out in the cold and dark, a long way from Alpha Centauri A and B, spacetime gets flat enough to go into hyperdrive, as they call it. At this point, you stop being in this universe, and where exactly you are stops making sense. Don't ask me to explain it, you can only talk about it in tensor calculus, which is hard to pronounce on account of all the funny symbols like little triangles and worse. As I'd explained to Vaemar, I didn't have to know things like that; mostly a pilot's job is telling the computer, which *is* the ship, what to do. If they ever get to argue back, we'll all be screwed. Sometimes they ask questions and most of a pilot's training consists of knowing how to answer them. When we set course for the Patriarchy, it didn't have any queries, it just accepted the command as placidly as if we were headed for We Made It or old Earth.

That was when the boredom started, but both Vaemar and I had plenty of ways of coping. He started work. The rec room wasn't very big, but it was big enough to have a good fight to the death if that was the sort of thing you wanted, and Vaemar did. He didn't fight me of course, he fought killer robots programmed to simulate a kzin warrior, only running fifty percent faster than almost any kzin can move. Kzin run their metabolisms about twice as fast as a human being does, and Vaemar went faster again.

When I practice, which I do quite a lot, I make sure my killer robots can't actually kill me, or at least, not very easily. The weapons aren't made of matter, they're made of fuzz, which normally barely interacts with ordinary matter at all, but can be programmed to. So when a fuzz *w'tsai* or saber goes into your belly, it looks just like a real one. It is programmed to hurt like hell, but it doesn't actually do any damage. Likewise if one slices your arm off or your head. Painful, but not actually dangerous. I discovered about the third week out that Vaemar didn't do it that way. His killer robots were armed with real weapons. I found out because he had to spend three days in the autodoc, staggering to it and leaving a trail of orange and purple blood dripping from a nasty wound in his shoulder and another in his gut.

"My blunder," he growled as he went past me.

Of course.

Vaemar had had the usual education of the Riit, which was mainly about how to kill other kzin before they killed you. They trained kits with killer robots in those days, and the Riit always aimed to run fifty percent faster than the norm. I suppose they started a bit slower to make sure they didn't kill all their male kits; all the same, the sex balance was just right for each male adult to have a harem of anywhere from ten to fifty females. Duels to the death were just a way to pass the time on the kzin worlds. Those kzin would think the Wunderkzin a bunch of softies for using fuzz instead of steel.

I watched him train after he'd got out of the autodoc, first checking that the robotic buggers weren't going to attack me. I had my own robotic buggers, smaller than Vaemar's and not nearly as lethal. I was invited to make suggestions in my capacity as seventh dan synth expert, and did. He had been doing mainly orthodox kzin combat forms up to this point, and he was damned good at them, but there are some additions, some devised by Wunderkzin, and some from the humans who have their own traditions of martial arts. I showed him some judo moves which are quite different in style to anything the kzin have devised. Also some aikido, which has to be modified quite a lot for kzinti because the joints are different. And quite a few other things.

In synth you used whatever weapons were to hand, which in the case of the kzinti includes built-in daggers in four independent sets.

But there are subtler and more devious weapons, some of which require considerable imagination. I shan't tell you any of them, if you want to learn how to kill people in ingenious ways, learn martial arts from a proper instructor. There's a certain amount of discipline required, and the thugs who just like violence don't survive for long.

So Vaemar spent all his time with his robotic killers, which he had now programmed to fight even dirtier. I did a certain amount in my time in the dojo, but not with the sort of ferocious dedication Vaemar did. I studied, I painted and I composed music as well. I have the most appalling collection of really bad paintings in the universe and some really terrible songs. But it's fun making them, even if visiting them on anyone else would be a capital offense in any right-thinking society. I store them on my wrist-com, and if anyone steals it and manages to break into it, they'll deserve all they get.

It took forty-one days to exit FTL drive and another two to get within range of Kzin-home. All this time, Vaemar was practicing killing robots, and he was now damned good at it.

There we were met by a dozen fighter craft, nasty looking things. We got a communication from their leader, a black-and-lemon striped kzin with a mean look that matched his ship.

"Identify yourself or face destruction," he spat at us. Vaemar answered him calmly.

"Vaemar of the house of Riit to talk with the Patriarch," he said. "Please assign us a landing site."

The kzin stared at him. What he really wanted to do was blast us, I could tell. He asked:

"Have you been sent for?"

"No. I come as a courtesy to present myself to my great uncle. I bring him news of the situation on Wunderland."

"We already know the situation on *Ka'ashi*," the kzin spat and snarled.

"Perhaps not all of it," Vaemar said. "Should the Patriarch have questions I will gladly answer them."

"Should the Patriarch have questions, you will certainly answer them," the captain of the warship told him. "You will be boarded, and your ship put in orbit around the Hunter's Moon. Then you will be transferred to Home World, to the pleasure of the Patriarch."

"That will be acceptable. We stand by for your boarding party." Vaemar switched off the transmission. He turned to me. "Do not permit yourself to be intimidated by their manner. The kzin of the Home World are rather more peremptory than the Wunderkzin, but they will despise you if you are too co-operative. Obey orders, of course. They are in charge around here."

That was obvious enough. I felt a tingle in my spine. This was another world, a whole lot of different assumptions governed it, assumptions I'd have to guess at. It looked all too likely I'd be dead before another day had gone by. For some unconsidered offense against local standards, like breathing.

The boarding party covered the port with some sort of globe of plastic and banged on the door when it was sealed, so we let them in. They turned out to have laser cutters ready to open it themselves, but we were prompt enough that they didn't have to unload them. Four big kzin filed in, their helmets back, and their leader looked us up and down and sneered at us. I followed Vaemar's advice and sneered back. The three underlings checked through the ship and made sure we were the only living beings aboard, and found the sealed engine room.

"Open it," the leader said, when he got the image from his understrapper who had found it.

"It is not possible to open it without destroying the ship and giving the Patriarch a severe case of sunburn if his palace is on this side of Kzin-home," I told him, helpfully. "He won't be grateful to you, but you need not fear his displeasure, you'll be plasma." He glared at me. Baleful wasn't the word, his glance was so full of bale there wasn't room for anything else.

He wasn't stupid. He knew decisions on this were above his pay grade and probably so was killing me.

Probably.

We were shuttled down to the Patriarch's palace, which was as big as a small city in its own right. It was basically a big castle, bulking against the skyline as we landed. There was a second city spread around the foothills of the castle, but we never went there and I saw it only from the air. Then we were taken to an anteroom and waited. And then we waited some more. Seeing Patriarchs takes time, and they like you to know they have more important things to do than deal with foreigners. Neither Vaemar nor I had anything more important to do than deal with Patriarchs, so we carried on waiting. I had plenty of time to admire the furnishings and the company.

The company consisted of five guards, each carrying a spear bigger than himself with a sort of hook in the blade. They stood to attention impassively, not looking at us, in a line next to the door. The room itself was huge, the ceiling towering off into the darkness, and the walls were covered with banners and shields, each with a different symbol. None of it meant anything to me, I'm not big on Kzin heraldry. Or any other.

It was darker than I was used to, and the color schemes seemed to have been chosen for contrast rather than harmony. The musical equivalent would have been raucous, with horns blaring and pipes squealing. Some of the symbols looked like abstractions of beasts, nasty ones. I had heard that Leonardo da Vinci had once been commissioned to put a picture so revolting on the duke's men's shields that the enemy would be struck down with sheer horror, and these looked like practice attempts.

Vaemar was admirably detached. He never spoke, but seemed to be meditating on infinity, which naturally takes a long time. I'm not the meditating type, and I started to get excruciatingly bored, which just goes to show something or other. I reminded myself that I was likely to be inspecting my own intestines shortly, but it didn't cheer me up.

After hours that seemed to have been stretched into weeks, the door opened and a flunky gestured to Vaemar imperiously, and Vaemar followed him. I followed Vaemar, and nobody tried to stop me.

We processed solemnly down long corridors of cold stone lined with what looked rather like carpets hanging on the walls, and the wind whistled under them and flapped them mournfully. It was not the sort of place you'd want to hold a party. It would have driven Santa Claus into suicidal depression, and even I wasn't my usual sunny self.

We passed through what must have been the throne room, which was full of large kzin spitting and snarling at each other but didn't contain the Patriarch, although there was a sizeable throne against the wall at the far end. The décor was similar to the waiting room; archaic and barbaric splendor with a touch of the cold horrors and lots of additional screaming. Then we passed out again and into another room, which also had a throne in it, although not quite so big. This one was occupied.

The Patriarch was big, bigger than Vaemar, and would have come last in a Mr. Congeniality contest. The throne was set against the far wall, had two soldiers armed with spiky spears on each side, and you didn't really notice them because the Patriarch rather took all your attention. We slowly walked up to him.

Most Kzin have violet eyes with intensely black pupils, the Riit tend to red fur, and eyes that are a sort of greeny-gold which is rare enough to be striking. The Patriarch's eyes were not just greeny-gold, they seemed disproportionately large and he stared, and looked at us with uncommon malevolence. Our guide stopped about five yards short of his throne and threw himself horizontal.

"The outworlders, Dread Lord," he hooted. Then he slithered off, taking good care not to turn his back on his monarch.

The Patriarch looked Vaemar over slowly and carefully. He ignored me totally, and I was rather glad of it. Facing up to that malevolent stare would have turned my guts to water.

"And who are you?" he asked.

"I am known as Vaemar," Vaemar told him. He sounded quite placid about it. "I am the leader of the Kzin of Ka'ashi. Wunderland as it is known to its inhabitants."

There was a long, loud silence while the Patriarch tried to outstare him. Then he grunted.

"And why are you here?" he asked.

"Great Lord, your younger brother was my grandsire. I am the son of Chuut-Riit. I am here to claim my patrimony." Vaemar spoke in the civilized speech of the Wunderkzin, which sounds a lot less aggressive that the speech on Kzin-home. It rather stood out, in an odd sort of way. It sounded rather as if Vaemar didn't have to impress anybody and didn't care whether he did or not.

"Kill him," the Patriarch said to the closest of the four guards.

The kzin reacted instantaneously, as one does if in the service of Dread Lords, and lowered his spear and leapt, screaming as it tried to stab Vaemar's gut. Vaemar batted it aside with his left paw, and took out the guard's throat with his right claws. The body fell at the Patriarch's feet and he considered it briefly. Vaemar just went back to standing there patiently, licking the blood off his claws, carefully. There wasn't much, most of it was in a great pool around the body.

These things happen very quickly, much faster than it takes to tell. I mentally chalked up a point to Vaemar. I suppose it was the first and most basic test; if Vaemar hadn't been able to defend himself against a guard, he wasn't fit for including in the Riit hegemony.

"Hmm. Not totally incompetent then," the Patriarch said, and he gave the ear flick which was the equivalent of a chuckle. An evil chuckle.

"If you are to be considered a Riit, you will have to take on someone of much greater ability than a mere guard. Where shall we begin, I wonder? At the other end perhaps? Would you like to fight me?"

"No, Great Lord," Vaemar said, after due consideration.

"Afraid?" the Patriarch asked with a sneer.

"No, my lord and kinsman. But I don't want your job. I expect to have to rule Wunderland in due course, and I do not look forward to doing so. Running your Empire of a Thousand Suns would be even more dispiriting."

The Patriach looked at him and favored him with an evil grin. For Kzin, a grin does not connote humor. All the same, the Patriarch seemed amused by Vaemar rather than annoyed.

"I see. But *you* must see that I cannot simply accept your story at face value. You may indeed be the son of Chuut-Riit; or then again you may be an imposter. Tests are necessary. And even if you were of the line of the Riit, you must show you are capable of maintaining the traditions of the Riit. I think a death duel with someone of established prowess is the way to go. Don't you agree?" He managed to sound like a civilized person discussing legal technicalities while looking like an evil monster longing for blood.

"Certainly, Great Lord. I would expect no less. I ask only that I be armed as my opponent." Vaemar still spoke in that relaxed, unthreatening voice. He wore no *w'tsai* at his side, he had left it in the ship. He wouldn't have been allowed near the Patriarch with one anyway.

🐾   🐾   🐾

Death duels are a very convenient method of getting rid of possible contenders to the throne. A wise Patriarch ensures that any possibilities are matched against each other. Prudence is not a Kzin virtue, but the more intelligent dukes and princes saw the advantages in going forth into space to conquer new worlds for the Empire rather than chance staying at home and fighting duels until they were defeated and consequently dead. This kept them out of the Patriarch's fur for a very long time. Win-win as far as the Patriarch saw it. Of course, he was obliged to fight some of them himself, as a few scars testified. But he was good, and smart enough to ensure he only took on those he could easily beat. Not that anyone on Kzin-home was likely to point this out. The average Kzin had a strong sense of honor and wouldn't have done anything like that, but Patriarchs have to be smart and hence cynical. Those who aren't don't hold the job for long.

The duel was organized very quickly. In fact there were scheduled to be three of them. It was, of course, a public spectacle, held in an amphitheater, and if Vaemar lost his first match, the other two would fight each other. There was a grand duke who was on first and then two princes of the blood. If he killed the lot of them, Vaemar would get his name and be acknowledged as a Riit by the Patriarch and everybody else. I guess Vaemar had expected exactly this, so he must have thought this really important. I don't see it myself, but then I'm not in the running for leader of the Kzin on Wunderland. I suppose this thirsting for recognition and glory is natural for the Riit but it does nothing for me. To be fair, Vaemar seemed to believe it was more a matter of getting stability among the Wunderkzin than getting honor and glory. Whatever. What it meant for me was that the Riit on Kzin-home were all nuts, and the Patriarch was clearly the nuttiest. A kzinicidal maniac if ever I saw one.

Mind you, the duke was a close second. I forget where he was duke of, but he wasn't a Riit although he had the same outlook on life as the Patriarch's immediate family. MSR is the technical term, I believe. It stands for 'Mad as a Shithouse Rat'.

If you are thinking I might be a little prejudiced, well, yes. Being brought up on Wunderland gives you a clear appreciation of other cultures when you meet them. They're all worse. Try some if you don't believe me. There are a few loonies around who insist all cultures are as good as each other.

They're wrong.

Sorry, I'm getting all philosophical when I should be telling you about Vaemar in the amphitheater facing the duke of wherever. I was given a front row seat and two of the Patriarch's guards stood by me; I don't know it they were guarding me from the crowd or the crowd from me. I don't need to say I was worried. I knew Vaemar was pretty good, but the duke had to be pretty good too, or he wouldn't have got his dukedom on Kzin-world. Duking was a very competitive business after all.

He certainly had some scars. There were places where his fur hadn't grown back properly. Of course Vaemar had been wounded too, but he'd had the benefit of an autodoc, and it was a good one, and they don't leave scars, so he looked quite clean and innocent by comparison. Anyway, it was one scarred striped beast with a nasty glint in his eyes and a look of smug confidence, holding a thing like a trident with three big nasty prongs on it, and a net. Vaemar had the same. I was pretty sure Vaemar had never practiced with anything like it before. You could see what the idea was, you caught the enemy in the net and then stabbed him with the trident.

The nets had weights around the edge and the duke was confidently waving his around in a circle, so the net spread out. Vaemar looked placid and almost uninterested, but he was watching the duke carefully all the same.

They were walking on sand, so it was much like a Roman amphitheater, where the sand was designed to soak up the blood of the vanquished and could be raked out and replaced by fresh sand in between bouts. The audience saw it as a Roman holiday too, the places were more than half filled, and the Patriarch sat in the best seat, looking bored.

The duke screamed, sprang with his trident out and as Vaemar dodged to one side, the net was sent out. Vaemar grabbed it on his trident and swept it aside, dodging back the other way, and nearly got caught by a stab of the duke's trident, but not quite. Vaemar's trident was way out, half entangled in the net still, his own net still bunched up. Then he swung the net, still tightly wound up, smack in the duke's face. It made him pause for a microsecond or two, during which time Vaemar dropped his own trident and went for him completely unarmed. He was too close now for the duke's trident to be of any use to him, and he got the duke with his leg, or rather the claws on his leg. They ripped into the duke's belly and down, taking everything with it. Purple blood spurted, and the crowd roared. Literally. Then Vaemar was at the duke's side, while the duke's intestines fell out. One slash at the throat with a casual claw and the duke was down with his throat pouring blood as well.

Vaemar stepped back, still keeping an eye on the duke, which was just as well, because Kzin are hard to kill. The duke was already dead but refusing to acknowledge it; he rose, screamed and leapt at Vaemar, stepping on his own looping intestines in the process and dropping his trident but mad with rage, guts falling out as he sprang.

To meet Vaemar's trident in his throat. Vaemar put the central prong right in, and twisted. The duke still didn't give up, but there was nothing he could do except stand there, swaying, as the blade bit into him. One last sideways sweep and his head almost came off, and he went down. The whole thing had taken less than a minute.

The crowd roared again, and Vaemar lifted the trident high. Four kzin hurried out to confirm that the duke was dead, completely and finally dead. Since his head was almost off, this didn't take long. They dragged his corpse out by the hind legs and he left a trail of blood behind him which was rapidly raked over to give a fresh surface for the next contest.

I can't say I care for violence myself. All that blood is somehow disgusting. I think disagreements should be settled by reasoned argument or maybe a game of chess as a last resort. On the other hand, if someone tries to kill you, you just have to kill them first, and the quicker the better. And it wasn't as if Vaemar had much choice in the matter. If he'd tried to back out, the Patriarch would have had him blasted, no doubt at all. He'd have been considered guilty of cowardice, and expressing a preference for an argument or a game of chess wouldn't have cut much ice.

So Vaemar went to collect his new weapon, just a *w'tsai* this time, and stood patiently waiting for the first of the Riit princes.

The *w'tsai*, in case you don't know, was something like the Roman gladius, a relatively short weapon, not much more than a knife in size. There were human hunting knives, the bowie knife in particular, that could be about the same blade length as the gladius, which was less than two feet, only about twenty inches in fact, and the *w'tsai* was scaled up for kzin size to between three and four feet long. Bigger kzin tended to carry longer *w'tsais*, but I've never seen one with more than four feet of blade, and some are noticeably smaller. The one Vaemar held was a very standard one with a blade of about three and a half feet long. It would make a very substantial sword for a human being, although the handle would need two hands because of its thickness. For a kzin it didn't look a very serious weapon at all, more like a hunting knife. Unlike swords or hunting knives, most of the *w'tsais* had hooks sticking out of the handle end, as did Vaemar's. So either end could do damage, and close fighting often used both parts. It could be thrown, but if you didn't kill with it, you faced your enemy with no weapons other than those provided by nature, and kzin claws are only about six inches long, and although there is a sharp edge to them, they aren't to be compared with a *w'tsai*.

The prince emerged, with his own *w'tsai* in his paw. He was wearing a red cloak, which he took off rather grandly and threw down for an underling to catch. Then he marched up to the spot in front of the Patriarch and did a sort of bow. Vaemar just stood there, watching him.

The prince turned and looked around lazily, until he spotted Vaemar. It was all an affectation, he had known exactly where Vaemar was from entering the arena; there weren't any rules, and Vaemar might have been waiting to pounce on him as soon as he came into the arena, cloak or no cloak. The prince just stood there, then gestured to Vaemar, urging him to approach. Vaemar strode forward to about the halfway point and then stood. Then he made the same gesture to the prince. 'Come and be killed.' It seemed to annoy the prince, who started running toward Vaemar until he had the momentum of a flying battle-tank. It was about twenty paces, kzin paces. He brought around his *w'tsai* in a sweeping blow at Vaemar's neck that looked unstoppable. Vaemar moved like greased lightning, he went in toward the prince, his left arm grabbing the other's right, he put his right paw on the prince's head and pushed it down, and then he swung, spinning himself and the prince so the prince's own momentum carried him off his feet. The prince went sprawling, went into a break-fall and recovered. He sprang to his feet and turned on Vaemar with a snarl.

Unfortunately for him, he had dropped his *w'tsai*. Or maybe fortunately, since he could easily have impaled himself upon it, which may have been Vaemar's intention. Vaemar stooped and picked it up with his left paw. He now had two *w'tsais* against an unarmed enemy. Then he did the dumbest thing you could imagine: he threw the *w'tsai* in his left paw. It spun shining in the sunlight and dropped at the feet of the prince. The prince rose to the occasion. He picked up the *w'tsai* in his right paw, and then bowed to Vaemar. Then he attacked again.

He was more cautious this time, Vaemar's spinning move had come as a nasty shock, being nothing like the standard Kzin fighting pattern. He came within a pace of Vaemar, his weapon held out and then stabbed and screamed. The blade should have gone up under Vaemar's rib cage, or at least the place where the ribs separate because Kzin ribs go right down the body.

The screams that fighting Kzin use are intended to instill fear and distract. The sounds from the dojo when Vaemar had been practicing were even louder, although Vaemar never screamed back. "Waste of breath," he had said curtly when I asked him about it.

The blade was caught by Vaemar's and deflected. Then Vaemar struck on the riposte, his blade going into the throat and out the side with a twist, Vaemar's body moving in the same direction, his left paw gripping the prince's right arm and pulling him. The gout of arterial blood went all over Vaemar, then he ducked down and struck the prince's leg right on the joint. The blade of a *w'tsai* is incredibly sharp and it sheared through meat and bone like a laser. When the blade had cut through one leg Vaemar rose and the blade went up into the prince's crotch and didn't stop.

The prince was almost in three pieces, but he intended to kill before he died. His blade came around just as Vaemar's emerged from his body, Vaemar stopped the blade with his own and then cut the arm holding the *w'tsai* clean through. It fell, still grasped by the prince's paw. Now the prince *was* in three pieces. He was balancing on one leg, his head half off, and he attacked Vaemar with one claw. It was a slow movement, more a matter of training than planned, and Vaemar chopped the paw off. The prince tottered, blood pouring out of both severed arms, and Vaemar finished him off by cutting his head off and sending it three meters to roll in the sand and color it purple. The body collapsed at last, Vaemar pushing it away gently, to land on its back.

Two down, one to go, I thought.

Vaemar looked terrible, his fur all matted and blood-boltered. None of it was his so far as I could tell, but he needed a shower badly. He looked down at himself and seemed to come to the same conclusion, because he went to the great gate through which contestants entered the amphitheater, accompanying the Kzin slaves who were towing the bits and pieces of the prince back to wherever they wound up. Possibly a dinner table, some Kzin believe in eating fallen heroes. He disappeared into the gate, still carrying his borrowed *w'tsai*.

There was a pause, and the second prince came on. He looked around for Vaemar and didn't see him of course. He seemed a bit put out. This one was wearing a purple cloak and a long sword over his shoulder as well as a *w'tsai* on his right thigh. The business end of the sword came well below his cloak hem. He marched up to the spot in front of the Patriarch's seat, bowed, and said something. It looked as if he was claiming a win on account of Vaemar not being present, and the Patriarch said something in his cold, icy voice. It must have been an order to wait. The Patriarch seemed to be fairly sure that Vaemar hadn't done a runner, and so was I. Given the speed with which he'd taken out a duke and a prince of the blood, there was no reason to suppose he'd suddenly gone chicken.

The crowd was starting to complain. They were used to getting blood, gallons of it, and weren't inclined to patience. Neither was the second prince, who was looking daggers at the Patriarch, as if thinking of challenging him. The crowd started chanting, although I couldn't make any sense of it. Fifty thousand kzin all complaining loudly in deep voices and screams is not a very cheerful sound.

Then Vaemar came back. His fur was fluffy, obviously he had showered and air-dried himself. He looked neat and clean and entirely unconcerned. He had an enormous sword on his back, held on by an elaborate belt, and was carrying his *w'tsai* in its sheath. He acknowledged the second prince with a curt nod of the head. I suppose the prince was an uncle or cousin or something. He was a head taller than Vaemar, and sneered when he saw the acknowledgment. Vaemar stalked slowly into the middle of the arena, while his opponent watched him critically.

The second prince drew his sword. It wasn't very different from the king-sized sabers Vaemar had trained with. About seven feet of blade and a basket hilt that had spikes on it; nasty weapons close up. He took his *w'tsai* out of its sheath and held it in his left paw. He swung both weapons about in curving arabesques, changing and chopping. This isn't done to show off, though there's an element of that I suppose; it's done to warm up the wrists and make them more flexible. Then he approached Vaemar, with the sort of caution that comes from having seen him in action. Vaemar drew his own sword in his right paw, and the *w'tsai* in his left and turned slightly to face him. The crowd had gone deathly silent. They knew this was the decider.

The swords clashed and drew sparks. The two circled, both light on their feet, and probed for weakness. Then the second prince stepped back two paces and flipped the sword with the *w'tsai*, taking the sword in his left hand. Vaemar attacked while this was going on, and thrust with his sword, but the prince deflected it in time with the *w'tsai*. Then he struck against Vaemar's left arm with his sword in a powerful sweep. Vaemar tried to block it with his own *w'tsai*, but the blow was too powerful, and the sword cut into his arm. Vaemar dropped his *w'tsai* and fell back, seeming shocked by the wound. The prince snarled in triumph and cut again with his sword at Vaemar's left arm. Vaemar threw up the arm to defend himself, and the sword cut into the wrist and severed Vaemar's paw.

With unbelievable speed, Vaemar turned his severed arm so that the jet of blood went straight into the face of the prince and covered his eyes, briefly blinding him. At the same moment Vaemar pivoted and his sword flashed at the prince's throat, cutting off his head. Vaemar jumped back as the prince swayed and fell, dropped his sword and used his right paw to stem the jetting blood flow from his left stump. Then he raised both arms above his head, and the crowd roared in approval. It had been a classical sacrifice play, not perhaps quite so spectacular these days when the hand could be regrown in an autodoc, but maybe the Kzin here didn't have them.

And that was basically it. Vaemar got his stump bound and reclaimed the severed hand and his *w'tsai* as the third corpse was dragged off. Then he marched up to the spot before the Patriarch and bowed to him. The Patriarch gave him an amiable wave, and a brief nod, then rose. The entertainment was over. Vaemar had rid the Patriarch of some irritating potential threats and all in exchange for a recognition that Vaemar was one of the family, which didn't cost him a cent. Not to mention providing the crowd with some rather bloody entertainment, helping cement his position.

We were back in the smaller throne room, this time with a much reduced waiting period.

"You have made your point, I think, Vaemar-Riit. I don't think I would dare argue with the crowd, and they have accepted you. I heard them screaming for Vaemar-Riit as I left."

Vaemar shrugged, which was an understandable gesture on Wunderland, but probably not here.

"I shall return to Wunderland then, my lord and kinsman, my task here is complete. It seems unlikely we shall meet again."

This would have been good news to the Patriarch, you'd think, who now had Vaemar on his list of those who might be a threat to him at some point.

"Not so fast, Vaemar, my great-nephew. Don't you think you should now show your loyalty to your lord and kinsman by revealing the secret of the FTL drive? We have been going to inordinate efforts to suborn some of your people to obtain it, it would save me a good deal of money if you would merely tell us. Or give us some useful hints, even."

"My lord, I have no idea of how it works. You may gladly employ a telepath to confirm that. The same is true of my pilot here. He can fly one, but does not know how to make one. The chauffeur who flys your aircar would have no idea how to make one, and no more does he."

The Patriarch looked at me speculatively, and it was as much as I could do to look back at him. He could have had me tortured to death by way of temporary diversion. His mad, greeny-gold eyes stared into mine. Not that mine were greeny-gold of course. I wasn't one of the Riit clan, and rather glad of it. The Wunder-Riit seemed to have the slightly priggish air of virtue unrecognized, while the Kzin-home Riit looked to be completely insane. MSR in spades.

I felt something like an instant headache, and knew that I was being probed. Much good would it do them. Somewhere in my subconscious I might be visualizing formulae, but nothing that would make sense to a telepath. Anyway, they'd be the wrong formulae. I had trouble remembering the one for solving quadratics, and I'd never even glanced at any of the math for FTL drives. It would have been ten years hard work to find out what the symbols meant.

The Patriarch was getting information through one of those comm systems embedded in his skull I expect. Anyway, he nodded in a resigned sort of way.

"I see I shall have to come and get it by force," he said. "Either that or carry on with looking for a traitor on Earth or *Ka'ashi*. There are always plenty around, but most of them are woefully uneducated, alas. Traitors, inevitably, come from the class of losers, and there are reasons they are losers."

"If I might suggest it, lord and kinsman, there are good reasons for leaving Wunderland alone. It is an interesting experiment. We are living with the humans, and evolving a new and different culture. We take their best ideas, and they take ours. Even you must admit they are formidable fighters. And it is sure that someday, either humans or kzinti will come across something in the blackness of space which will be a greater threat than we are to each other. If we can share each other's strengths, it might be that together we could defeat some horror before which either alone must fall. I have heard tales that suggest this has been devised by some other race of star-travelers, that our meeting up with the humans was by design. This may be some nonsense, yet forming an alliance with Man may be in the best interests of Kzin eventually. Maybe it cannot happen, but if it can, Wunderland is a place where it is more likely than anywhere else."

"Ah, so you have the strategy gene," the Patriarch said looking hard at Vaemar. It was not a word I recognized, I didn't know there was any such word for the concept in the Heroes' Tongue, but it had to mean that.

Obviously, the Patriarch had it too. It wasn't exactly common in the Kzin species; taking the longer view wasn't particularly likely to improve life expectancy on Kzin-home. Strong wrists and good reflexes counted for a lot more. Obviously, to get to be Patriarch, you had to have the lot.

The Patriarch looked quizzically at Vaemar who looked calmly back.

"Very well, my great-nephew, you may go back and rule *Ka'ashi*," he said. "Eventually. No doubt in that strange, so-called democratic manner in which the mob demand the wealth of others and the weak provide it in order to win votes. It is not likely to endure long, this folly. It will turn to chaos, and then strong individuals will need to rule by force. And so the wheel turns. A foolish and pointless business, wouldn't you say?" He squinted at Vaemar with his head on one side.

"At present it is beyond our control," Vaemar said equably. Settling into a philosophical debate with an insane monster seemed to give him no problems at all. "But that may not always be so. I was hoping to develop some mathematics which might have given insights into the processes you mention, and eventually perhaps, one day, to control them. But I was diverted, alas into practical politics. The immediate takes over from the long term, the pressures of the day win out over the long view. It is folly, but that is the nature of the world, this one as well as Wunderland."

"Ah, well, the fools and knaves will win unless stopped hard; they have, after all, the numbers," the Patriarch said. He sounded almost melancholy, as though he too would have preferred to spend his time on mathematics. It wasn't impossible, Napoleon regretted that he'd been obliged to take up emperoring when he'd have preferred math. I never believed it, but that might be why I wasn't in line to be an emperor, not having any talent for either.

"Perhaps someone else can do it, and one day we shall understand ourselves a little better than we do," Vaemar said politely. For just a moment, seeing them look at each other and get all sentimental about algebra and suchlike, they looked very similar. The Patriarch was older, of course, but there was something about the two of them . . . I shook my head to clear it of nonsense.

He let us go. Before we left, the Patriarch made Vaemar two presentations: a gold medallion bearing his sigil and an ornately crafted jar containing his own urine. With Vaemar the hero of the hour (of course, the very word 'kzin' means 'hero' in our tongue), it was more entertainment for the court, although somewhat less bloodthirsty than they'd have preferred.

"That should convince your subjects of your legitimacy," the Patriarch remarked. Then he added, *sotto-voce*, "And do be sure not to return."

We were taken back to our ship, the troop of soldiers now being most respectful to Vaemar, and even tolerating me. We strapped in and started for the edge of the star system so we could go FTL, and the kzin warships escorted us out.

We went FTL, and the universe went out. We were alone. Vaemar stood up.

"And now I need to grow my paw back," he observed. "No doubt it will take some days. But I should like to be fully functional before we get home to Wunderland. Not that I expect to do any dueling there, but you never know. So I shall put myself in the autodoc for as long as it takes. Check on me periodically."

So I was on my own. Nothing to do. After what I'd seen, I figured I needed all the combat practice I could get, so I set up the dojo for some high-speed fighting. You never could tell. One day I, JimSono'Rruat, might find myself back on Kzin-home, and it might be *me* in the arena.

JUSTICE

by Jessica Q. Fox

❧ JUSTICE ❧

2987 AD, en route to Wunderland

"SORRY DARLING, but you're going to have to put up with a certain amount of inconvenience," Mimsy said.

"Huh?" Evan was bewildered. His girl had just come back from some sort of meeting with the rest of the crew, and it looked as though there'd been some sort of joint decision. But why should it affect him? He was the pilot. Pilots didn't get to be told what to do while on board a starship, they were god-like beings whose word was law. He'd have, he thought, a certain amount of difficulty getting this idea over to Mimsy. She'd probably laugh at him.

"We checked and we have a stowaway."

"Impossible," Evan said emphatically. "There was nothing on Kr'argon that . . . Uh oh. You mean we have a ghost?"

"Yup. It was pretty much inevitable, and I guessed it as soon as I had time to think about it. You and I were crawling with the stuff, and although we vacuumed everything, and although your nanites and mine killed the bits that were eating us, we didn't get it all. And it's been growing slowly since we left BigEars."

The ghost was an acellular life form; you could think of it as a swarm of bees, except that the bees were just protein molecules. Big as molecules go, but far too small to see. And the monster they had met on Kr'argon which was dense enough to actually be visible had shown signs of intelligence. It had also killed two of their company and had made a good attempt to eat Evan and Mimsy.

"What do we have to do?" Evan asked.

"We have to go into quarantine in the Serpent Swarm. There we suck up every particle of air and filter it. And then we sterilize the whole ship, with enough radiation to give our nanites something to think about. Then we wait for a month to see if we've got every bit of it. If we haven't, we do it all over again. It could take a while."

Evan groaned. "I'd been looking forward to getting home," he said. "I want to go out and get drunk. I want to go home afterwards and find you there to soothe my fevered brow." Evan had hopes that his relationship with Mimsy was going to turn into something permanent and that they'd live together. He'd never had the nerve to mention it until now.

"Nuts. I'll be getting drunk too. Good disinfectant, alcohol. Applied internally it should take care of the odd bit of ghost. In fact I think we should start as soon as we've done the air filtering."

Evan considered. She hadn't scorned the idea, at least. He brightened. Finding an excuse for getting even slightly squiffy on a starship wasn't easy. Most of the usual ones had been tried and banned over the years.

"What do we do with the stuff we filter out? Space it?" he asked.

"Oh Evan, you're hopeless," Mimsy told him fondly. "It's the only trace we have of an intelligent ghost. I don't expect it's got much intelligence now, but if we culture it and grow it in the right environment, we might be able to get it back again."

"Get it back? But it tried to kill us," he said indignantly.

"It won't have any memories of that," Mimsy said. "We can study it if we can grow it."

"You scientists are all the same," Evan grouched. "You find an alien life-form and before anyone can stop you, you're trying to make friends with it."

"We like learning, Evan. You should try it, you might enjoy it."

Evan shuddered. Not if it led to trying to buddy up with a bunch of molecules that would eat anything it found, he decided.

"I reckon BigEars turning nova was the universe deciding it didn't like intelligent ghosts, and in my view the universe has the right idea," he declared. "I vote for spacing it."

"But Evan, it's a unique chance to learn something about an alien life form," Mimsy sighed at him. "Something really different from us."

"I'll say," Evan gloomed. "An invisible thing that could be any-where. It doesn't have to leap out from behind things to give us a nasty shock, it's already here. What the hell are you planning to do with it?"

"Oh that's fixed," Mimsy said sunnily. "There's a new settlement planned in the Serpent Swarm. An empty asteroid that's already got air and water. They were going to put some settlers in it next month, but we bought it for our ghost. May have to put some methane in it, make it more suitable for the little beastie. And we shall load it with instruments to measure and observe everything that goes on inside it, and some telepresence robots. There'll never be a human being goes into the place."

She was wrong about that.

Alyssa was two miles long and a mile wide and had been trimmed down from something the shape of a potato to a tiny worldlet that could spin on its long axis without any detectable wobble. It had three-quarters of a standard g inside at the hull, and contained lakes, trees, grass and air at rather lower pressure than would have been entirely comfortable, but disks were passing more air in from nearby asteroid bases that already had plenty. The crew of the *Busted Bird* were having enormous fun making modifica-tions, including putting in methane and bits of ghost.

"The methane is probably the main source of amino acids, but we shall need some lightning inside to assist with their production," one of the biochemists had lectured. "On the other hand, we cannot put too much in or it will kill off the existing animals. Which should also be a good source of protein for the ghost."

"Won't the strange environment kill off something?" Evan asked. "I mean, either the ghost wins and eats all the animals or the ani-mals win and the ghost dies."

The biochemist sighed. "Systems of any complexity either go into positive feedback and die or they hit an equilibrium," he told Evan. "Most biological systems have very complex negative feed-back loops to ensure their survival. Were it not so, there would be no human biosphere."

This was not entirely gobbledygook. Evan knew that modern starships were about as complex as some living organisms, and could repair themselves and even make copies of themselves, given time. In fact Wunderland had won a war that way not so long ago, back in the golden age, when there were interplanetary and even interstellar disks. Now there were only disks that could operate at short distances, about a light-second. So they could pour air from one asteroid to another only while they were in range, which left a lot of time when they weren't. But feedback loops in complex systems were bread and butter to engineers.

"Are we clean and able to get back to Wunderland?" Evan asked the man.

He shrugged. "We are in no hurry. I believe the checks were satisfactory and all the ghost was transferred to Alyssa, but why should we leave now? There is fascinating work to be done, and we want to monitor the organism."

Evan sighed. Sometimes he hated scientists.

The physical scientists, mostly kzinti, had no more interest in the fate of the ghost than Evan, and although Mimsy was interested in everything, she agreed that the odd check would be sufficient to satisfy her curiosity, so when it had been established that the ghost was surviving in its rather spacious zoo, most of the crew returned to Wunderland. Mimsy moved in with him, and Evan thought that was wonderful. It was true that she disappeared to the university for long periods, but he was determined to be an indulgent and understanding man. He thought of marriage, being old-fashioned, but was too frightened at the thought that she would laugh at him. So life went on in the disorganized fashion it does, and both of them were happy in the way most people are when they don't think about it too much. Evan studied, because there was always another examination to pass, and Mimsy sometimes helped him with the mathematics, and sometimes made things worse by explaining the ideas to him. But she was a kindly girl, and when she saw the look of dumb agony in his eyes, she usually settled for just telling him how to do the sums and gave up explaining why they worked, and how anyone had hit on the idea, the only bits that interested her.

It was two years and six months after Evan and Mimsy and the others had returned to Wunderland. In a large asteroidal base, a man known to the few acquaintances he had as Racin' Jason Heyson was trying to escape. He suspected he didn't have long. He was checking out disks big enough to get through, and they were not uncommon, but most went to well-policed locations and carried monitors to say who was passing through them. But he had what he saw as a wonderful opportunity. There was a disk which had been open two and a half years ago, but was now closed. At that time, it had been close to some dump of a rock and was sending air to it. Then the thing had gotten out of range, and the disks were closed, but now the rock was back in range. There was, presumably, no need to send any more air, but it could send a man, Jason thought. And whatever was on this dump of a rock, if it had air it probably had water and plants and animals. It would be like camping out, he decided, and if he could get away for another two and a half years, the cops would have given up on him and he could get back. When the heat had died down. Of course, killing someone was the kind of thing that got the cops riled up, and most of them were Kzin and took a dim view of murder. Particularly child murder.

Jason had killed a small boy this time. He had painted himself all over first so as to cut out any DNA particles being left behind, and switched off his phone somewhere far from the murder scene. He was fairly sure he had left no trace. And a boy, he thought, would be less trouble than a girl, he had got close to disaster the time before, when it had been a girl. But boys were nearly as good. The look of terror on their little faces as his hands began to squeeze around their necks was just so exciting. Afterwards he'd had to exercise restraint, the temptation to rape the warm bodies was powerful, but he knew it was too risky. But going home and jerking off to the memory of the look on their faces was nearly as good. He could get a hard-on just thinking about it.

"Get on with it, you can connect, now!" he told the disk. And it worked. The disk was black, but he could feel the sudden lack of resistance as it made contact. He pushed a lens through on the end of a length of cable.

On Alyssa, a metallic probe suddenly popped out of nowhere. It turned and surveyed the world. Jason's mouth went wet as he looked. Water, yes, light from the central column that went the length of the inside of the asteroid. There was a good-size lake.

There was grass waving in some sort of synthetic wind. It was big enough to have something like weather, there were clouds in the sky. And there were animals, deer and maybe pigs and chickens pecking about. He could live there. And not a sign of a human being. It looked perfect.

Jason threw some cases through and made sure with the lens that they were undamaged and had not had far to fall. Then he set the disk to switch itself off and delete all memory of having been on. Then he took a deep breath and pushed himself headfirst through the disk. He fell only just over a foot, skidded because of the coriolis force, rolled forward and looked around.

Yes, it looked perfect. Home for about two and a half years.

"There is a human being in the habitat," the chief biologist, a kzin, pointed out to a colleague.

"Impossible!" the human colleague said. Then he looked and swallowed. The video sensors were probably the least important for keeping track of the ghost, which was almost undetectable by most modes. One had to look for the tiny microwaves which the constituent protein molecules used to signal each other, although there were some infrared lines in which the proteins could be made to fluoresce briefly. So it was not surprising that Racin' Jason had been there for a month before anyone noticed him. In this time he had made a campsite, built fires and roasted pigs and chickens. He'd have gotten away for longer but the ghost had found him, and the scientists had followed the ghost.

The ghost was cautious. It had found the animals earlier, and discovered that they were a useful source of complex proteins, and it had grown bigger. It had no conception of limiting its diet, food was there to be absorbed and modified into body mass, but there was plenty of it, and just absorbing bits of skin served perfectly well. At the moment its body mass was not much more than that of a dozen human beings, but spread about a volume nearly a tenth of the interior of Alyssa, so the effect on any one animal was seldom enough to kill it immediately. It had shown not the slightest signs of intelligence greater than that of a jellyfish. The difference between the behavior of Racin' Jason and that of the other animals was not apparent to the ghost. It had no real vision, although it could react to the changes in intensity as the huge lights on the central column of Alyssa cycled slowly to simulate day and night. Its sensors could best be described as an ability to scent a huge variety of molecules by interacting with them directly. It liked the smell of Racin' Jason. No human being would have, and certainly no kzin, but the ghost found him quite fragrant.

Seen from the ghost's point of view, Racin' Jason was a complicated bag with lots of holes in. His eyes were damp as were his lungs, and mostly best avoided by the soluble parts of the ghost at first, but it was not difficult to saturate them and then they became very tasty.

"How do we get him out of there?" the human asked. "He's a danger to the experiment."

"I don't know," the kzin answered. "I would like to know how he got in. And he is no more a danger than the other animals."

"But the ghost may eat him, we know it eats some of the animals."

"True," the kzin answered placidly. "But he is there illegally. I think I shall consult the police. The Serpent Swarm police is not a large body. One of my cousins is a senior person in the force. Garcharr may be able to advise us as to how the human got into Alyssa. I shall take him some of the images and see what he says."

"Ah. We were hunting him. He is wanted for murder. Several very nasty murders," Garcharr said. "His name is Racin' Jason Heyson. He left behind enough breath particles on his last murder to make identification certain. And knowing where he is now we were able to track his method of getting into your habitat. When we get him, he will have his brain rewritten very extensively. And his genes edited."

"It may be difficult to get him out," the other kzin said. "We have no entrances and exits ourselves. We might be able to push him back through the disk he entered by; we have surveillance telepresence robots. But they are not very strong."

"The disk he used for entry will not be available for another two years," Garcharr said.

"I see. So he is there for an extended period." The kzin's eyes gleamed. "It seems as if he is going to be part of the experiment for some time then."

🐾 🐾 🐾

Racin' Jason Heyson felt a faint breeze in his ears. Strange. He coughed. There was a faint smell of burning rubber. And his eyes were stinging.

The brain begins in the nasal cavity, and is directly connected to the smell sensors. Also, once through the eye, there are huge ribbons of neurons with lots of very interesting neurotransmitters.

It was two weeks before Racin' Jason knew for sure he was being eaten alive. It was more like a gentle nibbling really. It wasn't so much painful at first, it tickled unendurably though. Later it became agony. And it took over a year for the entire body to be consumed, although Racin' Jason was dead halfway through that. He had wondered at times whether this was some sort of punishment for his crimes, for he knew that he deserved something bad. He wept a great deal in the last months, through sockets where his eyes had once been, and he apologized to all the gods he could think of, but it made not the slightest difference. His nanites fought back, but it just made the battle that much more drawn out.

"I think it is justice," Garcharr said, looking at the bundles of chalk that was all that was left of Racin' Jason Heyson. All the collagen had been eaten long ago.

"Yes. Also of great scientific interest, although some of my human colleagues were squeamish about it towards the end," the kzin biologist said. "I would not have tolerated it for an innocent man, even if I had been forced to damage the experiment by cutting into the habitat. But he was far from innocent. When the humans protested, I showed them pictures of the mankit that he had killed. I refused to countenance heroic measures to save so worthless a life. It was indeed justice."

Six months later, the ghost started to show some small signs of intelligence. Whether this had something to do with an improved diet was never established, but it is just possible that Racin' Jason Heyson did make at least one positive contribution to the universe.

Evan and Mimsy were finishing their after-dinner wine, a copy of an old French classic St. Emilion. Evan had prepared the dinner, mainly a matter of selecting a menu from a list and pressing a few buttons. He had the time, as Mimsy had spent all day at the university, thinking hard. It seemed a fair division of labor to both of them. Evan was drinking a lot of the wine so as to get the courage to propose.

"That bastard in Alyssa finally died, I see," Mimsy said.

"Yes. I thought that was terrible," Evan said with a shudder. "I couldn't bring myself to watch it. Shows what we escaped on Kr'argon."

"Mmm. Guess so. Still, we were monitoring his nanites, so we'll be better prepared for defending people from the ghost next time."

"All the same, we should have done something to save him. Those kzin have no conception of mercy."

"Well, no, they don't. But they understand justice. And face it, the guy would have died even if we'd got him out. There was no way he'd have got away without having a major brain rewrite."

"That wouldn't kill him," Evan argued.

"Yes it would. Oh, his body would survive, but it wouldn't be him inside it any more. He'd have gone under the brain rewiring, and a damn good thing too. I saw the pictures of the kids he'd killed."

"It makes me feel awfully uncomfortable though," Evan complained. "It was as if we were torturing him."

Mimsy shrugged. "They offered him a suicide pill. One of the robots went out and gave it to him and explained it would kill him painlessly. It took a lot to talk the chief kzin biologist into doing even that much, kzin think pain is just something you put up with, and he said rude things about humans being morally feeble and squeamish. But he let them do it. But the bastard wouldn't take it. He played with it a certain amount, but he never got around to actually swallowing the thing. So we didn't torture him, he did it to himself."

"I still feel awful about it," Evan fretted. "It's a lot to ask a man to commit suicide."

"We wouldn't have let him live anyway," Mimsy pointed out. "He was going to get a major brain rewrite. And to be quite candid, torturing someone like him wouldn't worry me all that much. What he did to those poor innocent children should be met in kind. An eye for an eye, a tooth for a tooth. And if he died in pain and terror, so did those kids. I mean, how else can you show you take that sort of crime seriously? In the old days, they'd have put him in prison for twenty years and then let him out on the advice of the so-called experts. Whose grasp of brain functioning was no better than witch doctoring. Probably worse than the average witch doctor."

"Women are hard," Evan sighed.

"Women are realists, men are sentimentalists," Mimsy said promptly. "And we care about children more and insane murderous perverts a lot less."

Evan sighed. He wasn't exactly sensitive to atmosphere, he was an engineer, but something told him he'd better postpone proposing to Mimsy for a week or so.

SAGA

by Brendan DuBois

❧ SAGA ❧

WHEN THE SLEEP-DEATH CHAMBER opened up in his stolen ship's landing module, Trask-Weapon Technician groggily awoke to thick smoke and flames roaring around him. He roared in return and stumbled out of the kzin-sized chamber, feeling heavier than he should. It instantly came to him: They had arrived on a strange world and their mission had been fulfilled. About him were broken struts, crushed bulkheads, dangling conduits and wires. He pushed through the wreckage, coughing from the smoke, grumbling as flames licked at him, scorching his fur and footpads.

Mission fulfilled, but too soon to see if it was a success.

With the module wreckage about him, the flames still flickering—the fire-suppressant system had to be off-line—it took a few moments to get his bearings. Then he went down a short passageway and—

A thick spar blocked his way. He touched the metal and yelped. It was hot to the touch.

But he needed to get down that passageway. He would not be blocked.

He grabbed the spar and howled in pain and in anger, and tore the spar away, opening up his path. He had to crawl some but then he came out into another compartment, its upper bulkhead crushed. But the second sleep-death chamber in this landing module, once belonging to the stolen star vessel *Fanged Revenge*, was still intact.

Trask moved forward, ignoring the burns on his body and feet, checking the glowing instrumentation, the dots and commas of his

191

language. The system was still working. It had survived the crash landing.

A brief soft yowl of triumph came out, and Trask manipulated the controls, and then sat back against a creased and damaged bulkhead that creaked in protest from his massive bulk.

There were noises, hissing, chuffing sounds, and then the chamber split open. Cold condensed air billowed out, and still he waited. He remembered what he had learned . . . Fanged God, it seemed like just a handful of days ago, but of course, it had been much, much longer. But he had remembered well: Let the chamber do its work, don't be impatient, don't rush it.

Just wait.

Trask hated waiting.

But he knew what had to be done.

So he waited.

Eventually something inside the chamber coughed, whimpered, and Trask walked over and looked down at the chamber's occupant.

A female kzin, her belly swollen with four kits safely inside.

The kzinret's name was First Daughter of Jarl-Geneticist.

He softly growled, touched her large belly.

The four kits inside—two male, two female—belonged to him.

First Daughter of Jarl-Geneticist was his mate, at a time when the Patriarchy had forbidden mates, had designated all kzinretti to be judged and tested for their intelligence, to breed them low and breed male kzinti high. Trask would not let that happen to First Daughter. It was why he had become a criminal, and an exile.

But she was alive.

Mission accomplished.

He helped her through the wreckage—most of the fires had now sputtered out—and then they climbed up the soft dirt of a long trench, caused by the module's searing crash landing. Atop the trench, claws extended and ears at full mark, Trask looked around in the night. He couldn't smell nor see anything approaching in the darkness, but he noticed the lushness of the grass and local vegetation, and the tall trees in the distance.

He leaned his head back, looked up at the hard, indifferent and alien stars.

"Do you know where we are, m'lord Mate?" First Daughter asked, standing next to him.

"No," he said. "I don't think we'll ever know. I doubt the landing craft's computer survived."

First Daughter grumbled. "So we might not know where we are, or when we are . . . how long we traveled from Kzin."

"Far enough," he said. "Far enough."

He gave the near land one more scan of his ears, eyes and nose. Nothing else seemed to stir here. Had the module's loud and bright landing scared away the local creatures or inhabitants?

If so, that was a bit of good luck. He would take it.

He looked to the horizons. No glow of artificial light, of settlements, of cities.

Could this world be empty, just for him, his mate, and their four soon-to-be-born kits?

"Stay," he ordered. "I'm going to see what can be salvaged."

"As you say, m'lord Mate," First Daughter replied, as he scampered back down the soft soil of the trench side.

He moved as best as he could through the crushed metal, the spars, the flickering and sparking coming from the module's electronics. There . . . the autodoc, gone. The ship's kitchen . . . gone. Computer unresponsive. The weapons locker . . . all the weapons in there were crushed, shattered, destroyed. In a rage he pawed through the locker, tossing everything behind him, cursing his life, his position, the damn Patriarchy that had brought him here to exile.

For Trask and his illegal mate had escaped from Kzin aboard *Fanged Revenge* in a desperate journey to escape the Patriarchy and certain execution. In experimental death-sleep aboard *Fanged Revenge*, they would travel out of Kzin space and to an undiscovered world, and once the ship's computer had located a star system with a planet that was suitable for Kzin, the passenger module would be ejected. He and First Daughter would be roused from death-sleep, ready to settle a new world.

But his plans hadn't included a crash landing that would destroy nearly everything of value.

He breathed hard, at last finding a portable medical kit. He opened it and was able to smear burn salve on his wounds, and the pain started throbbing away. Good. He went outside for a moment. A wind had come up, blowing away most of the smoke. He could see better now, and he returned to work. He moved methodically, removing some ration packs, containers of water, and scraps of fabric that could be used as covering if this place grew too cold.

But weapons . . .

He needed to be armed.

Trask moved forward, to where the damage was greatest to the landing module. He found a pointed arc of ship's ribbing, broken away. He ran one finger along the edge. It was sharp. Not as sharp as it could be, but it would work, and the makeshift sword was long enough and light enough that he could carry it without fatigue.

He needed a handle.

He went back to work.

Dawn was coming to this alien world when he was done, having fashioned a hilt out of another, duller piece of metal, and using a small supply of ship's adhesive to make a grip. He swung the sword around, growling with pleasure.

Now he was an armed warrior, a member of the Heroes' Race, here on a strange world.

With their meager belongings carried in a sack, he raced up the trench, sword in hand, and nodded to his mate, and dropped the sack on the ground. She clumsily got up, her pregnant belly swollen, and came to him.

"This is all we have," he said.

First Daughter said, "We were fortunate to survive."

"Yes."

"Is there life on this world?"

"Plants. I've smelled nothing to hunt."

She nodded, her ears fully open, and she rubbed the top of her paw on top of his strong forearm.

"We will live, you and I," she said. "We will thrive on this new place, and"—she stroked the fur over her distended belly—"our kits will thrive as well, and their kits will grow . . . and this world, all of it, will belong to us and our descendants."

Her words thrilled Trask, and he enjoyed her touch, and then, her voice shy, she said, "M'lord Mate, forgive me for saying so, but I hunger."

He growled, went into the sack, took out an emergency ration brick. She tore it open and ate it in two large tearing snaps, and he said, "I will go and hunt. Stay . . . and take care of our future."

"I shall do that, m'lord Mate," she said.

With sword in hand, Trask loped away from the wreckage and torn dirt. He was soon in grassland, and for a moment he thought of the fields on Kzin, but this grass . . . it was lush and moist. So different. And the scents . . . he turned his head to and fro, his pink ears extended, his tail flicking back and forth. There was the scent of water, and he tracked it to an open stream. He spent a long time, looking and evaluating, and when he was satisfied that no enemy was nearby, he leaned down, lapped at the water until he got his fill. The water was cold and clear, and tasted fine.

His thirst satiated, he stood up, breathing hard, sword in his paw.

Something came to him . . . something deep and stirring. This entire world . . . was his!

An entire planet!

He was the Patriarch here, *he* was the ruler, *he* was the conqueror!

He started racing, running, feeling a fierce joy in him, that of the hunter, of the conqueror, fearing nothing, nothing at all. On Kzin there was no place like this, where one was alone, when one could stalk, fight and kill, to—

A four-legged animal with short horns on its narrow head burst from the wooded area to the right, started racing, running, jogging to the left and right, desperately trying to outrun him.

He dropped his handmade sword, growled in a large shout, and in a matter of moments was on the running creature, tumbling it to the ground, tearing at its flesh, blood spurting into his mouth, as he rolled and sliced and tugged.

The next thing he knew he was on his knees, breathing hard, the creature's blood matting the fur around his mouth, his belly full of the meat he had torn away. The taste . . . nothing like he had ever sensed before, but it was not unpleasant. He panted, knowing the full joy and thrill of the hunt, of taking down a prey.

The creature's remains were scattered in front of him, its entrails steaming in the morning air.

Food . . . now at least they had food.

He tore off and ate some more, slowly this time, cherishing the raw taste and freshness of the meat. Trask got up, wiped his right arm across his face, panting in joy. A torn leg and joint was on the ground, and he easily picked it up, and retrieved his sword, and when he got back to the shelter, First Daughter growled and hissed with joy, and something else came to him, the fierce pleasure of a warrior providing for his mate.

He moved them to a hilly area that could be defended, in the middle of a wide, wet range with low grass and expanses of mud that would slow down any approaching enemy. The idea of "defense" made him growl with anger, but as First Daughter's mate, he had a responsibility. And she was carrying his four kits, enough to populate this world with enough work, luck and the use of his sword.

The top of the hill had low brush and plants, but had a good view of the surrounding territory. Trask placed trimmed sharpened spikes of wood on the easy approaches to the hilltop, and soon the only way to their encampment would be from a creature like a Kzin, scrambling up steep rocks.

A smoldering fire was kept going, day and night by First Daughter, and one night, as the coals glowed, they were together, sharing warmth, looking up at the unfamiliar stars.

"M'lord Mate," First Daughter whispered. "Can you tell how far we might be from Kzin?"

He growled. "Very far. Without optics and the ship's computer, it will be up to our descendants to learn who we were, and where we came from."

"Can that be done? For them to learn so much?"

A softer growl. "With our kits and with your father's knowledge, I have no doubt."

He stroked her bulging belly and thought of her father, Jarl-Geneticist. He worked for the Patriarchy and plunged the depths of Jotoki biotechnology to raise stronger and smarter kzinti, and—in a matter of controversy to some—to breed the kzinretti to be less intelligent and more suited for breeding. But secretly he and a small band of others did what they could to soften the blow, and it was he who had helped Trask steal the experimental star craft to take them away from Kzin.

Another stroke of his paw against his mate's swollen fur. The work of her father was also within those unborn kits, for he had changed their genetic line, so each would have their own genes, their own bloodline, so that inbreeding and the associated defects would not arise generations from now.

"We are fortunate, you and I, for we have this world to conquer as our own, and our Names will live forever," Trask said. "At some point, sagas will be written about us."

They stayed together that night, huddling for warmth, and on the next day, the monsters came.

Trask was hunting in another stretch of woods, some leagues away from their encampment, when he heard odd sounds coming from the near field. So far the hunt had been unsuccessful—Trask thought the meat creatures he had killed had now learned his scent, and were keeping far, far away—but now he stopped.

Noises.

Voices.

What was it?

He growled, lowered himself, his ears open, listening, and he crawled to the ragged edge of the woods, and stared out, seeing the monsters that had suddenly appeared.

There were four of them, large, with short hair and four legs, and a thick tail. Two heads were mounted on the thick body, and it had upper arms as well. The first, lower head had small eyes, long nose and teeth covered by flapping lips. The second, upper head was smaller, and could rotate in a wide range, much further than the larger head.

Even at this distance, he noted the intelligence in the smaller head, which wore a helmet of apparent metal.

The upper creatures wore—

Hold on!

He growled again. Trask had been wrong.

There were two creatures, not one large one. The smaller one clambered off the four-legged animal and walked around on its two legs. They wore worked metal in addition to their head helmets, and he saw they had cutting tools—swords much smaller than his own— and that the creatures were smaller than him.

Monsters.

No, not monsters, but they were creatures, walking upright, armed, and they talked in grunts and chatter.

He licked saliva from his mouth. It would be kit's play to slaughter these four bipeds, and perhaps even the larger creatures they rode on . . . but no.

They had worked metal. They were primitive, yes, but truth be told, Trask was primitive as well, had traveled through the stars to end up in this low position.

But they were a threat.

He could not let them live.

But first, he needed to know more about them.

Back at his lodging, First Daughter said, "M'lord Mate, I hunger."

He sat down, breathing hard. Scrambling up the rocks on an empty belly was getting harder and harder.

"I hunger as well."

"But m'lord Mate, I am carrying our four kits, and I—"

He struck her with anger, growling, "For Fanged God's sake, close that mouth!"

First Daughter rolled away and then, moving quick for a large kzinret, came at him, fangs exposed, claws extended, and he grabbed his sword and held it to her neck.

She spat at the ground. "You may have me now, m'lord Mate, but at some point you will doze . . . and what will you do then?"

His anger and heart were racing, and he hissed: "There are times like this, First Daughter, when I agree with those who want to change your kind into nothing else but breeders."

"That is on Kzin, not here. Here, we are alone."

They stood there, staring at each other, and Trask lowered his sword. "We are no longer alone. There are creatures here. Armed."

"Civilized?"

He put his sword down. "No. But they are armed as I am, with sword and some metal. But they are small, and move slowly."

"What shall you do then, m'lord Mate?"

He went to the small fire, warmed his paws. "I will find where they live, and put them to the sword, and have them swear allegiance to me, their Kzin lord."

He went back to the field where had first spotted the odd creatures, and was able to follow the spoor of the creatures that they rode, using both sight and scent. The grassland led to an area of ordered crops, and a path, and then there was smoke rising up from small structures. There was also an area of flat water, and narrow wooden watercraft drawn up on sand. Off to the right was a larger building, long and low.

He counted about forty or fifty of the creatures, moving about. Some wore cloth around their legs in a tube-like fashion, and others wore cloth around their legs in a wider, singular tube.

Trask moved along the wood edge, keeping as low as he could, and his stomach growled at seeing a stone enclosure, holding smaller, fat animals, also with four legs. These weren't big enough to ride, so they were being kept for something else.

Food.

Trask waited until night, and saw a line of the two-legged creatures go into the low building, and there were voices, and some rhyming noises and loud voices. The sound disturbed him but that was all right, for he was not planning to spend the night here.

Instead he leapt into the stone enclosure, crushed the skulls of two of the small animals. There were noises, shouts, and the door to the low building opened up, revealing dim light, but by then Trask was gone. He raced back to his mate holding two of the small dead animals, one under each arm.

For the next few nights he returned again and again, slaughtering the meat animals, bringing back enough for his mate to feast on, for her and the kits.

On the fourth night, they were waiting for him.

The two-legged primitives howled and rose up from the stone enclosure, hiding among the smaller animals, and came after him with their short swords.

Trask howled in reply, and he was pleased to see two of the creatures break and run away as he waded forth, jumping at them, swinging his sword. The clash of his sword on their armor, their blades—oh, what a sound that was!—and the feel of it cutting through them, slicing, cutting again, gutting. . . .

He whirled, sliced, and picked up one of the creatures and tossed it at the near stone fence, shattering its spine, and in a moment, the battle was over.

Trask stood there in the light of the odd moon, the small animals bleating and cowering in the corner, the two-legged creatures dead and slaughtered before him.

He tilted his head back, howled up at the night sky, and then killed two more of the small meat animals, and went back to his shelter, and First Daughter was awake, near the fire, her eyes wide with excitement.

"The wind . . . it shifted," she said. "I could hear you, m'lord Mate. I could hear your battle cries . . . oh, what a wonder it must have been."

"It was," he said, dropping the bloodied bodies of the meat animals at her feet. And First Daughter growled and he was waiting for her to fall upon the animals, but she said, "Wait, m'lord, I want to show you what I have done in your absence."

She slipped out beyond the light of the fire and then came back, bearing . . .

A weapon.

A sword, shorter than his own, but a weapon nonetheless.

She passed it over to him, almost shyly, and he knew what would have happened had this occurred on Kzin. She would have been imprisoned, or struck down, because the thought of a kzinret creating a weapon . . .

Trask passed it over to her.

"A fine sword, First Daughter," Trask said. "You should be proud."

She lowered her eyes. "With your sword and mine, m'lord Mate, we will rule this world."

Back again at darkness. Trask realized these creatures didn't fight well at night, that they seemed to fear the darkness. He would use that to his advantage.

This time, he didn't attack, didn't grab a meat creature, or kill anything.

He stayed in the near woods, howling and crying, to keep them awake, to make them fear him even more.

Trask did that for three more nights, and then on the fourth night, he attacked again.

This night, he moved quietly, even though the meat animals bleated and moaned at smelling his scent. There was enough meat back at their small camp to last for several more of this planet's days, and he was no longer interested in killing for food.

He had other plans.

Trask moved closer to the large building, and he could smell so many different scents, from wet fur to the smoke of burning wood to the thick, gamey scent of these creatures. The door was heavy, wide and tall. There was a worked-metal grasping handle in the center. He pulled. The door wouldn't budge.

He pulled again.

Again, it didn't move.

In the moonlight, Trask smiled, walked away a few paces, and with a roar ran at the door and broke through.

After smashing through the door, Trask found himself in a long and wide room, with small fires and embers burning, smoke drifting up to the peaked ceiling. There were shouts and screams from the two-legged creatures as they bestirred themselves, and there was also yelping and sharp noises from four-legged furred creatures that raced to him.

No matter.

He roared out his challenge, began swinging his sword, slicing and cutting. Trask pushed forward, and two of the small furred creatures tried to snap at him, and with one sweep of his left arm, he gutted and tossed both of them to the end of the long building.

The scent of blood and terror from the creatures made him roar even deeper, as the blood lust stirred through him, as the creatures tried to come at him, swinging their own short weapons. None could get close to him as he pushed his way through.

Slice, stab, and with his other arm, any creature coming closer to him was torn and ripped apart, tossed away, gutted and dying.

At one moment, they were around him in a circle, banging their swords against round shields, chanting in a guttural sound, and then he knew it was time to leave these primitives. He roared once more, broke through the circle, grabbing one creature by its shoulder, dragging it behind him as he raced out of the long building.

He moved fast, shouts echoing behind him, and then he was away, moving along to the wet area and rocky outcropping that marked his settlement, and he turned to look at his prisoner. Killing and slaughtering was the pleasure of a Hero like himself, but if he were to conquer this world, he needed to communicate, to ensure some language between them, and this prisoner would be a start.

Trask turned in the light from the strange moon, to look over his prisoner.

He growled in disappointment.

The creature's head was dangling from its shoulders, held up by a few muscles and tendons.

He tore the head off, continued to move afar from the creature's village.

This dead prisoner would be a good meal for his mate.

Twice more he raided the long building, and twice more he tried to return with prisoners. Once a captive managed to break free and race into the woods until it was out of sight, and another time, a captive had stabbed Trask with a short blade. The pain was unexpected and sudden, and in fury, he had disemboweled the creature before he even got to the wetlands.

Now, he was going out again to the village of the creatures, and First Daughter caressed his back.

"Go and be a Hero, once more," she said.

He growled with pleasure at her words.

"Find one to learn our Heroes' Tongue, so together, we can take this world," she said. A paw went to her belly. "Soon . . . soon our kits will be birthed, and someday, ships from the Patriarchy will come here, and they will find a home populated by our descendants, and your Hero Name will shine for generations to come."

With those words still pleasing him, Trask raced away and through the wetlands, moving to the forest and along the now-familiar trail, seeing well in the night. He moved quietly and quickly, and then he came to the village, and paused.

Something was different.

He scanned the area, long hairless tail flicking back and forth, his membrane ears wide open.

The building he had attacked over and over again was still there, of course, with its door repaired and buttressed with more wooden beams, but it would be nothing serious to break through again.

There were creatures in the building as well, and he could smell and hear them, but there seemed to be more of them.

Good.

Perhaps one of them would be bright enough to learn the Heroes' Tongue.

He looked again, feeling again something out of place.

Ah.

There it was.

More of the watercraft had come to the sandy shore.

Reinforcements?

He breathed in, picked up his bloodstained sword. So be it.

He raced across the bloody ground where he had fought, howled once more—he knew his Heroes' Tongue put fright into these creatures—and broke through the door again, tearing away the planks and beams, entering the low hall, finding again the small creatures with their short swords and round shields, and as he screamed again, tossing aside the bloody and torn savages, a sharp and wary part of him thought, there is something unusual here, something different.

There was a group of the creatures, who smelled different, who kept their ground, who stood ready, and Trask didn't smell as much fear coming off them as the others. He growled and leapt at them and—

Something fell upon him.

A rope.

And another.

He twirled, slashing, and the ropes were separated, but more descended, close-tied sheets of rope, and as much as he growled and sliced, the ropes started to slow him down.

He yelped as a long spear pierced his side, and another . . .

He tore more.

Another spear.

One of the creatures came forth with a sword, and as he battled that one, another came from behind, hacked at his arm.

The pain made him yowl as he struggled.

More ropes and then his wounded arm . . . the one that carried his sword, now on the dirt floor, it was bound and stretched out. Two more of the creatures came at him, and he tore the head off one, and tore the chest and guts out of the other.

The creatures were yelling now, not in fear, but in triumph and boldness, and his right arm was extended out and he couldn't move it, as much as he tried. More ropes were around his legs. He kicked, snarled, and then a larger creature came forward, with the largest sword he had seen among these barbarians, and the sword came down.

Hacked at his right arm, where it joined his shoulder.

Again and again.

Hacked one more time.

Trask bellowed in pain, as his right arm was finally severed.

He fell.

More jabs and hacks.

He whipped out with his left arm, catching one more creature, and then it started getting dark, and his last thought was, First Daughter, oh, First Daughter . . .

Dawn came up and First Daughter sat by herself on the bare rock of their settlement, watching over the wetlands, her sword nearby. It had been a troubled evening, for her Lord Mate had not returned. She had been keeping a secret from her mate, that when he went out at night to raid the village of the barbarians, she would sneak out behind him, to at least hear his roars and bellowing challenges as he fought as the Hero he was.

Was.

The word stuck in her throat. Last night she had heard the familiar yelps and howls of her Trask, and then his cries of pain and then . . .

Chanting and words of triumph from the two-legged barbarians.

And she waited. And waited.

And her Trask had not returned.

The smart thing would be to stay hidden, to bear their four kits, to raise them and tell them of their Hero Sire, of how he had spirited the two of them away from Kzin to settle here on this moist and green planet, to kill and conquer the two-legged creatures.

That would be the safe route as well.

She howled, brought herself heavily to her feet, picked up her sword and started to the wetlands and then to the barbarian village.

She would not be safe.

She was First Daughter of Jarl-Geneticist, and she would avenge her mate.

2859 AD

ON THE ISLAND OF ZEALAND, off the coast of Denmark, Noah Hansen waited for his visitor while standing next to the wide archaeological dig site. Two floaters hovered nearby. Noah had been with UNESCO for a dozen years, working as a site supervisor for archaeological digs from Kazakhstan to Cambodia to Vandenberg, but this was the oddest one he had ever been involved with.

And all because of his . . . visitor, striding over to him under the warm European sun, having emerged from a recently arrived floater.

A male kzin, tall, orange and black, muscles rippling under his fur, pink tail flickering, wearing a simple leather belt and pouch around his waist. Noah swallowed, remembering a visit as a child in Boston, going to a friend's cube—Hap, that was his name—whose great-great grandfather had fought in the last Man-Kzin wars. One of the souvenirs, carefully wrapped and hidden, had been a wallet made from kzin skin.

The kzin came closer, flanked by two female UNESCO officials from Paris, and introductions were made, and the kzin was identified as Seeker of Glorious Past. This was the first time Noah had ever seen a kzin face-to-face, and perhaps it was something in his ancestral genes, but seeing a large cat like this made the old part of him want to turn and run.

He swallowed again, looking up at the alien. "Seeker of Glorious Past, if you will accompany me . . ."

The kzin growled back at him in Interworld. "You may call me Seeker. That will do."

He turned and the kzin followed him to the edge of the wide trench—covered overhead with a floating thin roof to protect it from sunshine and news drones—and Noah gave a memorized lecture of how this dig began as a wider archaeological effort to excavate the suspected remains of a great hall used by local Dane kings in the time of 600 AD or thereabouts, and how the foundation and remains of a long hall had been excavated, along with a village and other supporting structures.

Off in the distance, the grad students and professors from a number of European universities waited near the temp tent structures, ordered to stay there while their visitor from the stars toured the dig site.

Noah went on with his prepared remarks, indicating that after the initial digs and probes, biological-based penetrating examination revealed the presence of bones, but an odd type of bones, and further excavation revealed . . .

"Uh, well," Noah said, "this is what we found."

Seeker leaned over, and Noah did the same. Tumbled in the grave were a heap of bones, and Noah took out his sectry and flashed through a screen, and held it up to Seeker.

"We've left the bones *in situ* for now, because of . . . uh, well, diplomatic and religious concerns. But we've done an analysis and re-creation and this is what we have."

In the sectry's screen two reconstructed skeletons were shown in slowly revolving 3-D, displaying the tall and interlocking bones of two adult kzinti. The larger of the two kzin was missing its right arm.

"And . . . with the smaller kzin, there was this . . ."

Noah touched the screen, brought it back up to Seeker. It showed four smaller kzinti, apparently newborn or fetuses.

Something like a sigh and grumble emerged from Seeker's large chest. "Ah," he said.

Noah lowered his sectry, looked down to the trench. "We haven't officially released our findings, but you can be sure that there'll be lots of interest here and on other worlds once it's announced. There's more archaeological research to be conducted, but it seems like Earth was visited more than two thousand years ago by a Kzin couple, with the female being pregnant, and that they, uh, encountered the locals and uh . . . well, there was conflict . . . and uh . . ."

Even now, after the late night meetings and arguments and heated discussions with the rest of the dig crew, Noah still found it hard to say the words.

"It, uh, seems that these two kzinti were the basis and inspiration of an ancient epic poem, a saga called *Beowulf*, which is about—"

Seeker spoke deep and low. "I am quite familiar with your *Beowulf*."

"Oh," Noah said. "Well, if you recall, it told the tale of a king and his warriors, attacked night after night by a creature called Grendel . . . then reinforcements arrived, and Grendel is defeated when its arm is severed . . ."

Seeker said, "Then Grendel's mother, distended and ugly, she in turn attacked the warriors, and was herself killed."

"That's correct."

Seeker said, "Yes, I know of *Beowulf*, along with humanity's other tales of war and heroism. To this day . . . we still don't quite understand you."

Noah said, "Sometimes I don't understand us either."

Seeker looked down for long moments, and said, "We have our own tales. And there are old stories of renegades who fled Kzin, some of them criminals, who left to escape justice and to also seek new worlds."

Noah stayed quiet. The two female UNESCO officials stood back there, looking impatient, but Noah wasn't going to do or say anything to anger this visiting Kzin.

The kzin stepped back, and again, there was that low grumble that marked . . . sadness? Happiness? A mix?

Seeker said, "Your *Beowulf* is an amazing tale, but if these two and their kits had lived, oh the legends we would be telling now."

"What kind of legends?" Noah asked.

With sincere regret, Seeker said, "A noble saga, that we were able to conquer and enslave you humans, before you could ever become a threat to us."

And the kzin smiled, barely revealing its razor-sharp and always deadly teeth.

SCRITH

by Brad R. Torgersen

☙ PROLOGUE ☙

THE CLASSIFIED MUSEUM of the Amalgamated Regional Militia was located a full ten stories beneath the barren soil of the Antarctic dry valley. Officially, the museum did not exist. Just as its satellites in Los Angeles, London, St. Petersburg, Sao Paulo, and Cairo did not exist. For the better part of a thousand years, the museum had served as both a library, and a repository for artifacts deemed too sensitive—or dangerous—for public inspection. Its labyrinthine array of carefully maintained galleries was seldom visited. And then, only for official business. No human came to this place on a whim. There were no transfer booths, like those servicing the Smithsonian, or the Louvre. Just a set of mechanized, controlled-access, armored service lifts, which ran up and down two shafts. One located at the museum's north end, and one located at the museum's south end.

Mantooth Strather was fascinated by the lift cars. Riding one of them down from the nondescript lobby building on the surface had been like taking a voyage into a different world. A world which sleepily remembered humanity's more savage, desperate, and brilliant moments. There was no crush of gayly laughing tourists to greet him when the doors opened. Just a single desk, over which hung a single lamp, illuminating a single plain-clothed ARM custodian—who checked and verified both Manny's credentials and his orders.

Presently, Manny wandered among the exhibits. And marveled at

211

the hulking behemoths of main battle tanks, intercontinental strategic bombers, cutaway replicas of a dozen different fission and fusion bomb designs, primitive antisatellite particle beam cannon, and countless types of small arms: from Webley top-breaks and Browning potato-diggers, to one-man recoilless guided-rocket guns—which had gone with the first hyperdrive fleets sent to liberate the colonies of men from the Kzin Patriarchy.

Manny's fascination with the place could not be overstated. He didn't even notice when his boss slipped up beside him—peering down at a Kzin skull under glass. The skull had a single large hole in it, made by a bullet which hadn't been manufactured in centuries.

"A big enemy deserves a big caliber, don't you think?" said the small, female voice.

Manny started for an instant, then recovered himself.

"You didn't make any noise, coming from the security checkpoint," he said. "Uncanny how you do that."

"At my age you get to have all sorts of tricks up your sleeve," Manny's boss replied, staring up at him—with a crooked smile on her lips. The top of her head barely came to his shoulder, and she had that quality of refined agelessness which typified those who'd survived a long time on boosterspice. Nobody who'd ever worked for Cedara Kellerman knew exactly how old she was. Some wondered if she had been around since before humanity had hyperdrive.

"But you didn't answer my question," she said, turning her head and looking down at the felinoid skull in front of them.

"For as long as we've known the Kzin," Manny said, "we've been inventing more effective ways to kill them."

"Your great-great-great-great-grandfather certainly got things started with a bang," she said, her crooked smile growing just a bit larger.

Manny grunted. "Greatly Jack would have been a menace to society, if he'd been born any earlier. It's amazing his descendants were allowed to have children at all, given his, ah, *specialness*. Even now, each and every one of us who share his bloodline have to get an autodoc checkout once a month. Just to be sure the schiz isn't manifesting."

"It was the schiz which allowed him to see what so many of the rest of us in the ARM—at that time—didn't want to see," she said. "And who in their right mind uses a starship launching laser to do battle with an invasion fleet? That alone bought Jack Strather's children the right to have kids of their own. You said he would have been a menace in an earlier time. Sure. And if the Patriarchy had discovered humans any earlier, you and I wouldn't exist. And neither would this collection of relics. Earth would be just another Kzin slave world, with a Riit descendant sitting on the governor's fooch."

Manny nodded. The facts of the wars with the Kzin were well known to him. He'd studied those facts ever since entering the ARM—riding on his ancestor's name. A name which meant very little to anyone not allowed to visit museums like the one Manny and Cedara stood in now. The ARM prized schizies.

"So, boss," Manny said, turning away from the skull, and facing Cedara squarely—his arms folded over his chest—"why bring me all the way to McMurdo to see war machinery, and the bones of dead rat-cats?"

"We're not here for that," she said. "I needed you to come to Antarctica because I've got something much more interesting to show you."

Manny's eyebrow raised, and he allowed himself to be led onward, as his supervisor's slippered feet lightly whispered over the floor. Her business suit was drab maroon, with a narrow waist, and just a little extra padding at the shoulders. When she had been younger, Manny imagined she would have been cute, without being beautiful. Now? The mere force of her personality radiated outward like a physical phenomenon. She'd been places and seen things the likes of which most of her subordinates could only guess. In ten years working for the lady, Manny had learned: The more he knew, the more he realized how much he *didn't* know, and Cedara seemed perfectly happy to keep it that way.

It took them ten minutes of walking before they reached the display she wanted him to see.

A fourteen-centimeter shard of what looked like milky glass was perched next to a holographic projection of a woman. Except, she wasn't *quite* a woman. Her lipless mouth cut across her face under her nose in a straight line. And her head was completely bald, except for the strands of thick hair which sprouted from a half-circle running from one ear all the way around back of her skull to the other ear. Her clothing was clearly contemporary Earth manufacture, but she seemed to wear the jumper uneasily—like it bothered her skin.

Plus, those eyes . . . they were not happy eyes.

"Who is she?" Manny asked. Unlike every other display he'd seen so far, this one had no computerized plaque for showing details.

"Halrloprillalar," Cedara said, with the precision of someone pronouncing a foreign language.

"Halla-*who?*" Manny blurted, half-smiling at his boss.

"She's dead now," Cedara said matter-of-factly. "We killed her."

"She must have done something pretty bad," Manny said, deadpan. Though he swallowed a bit harder than normal, catching the regretful tone in his boss's voice.

"Nothing bad at all," Cedara replied. "Halrloprillalar came to us, completely trusting that we could help her, and we failed. We failed because we didn't believe anything she told us. Until it was too late. We thought she was human. We *insisted* she was human. We were almost right."

"*Almost* right?" Manny said. "If she's not human, then what is she? Not a Crashlander. Too short. And not a Jinxian either. Too tall. Is she a Belter mutant? Some of their more scattered habitats—both here, and in the Serpent Swarm around Alpha Centauri—still get too much solar and cosmic radiation, even to this day."

"It would have been so much simpler, if one of your guesses were correct," Cedara said, reaching a hand out to reverently play her fingers through the hologram. It briefly distorted and rippled, until Manny's boss pulled her hand back, and the image of Halrloprillalar steadied once more.

"But . . ." Manny said.

"But, it's all wrong. Genetic tracing doesn't tie her to *any* human lineage. Not on Earth. Not anywhere in Known Space. She's a cousin, though. A cousin so damned close, we kept thinking the blood sampler was just making a mistake. But it wasn't. She's like . . . what might happen if you took a population of great apes, then gave them enough room—and time—to evolve up to *Homo sapiens* standard. Or at least as close to *Homo sapiens* standard as can be done, with that stock. About as smart as we are. And about as capable too. The man who brought her to us told us he'd actually had an ongoing sexual relationship with her. But no children. He was from Earth. She's not from anywhere."

"A colony nobody knew about?" Manny said. "There were lots of slowboats in the early days. And not all of the records are clear about who wound up where." He was trying to keep up with the implications. Cedara was many things, but she was not a prankster. And this place? It was not a setting for jokes. She was showing him this hologram for a reason related to his job.

"The only thing we have to tie her back to her true home," Cedara said, pointing to the milky shard, "is that. Go ahead. Pick it up."

Manny hesitantly reached out to grasp the shard. It looked sharp. When he lifted it, it was far heavier than he expected it to be. Heavier even than the heaviest of industrial-grade steel, for an object of similar size and volume.

"What is it?" he asked.

"Halrloprillalar called it *scrith*," Cedara said.

"Feels solid," Manny said, using both hands to carefully apply torsion, without opening up the tips of his fingers. The material was extremely smooth, too. Almost slippery to the touch.

"This was a splinter, jammed into the hatch of the General Products hull which carried Halrloprillalar away from her home."

"You said a man brought her to you," Manny said. "By that I assume you mean he brought her to the ARM. Why not ask him for more specifics? Surely he didn't walk away without us doing a good, thorough interrogation?"

"We'd love to quiz him some more," Cedara said. "But he's vanished. Gone. We have a name, and details of his last known residence on Earth, but where he's disappeared to since then . . . we can't say. And you don't need to be told how unusual *that* is. Not a single soul on this planet dies, nor is born, nor travels off-world, without the ARM knowing about it. Except *this* gentleman. Well, like I said, when you get to be my age, you get to have some interesting tricks up your sleeve. And he is no exception, apparently."

Manny kept testing the shard. It felt impossibly strong.

"You said this was *jammed* into a General Products hull hatch?"

"The story we got is that Halrloprillalar's ship was crippled, and had to be dragged across the surface of her world, to the top of a gargantuan, hollow mountain, at which point it tipped over the edge at the summit . . . and fell into interplanetary space. Where they used the hyperdrive motor to return to civilization."

"Sounds like a hell of a tale," Manny said, his eyebrow once again raised. "If all I had was somebody's say-so, I probably wouldn't buy it either. How does a ship *fall* from the summit of a mountain, into space? And how does anything get *jammed* into a General Products Hull?"

Cedara tapped a finger to the side of her nose.

"That's the real question, isn't it? We've put the *scrith* through every form of physical and chemical analysis in the ARM laboratories. It's not like anything we've ever seen. Not even like a General Products hull, though who the hell knows how *those* get made. We've been trying forever to unravel the General Products secret. So have the Kzin. And we're all stumped. But this? *Scrith* is something different. Maybe almost as good as a General Products hull? Enough to make a world out of it."

Manny just stared. Then he silently put the shard back in its place.

"What do you need me to do?" he asked.

"If we know about the *scrith,* then the Patriarchy knows about it too. Doubtless they're as intrigued as we are. The ARM doesn't know precisely where it came from, nor are we completely sure of Halrloprillalar's point of origin—beyond the fact it's well outside the borders of Known Space. We reason that her world wasn't manufactured without somebody doing a hell of a lot of materials research and development first. Possibly even prototyping?"

"Wait," Manny said. "You keep saying 'her world' like it's artificial, and that doesn't make any sense. Did she live on a large space station?"

"You might think of it that way," Cedara admitted. "Look, somewhere out there is the laboratory which cooked *scrith* up. And refined the manufacturing process. Then scaled that process up to a phenomenal level. Sooner or later, somebody is going to find the source. If not us, then the Patriarchy. And there's absolutely no way in hell the ARM can allow the Patriarchy to get its claws on this material first. We already dodged that bullet once, with the new hyperdrive design."

"*New* hyperdrive??"

"Look, Mantooth, the point is, the balance in Known Space is shifting. We've been at peace with the Patriarchy for a long time. A peace which has saved millions of lives. Both ours, and theirs. But a djinni is out of its bottle now, and things are developing so quickly, things could get very bloody for all of us, very fast. Unless we act."

Manny felt her hand gripping his bicep like a vise.

"Stet, boss," Manny said. "Stet. Just tell me where I start."

"Remember the kzin researcher we had you get acquainted with five years ago? The one you're still in touch with from time to time, as a matter of ARM niceties?"

"I thought you just told me we were trying to keep the Kzin *out* of this . . . whatever it is we're getting into."

"Sometimes the best way to keep someone out of something," Cedara said, "is to get them so totally *into* it, that they can't seriously hurt you without also seriously hurting themselves. Anyway, you remember the one I am talking about? Multicolored fur."

"Zrarr-Professor. Very urbane, for a Kzin."

"Him. We've got to line up a joint mission. ARM and Patriarchy combined. He's the key."

"Why do I suddenly have the feeling this is all going to get far more complicated than any sane man should want it to be?"

Cedara's crooked smile returned. "That's my boy."

☙ CHAPTER 1 ☙

SFISST-CAPTAIN was an imposing kzin. The nude lines of scar tissue—running like shallow canyons through his tabby-striped fur—told of an officer who'd won his command the hard way. And as the only other Hero onboard with a partial name, he technically shared his command with the newly arrived Zrarr-Professor. But Zrarr was certain that if claws came to bellies, Sfisst would guarantee that no academic stranger got in the way of Sfisst's orders. It was *his* ship. Zrarr was just borrowing it for a while.

To that end, Sfisst had demanded an immediate report the moment Zrarr's shuttle disembarked. Without even taking the time to deposit his spacer's travel kit in his stateroom, Zrarr had found his way through the innards of the Patriarchy long-range reconnaissance cruiser *Glaring Eye*, eventually to be greeted by Sfisst alone—in the ship's tactical planning chamber.

Zrarr looked around, noting that every single holographic projector was off. But the almost inaudible hum of sound-deadeners made Zrarr's pink ears unfurl—like two collapsible satellite dishes.

"We are secure from eavesdropping," Sfisst rumbled in the Heroes' Tongue.

"I didn't realize we had reason to distrust others aboard," Zrarr said.

"Don't be stupid," Sfisst sniffed, his pink tail lashing once behind his chair. "All of these kzinti are loyal to me, and to the Patriarch. If I thought any kzin on my ship posed a threat, I'd have killed him before your arrival. This is strictly about need to know. And while I am bound to execute the Patriarch's orders, I won't move us so much as a light-year before I feel like I understand just what it is we're supposed to accomplish. I was told you would provide answers upon your arrival, Zrarr-Professor. So, provide them."

Zrarr's calico coat didn't have nearly as much scarring as Sfisst's, but he made sure to flex his muscles as he slowly set down his kit—so that Sfisst could get a good look at the naked lines running over the right side of Zrarr's torso, and down his right leg. Researcher he may have been, but Zrarr hadn't gotten a partial name through brains alone.

"Are you familiar with a Hero named Chmeee?" Zrarr asked. "He was formerly Speaker-to-Animals, on assignment to the Patriarchy embassy on Earth."

"No," Sfisst said flatly.

"It was while he was detailed to the embassy that Chmeee embarked upon the adventure which earned him a full name. Some of the details of that adventure remain Patriarchy secrets, which even I am not privy to. But other information is known to me. Such as the fact that Chmeee returned to Patriarchy space with a mighty technological prize, which the Patriarch's best engineers and theoretical physicists are still examining. Chmeee also produced *this*."

Zrarr's huge claw-tipped fist dropped a thin, cloth-wrapped object onto the darkened control panel in front of Sfisst-Captain.

The officer curiously unwrapped the artifact, holding it carefully in an upturned paw.

"Feels heavier than it should," Sfisst remarked.

"It ought to," Zrarr said. "This was one of two pieces embedded in the hatch of a General Products hull. It's stronger than any material which Patriarchy science understands. According to the story of Chmeee, there is an entire world of this substance, somewhere far beyond the Patriarchy's reach. How Chmeee traveled there, and returned, is still something I've been unable to learn. But I've been given access to this one sample, with a directive from the Patriarch himself to discover where and how it was manufactured."

Sfisst's nose sniffed instinctively at the air, as he brought the object up to his face.

"A new material for battle hull construction?" he opined.

"Now you seem to be getting the idea," Zrarr said. "The Patriarchy believes this material—Chmeee named it *scrith*—might be just as useful as that which makes up a General Products hull. But only if we can find out how it's made. It is a purely artificial element, completely off the table of known and synthesized elements familiar to both Kzin and men."

Sfisst-Captain made a distasteful noise.

"*Men.* I gather the Patriarch wants us to uncover the secret of *scrith* before the sthondat-humping ARM does?"

"Quite the contrary," Zrarr replied. "We're under the Patriarch's specific orders to work *with* the ARM. Just as Chmeee worked with his human companions during his classified voyage to the *scrith* world."

More distasteful noises from the ship's head officer.

"I would not cooperate with the ARM even if my life depended on it," Sfisst remarked coldly. "Humans I can tolerate. I've done it before. In their own way, they can be useful, and even manifest courage approaching that of an average kzin. But the Amalgamated Regional Militia of Earth? That is an enemy to all of us. Without exception. The ARM would have us exterminated down to the last kit. Is the Patriarch mad? Come, let us perform the search on our own. *Glaring Eye* is a capable ship. If *scrith* has as much potential value as you've implied, it's worth every kzin aboard. Yourself and myself included. A war fleet, equipped with near-invulnerable hulls, could be just the thing to put the universe back in balance—between the Patriarchy and the worlds of men."

There it is, Zrarr-Professor thought. *The secret dream of every kzin warrior raised on tales of the old Patriarchy. To put the humans back on their heels. Make them swallow their own teeth. As if all that's necessary to restore the Patriarchy to its former stature is the sweeping aside of the Amalgamated Regional Militia. Sfisst-Captain, do you have any ideas how much the centuries have changed us? Would one of your counterparts from the First Invasion even recognize you for what you are? Surely such a Hero would not recognize me.*

Zrarr did not give voice to his ideas. He needed Sfisst's cooperation. Not an instant duel to the death, which such ideas would surely invite.

But how to proceed?

"I suspect strongly that the ARM's invitation to participate in a joint mission is as much about preserving the peace, as it is about discovering the origins of this new material. Sfisst-Captain, the men of Earth are not murderous. Not now, at least. The summary report of Chmeee indicates that his human companions could have abandoned or killed him several times, yet they did not. They helped him. And he helped them in kind. I know it's difficult to ignore the past, and that the ARM has its claws covered in our ancestors' blood. But we inhabit a very small part of a very big galaxy. If Chmeee's suspicions are correct, there may be things out there—far more cunning, and dangerous, than either kzinti or men can imagine."

👣 CHAPTER 2 👣

JAVELIN was mostly fuel tanks, and a single, gargantuan neutrino sensor, wrapped up in a thick-walled cylinder of hull steel. Christened just days earlier at the dedicated ARM shipyard in Earth orbit, her essentials felt sound. But there'd been no time to give her a proper shakedown. Her off-the-shelf bridge, crew accommodations, and life support were jammed into an oblong blister running the length of the ventral surface, which itself sprouted over a dozen robustly built ship-to-ship grapplers. Her dorsal surface had but one feature: a wide-mouthed one-hundred-meter cup, into which the business end of an even larger General Products #4 hull had been depressed.

A separate ship in its own right, the mammoth spherical #4 GP hull was acting as a hyperdrive "booster" for this mission—using a type of motor no man had ever constructed. The #4 hull's origin and designation were ARM secrets, but her purpose was clear: to go places well beyond that which could be easily reached using conventional means.

But first, Mantooth Strather had a date with the Kzin.

It had taken weeks to get everything arranged via hyperwave. Officially, the Patriarchy was sending one ship, appropriately classed for longevity and exploration. *Glaring Eye* was expected to be of a certain size and a certain mass, so that *Javelin* could latch on and use the Quantum II hyperdrive motor in the #4 hull to transport the three ships as one. Neither *Javelin* nor *Glaring Eye* had a large crew.

But then, neither ship needed a large crew. More people just meant hauling more consumables. And there was no telling how far outside the boundaries of Known Space they'd have to go, or how long it would take them to make the round trip. Assuming there was even a destination worth reaching.

All Manny had to go on were educated guesses.

"So far, so good," *Javelin*'s commander said reservedly, her arms folded over her chest. She was perched in her seat at the rear of the *Javelin*'s miniscule bridge module. Like so much else about the ship, the module had come off the assembly line intended for an entirely different type of vessel—and been hastily repurposed for *Javelin*'s use.

Detective-Major Pryce Spalding was an experienced ARM officer who'd done over a dozen missions beyond the worlds of men, many of them involving covert watches on the Patriarchy. She'd come recommended by Cedara, who'd had dealings with Detective-Major Spalding before, though Pryce didn't report directly to Cedara's office, the way Manny did. Technically, Pryce—and every other crewperson aboard—were on loan from the ARM's officially unofficial stealth navy, which made routine checks on Patriarchy territory, just to be sure the rat-cats weren't making any sudden moves.

Spalding's executive was a muscle-bound man. Detective-Captain Benitez seemed to have no seat on the bridge module. He merely wandered from station to station, staring over shoulders. If he noticed Manny, it was only to occasionally glance in the Science-Inspector's direction—eyes unwavering, face never betraying emotion. Manny tried to ignore him, but felt scrutinized just the same. So, Manny diverted his attention to the #4 hull and its remarkable engine.

"I'd say the Quantum II motor is working well," Manny remarked, sitting at the guest station where he had auxiliary access to most of Javelin's systems status displays.

"It's certainly the shortest time I've ever spent getting this far from home," Pryce replied, a finger tapping idly on her bicep. Like all of the crew, she wore a light-blue military-fashion space coverall, with pockets up and down the limbs. She also wore soft spacer's boots, which could double as grip shoes in the event that the gravity motors went out. Her hair was cut spacer short—almost buzzed down to the scalp—and looked like a layer of iron filings being stood up on the surface of a magnet.

"You watching the log computer?" Pryce said to her young subordinate, who was sitting opposite to Manny's chair. The young officer was obediently staring into his array of computer screens.

"Every second of Quantum II hyperdrive activity has been faithfully recorded, ma'am," the young ARM spacer replied. "The motor appears to be operating within expected parameters."

Detective-Major Spalding made a scoffing noise.

"How can we even know, with a prototype based on an alien design we don't fully understand yet? By rights, *Javelin* should spend her first year doing trials between the Oort Cloud and Wunderland. We're now tens of light-years beyond that, and depending fully on the Quantum II unit to take us tens, or even hundreds, of light-years more. Maybe thousands?"

Every head on the bridge turned—their eyes glancing at their boss's face.

"Yes, you heard me," Pryce said, raising her volume for emphasis. "We're all ARM interstellar veterans. Trained to push the outside of the envelope. Even Science-Inspector Strather. Don't let me catch you not on your toes. We're about to rendezvous with a kzin craft, at which time Sci-Spec Strather will be our liaison to a kzin crew. Anything might happen. Though, hopefully, it won't. Strather, care to tell us any more about what we might expect from our partners?"

"I can only tell you what I know about my counterpart," Manny said. "Zrarr-Professor is not warrior caste, but he's got a partial name, so that tells you something about his clout among his people. My boss back on Earth ordered me to use a previous affiliation to secure Zrarr-Professor's interest in this joint effort, knowing that Zrarr'd have the wherewithal to get us a good Patriarchy ship crewed with, we hope, a good Patriarchy crew."

"For whatever definition of 'good' applies to a kzin," muttered the young spacer who'd reported on the Quantum II motor.

"Stow it," Pryce snapped. "None of us have to like the kzinti, any further than we can throw them. Stet? Again, we're ARM interstellar veterans. Doing difficult things is in our blood. Taking risks is what we do. It's what we're good at. We've maintained the peace for not just Earth, but Jinx, Wunderland, We Made It, and every other human colony in the galaxy. So far as I am concerned, this is just more of the same."

A little chorus of *affirmatives* went around the bridge, and then Pryce was nodding her head at Manny—to continue.

"At this point," he said, "the Patriarchy knows as much as we do. We have access to the same relative sets of data, as well as the Quantum II hyperdrive—which is a *joint* commodity, by the way, shared equally between the ARM and the Patriarchy. What's more, we have evidence pointing to a potentially human-like civilization far beyond the ordinary reach of Earth or Kzin-home. This civilization may have discovered a way to mass produce a substance potentially as durable and useful as that of a General Products hull. Only problem is, we don't know where this civilization is. And neither does the Patriarchy. We only have a vague notion of which direction to go in, and just one potential telltale to guide us in our search."

"And what's that?" asked one of the other *Javelin* crewmembers.

Manny pulled out a clear plastic case, in which rested the *scrith* shard he'd first seen in the ARM museum.

"This substance blocks up to forty percent of neutrino emissions."

"Impossible," blurted the 'Tec-Major. "No element can do that."

"This stuff—called *scrith*—can," Manny said, and gently placed the case into the hands of the ARM spacer nearest him. Slowly, the case passed around the bridge, until it ended up in the hands of Spalding.

"We'll be looking for what I expect to be a miniscule neutrino shadow," Manny said, addressing the entire bridge, but with his eyes on the ship's commander in particular. "*Javelin* has the sensing capability for the job. *Glaring Eye* gives us the all-purpose exploratory piece. Both ships have weapons, if needed in a pinch. Though I sincerely hope it doesn't come to that."

Manny took the case back from the 'Tec-Major.

"How did ARM obtain your sample," Pryce asked, "without knowing exactly where it came from?"

"I am sure that's a question which has bedeviled the Patriarchy too," Manny said. "I can tell you that at least two humans and one kzin made it there, and back, though our intel suggests they weren't necessarily doing it on their own. Somebody—or something—else was involved. And that's where the Quantum II motor discovery comes in. I know it's frustrating to be doing all of this half-blind, but the time for doing it is *now*. A man and a kzin both went to a lot of trouble to ensure that the Quantum II technology came to men *and* kzinti at the same time. In so doing, they averted a war. We're trying to live up to the spirit of that bargain, in the quest for *scrith*. So, working with the kzinti now, at this moment, hopefully ensures we won't be working *against* them in the future. Stet?"

"Stet," Major Spalding said, nodding her head.

☙ CHAPTER 3 ☙

"**URRRRR,**" Sfisst-Captain uttered, as *Glaring Eye* came into visual range of the ARM ship with which he was to rendezvous. Zrarr-Professor had assumed his place at Sfisst-Captain's side. A second couch had been installed somewhat below and in front of the commander's seat, which itself was installed on a dais at the center of *Glaring Eye*'s control center deep in the guts of the ship. Several kzinti were arrayed on the perimeter of the dais, their faces peering into screens or holos displaying information on gravity control, hyperdrive engine stress, environmental plant status, weapons readiness, and so forth. Some of them had the scars of veterans. Some of them had the unblemished pelts of youngsters. Each of them had earned the trust of Sfisst, in one way or another. Though Zrarr knew he himself had a long way to go, in this regard.

"Impressive, is it not?" Zrarr-Professor said, as a magnified image of their intended target was displayed on the holo at Sfisst's elbow. A huge, globe-shaped General Products #4 hull was mated to a much narrower cylinder, which itself appeared to have been equipped specifically with grapplers designed to handle a kzin ship.

"If the General Products hull is co-owned," Sfisst said, "why do the humans have it, and we don't?"

"I don't know the diplomatic specifics," Zrarr replied. "I can only tell you that the Quantum II motor fills the majority of the Number Four. Patriarchy engineers have examined it firsthand, as have human engineers. Neither we nor the ARM have managed to duplicate the design, yet. Its secrets remain a mystery, even if the design itself is functionally sound. The Quantum II hyperdrive will be necessary for us to scout out the location of *scrith*'s origin, in something approaching a reasonable period of time. Otherwise, *Glaring Eye* could devote a life's age to the search, and never come close to finding what the Patriarch wants."

Sfisst's paws were gripping the arms of his seat, the claws on the tips of his digits reflexively poking out of the fur. His whole body posture screamed, *alert!* The mere sight of the ARM ship—equipped with a puissant and exotic piece of technology, in the form of the Quantum II hyperdrive—no doubt triggered all of Sfisst's fighting reflexes. Yet the kzin warrior kept his composure, and applied his mind to the task at hand.

Unlike so many other officers of wars before you, Zrarr thought to himself.

"Have they responded to our announcement?" Sfisst asked. "Of our intentions to match course and speed, for docking?"

"Affirmative, Sfisst-Captain," said the communications station operator. He was the youngest kzin aboard. And eager to impress two Heroes with partial names. "The human ship is agreeing to our request. Our pilot is free to proceed with the maneuver. Shall I inform the ARM vessel that we are beginning our trajectory adjustment?"

"No need," Sfisst sniffed. "Their equipment will tell them what we're doing, as readily as we can voice it. Send them the Patriarch's standard regards, as scripted for this mission. Inform the human commander that I also send my regards, per the script."

Good, Zrarr thought. *You argued with me at first, Sfisst, but in the end, even you recognize the necessity for diplomatic niceties—if our mission is to be successful.*

Sfisst considered. "With a mountain like that on their backs, their center of mass is going to be extremely off. Doubtless the humans have compensated. But still, didn't you tell me, Zrarr-Professor, that the bottom of the General Products hull has four outlets for fusion thrusters?"

"It does," Zrarr said.

"So, conventional thrust is accomplished entirely by the smaller ship?"

"That is correct. The Quantum II hyperdrive fills almost the entirety of the Number Four, with only a small amount of room reserved for life support, and a crew cabin for the pilot."

"The Quantum II performs and behaves similarly to extant hyperdrive?"

"Also correct. A sapient mind must be constantly observing the mass detector at all times, due to the fact that the craft moves at such a quickened pace, compared to usual hyperdrive velocity. There isn't time to look away. I imagine the humans have had to pilot in shifts, so that a fresh-minded operator can always be at the pilot's couch inside the Number Four hull."

The angle on the view began to shift, as *Glaring Eye* adjusted thrust to match with the ARM ship. Equipment hummed or whirred, as many, many gravities were applied during the maneuver. It took several minutes to close on the human craft, then do a delicate dance with the computer docking interface which guided *Glaring Eye* into position. The kzin ship slid up into the *Javelin's* shadow, at which point the grapplers closed tight, and *Glaring Eye* became a captive to its human parent.

"To the docking tunnel!" Zrarr-Professor said, standing up quickly from his seat. When nobody moved—and every kzin aboard eyed the Professor with a look of surprise—Zrarr remembered his place. "If it be the will of Sfisst-Captain, of course."

"Of course," Sfisst-Captain growled, his tone making his annoyance plain. Then he too rose from his seat, and led Zrarr-Professor out of the control center. Where they immediately picked up a small entourage of bodyguards. It had taken Zrarr even more argument to get Sfisst to disarm his security detail. But Zrarr felt it was imperative to greet the ARM officers on the other side with nothing but signs of magnanimity.

Once at the hatch for the tube proper, two of the security detail assumed their places in front of Sfisst, operating the controls which released the hatch. A hiss was heard, then the hatch swung away, and suddenly all concerned were staring up into a well-lit cylinder lined with grips and pawholds. There would be no gravity for the crossing. Zrarr felt his equilibrium flutter as they crossed the threshold. He'd done his time in microgravity, like any other kzin of similar social stature. But the experience was still disconcerting. By the time they swung through the open hatch on the other end, Zrarr was thankful for the resumption of weight—albeit not as much weight as on *Glaring Eye.*

There were seven ARM humans waiting in the *Javelin*'s small reception bay. All of them wore the same coveralls, and one of them—the female—appeared to have a security detail similar to that of Sfisst. Like Sfisst's, the ARM detail conspicuously lacked weapons, and the female was careful *not* to display her teeth, when she offered her visitors a diplomatic monkey's smile.

"Welcome aboard, *Sfisst-Captain,* and *Zrarr-Professor,*" she said, with what Zrarr considered to be excellent inflection on their partial names. It wasn't easy for human mouths to replicate the Heroes' Tongue. This female had obviously practiced.

"The Patriarch honors you," Sfisst-Captain said, using Interworld—also practiced.

Zrarr searched the faces of the humans—men looking so much alike, to kzin eyes—until he was sure he'd spotted the one he wanted. Science-Inspector Strather had his lower arms placed behind his back, and his feet set shoulder width on the deck. He too was monkey-smiling, though not with teeth.

"I'm Detective-Major Pryce Spalding," the human commander said, "of the Amalgamated Regional Militia. We embrace the Patriarch's trust, and extend mankind's trust in turn. It's a pleasure to be working with Heroes of such prowess and stature."

"Urrrr," Sfisst rumbled, somewhat surprised at the human female's recognition of the half-named. "You command a mighty prize, 'Tec-Major. The General Products hull would be valuable enough in its own right. But the new hyperdrive engine inside? A treasure without equal. I am eager to see it in action. May we proceed directly to an inspection of the Number Four's control center? As an experienced pilot in my own right, I am curious to see the prize's inner workings."

This was unexpected, as Zrarr had only planned for a formal greeting, followed by a face-to-face conference regarding the plan for the neutrino shadow search. Sfisst was asking for access the human female might not want to give. But what could she do? The Quantum II motor did belong to both species.

"Very well," Spalding said. "If you will please follow me."

The Detective-Major led them at a brisk human walk through the interior of the ARM vessel—amounting to a leisurely stroll for the much larger kzinti. The ceiling was just barely adequate for the height of an average kzin. Sfisst's entourage scanned alertly about themselves as the party traveled. Occasionally human crewmembers would step into the party's path, from an adjoining corridor, then quickly step back. If any of those men and women were alarmed, they didn't show it. All of them looked far too young to have participated in any of the fighting from the past.

They hadn't yet learned what a grown kzin could do to a grown human in close combat.

On the other hand, none of the warriors in Sfisst's entourage had learned to fear the monkey ferocity of the humans, either. Men were smaller and physically weaker, of course, but no less cunning and clever. A properly equipped and courageous man could easily fell a score of Heroes, if those Heroes took the man for granted—as had famously happened in the case of a certain man named Harvey Mossbauer.

Eventually the party passed through a second cylindrical corridor, this time crossing the body of the *Javelin* until they were at the open hatch at the bottom of the General Products hull. Like any General Products design, the hull material itself was completely transparent. As Zrarr passed up and into the ship, he quickly realized that the *Javelin*'s cramped interior was positively roomy, in comparison to what waited inside the Quantum II ship.

"One at a time," the 'Tec-Major cautioned.

Zrarr backed off, as did Sfisst's entourage. They waited as their commander proceeded up into the General Products hull, with the 'Tec-Major in Sfisst's wake.

"We'll remain here," Zrarr announced. "I have no need to view the controls, suffice to say if they work, they work. I doubt the Number Four can accommodate another kzin, beyond Sfisst-Captain, at any rate."

The entourage hesitated, peered up into the claustrophobic interior of the General Products hull, then voiced their agreement in terse Heroes' Tongue.

"Hello, Zrarr-Professor," said the human Zrarr had previously identified as Science-Inspector Strather.

"At your service," Zrarr replied, using the human Interworld idiom.

"How was the journey from Kzin-home?" Strather asked.

"Uneventful. Though I imagine your journey from Earth was much quicker than ours?"

"You'll be truly surprised by the velocity attainable with Quantum II."

"When we're able to replicate it, the face of Known Space will change utterly."

"Assuming we *can* replicate it. I don't think I'm giving away a secret when I say that the Quantum II motor baffles us. It might take the full focus of ARM and Patriarchy both—working in concert—to crack the Quantum II puzzle. Until then, we at least have the one functional prototype."

"If it can be built once, it can be built many times. I myself confess no small desire to see the horizons of Known Space expanded dramatically. We have only seen a tiny portion of our galaxy. What more may be out there, for men and kzinti alike to discover?"

"Indeed."

Several moments of silence followed. Zrarr got the sense that Strather wanted to say more, but didn't necessarily feel comfortable speaking his mind in mixed company.

Eventually Sfisst-Captain and the 'Tec-Major returned.

"It looks almost no different from any ordinary human-operated hyperdrive control arrangement," the kzin commander said. "I look forward to seeing the drive itself in operation. But where do we propose to go first?"

"Let's talk about that," Science-Inspector Strather said to the group, and proceeded to take the lead from the 'Tec-Major. They went back down the cylinder, into the horizontal realm of the *Javelin,* and ended up at a somewhat sizeable—for the ship considered—conference cabin. Seating built to accommodate two kzintoshi had been provided at one end of the table. Zrarr and Sfisst took their places, with the kzin entourage standing at their backs, while Strather and Spalding took chairs on the opposite side, flanked by their own security. The 'Tec-Major tapped controls on the tabletop in front of her, and the doors to the conference cabin slipped shut. Followed by a low chime, which may have indicated that their conversation was now secure—an almost inaudible hum, similar to that formerly heard aboard the *Glaring Eye,* tickled Zrarr's sharp kzin hearing.

"ARM has devoted a lot of time to the question you've asked," Strather said. "We have the documented testimonies of both the human and the Hero who discovered *scrith*—identified as Wu, Louis, and the now-titled Chmeee—and there are no specific coordinates to which we might point. Simply, there is a thirty-degree arc of space, relative to Earth and Kzin-home alike, in which their adventure occurred.

"We also know that one of *scrith*'s unusual properties is the blocking of neutrinos. Up to forty percent, we estimate, which should—if the stated scale of the artifact Wu and Chmeee found is accurate—leave enough of a neutrino shadow for *Javelin* to detect. Provided we do a systematic, comprehensive search."

"I don't even know what this 'artifact' is supposed to be," Sfisst groused. "Zrarr-Professor has been able to provide some details, yes, but neither he nor I have been privy to every single piece of information the Patriarchy may have collected. What can ARM tell us that our own people cannot?"

Strather audibly sighed, then stood up, and began pacing back and forth behind his chair.

"I am afraid I am limited to the same information as my counterpart," Strather said. "What we know is that there is a significantly-sized artificial habitat in orbit about a G-type yellow dwarf sun, somewhere in here . . ."

With a wave of his hand, Strather displayed bright holos over the table: showing a three-dimensional replica of the galaxy. Known Space was a tiny pocket along one of the galactic arms, and Strather was drawing circles with the tip of his index finger—some several hundred light-years away from their current position.

"If the account of Chmeee is accurate," Zrarr said, "the artifact in question is composed almost entirely of the *scrith* material. It's a habitat, populated with hominid-type sapients who have multiplied innumerably across the surface. We don't know who or what built it. We don't know how or why hominids dominate the artifact. We do know that these hominids persist in a more or less degenerate state of technology."

"No Builders in sight?" asked the 'Tec-Major.

"None that either Wu or Chmeee could identify," Strather said. "Though there was a single individual who returned to Known Space with Wu. She claimed to be of the hominid race which built the artifact—though the ARM officially considers certain aspects of this individual's testimony to be suspect."

"Is this Legal Entity presently aboard?" Sfisst asked. "She would be our greatest source of intelligence for this mission."

"Unfortunately," Sci-Spec Strather admitted, "that particular LE no longer lives."

"Urrrr?" Sfisst questioned, his tail lashing. "What happened?"

"My superiors didn't release the specifics of her death to me."

Zrarr felt his own tail lash reflexively. He'd not been told this beforehand. His eyes darted to Sfisst-Captain, whose perturbed state could be smelled. Then he looked back at Strather, who was clearly uncomfortable with the situation.

Many seconds of silence elapsed. Then Sfisst said slowly, "Very unfortunate. Especially since the Patriarchy was never permitted to have access to this female. And now she is deceased, taking everything she knows with her."

Strather's eyes looked down at Sfisst's paws, where his claws were once again reflexively poking out of the fur.

Detective-Major Spalding cleared her throat.

"Regardless of that particular LE's status, I am confident *Javelin* can sniff the galactic wind sufficiently to guide us to our objective. Ninety percent of the volume of this vessel is one gigantic neutrino detector. The largest, by far, ever put into space, by humans. And for one and only one purpose. Upon arrival at the objective, we will need *Glaring Eye*'s scout capabilities—as well as the bravery of the kzinti aboard—to discern whether or not *scrith* is a technological artifact we from Known Space can understand, as well as duplicate."

Sfisst-Captain's claws slowly disappeared.

"*Glaring Eye* is a worthy Patriarchy ship, and every kzin aboard a worthy servant of the Patriarch proper. We will see it done."

☙ CHAPTER 4 ☙

THE THREE-DIMENSIONAL "pie wedge" of space, into which they would be peering, was divided up into sections. As they progressed along their route, *Javelin*—combined with *Glaring Eye*, and the #4 hull—would be stopping dead center in each section, where *Javelin* would perform a thirty-minute sensing session with the neutrino detector. Theoretically, the mission would only have to discover a shadow in two of the sections to give them a rough point-to-point bearing back to the source. Assuming the neutrino detector worked as advertised. And assuming the shadow became more pronounced, the closer they got to the origin.

If it *didn't* work . . . well, Strather was committing the crews of both ships to what would likely amount to a months-long wild goose chase.

How a Hero such as Sfisst-Captain would react to *that* kind of debacle was something Manny hoped very much they'd not have to find out.

Just before their first combined-hull Quantum II jump, Manny caught up with 'Tec-Major Spalding just outside the hatch to the bridge module.

"Sfisst thinks the ARM is lying to him," Manny said matter-of-factly.

"You noticed that too?" she said. "Well, if the situations were reversed, and he was telling us a humanoid of the sort described— this Prill woman, according to Louis Wu's statements—had perished at Patriarchy hands, I'd suspect they were lying, too. She'd be far too valuable to let her die, if it could be helped. I know Cedara couldn't reveal to you how or why the alien humanoid perished. But I don't blame Sfisst-Captain for having suspicions. Any competent officer in his position would."

"Zrarr-Professor wasn't thrilled with the news, either. I'm going to have to work hard to reassure him ARM is playing things straight."

"*Are* we playing things straight?" she asked. "I have you and I have your boss, directing me and my crew on this trip. We're relying on both of you to tell us the full story, and we both know that the ARM loves operating on a need-to-know basis. Those not deemed as 'needing' don't get the information. If the humanoid female *is* alive, somewhere in an ARM facility on Earth, that's a big vote of no-confidence from the ARM brass to us. And, frankly, it would be returned in kind. I'm as loyal as any commander in the stealth fleet. I've devoted my life to watchdogging the Patriarchy, and to keeping the worlds of humanity safe from future Patriarchy aggression. If *I* don't qualify as 'need-to-know' then who does? Sfisst-Captain is right. It's hugely unfortunate that we don't have Prill with us, to help us find her home again."

"Assuming she even wanted to go home," Manny said. "The report from Wu indicated that he thought he was doing Prill a favor."

"Then what we really need now," she said, "is Wu himself."

"Also unavailable," Manny said.

Spalding quickly ran a hand over her short-haired scalp—her exasperation palpable.

"So we've been told! Amazingly, the two key people we'd need to make our job easier aren't here. And neither is the lone Hero who'd be able to help us from the other side. Consider *that,* if you get too deep into the weeds with Zrarr—regarding the fate of Halrloprillalar. Part of me thinks Chmeee should be on this ship. So why isn't he?"

The question hung in the air between them. Then the 'Tec-Major turned and went through the hatch.

When they ultimately made the jump, the kzinti expressed surprise that it wasn't any different from an ordinary hyperspace shunt. Whatever Zrarr and Sfisst had been expecting, they were disappointed. Until Sfisst made his way back to the pilot's couch in the #4 hull, and directly observed the mass detector while under Quantum II. Upon descending back through the tunnel into the crewed portion of *Javelin,* Sfisst's manner was that of a kzin who'd been impressed.

"Not in my many years of service to the Patriarch would I have thought such speed was possible," the kzin commander said. "There are scientists and researchers on Kzin-home who have theorized that Quantum I hyperdrive is the absolute limit. We will never get beyond it. Thus our practical horizon in the galaxy is very near. But with this? Thousands upon thousands of stars may be within the reach of every species in Known Space. Which begs the question: Where did the Quantum II unit come from, and who built it? Even Chmeee could not say. Or if he could say, this information was not released to either myself or Zrarr-Professor."

"We've got our theories, on the ARM side," Manny said, as he walked with both Sfisst-Captain and Zrarr-Professor through the innards of the *Glaring Eye.* Unlike when the kzinti themselves had boarded *Javelin,* aboard *Glaring Eye* Manny felt like the proverbial Lilliputian. Everything was sized for creatures who were the better part of three meters high. He almost had to jog to keep up with the two partially-named Heroes. So, he talked between breaths, until they arrived at the *Glaring Eye*'s single, cavernous launch bay.

"We carry three planetary landers of different sizes and capacities," Sfisst-Captain said, gesturing to the three craft which inhabited the bay. Each of them had the streamlining of ships designed to operate in-atmosphere, as well as practically located nozzles for reaction control systems—which would provide the kind of precise maneuverability gravity planers couldn't match. These landers were designed to fight, as well as explore.

"Chmeee's report indicated that they used individual craft when exploring the artifact," Manny said. "Though I gather this was not Chmeee's choice."

"A great deal about that particular Hero's voyage appears to have not been his choice," Zrarr-Professor said. "I've studied Chmeee's statements extensively. There are certain things he's not at liberty to say, even to a Patriarch's Inquisitor. And Chmeee is prepared to sacrifice not only his life, but his name, to protect that information.

We who've been assigned to follow up on this peculiar and tantalizing nest of mysteries have been debating the meaning behind Chmeee's silence. For quite some time."

"Well, it won't matter soon, hopefully," Sfisst-Captain said. "If *Javelin* is as effective a tool as your 'Tec-Major says the ship is, we should ultimately be able to get to the bottom of things. And if not us—though, I would have the ears of anyone who said we weren't up to the task—then someone else. Both the Quantum II drive and *scrith* point to interstellar cultures far in advance of our own. What has ARM done about conceptualizing or quantifying the threat?"

The kzinti weren't paranoid in the human sense. But they were hyper-vigilant when it came to looking for threats beyond their borders. Maybe that was because, until they stumbled across humans, and until humans had the Quantum I hyperdrive, kzinti themselves *had* no borders? Having essentially been reverse-conquered—through successive failed attempts to thwart and enslave humanity—the Patriarchy had finally tasted some of its own medicine.

"ARM is keenly curious about the capabilities of the *scrith* culture," Manny said. "We're guessing at mass-engineering capabilities and matter transmutation which would revolutionize human manufacturing techniques, on various scales. What we've been asking ourselves is: If this culture is so theoretically close to Known Space, why haven't we seen anything of them, or heard from them, by now? A scout mission? Probe ships? Unless the Patriarchy knows something the ARM does not, we speculate the mystery culture is either so alien we cannot comprehend their motives, or they have fallen into a dark age."

"Chmeee's intelligence suggests the latter," Zrarr-Professor stated. "But it is in our mutual best interest to confirm this, with hard evidence."

"Agreed," Manny and Sfisst-Captain each said almost simultaneously.

Suddenly, the overhead speaker in the launch bay came to life.

"Sfisst-Captain," said a kzin who was speaking Heroes' Tongue, though Manny knew enough to make sense out of it. The officer's tone was urgent.

"Speak, lieutenant-of-the-watch," Sfisst commanded.

"There's been an incident aboard the human vessel."

"An incident?" Zrarr-Professor said, his posture suddenly going stiff.

"One of the humans, and one of our own, have been killed!"

Sfisst-Captain was off like a shot, with Manny and Zrarr-Professor pelting along in the kzin officer's wake. They made the docking tunnel—crossed microgravity hand-over-paw—and were met by ARM security, who led them to the scene—cordoned off, of course.

Kzin blood, as well as human blood, was everywhere. Both the ARM crewman and the kzin lay in pieces. The human, dead from the force and sharpness of the kzin's claws. The kzin, dismembered by an apparent vibrofiber blade, which had cleanly lopped off one of the kzin's arms through the shoulder, and also part of the torso.

"The autodoc—" Manny blurted, but one of the ARM ship's security shook her head.

"This happened almost twenty minutes ago, sir. Too much time for either Detective-Three Gates, or this kzin, to have any chance. They mutually bled to death within seconds."

"How does a fight like this occur, and no one stops it?" Zrarr-Professor demanded.

"We're not sure, sir," the woman said. "We're going to pull the deck and corridor camera logs, to see if we can determine what happened. The crewmember who discovered the scene called us immediately. We're still trying to discern what could have happened."

"Is this a part of the ship which is frequently traveled?" Manny asked.

"We're in the corridor leading to the raw consumables storage tanks," the security woman said. "Through that hatch down there. The only people who need to come and go through that hatch would be the processor maintenance chief, or one of his assistants."

"Is 'Tec-Three Gates either of those things?" Manny asked.

"No. 'Tec-Three Gates is security, like me," she said. "But he was off duty."

Manny felt the bottom of his stomach drop out. They'd just barely begun the search, and already a kzin warrior, and one of ARM's own . . .

Detective-Major Spalding arrived, almost at a run. She took three seconds to stare at the gore, then turned to Sfisst-Captain.

"Who was the kzin?"

"A maintenance specialist," Sfisst-Captain said.

"Why would he have come aboard in the first place?" Spalding asked.

"He was not authorized to be aboard—I didn't put him on the list given permission to visit the *Javelin*."

"If you ask me," said the security woman, "it was self-defense on 'Tec-Three Gates's part."

"Are your personnel in the habit of carrying vibro weapons during their nonduty time?" Sfisst-Captain said, his lip curling back to reveal the tips of his pointed teeth.

"None of my personnel are authorized to carry private weapons of *any* kind aboard this ship," Spalding replied hotly.

"So," Zrarr-Professor interjected, "it seems we've got a case of two individuals—neither of whom had any business being in this particular corridor—hacking each other to pieces. For reasons unknown. Sfisst-Captain, it might be prudent to suspend current operations until we can get to the bottom of this incident. As word of this is already travelling through our separate ranks, emotions among humans and kzinti alike are going to be running high."

"No," both Sfisst-Captain and 'Tec-Major Spalding uttered in unison.

Manny looked at Spalding, his eyebrow raised.

"I'm inclined to agree with my colleague," Manny said. "As anxious as I am to continue the mission, this demands resolution before we go further."

"The Patriarch made it plain," Sfisst-Captain said. "We were to proceed with haste, for the good of Kzin-home, and all kzinti everywhere. We *must* discern the location and nature of the civilization which produces *scrith*. The Patriarch *will* know the size and potency of the threat!"

"ARM brass feels the same," Spalding said. "I was told—before you came aboard, Sci-Spec Strather—that once we were underway, there would be no delays. We're dealing with a potential threat to the whole of Known Space. It takes *Javelin* mere minutes to do what a standard ARM ship does in days. We'll have to figure this double murder out *while* we continue the survey."

Manny swallowed hard. And not just because the sight of so

much human and kzin blood—spread over the bulkheads and deck—revolted him.

Zrarr-Professor merely lashed his tail several times, then looked at Sfisst-Captain.

"Sfisst-Captain, I suggest we post a guard at the entrance to the docking tube. 'Tec-Major will no doubt be doing the same on her side. Absolutely *no* unauthorized humans are to have access to the *Glaring Eye,* and absolutely no kzinti should be allowed to cross to the *Javelin* without your specific say-so."

"We were naïve not to institute such a protocol in the first place," the kzin commander said, obviously irritated, and looked at his human counterpart. "Now, 'Tec-Major, I demand to see the camera logs."

☙ CHAPTER 5 ☙

The lone kzin appeared to be wandering aimlessly. He'd come up the docking cylinder by himself, and gone down several different corridors, occasionally switching back at random. Not every hatch would permit him, just as not every hatch was accessible by every human aboard, either. When he hit dead ends, he retraced his steps, and chose a new route. Though Zrarr-Professor was hard-pressed to determine what was going through the dead kzin's mind.

Finally, the kzin began walking down the corridor toward the raw consumables hatchway. Detective-Three Gates bumped into the kzin—from an adjoining corridor—and the two of them appeared to have a conversation. Then the cameras went black. For just long enough to shroud the violence which ensued. At which point the cameras came back, and the two LEs lay where they'd been found a few minutes later. No audio available.

Sfisst-Captain's demeanor betrayed no emotion. Which—Zrarr suspected—meant the *Glaring Eye*'s commander was having to use more self-control than ever before to keep from unleashing his temper on the humans in the conference cabin.

"Care to explain your ship's technical problems, at the instant of lethal contact?" Sfisst asked.

The 'Tec-Major didn't reply at first. She merely ran the footage back, and forth. Back, and forth. Then she pivoted her chair so that she was facing Sfisst-Captain directly.

"I can't explain it," she said coolly.

"If you were in my place, what would you think?" Sfisst asked.

Spalding's tongue ran along the inside of one cheek, then she laughed. It was a hard sound.

"I'd think you—or someone aboard your ship—jumped my crewmember, and that you'd erased what you had to erase, to avoid things looking any worse than they already did."

"Precisely," Sfisst almost purred.

"But," Spalding continued, "I'd also wonder what the hell my crewperson was doing aboard *your* ship, without authorization or need to be there. And if such an individual had returned to me in one piece, I personally would have been tempted to cut him to ribbons. Merely for being catastrophically stupid! What the tanj was your maintenance specialist doing wandering around like that, Sfisst-Captain?"

"I . . . do not have an answer to that question," Sfisst confessed.

"I can assure I did not order *any* of my security personnel to molest him," Spalding continued, "though I admit I am now feeling stupid for having allowed your people unrestricted access to *Javelin*'s common spaces. I thought it would be a good idea, to encourage cooperative amity. Well, so much for that."

"And it *was* a good idea," Zrarr-Professor said, trying to soothe things. Though he was quite certain no sane human would have had the audacity to go alone to *Glaring Eye* and begin wandering around without an escort.

"So, who or what blanked the file?" Sfisst demanded, his claws digging into the arm of his oversized chair. "Until or unless *that* question is answered, 'Tec-Major, I am going to assume that 'Tec-Three Gates was not acting alone. Someone on this vessel intends harm to the crew of the *Glaring Eye*. I will have justice for my dead crew, one way or another. Is that understood?"

"We're assuming," Zrarr said, being careful with his choice of words, "that our maintenance specialist was not the aggressor in the affair."

"Why blank the camera—and the sound—if it was our kzin's fault?" Sfisst spat in annoyance.

Sfisst's tail swiped this way and that, his lips withdrawing to reveal the tiniest hint of teeth.

"It's all very confusing," Zrarr said. "But if we cannot delay the mission, we have to proceed in a manner which will still allow us to trust one another."

"*Trust,*" Sfisst said, with a kzin inflection meant for mocking, "I've thought it over, and I have a serious problem with the 'Tec-Major restricting our access to her ship. Passing through *Javelin* is the only way to get to the Number Four hull, which belongs to both ARM and Patriarchy."

"Sir," Zrarr continued, "if you will remember my original suggestion, I didn't propose a total ban. Merely hard enforcement of the extant access rosters. The security details posted to either side of the tunnel need only ensure that the list is not violated going forward. This ought to prevent any more accidents like this from happening."

"Accident!?" Spalding said, her voice rising.

Sfisst-Captain's lips pulled back even more.

"Please, please," Strather said, standing up from his seat and placing himself between the two ships' commanders, his hands poised in the air as if to push Spalding and Sfisst apart. "We're not going to get anything done if we bicker over semantics. I think Zrarr-Professor has a good idea. I also think Zrarr-Professor and myself are the only ones on this mission capable of investigating impartially."

"Why?" Spalding asked.

"Because neither Sci-Spec Strather, nor myself, are members of either crew," Zrarr said, quick on the uptake. "If the underlying assumption is that 'Tec-Three Gates could not have acted alone, this assumption works the other way as well. There may be more than one kzin aboard *Glaring Eye* who proposes to do the mission harm."

Both commanders turned their heads to look at Zrarr, then Strather, and finally at each other.

"I believe this may be a logical course of action," Sfisst said. "But if you will excuse me, I need to return to *Glaring Eye* to make arrangements for the receipt of our fallen comrade. Not to mention issuing new instructions regarding ship-to-ship access."

Zrarr followed in Sfisst's wake, until they were entirely clear of the kzin side of the access tunnel. At which time Zrarr pawed a switch, opening a side hatch to a small equipment room, then unceremoniously steered Sfisst into it.

When the hatch snapped shut, Zrarr let his own lips peel back from his teeth.

"Out with it," Zrarr demanded in the Heroes' Tongue.

"Beware the ground on which you tread," Sfisst said. "You are in no position to intimidate me. Every kzinti on this ship would claw your belly open at my merest whim."

"Which is exactly why I need to know what is going on!" Zrarr snarled. "That maintenance technician didn't board the *Javelin* by mistake, and he wasn't there for a personal tour, either. He knew he wasn't on the access list, but he went anyway. Which tells me he either experienced a moment of pure insanity, or he was over there on your *orders,* Sfisst-Captain."

Sfisst and Zrarr stood eye to eye for several moments, then Sfisst's posture changed from one of defiance, to one of resignation.

"All right, Zrarr-Professor, you're correct. That young kzin was aboard the *Javelin* with my instructions. Since Detective-Major Spalding was so generously allowing us to have access to her ship, I felt it was imperative that the Patriarchy have a look inside. Someone from my own security detail would have been a poor choice. But a maintenance technician would have good eyes for mechanical details, and be able to commit deck arrangements to memory, speculate on the nature of special or unusual equipment, and so forth. The fact that he was killed near their 'raw consumables' hatchway tells me there may have been more behind that hatch than the 'Tec-Major cares to admit."

"Why are you making this so much harder than it needs to be!?" Zrarr almost roared, no longer caring whether or not he was out of line.

"I have my duty to the Patriarchy," Sfisst hissed, spinning away from Zrarr and stalking once in a circle, before coming back to stare Zrarr in the eye.

"But mark my words," Sfisst said coldly, "the ARM is going to prove every bit as treacherous as I told you they'd be. Mission to discover *scrith,* or no mission. They are a military force with just one purpose: to contain the rightful expansion of the kzin people, while they engineer our docile descent toward extinction! Not immediately, mind you. But piecemeal. A bit at a time. Until we have utterly forgotten ourselves. How many of our erstwhile brothers languish in a delusion, on human-owned worlds where kzinti are permitted to participate in *human* society? Kits born and raised without true Heroes to guide and inspire them! Bereft of proper kzin culture. Partaking in the fantasy that men and kzinti are equals!"

Now it was Zrarr-Professor who had to exert utmost control, lest his temper get the better of him. With every statement, Sfisst had insulted Zrarr deeply. Though Sfisst had no way of knowing what he was doing. It was almost more than a grown Hero could take. But because he *was* a Hero—despite everything Sfisst thought—Zrarr kept his emotions in check.

"I will uncover the truth behind your young technician's death," Zrarr said coldly. "Meanwhile, you must *not* do anything else to foolishly sacrifice the gristle of trust which now tenuously holds this expedition together. If I were the 'Tec-Major I'd be sorely tempted to cut *Glaring Eye* loose in space, and conduct the *scrith* shadow survey on my own. She knows *Glaring Eye* has no hope of keeping up. And at this point, every kzin aboard must be seen—by her—as a potential liability."

"We could make it easy for her," Sfisst said. "Take *Javelin* and the Number Four by force. You've seen how few they are. If I committed just half the kzinti on this ship, we'd have *Javelin* before the end of the day. And there wouldn't be anything any of the humans could do about it. We then conduct the survey ourselves, and return the knowledge of *scrith* to the Patriarch in secret. Both *Javelin* and *Glaring Eye* are reported missing, along with the Number Four hull."

"Are you so sure?" Zrarr said. "It took just a lowly 'Tec-Three to dispatch your maintenance technician, kzin though he may have been. Kzin commanders bolder and more audacious than yourself have proceeded under assumptions similar to yours, and paid the ultimate penalty. Don't prove yourself to be their equal in limited thinking, Sfisst-Captain."

The small equipment room suddenly became thick with the smell of violence, but just barely contained. Both of the partially-named Heroes waited for the other to scream and leap.

The voice comm panel near the door interrupted.

"Sfisst-Captain, this is the lieutenant-of-the-watch, respond, please, sir."

Sfisst glared angrily at Zrarr for a few more moments, then marched over to the hatch and slammed the comm panel.

"Sfisst here, speak now," he said peremptorily.

"Sir, the *Javelin* is reporting that the neutrino sensor reports negative for this sector. They are asking if we are ready to proceed to the next target sector."

"Tell them yes," Sfisst said. "Also, post a trio of guards to the access tunnel to *Javelin*. Any human who tries to cross without explicit kzin escort is to be killed immediately. Any kzin who tries to cross against my specific instructions will be detained until I can personally interrogate him. Is that understood?"

"Understood clearly, sir," the comm speaker said. Then the light went dark.

"This test of wills is not over between us," Sfisst said over his shoulder as the hatch opened. Then he pounced through it, and was gone. Leaving Zrarr-Professor to sag his full weight against a support column, where he slowly calmed his nerves and allowed the battle reflex in him to wind itself down. He'd come to blows with his own kind before. Even killed his own kind, when honor demanded it. But he still needed Sfisst.

When Zrarr went back up the docking tunnel, he could see ARM guards, and Sci-Spec Strather, waiting for him on the other side.

"Keeping that Hero placated must be a full-time job," Strather said, in the joking manner Zrarr had learned humans used to cover up for embarrassment, or discomfort.

"He is a true warrior of the Patriarch," Zrarr said, and meant it.

Despite the fact that Sfisst's decision had precipitated an unexpectedly deadly debacle, part of Zrarr grudgingly respected the fact that Sfisst had the same ambition which ear-marked classic Heroes of old—the kind of kzinti who populated the legends of their people. And made a kzin proud to be who and what he was. Modern difficulties notwithstanding.

Different though Zrarr might have been, he was still a kzin himself. The same blood that pumped through Sfisst's heart pumped in Zrarr's arteries as well. Zrarr merely had the wider perspective, allowing him to see to a farther horizon.

"Have you any idea why the camera log would blank like that?" Zrarr said, as Strather took Zrarr in tow, and led the big kzin to a part of the *Javelin* Zrarr had never seen before. Not the conference room the 'Tec-Major liked to use for official business. This was a more intimate spot, away from the busier corridors.

"My quarters," Strather said, waving his hand around. "Where I've already ensured we can talk privately, without the 'Tec-Major being involved. If we're going to conduct this investigation thoroughly, we have to assume that both chains of command might be tainted."

"Urrr," Zrarr said. "That is a prudent assumption."

"And no, I haven't the foggiest idea why the camera would blank. Not without assuming somebody with access to the ship's internal security network was watching the whole thing, and cut that specific camera out of the loop for as long as the fight ensued. Though, obviously, the melee finished almost the instant it started.

"But you have to tell me straight, Zrarr-Professor. What *was* that lone kzin doing wandering around the ship? I can't believe it happened without Sfisst-Captain being aware of what was going on."

Zrarr debated within himself. Though he'd managed to get Sfisst to divulge the truth, did Zrarr dare allow Strather into Zrarr's confidence so completely? How much could he share with his human counterpart before he was actually betraying the Patriarch's trust? He considered the issue for several moments, took a deep breath, then talked.

"Sfisst-Captain foolishly ordered the maintenance technician to perform an 'inspection' of *Javelin*. Not with malicious intent toward *Javelin*'s crew, mind you. I detected nothing of that. Merely Sfisst's too-curious nature getting the better of him. The maintenance technician was to observe, and report back. Except, he never made it back. What was the off-duty 'Tec-Three doing in that corridor, and how or why was he wielding a weapon which 'Tec-Major herself declared off-limits to human personnel?"

"That's something I'm going to have to find out," Strather said. "And quickly. There's no reason to think that the 'Tec-Major herself is involved. But if she's like Sfisst-Captain, she's going to be holding her cards close to her chest from here on out."

Zrarr-Professor had to search his memory for that particular human phrase, then caught the reference, and was pleased with himself for having done so.

"Neither your ship's commander, nor mine, have much incentive to trust each other, or this situation. I think you and I both knew that when we opened our dialogue on the *scrith* matter some time ago. It's a very wicked problem which may sabotage this mission yet. I believe you and I represent the only two voices capable of speaking sense to either side in this matter. Do you agree?"

"Yes, I think so," Strather said.

"And do you think we, ourselves, can learn to trust each other enough to do what's necessary?"

"If we don't yet," Strather said. "Now is a perfect time to start practicing."

☙ CHAPTER 6 ☙

"WE NEED TO TALK," Manny said as he entered the *Javelin*'s bridge module. Several of the bridge staff turned their heads to look at him over the headrests of their chairs, but it was obvious to all concerned whom Manny had been addressing.

"Okay, let's talk," Detective-Major Spalding said.

"Privately, please," Manny said.

The 'Tec-Major looked around at the faces of her crew, then nodded to Strather and got up from her seat. Together they ducked into the small ancillary control room just off the bridge module proper. When the hatch slid shut, Manny got right to the point.

"You knew an unauthorized kzin had come aboard, so why didn't you stop him immediately?"

"I was curious," Spalding said. "When my security alerted me to the fact that a kzin *not* on the authorized list was clumsily snooping around, I decided to let things play out. See where the rat-cat wanted to go. Maybe figure out what, specifically, Sfisst-Captain had sent him to accomplish aboard the *Javelin*?"

"And when one of your security officers took matters into his own hands?" Manny said, his voice sharp edged.

"I still don't know why 'Tec-Three Gates did what he did. Nor do I know how he got a personally owned vibrowire weapon aboard. He was in fact off-duty when the incident occurred. And if you noticed from the camera logs, he did not cross paths with the kzin until almost immediately before their lethal altercation."

"Somebody with a family grudge against the kzinti?"

"Maybe," Spalding said, chewing at her bottom lip. "I didn't know 'Tec-Three Gates all that well. He had a clean ARM file, and came recommended from a previous 'Tec-Captain of a prior command. There's nothing in his record to make me think he had some kind of vendetta."

"We *must* find out how and why the camera blanked, along with the audio. It's the only way we're going to be able to earn back Sfisst-Captain's trust. *If* we can prove that 'Tec-Three Gates was acting alone."

"Sfisst-Captain is the one who ought to be earning *my* trust back!" Spalding snapped. "I'm not the one who sent a pawn across the docking tunnel, sniffing around for who knows what. I agreed to an open-access mission—ship to ship—only because of the previously agreed-upon access list. Sfisst immediately wadded that list up and threw it in the trash. I almost *want* to take credit for what 'Tec-Three Gates did. Just because I know it's the kind of move a kzin commander in my place would have done, upon detecting a human intruder."

"But you didn't send him," Manny said.

"No. I didn't. And now I have to write the whole damned thing up. There are 'Tec-Admirals who are going to be asking questions, and I will be on the hot seat for that—regardless of how this whole mission turns out."

"Speaking of that," Manny said, "how is the neutrino detector working?"

"Fine," Spalding said. "Either that, or our whole theory with the detector is wrong. We won't know until we've visited at least a dozen more sectors, and been able to compare the data. We're sitting on what should be the most sensitive neutrino detector in Known Space. If it can't find the expected shadows, then we're going to have to figure out some other way of tracking down where *scrith* came from."

"It'll work," Manny said—and hoped very badly he wasn't making a liar out of himself.

"For both our sakes, I want to believe you," Spalding replied.

After that, they reentered the bridge module, and Manny left Spalding to resume the watch.

Two days elapsed in relative peace and quiet. The Quantum II motor continued to perform as expected, and the triple-ship combination was able to cover more territory in forty-eight hours than either *Javelin* or *Glaring Eye* alone could have covered in three Earth months. Meanwhile, Manny set to work on the *Javelin*'s deck camera logs. Using his credentials as a Science-Inspector, he combed through the various smart programs, trying to determine if something had been rigged in advance, or if the cutout had occurred due to manual interruption at the source. He even went down to the corridor—now cleaned up, since there had been no forensics needed to determine cause of death—and took the cameras in the corridor apart himself. Looked at all the chips, and the wiring. Nothing seemed out of place.

Three times a day, Manny met with Zrarr-Professor. Either in Manny's quarters, or in Zrarr's own cabin aboard the *Glaring Eye*. As with the visit to the launch bay, going aboard the kzin vessel was like stepping into an adult world, but straight out of first grade. Everything was sized half again as large as anything on *Javelin*. And the crew who crossed Manny's path gave him a disdainful look. Not quite threatening. But hostile enough for Manny to make sure he was never out of Zrarr's sight while aboard.

Together, they pored over the personnel files for both the kzin maintenance technician and 'Tec-Three Gates. Trying to determine if there was some kind of oblique connection. Men and kzinti rarely killed each other blindly these days. If a kzin wanted a man dead, or vice versa, there had to be a reason. Especially since whoever had blanked the *Javelin*'s cameras didn't want a record of the killing.

On the third day, their investigation was interrupted by news that the neutrino detector had found something. It wasn't much. Just a slight drop in the overall ambient density of neutrinos in that specific sector of their search. But it was the first time the detector—very large, very specialized, and therefore very expensive—had given any hint that it was actually doing what it had been designed to do.

For a few hours, at least, the double homicide was temporarily forgotten, as the triple-ship combo tried all the adjacent sectors, and was unable to come up with a similar reading.

"Damn," Manny said, thudding a fist on the auxiliary readout board where he sat in the *Javelin*'s bridge module. "We had it. We had it!"

"Did we?" Sfisst-Captain—who'd made the unusual gesture of coming to *Javelin*'s bridge module without his escort—asked. "So far in our search, we've turned up very little. It's possible that the detector found a mere solitary pocket of decreased density, nothing more. I would think a true shadow of the sort we're imagining must exist would be more pronounced, urrrr?"

"Sfisst-Captain may be right," Zrarr-Professor said. "In our eagerness to pick up the *scrith* trail, we're liable to see things—in even the puniest bit of evidence—which may not be there. Let us not be discouraged. We have our sectors to be explored still. Hundreds of them, in fact. And I believe our methodology is sound. Let's continue."

So, continue they did. For three additional days.

Until an explosion in the *Glaring Eye*'s launch bay brought the entire mission to an abrupt halt.

From the perspective of the *Javelin,* all had been well. They'd been preparing for the next Quantum II shunt to the next sector when suddenly the ship-to-ship communications network lit up with traffic from *Glaring Eye.* The smallest of the three landers had been seriously damaged, and three kzinti were in the autodoc—two of them critical enough that their survival was not assured.

Once again, Manny found himself aboard the *Glaring Eye,* this time with Spalding at his back, and half a dozen armed *Javelin* security to keep both the 'Tec-Major and the Sci-Spec protected. Sfisst-Captain looked prepared to disembowel the lot of them, from where he sat across the compartment from the humans. His lips quivered with rage, and his speech drifted in and out of Interworld and the Heroes' Tongue.

"Unacceptable!" Sfisst spat. "I was almost prepared to believe that the incident aboard *Javelin* was a dreadfully timed blunder. But now I have *proof* of direct ARM action taken against this vessel!"

"Impossible," the 'Tec-Major said, trying to remain calm. "None of my people were aboard *Glaring Eye* during the explosion. And the last one specifically to enter your launch bay was Sci-Spec Strather, just prior to the double homicide aboard *Javelin.*"

"Yes," Sfisst said, focusing his baleful gaze on Manny. Ancient men who'd faced tigers in the jungles of Asia—and died—must have felt the same sensation that Manny did in that moment. He swallowed hard, and steeled himself.

"You were with me the whole time," Manny said. "What could I have done in the launch bay which would have escaped your notice?"

"I'm rapidly tiring of this," Sfisst said. "One of mine is dead, and three more are almost dead. And for what? A mission which has yet to yield anything conclusive. And now one of the three landers is so badly damaged, it may have to be scrapped! Not to mention the damage to the launch bay itself. It will take days to repair what needs to be repaired, as well as inspect the other two landers for additional sabotage."

"Sabotage?" Zrarr-Professor blurted.

"What *else* could it be?" Sfisst shouted, pure kzin speech.

"An accident—" Zrarr began to say, but was cut off.

"As of this moment," Sfisst announced, "I am placing both Detective-Major Spalding and Science-Inspector Strather under arrest. For crimes against the Patriarchy."

"You wouldn't dare," the 'Tec-Major said, this time letting her teeth show.

The security detail from the *Javelin* were suddenly surrounding both Manny and Pryce on both sides—weapons up. And these weren't police-standard needle guns either. These were combination projectile launchers with modified flashlight-lasers mounted beneath. Weapons designed explicitly for combat.

"I would *relish* the opportunity," Sfisst-Captain purred with a very-toothy grin. "Please, give the signal for your security detail to open fire. My warriors will make quick work of you, and then quick work of *Javelin*'s crew, too. Go ahead. Do it."

Manny felt his blood run cold. Sfisst wasn't kidding. He was almost gleeful in his anticipation.

But Spalding had not made 'Tec-Major for nothing.

"I don't think I'm going to give you the satisfaction of a stand-up fight," she said. "Sfisst-Captain, you should know that prior to boarding your ship, I gave explicit instructions. In the event that myself and Sci-Spec Strather are harmed—and my crew will know it, because my vitals, and the vitals of every human in this room are being relayed back to my bridge module—*Javelin* is commanded to eject *Glaring Eye* into the void. It would take you a long time to get back to Known Space, even at full hyperdrive. At which time you would be intercepted by a flotilla of ARM vessels, each with explicit instructions to capture or kill you before you ever reached the Patriarchy."

Sfisst snarled. His own security detail—at his back—advanced one step.

"Wait!" Manny shouted. "Nobody do anything we'll all regret."

"Yes, wait!" Zrarr also shouted, but explicitly in the Heroes' Tongue.

The entire compartment teetered on the edge of bloody mayhem.

"This is all too convenient," Manny said, his thoughts whirring through his head as fast as his brain could cogitate.

"*Convenient*?" Sfisst spat, incredulous.

"Yes," Manny said. "Someone—or something—clearly intends for this mission to fail. We don't know for what reason, yet. But I am convinced that the mystery of the double homicide, and now the unexplainable explosion in your launch bay, are connected. And I am beginning to think it's not anything either you, Sfisst-Captain, nor you, 'Tec-Major, are doing deliberately. Rather, there is a mind at work. Or minds. Which realize precisely how each of you would react to a specific set of circumstances. And now those circumstances are being created. So that the mission falls to pieces. Possibly costing us our lives."

"To what end?" Sfisst demanded. "Explain to me why I shouldn't haul both of you to my brig this instant, and hold you there while I conduct my own investigation?"

"You could do that," Manny said. "And risk retaliation from *Javelin*'s executive officer. Or you could kill us here, and suffer the fate which Spalding has planned for you in the event of our deaths. Or, you could allow myself and Zrarr-Professor to continue our co-investigation. We have one crime, compounded by another. Zrarr and I need to find out who is behind these events, and why."

"Yourself and Zrarr-Professor have so far yielded *nothing*," Sfisst said, emphasizing the last word, with his eyes on Zrarr. The academic kzin didn't flinch, though Manny thought a different Hero in Zrarr's place would have been livid to the point of clawing a belly open.

"We've just got to have more time," Zrarr pleaded. "Sfisst-Captain, I implore you. Don't cripple this mission. There's much more at stake here than either *Glaring Eye* or *Javelin*, or even the

Quantum II hyperdrive prototype. Unless we can return to Known Space with a successful reconnoiter of the *scrith* source, neither ARM nor the Patriarchy will be any the wiser as to the capabilities of the foreign state which created *scrith*. And that's not a risk either government can take. We've known as much since the beginning, and it's what's compelled us forward. Botching the thing, now, for the sake of petty brinksmanship . . . would be the height of foolishness."

Sfisst's glare swept the room, slowly.

Manny didn't say a word, and neither did Pryce.

When Sfisst's claws gradually began to withdraw back into the tips of his digits, Manny allowed his breath to slowly escape his lungs. While the security details on both sides relaxed their stances.

"Very well, Zrarr-Professor," Sfisst said flatly. "I am not partially named because I am an idiot who can't think. But I am giving you and Sci-Spec Strather an ultimatum. *Find me these perpetrators.* I do not like the ARM, but I like being manipulated even less! Four of my crew have already paid for our ignorance on this matter. If our mission *is* infested with a third party acting against both Patriarchy and ARM alike, I *will* have the satisfaction of rooting the infestation out. Do not fail in this, Zrarr-Professor."

With that, Sfisst stood up and swept out of the compartment, taking most of his detail with him, but leaving two kzinti to stand guard at the hatch through which Sfisst had departed.

"He's right," Spalding said, her chin dropping to her chest, while she used a palm to wipe at the sweat which had suddenly began to pop out across her face. "Things seem to be ratcheting up. I don't think this mission can take another mystery explosion, mystery altercation, what have you. *Find out* what is going on, Strather. Or I'm going to have to shove Zrarr-Professor down the docking tube, slam the hatch, and punch *Glaring Eye* off the grapplers. *Javelin* will have to finish the reconnoiter alone."

"And if these saboteurs remain aboard *your* ship, and continue to do more harm?" Zrarr-Professor asked.

Spalding merely stared at her hand—covered in perspiration—then she stood up, and marched her way out of the compartment.

☙ CHAPTER 7 ☙

FOUR ADDITIONAL days passed in painfully tense uneventfulness. Only Zrarr himself, and his companion Strather, were permitted to pass between the two vessels. The number of armed guards on either side of the tunnel swelled to what Zrarr felt were unreasonable levels. For ships already crewed at their functional minimums, pulling additional individuals away to watch the tunnel was a significant disruption in the duty rotations for both commanders. Spalding and Sfisst were both going out of their way to ensure that nobody was crossing or entering without significant force prepared to repel what both sides seemingly assumed to be imminent boarding action.

The mission was now well outside the farthest-known galactic exploration point of any Patriarchy scout, and Zrarr had no doubt that 'Tec-Major Spalding would sooner destroy *Javelin,* than see it—or especially the #4 hull—captured.

The two security forces eyed each other across the tunnel with what Zrarr could only call mutually enthusiastic suspicion.

If Sci-Spec Strather's theory was right, the perpetrator—or perpetrators—had pushed both ARM's and the Patriarchy's buttons to perfection. Meanwhile, close inspection of the totaled lander's remains revealed very little. The explosives had been knowledgeably placed where conventional demolitions might do the most damage. The three kzinti taken to autodoc were in critical and serious conditions, respectively. And neither Zrarr nor Strather was eager to face the commander of either ship empty-handed. So they kept at it. Sleeping only as much as necessary.

"We might assume that the kzinti taken to autodoc were themselves responsible for the blast," Strather said, as he and Zrarr made one more pass through the heap of scorched, melted, and burned evidence which had been pushed out of the way of the kzin repair crews. Those kzinti gave Strather a wide berth, showing a posture Zrarr knew instinctively to be half a step from violence. They viewed the Sci-Spec with contempt, and said as much in hushed Heroes' Tongue while performing their work.

"It's possible," Zrarr said, being sure to pay attention to his peripheral vision. Leaving Strather unguarded for even a moment might invite reprisal. "But it would take an insane kzin to willingly damage, through self-sabotage, a Patriarchy ship. Much less kill or injure other members of a Patriarchy crew. Merely for the sake of starting a fight. We are not so much like humans that we would 'false flag' in the human manner you suggest."

"The history between our two species suggests you're giving kzin character too much credit," Strather said dryly.

Zrarr dropped the piece of blackened machinery he'd been examining. It slammed to the deck with a very loud *thud*. The kzinti making repairs stopped what they were doing, and looked up from their work.

"And what exactly is your meaning?" Zrarr demanded. He'd been trying hard all this time to be diplomatic—especially with Strather— but even he had his limits. "We are a direct people, whatever you may think of us. Perhaps so direct it has been our undoing, when confronted with the war fleets of men. Fault us for this, Science-Inspector. But do not call us dishonest to the point of attempting to murder our own, purely for the sake of inviting a conflict. If it was the Patriarch's will to have war again, *we would have war again*. But it is the Patriarch's will that we *not* have war. Thus you and I are here, and we are trying desperately to keep our people away from each other's ears."

"My apologies," Strather said. "It was not my intent to offend."

"I know that," Zrarr said, then picked up the piece of equipment he'd dropped, and went back to examining it.

"The kzinti aboard this ship find me strange," Zrarr said, "but I am still one of them. And even though you yourself may find me easier to dialogue with than any kzin you've yet met, I am still a Hero. I have *pride*. Albeit not untouched by wisdom."

The air between them was silent for several minutes, and the repair crew went back to their business—the fluttering white light from welding equipment making strange shadows on the ceiling.

"You're correct about that," Strather finally said, leaning his hip against the metal table which had been brought in for the sake of the examination.

"About what specifically?" Zrarr asked.

"That you're the most easygoing kzin I've ever encountered. Especially around people. Human people, I mean."

"Perhaps that's just the kind of kzin I am," Zrarr said, using the claw on one of his digits to experimentally scratch at the scalded residue along one side of a small access panel.

"I've met Patriarchy kzinti trained for diplomatic jobs," Strather pressed, "and they have a polished professionalism that comes from extensive schooling—to deal with non-kzinti. But you? You *feel* different. Different from your diplomatic corps. Different even from kzinti who've been born and raised on worlds that men and kzinti share."

"The kzinti of human space are a very touchy subject," Zrarr said. "For those of us born to the Patriarchy proper, the human-world kzinti are regarded as being at once *us*—and yet also clearly *not* us. If that makes any sense?"

"It does," Strather said. "At least academically. One thousand years ago, Earth was a very divided place. Tribes and nations still violently fighting with one another. Conquered cultures being subsumed by conquering cultures. This was long before the ARM existed. Though identitarianism didn't stop being a problem after the United Nations put a stop to the wars between men. Identitarianism is merely controlled. Kept in check. Even now, the ARM exerts a lot of effort making sure that humans don't redivide to the point of shedding our own blood. On Earth. On other colonies. Hell, the alliance between the colonies themselves—born out of necessity, once the Patriarchy manifested—remains uneasy. It is the nature of men to seek excuses to hate and kill each other. If the Patriarchy had not forced us to unite—"

"Why tell me this?" Zrarr interrupted. "You are ARM. Why speak of your own people in such unflattering terms?"

Strather sighed, rubbing the heels of his palms into his eyes, then looked up at Zrarr with a monkey expression Zrarr had learned meant earnestness.

"Because," Strather said emphatically, "it's important to me that you understand I am not willing to critically examine kzin history— what it means to *be* Kzin—without critically examining men and our history as well."

"Give me an example," Zrarr said, intrigued.

"What would you say if I told you I have an ancestor who was directly involved in defeating the Patriarchy's First Invasion, against Earth and Sol? Though, to be honest about it, Greatly Jack didn't know what he'd gotten himself into—when he first took the job minding the launching lasers. Like everyone in his generation, the ARM ensured he didn't know about war. But he learned fast, once the war came. So did everybody else. Almost like the human race took a nice, lazy siesta from history—telling ourselves we were 'beyond' what we truly are—before reality reasserted itself. In the form of a Patriarchy scout fleet, which in turn was followed by still more waves of Patriarchy ships. Then we came back to being ourselves *real* fast."

"You don't believe in the lasting peace," Zrarr said, "even though you are ARM?"

"I don't believe in it precisely *because* I am ARM. We're the unlucky ones who get to know the truth. In all its uncomfortable glory. Just about everyone on Earth, and more than a few people out in the colonies, cooperate in this mutual daydream. The Man-Kzin Wars are over, we tell ourselves. Permanent luxury and abundance being the birthright of every human child. Nobody has to suffer. Boosterspice lets us have long lives, which we hesitate to waste on gallant adventure—or murderous foolishness, depending on how you choose to see it. Humanity *needs* it this way. We're too dangerous to ourselves otherwise."

Zrarr-Professor stared. This was an aspect of the question he'd never considered before. What he knew of men—of Earth—spoke mainly of their happy indulgence in an existence untroubled by hardship. That any man, much less a man of the ARM, should question the success of his species . . . For the kzinti it had been different. Once kzinti were unified beneath the banner of Riit, and ruling space with technology taken from the Jotoki, there was little thought given to internal squabbling. Heroes fought each other for status and honor, but only at the individual level. The pride-on-pride battles of ancient times were truly a thing of the past.

And now? Where *could* a warrior test his mettle? A large percentage of the kzin species had snuffed itself out battling against men. There was no more frontier for kzinti to tame. It had been taken from them.

Zrarr-Professor rested his paws on the table, and did not look up when he spoke.

"Shall I tell you what it is to be a shamed?"

"I don't understand," Strather admitted.

"Of course you don't. You were sired by men who slaughtered the First Invasion, and all subsequent Patriarchy military operations thereafter. You didn't see your most ferocious, most *kzin-like* Heroes go forward and take death as a sacrament. Because it is, for every kzin born in the Patriarchy. Our honor—our notion of who we truly are, deep down—is tied to this. And yet we *failed*. Death for the sake of victory is noble. Death for the sake of defeat? Is stupid. We have lived with that stupidity on our hearts for a very long time. Some part of us still yearns for another chance. Another turning of the great wheel of fate, so that every kzin kit can look up at the night sky of Kzin-home, and know in his heart that the stars belong to *him*. Not to the monkeys of Earth."

A pink flush had darkened Strather's cheeks—embarrassment.

"I honestly never thought of it like that," the Science-Inspector confessed.

"You have been candid," Zrarr said, straightening his posture, so that he could look Strather squarely in the face. "Probably candid beyond the boundaries of discretion. Therefore I have been candid as well. This mission is in jeopardy precisely because you and I navigate the waters of kzin shame, muddied by your ARM's justified fear of what that shame can cause. Your ARM knows from experience what it means to relax their watch. They would be stupid to extend any more trust to us than is absolutely necessary, even all this time after the end of the last openly declared war. Meanwhile, the Patriarchy wonders—at an almost unconscious level—when it will get another 'roll of the dice,' as men might say. A fresh opportunity to once again be victorious. If not by one angle, perhaps by another?"

Strather stared up at Zrarr, and for the first time the science-monkey appeared afraid of the scholar-kzin. Zrarr felt instinctual satisfaction in this—a part of his psyche Zrarr had spent his whole life learning to carefully manage. Zrarr therefore knew better than to trust this feral manifestation of his most basic kzin-self, and pushed the feeling back into the psychological paddock where such things belonged.

To his credit, Strather appeared to do the same—literally swallowing his fear.

The moment was interrupted by an audio alert from *Glaring Eye*'s lieutenant-of-the-watch.

"Speak," Zrarr said, acknowledging the officer.

"*Javelin*'s neutrino sensing system has found another dip in the number of neutrinos. Much more pronounced than the first."

Strather's eyes blinked several times, then he was quickly communicating with the other ARM officers aboard his vessel.

"Confirmed," he said, and appeared to be relieved on several levels.

"Shall we adjourn to *Javelin* to see what develops?" Zrarr suggested.

"Yes, please," Strather said emphatically.

☙ CHAPTER 8 ☙

THE NEUTRINO reading held true. And not just for one piece of the "pie" but for several in a row. Crew aboard both the *Javelin* and the *Glaring Eye* began communicating rapidly—hostilities seemingly forgotten in the rush to triangulate a direction for the cause of the neutrino shadow—then Sfisst and Spalding were co-ordering the largest single Quantum II jump they'd yet made. And at the end of it, the three-ships-in-one sat solidly astride a definite diminishing in ambient neutrinos. The available register showed the numbers for all to see, so that Mantooth Strather was almost giddy with relief. Not because the stress of the investigation had lessened, but because for the first time, all that stress—the sheer effort being made to keep the mission from flying apart—finally seemed to have a purpose.

Two more Quantum II maneuvers were co-ordered, until the trio of vessels were hanging at the very edge of a small red dwarf's Kuiper region, staring down the star's gravity funnel to . . . something that couldn't be easily identified.

"What is it?" Sfisst-Captain rumbled over the ship-to-ship link, as Manny sat in his seat in the *Javelin*'s bridge module.

"It appears to be a shadow *within* a shadow," Manny replied, using his workstation to collate as much of the *Javelin*'s neutrino sensor data as his controls could manage. It had been a fluke, really. One moment they'd been following the "road" of the initial neutrino shadow, when the number of neutrinos dipped sharply a second time. So much so that Manny asked Spalding to jump them back two paces on their navigation sequence, then forward again to their present location—just to be sure that it hadn't been an instrumentation issue.

"What do the telescopes tell us?" 'Tec-Major Spalding asked the ARM officer hunched over the equipment operations station which had full command of the optics suite installed during *Javelin*'s construction.

"No large planets of which I can be sure," the 'Tec-Two said, his voice dryly academic in tone, while his hands gently touched the telescope's controls.

"Is it the star itself that's causing the new reading?" Spalding asked, looking over at Manny. He imported the optical enhancements from the telescopes as quickly as they came in, then shook his head negatively.

"No," he said. "This is something else. Do me a favor? Take us on Quantum II to this red dwarf's pole, but at the same relative distance from the star proper."

Within a few minutes, the three-ship combo was in solar orbit roughly over the stellar "north" of the red dwarf, and the neutrino density had jumped up considerably.

Jumping back to their original position—in solar orbit along the ecliptic—produced the same sharp trough as before.

"So it's in the plane," 'Tec-Major Spalding speculated.

"But no planets," said the 'Tec-Two at the optics console.

"No ordinary planet—nor any star for that matter—blocks neutrinos," Manny said. "This must be something else. It appears to be constant. Can we get some more imagery of the star, please? Infrared, ultraviolet, x-ray. Are there any prominences?"

"No prominences," Sfisst-Captain said ship-to-ship. "But one of my warriors believes he has discerned a straight-line occlusion. We're still slightly above the ecliptic—judging by the Kuiper belt— but if we come down to the plane proper, the occlusion might manifest itself more clearly."

Another Quantum II maneuver, and the three-ship trio was looking at what appeared to be a black rectangle directly across the face of the red dwarf. The two poles of the star were still visible. But at least thirty percent of the star's surface vanished into a cleanly-bordered blackness which left thirty-five percent shining toward one pole, and thirty-five percent shining toward another pole.

"Neutrino readings are now down ten additional percent," remarked the 'Tec-Two who was minding the neutrino sensor workstation.

"Confirmed," Manny said, using his own controls. He stared at the imagery, then looked at the neutrino sensor's live data, then went back to staring at the imagery again.

"What is it?" 'Tec-Major Spalding asked.

"Impossible to determine at this great distance," Sfisst-Captain replied.

Then Zrarr-Professor's voice was also on the ship-to-ship.

"We can't go too deep into that gravity well on Quantum II or Quantum I. Perhaps now is a good time to separate ships? Leave *Javelin* with the Number Four hull and proceed aboard *Glaring Eye* to make a full system survey."

There was a sputtering yowl—Sfisst objecting.

"We separate *nothing*," he replied firmly in Interworld. "I will not risk *Glaring Eye* while sabotage remains a threat. If the saboteur—or saboteurs?—commandeer *Javelin* while *Glaring Eye* is exploring the space close to this star, *Glaring Eye* will be stranded. No. We will get as close as Quantum II permits, and then use our gravity thrusters to proceed the rest of the distance. Even though the fuel use—for thrusters—will be far in excess of normal, due to us having the mass of the Number Four on our backs."

"I think I am inclined to agree with my counterpart," Spalding said. "Until or unless the investigation produces culprits we can put in the brig, separation seems like the perfect way to give them another chance to hurt us. So we go in together. This phenomenon is unlike anything I've ever seen, during any survey beyond Known Space. And I have done a *lot* of surveying."

"As have I," Sfisst said. "We must determine the nature of the artifact."

"Artifact?" Manny said.

"What else can it be?" Sfisst replied. "Nothing natural can explain what the telescopes are showing us. That occlusion is cleanly bordered, and blocks neutrinos. Depending on what we discover, this too may prove to be a 'trigger' for sabotage. I would like the ears of whoever is working internally to wound us—be they human, or kzin."

Spalding was nodding her head in silent agreement. She coordinated navigation and thrust orders with Sfisst-Captain, then beckoned Manny to follow her out of the bridge. They wound their way across the deck, through several connecting corridors, until they were in an observation alcove far off from the busily traveled portions of the ship. Light from the distant red dwarf made it just barely brighter than some of the stars surrounding it—suns much larger and younger, but also much farther away. The dwarf itself was doubtless ancient. A grandfatherly relic which had been slowly turning hydrogen into helium for billions of years, while other stars—bloated with hydrogen mass—rapidly passed through their life cycles, to end as nova or supernovae.

Manny stared out into deep space, then asked, "Why here?"

"Because I am to the point where I am not sure if people in my command group aren't part of the problem."

"Trust has eroded that far?" Manny asked, his eyes going wide.

"What the hell else did you expect?" Pryce hissed. "We've got two dead and three in autodoc, and you've come up zero. Did going through the wreck of the lander tell you *anything* new?"

"No," Manny admitted. "Did your systems maintenance people turn up even a shred of computer evidence to tell us who gimmicked the deck cameras during the co-murder?"

"No," she admitted.

"So, whoever is doing this seems to know ARM systems and procedures quite well, and probably has the clearance to conduct operations without tripping the system to the fact that he is up to no good."

"Maybe, but this doesn't tell us who set off the demolitions in the kzin hangar."

"I can't figure that one out either," Manny said, "though I told Zrarr-Professor we shouldn't rule out that it might have been the three kzinti in the autodoc who did it. If they live, they'll be out of the autodoc in a few days. We can try to interrogate them then."

"I suspect the saboteur will hit before that happens," she said firmly.

"I think you're right. And there may not be a lot we can do about it, except wait for something to go down, and hopefully this time—due to heightened vigilance on both the ARM side and the

Patriarchy side—we catch him. Or them? Or obtain evidence which leads us closer. But . . . I think I've uncovered an even bigger problem."

"What now?" the 'Tec-Major said, rubbing a palm over her face.

"Zrarr-Professor pointed it out to me, and it goes way beyond the saboteur."

"What do you mean?"

"He said the kzinti are spoiling for another war."

"That's stupid, of *course* the kzinti want another war! They've been wanting to refight us all our lives. They're damned *kzinti* for Finagle's sake!"

"Right, but Zrarr's gotten me to thinking that a lot of this comes down to how the kzinti see themselves. It's a paradigm problem. They won't accept perpetual armistice because they see themselves as winners who've been temporarily embarrassed by the rightful losers."

"I'm not sure I understand," Pryce said.

"For their entire history, the kzinti conquered. It's in their evolution. Apex predators. Then they ran into us, just before we got the hyperdrive. Successively lost wars have beaten a lot of apex attitude out of their bloodline, but it hasn't been removed entirely. And maybe it never will be? Consider Zrarr himself. Have you ever dealt with a kzin who is that eloquent and mannerly? Most of the ones I've dealt with are like Sfisst. He's a known quantity. Zrarr, on the other hand, is special. Though I haven't been able to get him to tell me why, exactly. And even he feels the burn—the sense that his people have been done *wrong*. By humanity, surely. But also by events. Fate? What have you. And they're looking for the next chance to make it *right*, in their eyes. It's their version of Manifest Destiny. Humanity winning wars doesn't make the Kzin happy in their losing. It just weeds out the impatient ones, while breeding future generations of kzinti who are more willing to wait, bide their time, play the diplomatic game, and then . . ."

"And then *what?*" Pryce demanded, almost up in Manny's face.

"I don't want to think about it. It's too close to something my Greatly Jack left in his personal secure ARM memoir. He said that sooner or later, it might come down to exterminating the rat-cats. Full genocide."

"We've been living peacefully with kzinti on Known Space worlds for centuries," she said. "Culture and species aren't the same thing. It's the *culture* of the Patriarchy that needs to change. That's the long game ARM is playing."

"Zrarr-Professor would probably agree with you," Manny said. "But you didn't look into his eyes. It was haunting. That Hero might be an example of the closest we ever get to a fully urbane, *humanized* kzin. But he's got a spiritual pain so deep . . . anyway, if he's the best of their lot, even after all these centuries, what does that say about the *worst* of their lot?"

Again, Spalding ran a hand over her face.

"Does this mean you think he's intentionally thwarting your investigation?"

"No," Manny said, backtracking. "I'm not implying he's insincere in his motives. Just honest about the fact that his people—in the aggregate—have never accepted the outcome of the Man-Kzin Wars. You can't have sustainable peace with a species who are determined to have their due."

The 'Tec-Major drew in a big breath, then let it out slowly.

"We're both tired. Go get some sleep, and wake up ready to attack this investigation with fresh eyes. Let ARM back on Earth figure out the cultural strategy with the kzinti. You just figure out if you can find the saboteurs—and if Zrarr-Professor is hindering your investigation, or not. Be prepared to handle the project on your own, if it comes to that."

"Is that your order, as *Javelin*'s skipper?" Manny asked.

"Damned right it is," Spalding said. Then she walked away.

Manny returned to his cabin, feeling both anxious and depressed. He was a firm believer in the idea that there was no such thing as a no-win. But even if the sabotage was stopped, and the mission successful, what did that mean for the future? What would happen when men or kzinti cracked the technical secrets of Quantum II? Instead of encompassing dozens of inhabited worlds, the contest between starfaring civilizations would expand to include thousands. Men and kzinti, forever dueling with one another, as each species leveled up its technology. Other species being roped in, bought off, played against each other, and ultimately dragged down. Maybe even extinguished?

Manny physically shivered.

ARM possessed artifacts and clues, from a different war, approximately two billion years in the past. The Slavers and the Tnuctipun left only fragments of themselves. Two fascinatingly different species, each with radically different morphology and aptitudes. Or so ARM had extrapolated. The one species seemingly controlled by the other. But the Tnuctipun had not accepted their lot, any more than the kzinti. And when the Slavers discovered the full extent of the Tnuctipun rebellion . . .

Manny didn't even take off his uniform. He flopped into his bunk and clamped his eyes shut, trying not to think of Quantum II fleets vying for supremacy over Known Space. Colonies and home planets brutalized—yet again—by interstellar savagery. Because humans were simply too good at it, when push came to shove. And kzinti considered it too essential to their character to let it go.

In the quiet darkness—with the light shut off—Manny never saw the hands that suddenly clamped down on his throat. They were impossibly strong. Warm to the touch, and smooth like a human's skin, but as irresistible as iron. Manny gagged for help, and found that he couldn't speak. When he tried to sit up, the hands kept him on his back. He reached up and clawed at the arms attached to the hands. With his heart racing, and unable to breathe, Manny thrashed in futility, until a voice whispered in his ear.

"Try to call for help, and I *will* kill you. But if you relax, and talk to me, I will let you live."

Manny went still. After a moment more, the hands loosened, and Manny lay in his bunk gasping for air. Additional seconds elapsed while Manny got sufficient oxygen back into his blood. Then he tried to talk.

"Who . . . ?"

"Not important."

"Clearly it's important enough for you to threaten my life," Manny said, managing to find his sense of humor.

"Whatever you may think of me, I am not your enemy," the voice said.

"But you'll kill me if I—"

"I can't have you delaying the inevitable," the voice interrupted.

"And what, precisely, is it that's inevitable?"

"You're already beginning to see it, Strather. The fact that a new war is just around the corner. The kzinti have been wanting it for a long, long time. ARM pretends publicly to not want it either, but we won't be caught with our pants down this time. Quantum II is too important for us to risk the rat-cats having it first."

"Quantum II is an official secret, yes," Manny said, swallowing hard, despite the grip on his neck, "but it's an official secret openly acknowledged between the two governments. The kzinti have already had their shot at the Number Four hull. If they were going to scoop humanity on Quantum II's mysteries, I think they'd have done it already."

"Your optimism is adorable," the voice said. Male. Older? Manny was trying hard to tell.

"You believe my optimism to be misplaced?"

"No," the voice said, tinged with regret. "But when you've been alive as long as some of us have—seen what some of us have seen— you get used to the fact that all the optimism in the world can't change certain realities. Sooner or later, one species or the other is going to be able to understand and reproduce Quantum II. Humanity *cannot* allow the kzinti to have it first. They may have it eventually. But only after men have so thoroughly surrounded the Patriarchy with new colonies and new Quantum II police flotillas that the kzinti will have no choice but to abide our terms."

"And if the kzinti beat us to it," Manny deduced, "they reclaim their lost colonies, including Wunderland, while also conquering Jinx and Home and We Made It—among other places—before encircling Sol and Earth."

"It is the only possible outcome, if the kzinti have Quantum II before we do. Which will *not* be allowed to happen."

Manny swallowed several times more, his thoughts spinning through his adrenaline-edged brain.

"Suppose all of this is too cynical?"

"Where a kzin is concerned," the voice said gravely, "a man cannot *be* too cynical."

"But what if you—we, us, the ARM—have it sideways?"

"Strather, you're not dumb. But you're gullible as hell if you think the Patriarchy wouldn't see us all dead, or enslaved, before you have grandchildren."

"I've been thinking about it," Manny said. "The Patriarchy cultural ego is badly bruised. What they need right now is a new challenge against which to measure themselves. The worst part about the armistice—for them—is that we men are so damned *nice* in our victory. The mind of the kzin struggles to comprehend human magnanimity. So their disgrace is doubled. But what if they had a new direction in which to go? A new foe to face?"

"I'm not tracking," the voice admitted.

"*Scrith* speaks of a species with technology far in advance of anything ARM can produce. The kzinti instinctively seek to match up against the biggest, baddest kid on the galactic block. For the past few hundred years, the biggest, baddest kid was us. But now there is potentially a much bigger, much badder kid out there. Somewhere. Once verified, the Patriarchy will shift its attention to the larger threat. Even if they replicate Quantum II before us—and I seriously doubt that's possible—they won't waste themselves against the worlds of Known Space. Not until the superior threat is vanquished. They will throw themselves against the new power. Because there is not nearly as much honor in defeating the nice guys from Earth as there is in facing down whoever or whatever can make *scrith*."

The voice was silent for several moments. Had Manny actually managed to talk his assailant around to his viewpoint?

"Strather, even if you're correct in your assumption—and you're not, trust me—imagine how much worse it will be if the Patriarchy wields both Quantum II and *scrith*? Even if they put all their strength into a war with a different species, when they win, or simply grow tired of being rebuffed, they'll take whatever technology they've stolen or scavenged, and fix their eyes on the worlds of men once more. The Patriarchy has a very good memory. Their defeat at the hands of men will not be allowed to go unanswered forever."

Manny agreed on that point, but didn't say it. He instead tried to think of a third angle—some other eventuality—but the voice kept talking.

"Nobody wants to hurt you," the man said. "But this whole thing is so much bigger than the life of a single human being. This is about all of Known Space now. Somehow Quantum II hyperdrive, *scrith*, the disappearance of the Puppeteers, the Patriarchy having abided the peace for far longer than they should have, it's all quickly tying together. What's needed now to ensure human survival are people unafraid to act. You can either let us do what we came on this mission to do, or you can risk being a victim of events. It's your choice."

"I take it to mean you want me to stop looking for you in all the wrong places?"

"I don't care if you look for me, just don't stop me from doing what must be done. Not me, and not anybody else with me, either."

Aha, Manny thought with a tiny feeling of triumph. *An admission that there are accomplices!*

"I can't promise that," Manny said honestly.

"Sure you can," the voice said.

"No, I can't."

"If this is about your oath as Science-Inspector, you can—"

"It's not that. No. It's that I don't want to let my boss down."

"We know Cedara Kellerman sent you. There'll be no shame in returning to Earth without being arm in arm with the kzinti. She knows this better than anybody."

"Shame's got nothing to do with it," Manny said, and tried to sit up again. The hands slammed him right back down on his bunk, and clamped down on his throat once more.

"Stay clear, and let it happen, or *else,*" the voice said in Manny's ear—so close that Manny could feel the moist warmth of the man's breath.

Then, just as suddenly, the hands were gone, and Manny was leaping up out of his bunk, into a defensive crouch on the deck. His lungs heaved air while he listened for the sound of feet. But there was nothing. As if the stranger had vanished into the inky blackness. When Manny verbally called for light, nothing happened. Eventually he found his way to the small panel near the hatch to the cabin, and manually palmed the overhead lamps.

Manny squinted as the light suddenly came up. His bedding was half on the deck, with the pillow in the middle of the cabin. But there was no one to be seen. Manny immediately eyed the air circulation vents—all of which seemed entirely too small for a man to quickly disappear through—and noted that not a single one of them appeared to be out of place. All the grates were still fastened tight.

"Damn," he said, rubbing his hands at his throat. There would be bruising. What was he going to tell 'Tec-Major Spalding?

Then Manny's feet went dead cold.

What if 'Tec-Major Spalding had *ordered* the visit?

He suddenly felt very, very alone, on a ship filled with people.

☙ CHAPTER 9 ☙

ZRARR-PROFESSOR dismissed the two guards who had stood watch at the entrance to the autodoc bay. He didn't think he had anything to fear from a warrior still encased in swooshing, gurgling machinery. While the other two kzinti who'd been wounded were sedated—their mangled flesh still too tender for even a brave kzin's nerves to manage—the third warrior was now lucid enough to talk. Zrarr thought the kzin a sorry sight. Every follicle of hair was gone. The kzin's exposed, nude face showed fresh, pink skin. The kind an autodoc grows when there has been third-degree burning. If this particular kzin had had scars to show for his life of service, they were gone now. Something Zrarr himself—had the situations been reversed—would have found quite upsetting.

"Do you see and know me?" Zrarr said softly, using the Heroes' Tongue.

"You are the Hero called Zrarr-Professor," the kzin said, then licked his bare lips once, wincing at the fact that his flesh was exposed.

"Do you know why I have come to see you, even before you are declared fit to return to duty?"

The injured kzin's eyes lost focus for a moment, as he appeared to gather his thoughts.

"You want to know what happened," the warrior said.

"Yes," Zrarr confirmed. "But, more than that, I want to know *why* it happened."

"It was an accident," the kzin said.

Zrarr made the kzin equivalent of a scoffing sound. The injured kzin's pink ears curled up tight against his head.

"I have examined the wreck of the lander," Zrarr said, "and determined the nature of the sabotage. Myself, and the human Science-Inspector who works at my side."

"*Works* at your side??" the injured kzin said, his eyes becoming large. "Then . . . the *Glaring Eye* is still mated to the *Javelin*?"

"It is. And we are."

The injured kzin's expression—made sadly comical by his lack of fur—changed from bafflement, to sorrow.

"The demolition charges were expertly done," Zrarr said academically. "Just enough explosive in the right places to reduce the lander to scrap. But not so much that *Glaring Eye* itself was in peril."

"The men of ARM are monkey-clever," the injured kzin spat, his eyes narrowing.

Again, Zrarr made the kzin equivalent of a scoffing sound.

"I have had time, during your recuperation, to do a thorough chemical analysis. Demolitions leave residue. And while the wreck of the lander itself was too contaminated for me to deduce much, I took the liberty of inspecting the filters from one of the ventilators that serves the launch bay. In the moments following the explosion, a great deal of vapor was sucked through those ventilators before the automatics doused the entire wreck in foam. The chemical signature of that vapor is distinctly kzin in manufacture. So, either ARM is so monkey-clever as to sneak into our munitions lockers and steal our own explosives out from under our very whiskers, or this sabotage was homegrown. Tell me, Weapons Technician, was attempted murder always your plan?"

"Attempted murder??" the injured kzin said, his voice rising—as much as it could, given his delicate condition.

"Two others were caught in the blast—in addition to yourself."

The injured kzin did not blink for several moments, then he let his head slowly come to rest on the cushioned headrest that stuck out of the top of the autodoc. The noise of fluids moving through the machinery was very loud in Zrarr's attentive ears.

"Unfortunate," the injured kzin finally said.

"Almost. Like you, they should live."

"What then is your intention, Zrarr-Professor?" the injured kzin asked.

"Based on my deductions, we could hold you in confinement until Pilot Primary and Pilot Secondary are both healthy enough to challenge you in a duel of honor."

"They should not have been aboard," the injured kzin said firmly.

"I checked their training request—through command—for seat time, performing ground checks in the cockpit. Shall I tell you what I think happened? You were aboard—as you should have been, inspecting the lander's tactical stores—when you decided to place the demolitions. Given the potency of the plastic explosive used, it would not have taken much. But you were nervous. In a hurry. So you forgot to see who else would be aboard. Pilot Primary and Pilot Secondary arrived before you could effectively finish. Then you rushed to leave, and in your haste, something with your trigger or timing mechanism went wrong. A premature detonation occurred. Am I right?"

The injured kzin merely stared up at the lamps recessed into the ceiling of the medical compartment.

"They should not have been aboard," he said, after a lengthy pause—reasserting his initial statement.

"But they were. And even if you had managed to get all the way out of the launch bay before the charges went, I'd still consider you my number-one suspect. You were aboard the lander in the time prior to its destruction, you had access to the necessary demolitions, and also the know-how to use them properly. If no one had interrupted your work, the lander itself would have been destroyed without casualties. But Sfisst-Captain would have been sufficiently enraged to assume ARM responsibility."

"The ARM *is* responsible!" the injured kzin said, his teeth bared. "Sfisst-Captain should destroy the *Javelin* and seize the Number Four hull for the Patriarch."

"Doubtless your sentiment is shared by many aboard *Glaring Eye*," Zrarr said.

"Except *you*," the injured kzin spat with contempt.

"You dare to use that tone with a Hero?" Zrarr said, feeling his pulse quicken.

"Traitors to the Patriarchy deserve no better," the injured kzin said, his teeth still bared.

Zrarr-Professor experienced—for a brief instant—the lightning-fast urge to swipe at the injured kzin's neck, and watch the saboteur's life run down his claws. But he controlled his temper. There was much more at stake now that Zrarr was sure there were kzinti, as well as men, actively working to ruin the mission.

"I credit you with the courage of one who has discovered he has nothing left to lose," Zrarr said. "So, please, no more attempting to hide what cannot be hidden. That is unworthy of a warrior."

"We cooperate with ARM at our peril," the injured kzin said, turning his gaze away from Zrarr's.

"Every kzin aboard *Glaring Eye* realizes the risk we take while working with the men from Earth. But men have worked with kzinti before. Not every interspecies enterprise has ended in bloodshed. Some might even say that working with ARM at this particular moment in time is to our distinct benefit. Since for all we know, ARM has already duplicated the Quantum II drive. Can you be sure that renewed hostilities wouldn't result in another disaster for the Patriarchy? You—and others like you—are the proverbial kit who becomes obsessed with fire. Too enamored to keep yourselves from getting burned. Only, the rest of us will get burned with you. Such as Pilot Primary and Pilot Secondary."

"Spoken like the son of an expatriated sthondat," the injured kzin said, still not looking at Zrarr-Professor.

The injured kzin was goading Zrarr now. Trying to incite Zrarr to finish him. Before a proper contest of honor could be arranged.

"If we were carrying a telepath, I'd have him strip the thoughts from your skull," Zrarr said. "But Patriarchy Command decided it would not demonstrate good faith if a telepath were aboard *Glaring Eye*. ARM would have regarded it with suspicion. Unless, of course, such a telepath would have divined your treachery before it took place? So, there are two reasons why Patriarchy Command might want to send *Glaring Eye* without a valuable asset. Being on orders is the one thing that might spare you from total dishonor, Weapons Technician. I just need the identities of who sent you, and who else aboard might be under those same orders."

The injured kzin kept his mouth shut.

"Or I can just tell Sfisst-Captain that the whole thing was your idea, and I've gotten all there is to get out of you."

"Sfisst-Captain will elect execution," Weapons Technician said.

"Probably. But you know what? It would serve you right. Especially since you've made a liar out of me."

"I don't understand," the injured kzin said.

"Nor should you," Zrarr replied, sniffing disdainfully, then stood up from his seat, and stomped out of the medical compartment. He signaled for the guards to resume their watch before tracing his way back to his stateroom. Once there, he hesitated for a few moments—pondering if there might be some hidden danger awaiting over the threshold—and opened the hatch.

Mantooth Strather's sleepless, distressed face greeted him.

"You came on your own?" Zrarr asked with surprise.

"Yes," Manny admitted.

"That was either brave, or foolish."

"More like desperate," the Sci-Spec said.

"Have you discovered something?"

"Yes," the human said. "Somebody aboard *Javelin* threatened to kill me an hour ago."

"Who?"

"I don't know. They broke into my cabin and almost choked the life out of me, before disappearing."

"Perform a forensic DNA sweep on your cabin immediately!"

"I didn't dare," Manny admitted.

"Why?" Zrarr demanded, then noticed the two duffel bags sitting under Strather's feet, while Strather made himself comfortable in one of Zrarr's kzin-sized reclining chairs, which could also double as a g-chair under combat duress.

"You're afraid of your own people," Zrarr deduced. "*Glaring Eye* is your safe harbor now."

"I don't think I can trust a single soul aboard *Javelin*."

Strather must have noticed Zrarr's expression, because the man added, "Looks like maybe the sentiment is mutual?"

"This treachery is cutting both ways, Science-Inspector. Humans. Kzinti. I almost killed one of my own people today. Out of pique. He wanted me to do it. I stopped myself."

"Why?"

"Because . . ." And this was where Zrarr-Professor had to think about it. "Because, like Sfisst-Captain, I hate being manipulated. There are kzinti aboard acting on orders from someone in Patriarchy Command. Officers who decided, long before this mission was ever launched, to ruin us."

"Is Sfisst-Captain in on it?"

"Frankly, given the fact Sfisst-Captain has elected *not* to attack the *Javelin* or her crew, I think that Hero is blameless. He detests the ARM. But if he were in on it, he'd not have hesitated to initiate fighting the moment the lander went up. Somebody is trying to steer him into combat, in spite of our attempts—yours and mine—to avert the crisis. You don't need to steer a kzin to fight, whose mind to shed blood is already made up."

"True," Strather said.

"If you're aboard *Glaring Eye* to stay, this means you aren't affording 'Tec-Major Spalding the same benefit of the doubt."

Manny hopped down from his seat and began walking in a small circle.

"I don't know for sure that I think Pryce is in on it," the human said, "but I can't be certain she's innocent, either. It's a very difficult thing to break into a man's quarters aboard an ARM ship, then disappear without a trace. There are people aboard *Javelin* very interested in ensuring that I can't find out who they are. Though I can now be certain of what they will do. Word of my departure is almost certain to have reached them by now. They will assume the worst, and if I set foot on *Javelin* again, they're liable to keep their promise to kill me."

Now it was Zrarr's turn to have a seat. He reclined in the large chair opposite where Strather had recently been resting, and curled his digits thoughtfully beneath his feline mouth.

"Life for you here may be no easier than it was aboard your ARM vessel. Is the 'Tec-Major aware that you've left permanently?"

"I didn't say a word," Strather said.

"And the security at the crossing, what did they have to say about your luggage?"

"I told them it was equipment I needed for the investigation."

"What is it really?"

"Uniforms, toiletries, and my environment suit."

"The autochefs aboard *Glaring Eye* are not programmed with human cuisine. You may not like what you have to eat. Raw meats are not to the liking of most humans. Especially raw meats like a Hero can find on the banquet tables of Kzin-home."

"I brought some spacer rations too," Strather assured him.

Zrarr continued to ponder the situation.

"Even if staying here—in my quarters—assures you relative safety from those aboard *Javelin* who would do you harm, it will not assure you safety from those aboard *Glaring Eye* who intend the same. Perhaps it would be best if we took what we've found to Sfisst-Captain, and then 'Tec-Major Spalding, in that order? Sfisst-Captain is liable to be somewhat mollified, once he learns that it was one of his own who destroyed the lander. If he learns also that you yourself have been threatened from within your own ranks, he will be motivated to forge some kind of tripartite alliance. I suggest that if Spalding is not a good candidate, somebody else be chosen."

"Problem is I don't know any of them," Strather admitted. "ARM is very, very big. So big nobody is really sure how many humans it employs, on Earth, and elsewhere. It's impossible for one person to be friendly with everybody. Spalding and the others come from the stealth fleet that keeps an eye on Patriarchy territory."

Zrarr stared at the human.

"What?" the Sci-Spec said defensively. "As if the Patriarchy doesn't play that game too?"

Zrarr blinked a few times, wanting to retort. But couldn't. He wasn't privy to Patriarchy Command's current strategy at the same level as Sfisst-Captain, but even Zrarr knew that the Patriarchy had "dark ships" patrolling very far from the worlds of kzin ownership. Quiet vessels which watched the vast spaces between the stars. Waiting for any sign of aggression against the Patriarchy, whether that aggression came from the worlds of men, or somewhere else.

"Anyone I might suggest," Strather said, "is as likely to be in on the sabotage as not. Whoever threatened me seems to be conducting their operations aboard *Javelin* completely unimpeded. I can't say for sure that Spalding is dirty, but I don't know who gets away with things like that aboard an ARM ship without the skipper turning a blind eye."

"Perhaps we do this," Zrarr said, forming a plan in his mind. "We go to Sfisst-Captain now. Tell him everything we know. I believe he will be amenable to having you aboard as temporary party, beneath the guise of the investigation. We ensure that you never go to the *Javelin* unless I am with you, and you're never aboard *Glaring Eye* without my escort either."

"I confess I never thought I'd need a grown kzin to keep me safe from my own people, as well as his own," Strather said, putting both palms over his face and rubbing.

"This voyage may grow stranger yet, my friend," Zrarr cautioned.

🐾 CHAPTER 10 🐾

TO MANNY'S great surprise, Sfisst-Captain took the news sitting down. Having dismissed his other officers from his presence, Sfisst conferenced with Zrarr-Professor and Manny alone, receiving their reports in turn, then devoted himself to several minutes staring out a porthole into space. When he was done with his reverie, he verbally granted Manny the Patriarch's protection aboard *Glaring Eye* and swore that he would do everything he could to ensure Manny's safety. Followed by peremptorily ordering the execution of the Weapons Technician still in the autodoc.

"Sfisst-Captain," Zrarr said, "we may yet need him."

"For information?" the kzin leader asked.

"Yes," Zrarr said.

"I think making a statement has become my first priority," Sfisst said. "If you are certain of that kzin's guilt—"

"I am," Zrarr said firmly.

"—then I will let every warrior aboard the *Glaring Eye* know that I do not tolerate sabotage. Whether your deduction that this warrior was acting on orders from someone at Patriarchy Command is correct, or not. Destruction of the Patriarch's property must be punished. Attempted murder of the Patriarch's own flyers must also be punished. If there are other kzinti aboard who intend the same actions as the Weapons Technician, they must understand that it will mean their deaths. Ignoble. Without honor. Lives terminated by a Hero with both the authority, and the will, to make it so."

"As you see fit," Zrarr acquiesced. "You might be right. Anyone plotting further sabotage could think twice, if one of their own meets such a humiliating end."

"As well they should," Sfisst rumbled. "Now, Sci-Spec Strather, you should understand that I don't trust you much more than I trust any other ARM. But I cannot deduce why a human in your position would seek asylum aboard a Patriarchy ship from his own kind. Not without it being a matter of expedient need. You say you cannot vouch for 'Tec-Major Spalding, or her other officers. If one of my officers said something similar about me, it would be an insult worthy of blood challenge. So, you are either foolish to do this, or acting as courageously as a monkey knows how to act. In either case, your protection hinges on your continued work with Zrarr-Professor. If at any point I deduce that you are acting contrary to the best interests of *Glaring Eye* I will expel you to *Javelin* permanently. Is that understood?"

"Perfectly clear, sir," Manny said. Then asked, "How will Weapons Technician die?"

"What?" Sfisst-Captain said.

"An ignoble death for a kzin. What does that look like?"

"We simply turn the autodoc off. He will never again stand on his own, aboard this ship. There will be no chance to challenge another warrior. No last moment of glory. Zrarr is right, in that both the Primary Pilot and Secondary Pilot have earned satisfaction in this regard, and it pains me as their commander to have to deny them what they are owed. But I have to make an example. A camera will capture the death of Weapons Technician as he slowly suffocates, blood and fluids leaking past his lips. He will be unable to move. Prevented by his own feebleness from uttering even a final scream. He will die the death of an impotent. *That*, Science-Inspector, is a fate to make any Hero shudder. It will have an even bigger impact on the unnamed still seeking their own chances for glory."

And so it was done. Just as Sfisst-Captain described. *Glaring Eye*'s bridge crew all paused in the conduct of their duties—as every kzin aboard had been commanded—to watch the death of the saboteur. Who could not lift a claw to help himself, dying with a look in his eyes that bordered on rage.

When it was over, Zrarr escorted Manny back to Zrarr's quarters.

"The effect on the crew has been noticeable," he said.

"How can you tell?" Manny asked.

"You would not smell it, but I do. Every warrior instinctively cringed. It was horrible for them to behold. Not a one of them would ever wish such a thing, not even on a hated rival. If Sfisst-Captain wanted deterrence, he may well get it. Even from kzinti who are operating on orders from above Sfisst. What's the reaction been on the 'Tec-Major's side?"

"She sent her regrets for the entire chain of events. And also passed along her hope that the mission can proceed without further incident."

"No mention of anything untoward happening aboard her own vessel?"

"She doesn't know about someone trying to strangle me in my bed," Manny reminded.

"Of course," Zrarr said.

The trip to the inner part of the red dwarf system proceeded without incident. Using gravity thrusters—versus the old fusion rockets of many centuries earlier—allowed the voyage to be made in a fraction of the time it might have otherwise taken. With no noticeable impact on either the *Glaring Eye* or the *Javelin*. Their crews experiencing the voyage at one Kzin-home g and one Earth g, respectively. When the three-ship trio was perhaps half an astronomical unit from the surface of the red dwarf—now burning brightly in their naked eye view, as well as on the telescopes—they assumed a roughly circular solar orbit, and took a closer look at what it was they'd stumbled upon.

"It's a solid mass," Manny said, having reassumed his place at the Sci-Spec station on *Javelin*'s bridge, but with Zrarr close at hand.

"Urrrrr," Zrarr uttered, his tail twisting back and forth in the air. "And moving. Note the tiny loops we now see at the edges of the thing? They pass perceptibly as the telescopes observe the star itself. And at regular intervals. Structures attached to the main object, though for what purpose it's not clear."

The expedition moved in, until almost the entire star had been obscured, and one whole side of space was a black nothingness which could only be discerned by starlight optics enhancement.

"The surface is variable," Manny observed, then used his controls to expand the enhanced imagery on *Javelin*'s main bridge projection system. A false-color holographic of the object appeared. Its surface was typified by geometrically precise shapes, either depressed below or raised above the median surface elevation. Squares, triangles, rectangles, hexagons, pentagons, all passing to *Javelin*'s starboard as the object moved—rotated? orbited?—about the red dwarf. Gradually, the large geometric patterns gave way to more intricate and also irregular shapes, which were then succeeded by what Manny could only describe as mountains, valleys, plateaus, and basins.

"It's a circle," 'Tec-Major Spalding said, staring into the false-color holographic imagery. "An enormous circle, like something a child might create to make the first link in a paper chain. Except this piece of paper is seventy thousand kilometers wide!"

"Bigger than Neptune is tall," said the 'Tec-Two minding *Javelin*'s telescope.

"The observable rate of motion is too fast for a solar orbit," Zrarr remarked.

"How can you tell that?" Manny asked.

"I have eyes," was all Zrarr said in reply.

Manny quickly computed the object's rate—surface features passing one after the other—and was startled to discover that Zrarr-Professor was correct. The rate of motion did exceed stellar orbital velocity for the object's relative distance from the red dwarf. And there were almost no observable breaks in the structure, allowing light from the red dwarf to get through, except for the occasional pinhole.

'Tec-Major Spalding ordered a position change, which Sfisst-Captain approved. Before long, the gravity thrusters had pushed the ships up above the plane of the ecliptic sufficiently for them to see past the object and into the red dwarf's heart. The star—with red-to-orange corona and yellow-to-white center—was still too bright to observe directly without instruments. But the object itself was clearly visible unaided. It looped around the red dwarf like a huge, thin belt. The underside—from *Javelin*'s point of view—was illuminated perpetually. The same geometric evolution which had been visible on the dark side was even more dramatically visible on the bright side: regular shapes in rows and formations, each giving way to still more complex patterns, until the landscape seemed almost recognizably terrestrial.

And then the entire thing cut off. A cleanly flat surface from one side of the ring to the other. And it appeared to remain this way for tens of thousands of kilometers before the geometric shapes began to appear again. First, in ones and twos. Then, becoming more frequent. And so on, and so forth. A pattern of least complexity progressing to most complexity, repeating itself at least twice across the entire object—from what they were able to tell at their distance.

The tri-ship expedition dropped back into the shadow of the object.

"Neutrino readings now in the basement," Manny reported. "If we wanted to find the source of *scrith*, I think we've done it."

"Any sign of other ships?" Sfisst-Captain's voice asked over the ship-to-ship net.

"None," 'Tec-Major Spalding said. "We've been looking constantly since we first arrived in this system. There's nothing. No radio broadcasts. No communications lasers. And we've not observed any vehicles nor vessels in motion about the object. Nor anything in apparent stellar orbit either. Though we'll keep looking. Even around a tiny red dwarf, space is still very, very big."

"I know that," Sfisst-Captain snapped. "My chief concern is threat awareness. I find it hard to believe that we could be allowed to approach this object without interception. The Patriarchy—were it in possession of such a mighty artifact—would never allow a foreign vessel anywhere near without proper escort."

"Accounts are of a potentially fallen civilization," Manny said, looking up from his controls. "Maybe the builders aren't around anymore to keep strangers away?"

"There's something else, too," Zrarr said. "Please do a temperature reading on the bright side."

One of the other *Javelin* officers—a female 'Tec Three—busied herself with her controls.

"Infrared shows an average ambient surface temperature of two hundred Celsius, give or take about twenty-five degrees, depending on the variable shape of the landscape."

"Too hot for liquid water," Zrarr said. "Urrrr."

"What's the problem?" Manny asked.

"The account of the Hero named Chmeee spoke of great amounts of liquid water. There is absolutely no evidence of that here. And as large as this object may be, it's not located at the right kind of star. Chmeee told of a yellow dwarf, not red. I am beginning to believe that if we have located the source of *scrith*, it's a different source from that which Chmeee visited."

"How can we be sure?" Manny asked. "Neither Chmeee, nor anyone else who originally used the Quantum II hyperdrive, was available to give us additional specifics. Or at least, ARM didn't declassify enough specifics for us to really get a handle on whether or not this . . . thing . . . whatever we're going to call it, is the same place the Number Four visited before."

"The Patriarchy has kept details classified to a similar degree," Sfisst-Captain said. "Nevertheless, according to my own computations, the stress placed on the object—spinning as it is—would be great enough to destroy even the strongest hull steel in the Patriarchy inventory."

"Could it be a Puppeteer artifact?" 'Tec-Major Spalding wondered aloud, her knees pressed together, while her elbows were on her armrests—rigid with the anticipation of discovery.

"That could be," Zrarr-Professor said. "But the Puppeteers are elusive. Coy. I do not understand why they would construct something of this scale, and out of a material approaching General Products hull quality, but not *at* General Products hull quality, just to abandon it. That would be careless on their part. I think we therefore have to assume that it's not Puppeteer in origin."

"It's not anyone from Known Space, that's for sure," Manny muttered, continuing to project a false-color view of the dark side of the ring as the geometric progression of the ring's topography repeated itself. Over, and over, and over again. Squares, rectangles, hexagons, pentagons, pressed into or extruded out of the artifact's material—presumably *scrith,* based on the neutrino shadow.

"Slaver?" Spalding guessed.

"Or Tnuctipun," Sfisst said.

"Take us in closer, please," Manny asked.

'Tec-Major Spalding simply stared into the various screens at her skipper's station, marveling at all the imagery and numbers coming through, then shook her head, and conferred with Sfisst-Captain.

The trio of ships closed to within ten thousand kilometers. At that distance, the rotational rate of the artifact was quite apparent, with formations racing past much faster than the tri-ship expedition traveled in its mere stellar orbit.

"The local gravity is negligibly affected," Manny said.

"Good," 'Tec-Major Spalding said. "I don't want us getting pulled into that thing."

"It's difficult to get an estimate for the object's total mass," Manny said.

On the visual spectrum, one of the formerly tiny pinholes zoomed past.

"Please take that back and replay it again," Zrarr-Professor asked.

One of the other bridge crew—a 'Tec-Three male—complied.

The point of light moved quickly, but the replay was slowed down enough for everyone on the bridge to get a good look at the starlight streaming through the hole at the bottom of an inverted cone, which marred an otherwise symmetrical chain of octagons.

Suddenly, Manny had an epiphany.

"How dangerous would it be for us to approach this close, only on the bright side?" he asked.

"Not any more dangerous than being on the dark side," 'Tec-Major Spalding replied. "Hull temps will go up, but we're still plenty far away from the red dwarf that it should not be a problem. Why?"

"I just need to see something, please."

Spalding and Sfisst complied.

"What's your thought, friend?" Zrarr said, placing one of his fur-covered, beefy paws on the back of Manny's chair.

"Something my boss told me before I left Earth," Manny said.

Within a few minutes, they'd repositioned themselves in solar orbit inside the loop's circumference. Now, the topography of the artifact blazed back at them in brilliantly visible sunshine, albeit dimmed and tinged orange, when compared to the blinding yellow-white of a Sol day on Earth. The same geometric formations flowed past them, gradually giving way to more and more complex patterns, before finally the artifact took on an almost terrestrial quality, until—the cutoff for the bright side was stark. All formations suddenly ended, in a straight line all the way from one side of the loop to the other. Giving way to nothing but a flat, perfect, featureless surface.

Except for the pinhole.

Only, it wasn't a pinhole. More like the perforated tip of a very large cone.

"Did we record that?" Manny asked.

"We've been recording everything for hours," Spalding said.

"Replay it."

The main bridge hologram transformed into an enlarged view of the cone as it swept by—again, slowed down for closer visual inspection. There was a period of about thirty seconds where the top of the cone, which was essentially a round, black hole, aligned with *Javelin* such that the *Javelin*'s scopes were staring straight through, and out into deep space beyond.

"Dragged to the top of a mountain, and fell through . . ." Manny said absently, a smile cracking the corners of his mouth.

"What?" Spalding asked.

"Nothing," Manny said, but kept smiling—in spite of the tension and anxiety of the past few days.

"What do you think it is?" Zrarr-Professor asked, staring into the holographic replay. "We've seen several of these now, at random points."

"Punctures," Manny said. "Probably the result of material on long-orbit trajectories—at Oort distances—eventually intercepting the artifact's surface."

"Versus asteroids?" 'Tec-Major Spalding asked.

"We didn't see anything like an asteroid field, coming in. Just like we didn't see any planets either. As a matter of fact, now that we're inside, we're not finding terrestrials. The whole system is *empty*. Except for this artifact."

"More proof that this is not Puppeteer," Zrarr said. "I doubt the Puppeteers would allow one of their structures to remain vulnerable to long-period comets."

"Urrr, concur," Sfisst-Captain said. "The leaf-eaters are obsessively thorough in their self-protectiveness."

"So it's not Puppeteers, stet," Manny said.

"But it's also not anyone who seems to be presently paying much attention to the outside universe, either," 'Tec-Major Spalding said. "Radio is quiet. Not a single foreign contact on our scopes. If they had ships, those ships have since gone away."

"Let's keep looking at it," Manny suggested. "There's a lot of real estate down there."

"Apparently disused," Zrarr said skeptically.

"Maybe," Manny said.

The expedition remained in solar orbit for half a day, taking additional neutrino readings—to compare the bright and dark zones, as well as getting a wealth of telescope data across the electromagnetic spectrum. All of which confirmed that the object matched the known properties of *scrith* so far as men and kzinti had been able to understand them.

"Thickness—the depth of the structure—doesn't seem to vary," Manny said.

"But the surface formations vary a great deal," Zrarr pointed out.

"Yah, but the actual width of the object isn't much more than fifty meters."

"How can you deduce that?"

Manny smiled, and was about to retort, *I have eyes!* Then thought better of it, and instead pointed to a table of aggregate measurements he'd taken since their arrival within close proximity to the *scrith* artifact. The thickness of the ring itself was consistent, whether at the bottom of a rectangle, or the top of a triangle. Even the formations approaching terrestrial complexity were consistent. The only exceptions were the circular areas surrounding the pinholes, where the thickness decreased from just over fifty meters down past six centimeter at the very top—or bottom—of what Manny had come to think of as extinction-event impact zones. Assuming anything had ever lived on the ring, or in the thickness of the structure itself. The energy released by a comet hitting the artifact at interplanetary speed was catastrophically sufficient to deform *scrith* to the point that it finally ruptured.

So, definitely not as good as a General Products hull. But damned better than anything men had ever learned to make.

"I've found something you might want to take a look at, sir," said the 'Tec-Two on the telescope.

"What?" Manny asked.

"I've been examining those hoops at the artifact's edges—the ones regularly spaced all the way around, on both sides—and I think I've spotted something that might be a ship."

"Let's see it," Manny and Spalding said in unison.

The telescope view was transferred to the big holographic projector, and suddenly the entire bridge was looking at a mass distinctly separate from the artifact, in stellar orbit just outside of the artifact's circumference. It was sixty degrees around the perimeter from where *Javelin* orbited with *Glaring Eye* on her belly and the #4 hull sticking up out of the metal cup on her spine. The motion of the new object was distinctly separate from that of the ring proper, as the tiny shapes of the hoops—function undetermined—passed in front of the object.

"Still no radio," Spalding said. "Whatever it is, it's not talking to us."

"Maybe they haven't noticed us yet," Manny speculated.

"With this great big transparent ball—and all the machinery inside—advertising our presence? I doubt it. If there's somebody still around to keep the pilot light on, they're either so unconcerned about visitors that they're not even looking, or we're dealing with an alien mind so *utterly* alien, it thinks in ways neither a human nor a kzin can understand."

"That is a distinct possibility," Zrarr said. "After all, what civilization would embark upon a project like this, simply to see it fall into disrepair?"

"We don't even know what this object *is*," Manny pointed out. "Does it *do* something? It's huge. Somebody put it here for a reason."

"Your Easter Island, on Earth," Zrarr-Professor said.

"Huh?" Manny blurted.

"The *moai* statues. Or perhaps Stonehenge is a better example? Not everything large or impressive—especially from the past—has an easily identifiable function. Kzin-home features similar archeological sites. I have visited a few of them. How or why ancient kzinti devoted so much time and work to these places is a topic for debate even to this day."

"But these . . . *people,* who created this ring," Manny said, "they were spacefarers. Intelligent sapients capable of producing not just modern materials and tools, but materials and tools which surpass anything we have in Known Space. It stands to reason we're not looking at the burial tomb of an interstellar pharaoh."

"Can you be so sure?" Zrarr-Professor said. "A very powerful ruler—of any species—might go to considerable trouble to commemorate his time on the fooch."

"Spacefarers always build in predictable ways," Manny said.

"Why do you believe this?" Zrarr asked.

"Because of the problems each spacefaring species has had to face in its history. The same physics problems which confronted humanity also confronted kzinti, and at some point far back in history, Puppeteers. Or the Slavers, and the Tnuctipun."

"I do not think the Slavers would have built something merely to see it populated with hominids. Who are entirely absent from both the bright and dark sides of this artifact. Mantooth, I believe that we have not in fact found the place described by Chmeee. Rather, this is something a lot like it. Built either by the same species responsible for the destination described in Chmeee's account, or by another species with equivalent materials technology."

"Which takes me back to wondering what it's for," Manny said, his thumbnail tapping on his teeth, as he stared at one of the bigger screens on his workstation. It showed the object the 'Tec-Two had located. Was it a piece of the actual ring, broken off, and now in close stellar orbit? Or something else again?

There was only one way to find out.

☙ CHAPTER 11 ☙

IT TOOK THEM AWHILE to cross the interplanetary distance to the far side of the loop, since the Quantum II motor wouldn't function this deep in the red dwarf's gravity well. When they arrived, Zrarr reassumed his place as Sci-Spec Strather's chaperone. Only this time they were aboard *Glaring Eye*, and observing events from the kzin perspective. There was much less chatter under Sfisst-Captain's watch. No subordinates tossing theories about. Just silence, and the occasional communications with *Javelin*. When Sfisst ordered something, it happened. When he asked a question, he got an answer. But the crew busied themselves at their assigned stations in the way good warriors should, without extraneous discussion.

Not until the new object was in full view did the bridge crew look up from their tasks, and marvel at the apparent size of the thing.

"Urrrr," Sfisst-Captain uttered.

"It has to be at least a thousand kilometers long!" Strather said, echoing Sfisst's sentiment.

The rectangle was clean edged, and orbiting the red dwarf perhaps half a million kilometers outside of the huge loop's path. Half illuminated by light from the red dwarf, and half in shadow, telescope observation revealed a great deal more variety than had been observed on the main artifact. There were huge bay hatchways—some opened, some closed—as well as what appeared to be stacked modules in regular geometric shapes. Great gantries and cranes were constructed around the bay mouths, and the edge of the rectangle featured the same smaller hoops which could be seen

294

at the edges of the main artifact. Plus, the object was covered by an absurdly large number of solar panels. Square kilometer after square kilometer of them.

"I'm only guessing," Strather said. "But it seems to me the hoops are there for attitude control. Notice how they come in clusters, and their axes aim in toward the star? Even this smaller object has them aimed toward the star, with the flat part of the object face-on. If the hoops are magnetic constrictors, the clusters could be ramjets."

"Utilizing the red dwarf's stellar wind for fuel," Zrarr said, finishing the thought.

"Yes," Strather said.

"But why not use gravity thrusters?" Sfisst-Captain asked. "Surely gravity thrusters would be more efficient, not to mention more effective."

"Good question," Strather said.

"Speaking of ramjets," Zrarr said, "what do you make of that?"

The commander's viewer—over which Sfisst had full control—was quickly slaved to Zrarr's workstation, showing one of the gargantuan, open bay mouths leading to the rectangle's interior. An elongated pill-capsule shape was suspended by gantries in the aperture. Its length was surrounded by several toroidal hoops, and there was a mushroom-shaped shield protecting one end.

"Not too different from what Earth used in the beginning," Manny said. "But Earth never built anything that enormous."

Dialing up the telescope magnification revealed line after line of portholes along the lozenge's side. Deck after deck? At least fifty decks, or more. But the portholes appeared dark. And there was still no indication that the builders were even aware of the expedition's existence.

"Not exactly a Lazy Eight, is it?" remarked the voice of 'Tec-Major Spalding.

"Urrr?" Sfisst-Captain voiced.

"One of our early colony boat designs," Strather explained. "Crew space was at a premium. Back before hyperdrive. I'd wager you could fit a hundred times as many people aboard *that* derelict."

"Portholes suggesting decks, which also suggest morphology similar to our own," Zrarr said, panning the telescope view carefully.

"We won't know for sure until we have a closer look," Strather said.

"Regional gravity is still negligible," Zrarr observed. "If the open bays are an indicator, the entire rectangle may be hollow."

"A hangar station for ships come to visit the main artifact?" Sfisst-Captain speculated.

"So it would seem," Zrarr agreed.

"Or a shipyard for constructing vessels capable of going to other stars," Strather thought out loud, flipping their speculation on its ear.

"But using *ramjets* of all things?" Sfisst-Captain said, incredulous. "It doesn't make any sense. A civilization capable of producing *scrith* would not bother with ramjets. They would have the hyperspace shunt before . . . urrrr, now I see it. If you have the hyperspace shunt, you can reach other stars with ease. Why go to the trouble of building on such a large scale? But if you *don't* have the hyperspace shunt, your incentive to build locally is greatly increased. Still, it is rather fantastic that sapients could be so far ahead of us in materials research and production, yet so far behind us in interstellar travel methods."

"Minds very unlike our own . . ." Zrarr said absently.

"Or they didn't come into contact with any species already using Quantum I," Strather said. "Like how Known Space got the hyperdrive."

"Begging your pardon, sir," said one of the nameless warriors who'd kept silent to that point.

"Speak," Sfisst-Captain said.

"When I examine the suspected vehicle suspended at the gantries, I do not detect *scrith*. The structure around the vehicle is definitely *scrith*. But the vehicle itself is more ordinary."

"Urrr?" Zrarr-Professor uttered.

A long moment of silence followed, while everyone in the compartment busied himself at his workstation.

"Urrr! Confirmed!" Sfisst-Captain said. "Spectrographic analysis seems to indicate something close to conventional hull steel."

"Why build their space dock from *scrith*, but not the ship itself?" Strather asked.

Zrarr-Professor's mind was churning. Again, he wished for a telepath. Someone who could reach across the distance of space, and

discern if there were other minds at work. Presently, the expedition
was blind. On the precipice of comprehension, surely. But not
knowing in fact. It was aggravating, like a mental toothache. Until or
unless they performed physical inspection—of the spacecraft, its
interior, and the space dock proper—they were merely spinning out
educated guesses.

"Sfisst-Captain, we must land," Zrarr said emphatically.

"With the Number Four on top of us?" Sfisst said.

"Docking is more like it," Strather said gently. "If that vessel—the
one we've been looking at—had tried to land under Earth-normal g,
it would have crushed itself beneath its own weight. We should
maneuver into position to mate with the space dock. Or at least get
ourselves close enough to go across in suits."

"Which would be far easier for *Glaring Eye* to accomplish if freed
from *Javelin* and the Number Four hull alike," Zrarr suggested.

"No," Sfisst replied.

"But—"

"I said it before, and I mean it: I do not intend to detach from
either *Javelin* or the Quantum II ship while there is the possibility of
sabotage."

"Which defeats the purpose of carrying *Glaring Eye* to begin
with," Spalding said, ship to ship. "This mission needed a vessel
capable of going where neither *Javelin* nor the Number Four hull
could. I understand your hesitation, Sfisst-Captain. Were I in a
similar position, I'd probably feel the same way. What if . . . What if
I offer to come aboard *Glaring Eye*? Accompanying Sci-Spec Strather
for the duration. No ARM officer aboard this ship would harm
Glaring Eye while I am aboard your vessel by my own consent."

Zrarr exchanged a quick glance with Strather, but neither of them
said anything.

Sfisst-Captain appeared to consider the offer.

"*Javelin*'s weapons are not what bother me," he said. "Ship
against ship, *Glaring Eye* is more than a match for your vessel—
assuming it becomes commandeered. It's the Quantum II drive
that's the real problem. So long as the Number Four hull remains
exclusively under ARM control, the fate shared by one must be
shared by all. As you say, 'Tec-Major, if you were in my position,
would you not feel similarly?"

"I think I would," Spalding said. "So . . . let's put a kzin aboard the Number Four hull. I go aboard *Glaring Eye,* your warrior goes aboard the Quantum II ship. It will be a tight fit, as you yourself have seen. But the Number Four hull carried one kzin before. It can do it again."

"This . . . may work. On one condition, 'Tec-Major. The kzin coming aboard the Number Four hull will be *me.*"

"Urrrr?" Zrarr uttered, suddenly turning in his seat to stare in shock at the kzin commander. As did every other warrior in the room.

"One field-grade officer for another," Sfisst-Captain said to his people, after cutting the feed to *Javelin.* "If somebody aboard the human ship is going to take the Quantum II motor and strand *Glaring Eye* here, they will do it over my dead body."

Zrarr turned his attention to Sci-Spec Strather, who was wide-eyed with surprise.

"It would seem our commanders are determined to keep this mission tied together. With their very lives, if necessary."

As before, Strather elected not to say anything. And for good reason. Whether or not the Detective-Major was party to the underhanded activities aboard her ship had not been fully determined. But Zrarr thought it took significant bravery for an ARM officer—and female, no less—to willingly board *Glaring Eye* without bringing her security team. Even more than Strather, the 'Tec-Major would be a target of opportunity for kzinti seeking to disrupt the mission.

It took only minutes for Sfisst-Captain to gather what he needed. Then he met the 'Tec-Major at the tunnel joining the two ships. She also had duffels, much like Strather before her.

"Permission to come aboard?" Spalding said across the distance.

"Permission granted," Sfisst-Captain said. "Who commands *Javelin* in your absence?"

"Detective-Captain Benitez. You?"

"Though he is not organic to the *Glaring Eye,* his partial name demands that I leave Zrarr-Professor in charge. All the routine command duties of the ship are being carried out by my executive, and Zrarr-Professor will hold the flag until I return."

Zrarr had accepted the responsibility without question, of course. Sfisst-Captain was going out on a limb, entrusting *Glaring Eye* to somebody not specifically trained for space war. Zrarr was therefore a figurehead, but with sufficient rank to stare down any challenger who might think Zrarr unfit.

The two skippers stared at one another across the empty air. Both of them seemed to know instinctively that there was tremendous risk in going over to the other side. But then Spalding quickly pushed her duffels through the microgravity between the ships—the bags being received by Strather on the other side. Followed by the 'Tec-Major herself. She gazed up at Sfisst-Captain for a moment, and he down at her. Then he pushed his own, kzin-sized flight bag across the tunnel, and followed it up into the *Javelin*'s interior.

"Communication is to remain open without interruption," Sfisst said back at them.

"Acknowledged and understood," Zrarr said.

Sfisst then vanished, taking a trio of human escorts with him.

"Welcome again, 'Tec-Major," Zrarr said. "Like Strather, you will be bunking in my stateroom."

"A male and female human bunking together?" she asked.

"It's the only place I feel you both can be truly secure. Is there a problem?"

"Males and females typically bunk in separate cabins, or at least segregated bays."

"We do not carry females on warships," Zrarr admitted. "This is not a problem kzinti are used to solving."

Spalding looked at Strather, them shrugged her shoulders.

"It'll be fine for now," she said. "Assuming kzin toilet facilities aren't impossible for a female human to use."

"It'll be a bit of a challenge," Strather said. "But I think you can manage."

Zrarr led them through the interior of the *Glaring Eye* until they were at the hatch to the stateroom. He looked this way and that, before opening the doorway. Once both humans had been ushered inside, he closed the hatch quickly.

"You still suspect saboteurs aboard *Glaring Eye*," Spalding deduced.

"Yes," Zrarr said. "I must also be frank in that I suspect the saboteurs aboard *Javelin* are operating very high up in your ship's command structure."

"Sci-Spec Strather will tell you I have the same suspicion," she said.

"What have you done to address the issue?"

"As much as I know to do, without openly accusing any single person. All corridors are now actively patrolled, in addition to the use of security cameras and microphones. Those assigned to the watch are being rotated randomly, so that no one officer is ever doing the same beat at the same time every day. Personnel files have been exhaustively perused, with scrutiny being given to otherwise benign details. Short of actually hauling some poor soul up on charges—for which we still don't have any conclusive evidence—I am not sure what else is within my authority. I can't just *kill* somebody, though I understand why that works on a kzin ship."

Zrarr thought over his next words very carefully.

"You should understand, too, that I am wondering if you *yourself* are involved. Sci-Spec Strather's presence aboard *Glaring Eye* aids the investigation, yes. But he is here primarily to escape a death threat."

The woman's eyes went wide.

"You never told me that," she said to Strather, her hands on her hips.

"I was instructed that if I raised the alarm to anyone aboard *Javelin,* it would be the end for me."

"When did this happen?" she demanded.

"Many of your nights ago," Zrarr said. "But that's not as important as the fact that until or unless the culprits aboard *Javelin* have been identified, and placed in your brig, *everyone* aboard is as much of a suspect, as any kzin aboard *Glaring Eye.*"

"Including myself," she finished, catching Zrarr's drift.

"Especially yourself," he said. "Sci-Spec Strather informs me that it is almost impossible for someone to break into an ARM officer's cabin, make threats, and escape again, without the captain of the ship being fully aware of the fact."

"They broke in??" she said, hands still on her hips.

Strather swallowed hard.

"Really, I only heard the one voice. Attached to an impossibly strong set of arms. He almost choked me to death, then we discussed the realities of kzin-human interstellar relations. He said he didn't want to hurt me, but he would if he had to. We talked about what was going on. And we disagreed about a few things. Then he let me go, and seemingly vanished without so much as opening the cabin's hatch. Though he did disable the cabin's audio controls."

"Did you perform a DNA sweep?" she said.

"No time, ma'am," Strather said. "I was exhausted. As well as afraid. I gathered what I knew I'd need, and left *Javelin* immediately. Zrarr-Professor has been my bodyguard ever since."

She looked the academician up and down, then said, "He's a heck of a choice."

"I was the *only* choice," Zrarr reminded. "And I asked Strather the same question. A thorough DNA sweep could have told us who it was. No Legal Entity in Known Space goes anywhere without leaving traces behind, be it hair or skin cells. In his haste, Strather cost us a remarkable opportunity."

"Not quite," Strather said. "When my assailant first attacked, I scratched at his arms. After I came here, I immediately checked under my fingernails, and put what little I could find into a specimen bag."

"You didn't tell me this," Zrarr erupted.

"Because it didn't matter as long as I didn't have access to the labs aboard *Javelin* that I'd need to try to make a positive DNA match. *Glaring Eye* doesn't exactly have database synchronization with ARM, stet? I thought eventually we might get a chance. But I also knew the minute you or I asked to use the labs aboard *Javelin,* that would tell my assailant—or assailants—what my intentions were. And then they'd be forced to kill us both."

"Give your sample to me," Spalding said. "I can cross back and order a forensic DNA test immediately."

"And if you're part of the conspiracy?" Strather said. "I have evidence which potentially exposes you, or at least one of your co-conspirators. What guarantee do I have that you won't destroy the sample?"

The Detective-Major drew in a long breath, and let it out slowly, her eyes closing.

"All this paranoia is really, *really* making me tired," she said.

"It's the same aboard *Glaring Eye*," Zrarr said. "Warriors side-glancing at one another as they cross paths. Far less talk in both the officers' and the enlisted banquet compartments. The stoic camaraderie which would ordinarily typify a Patriarchy ship has been gradually displaced by the sickness of suspicion."

"So why take a chance telling me all this, if I am a prime suspect on the human side?" Spalding asked Zrarr directly.

Strather looked away, his cheeks getting pink.

"I didn't discuss it with my counterpart beforehand," Zrarr admitted. "But since I am quite certain, now, that Sfisst-Captain is not involved, I felt compelled to bring you into our confidence. And for only one reason. If you *are* desiring a fight between men and kzinti, *Glaring Eye* is the last place you'd want to be. That you volunteered to come aboard, as a high-profile token of exchange—which Sfisst has honored in kind—tells me you cannot be part of the conspiracy."

"Maybe I'm a suicide martyr," Spalding said, with a tone Zrarr-Professor had learned among humans would be considered dryly humorous.

"A suicide martyr who openly permits a kzin Hero to post himself aboard the Number Four hull? No. I do not believe it."

"Sfisst-Captain just doesn't dare let the Quantum II drive out of his sight."

"Nor would you, 'Tec-Major, if the roles were reversed."

"True."

"So why offer yourself in the first place?" Mantooth Strather asked.

"I wanted to make a demonstration of good faith. Even if Sfisst-Captain would shoot me just as soon as look at me, I can respect his directness, as a Hero of the Patriarchy. He should have used the destruction of his lander as an excuse to fight. But he allowed himself to be talked out of combat. That impressed me. Enough so that when the time came, I decided to make a gesture of similar import. Though being here also allows me to fulfill a selfish desire. I can participate in the reconnoiter of the space dock. Sfisst-Captain would give his life to ensure that the Quantum II drive remains accessible to the Patriarchy. I joined the ARM because I want to *explore*. See places nobody in Known Space has ever seen. That space dock represents an opportunity I won't ever get again."

"Urrrr," Zrarr uttered. Hers was a motive he could understand.

He too felt the almost irresistible urge to cross space, and see the space dock up close. Without telescopes. Just the transparent face bowl of his space helmet separating him from the unknown.

Uncoupling *Glaring Eye* from *Javelin* was a routine affair, underlaid by tension. With Zrarr occupying the command seat which Sfisst had ordinarily used, the bridge of the *Glaring Eye* was on full alert for any mischief. But when the one ship was fully separated from the other, and *Glaring Eye* began to maneuver independently—no untoward actions taken by the ARM ship—the anxiety filling the *Glaring Eye*'s bridge began to draw down. Zrarr could smell it, and similarly allowed himself to relax.

"Find us answers," Sfisst-Captain said over the ship-to-ship net.

Zrarr peered at the small screen on the commander's arm rest. He could see Sfisst's face and eyes, as well as the small bit of machinery behind him. The #4 hull gave the kzin Hero precious little comfort room.

"Have the humans welcomed you aboard?" Zrarr-Professor asked, using the Heroes' Tongue.

"I would not use that phrase," Sfisst said. "They tolerate me. And I tolerate them. But no one has stopped me from occupying the Number Four hull's piloting station. I intend to stay here for as long as *Glaring Eye* conducts the reconnaissance. If I detect anything out of sorts, you will be the first to know, Zrarr-Professor. If *you* detect anything out of sorts, *I* should be the first to know."

"Agreed," Zrarr responded.

"Sir," said the Executive Officer, an older kzin warrior not quite as senior as Sfisst, but still bearing the scars of a soldier who'd earned his rank. Depending on how he conducted himself during their planned exploration of the space dock, perhaps there might be enough justification to earn the Executive Officer a partial name?

"Speak," Zrarr responded.

"What is the priority of search?"

"Let's do a close flyover on the alien Bussard vessel. Sci-Spec Strather seemed sufficiently impressed with it. Let's determine if it's as unoccupied as it looks. And if there are any obvious airlocks through which a scout squad might pass."

Freed from the mass of the #4 hull, and all the Quantum II machinery inside, *Glaring Eye* maneuvered gracefully through space.

The gravity thrusters had to work just a fraction as hard as they'd been working before, though internal gravity for the crew remained constant. Very quickly, *Glaring Eye* was passing within a thousand meters of the Bussard ship, gathering radio and radar data, as well as copious quantities of video. Zrarr counted fifty two decks in total, running the length of the craft. Each and every porthole was dark. Using the telescopes to zoom in on any single porthole revealed little. Though several closed hatchways which appeared to be airlock capable were identified.

"Without power, we'll have to pry them open," Zrarr said.

"Or the interior is already in vacuum," Strather replied, sitting alone at the station Zrarr had formerly occupied when Sfisst-Captain was still aboard.

"Only one way to find out. Wait, where are you going?" Zrarr asked.

"To suit up," Strather replied, heading for the exit.

Zrarr started to open his mouth to countermand the Science-Inspector, then closed his mouth. And got up out of the command seat. He too would suit up.

"Zrarr-Professor?" the Executive said, his tone forming a question.

"I will make the survey, with my counterpart. We will take eight of your best warriors, and the Detective-Major. Please maneuver us to within docking distance."

✌ CHAPTER 12 ✌

MANNY SLIPPED HIS HELMET over his suit, and dogged the latches at the suit's collar. A small, motorized sound filled his ears, as the suit's atmosphere circulator took over. A dry, odorless mixture of nitrogen and oxygen swirled around his face. His ears began to feel the change in pressure, as the suit automatically dropped from cabin normal down to the suit's operational pressure, which was much less than Earth sea level. Around him, the kzinti and the 'Tec-Major were doing the same. They occupied one of the egress prep compartments aboard the largest lander brought by the kzin side of the expedition. And though they had each been embarrassingly devoid of fur, the Pilot Primary and Pilot Secondary—now released from their autodocs—had requested the privilege of flying the squad to their destination. A request Zrarr-Professor had heartily granted.

Manny tested his communications with the rest of the squad, using an encrypted frequency that also linked *Glaring Eye* and *Javelin*. Then he switched over to a suit-to-suit link which was ARM exclusive, and tried his luck with the 'Tec-Major.

"Copy you," Spalding said.

"Roger, thank you," Manny said, satisfied that he could talk to the ARM commander on his own terms in a pinch.

"We follow the Special Tactics Sergeant," Zrarr-Professor said, indicating the senior-most kzin warrior who was finishing up his own battle suit checks. Compared to the relatively sleek ARM suits, the kzin environment suits were colossal. Mainly due to their armor.

An ARM suit was built with soft ballistics, and afforded maximum flexibility. The kzin suits were covered in hard armor plate, and surely weighed more than Manny and the 'Tec-Major put together, even for one kzin wearer. But the squad didn't seem to notice the extra mass. And it would not matter in any case, once they crossed to the alien Bussard ship. As soon as the lander left *Glaring Eye* they would be in microgravity conditions.

Once they were each satisfied that all of their suits—and weapons, for the kzinti, as well as the 'Tec-Major—checked out, the squad seated themselves in the lander's main passenger pod. Crash webbing was stretched across legs and torsos, but arms were left free to move. When Pilot Primary signaled his readiness to go, Zrarr hand-signed to the Special Tactics Sergeant, who also gave his affirmative—on the network—to go.

Nothing was felt for several minutes, until the lander left the launch bay, and then Manny's stomach was complaining. It was worse than crossing the docking tunnel between *Glaring Eye* and *Javelin,* because the sensation of falling did not end. Manny had to focus his eyes on the 'Tec-Major sitting across from him, and will his body into believing that he was not, in fact, plummeting to his death.

If any of the kzinti were experiencing the same discomfort, they did not show it.

Though Zrarr appeared to discern Manny's distress.

A small light illuminated in Manny's helmet display—appearing as a blinking icon in Manny's field of view—indicating Zrarr desired a private audio link. Manny verbally ordered his suit to comply, and then he heard Zrarr's voice coming out of the speakers on either side of his head.

"It's unsettling, isn't it?" Zrarr said.

"You do a wonderful job concealing that fact."

"Now would be a terrible moment for this Hero to reveal that he's not spent nearly as much time training in space as these other warriors."

"What do you expect we'll find once we're over there?" Manny asked.

"I hesitate to speculate. We may not even be able to open the doors. If the ship is made from standard hull materials, as seems to be the case, it may have sat unused in vacuum for so long that certain elements are now fused tight."

"I would think anyone operating Bussard ships would know to sufficiently lubricate all the moving parts," Manny said, "so as to avoid such a predicament."

"Urrr," Zrarr uttered.

"We are opening the pod for egress maneuver," Pilot Secondary said over the lander's internal link.

The pod ramp opened, and suddenly light from the red dwarf speared into the pod. Face bowls automatically went chrome or bronze, depending on the species, so as to protect the eyes of the wearers from damage. The lander itself maneuvered until the open pod was out of direct sunlight, and the Bussard ship itself came into view. The lander was incredibly close, to Manny's relief. Almost so close that a man could have stepped directly from the edge of the ramp onto the Bussard ship's hull with one stride.

"Up," the Special Tactics Sergeant ordered.

His warriors moved with the coordination of training. Zrarr, Manny, and Pryce Spalding moved behind, trying to keep out of the way. In twos, the Special Tactics squad leaped over to the Bussard ship. The soles of their suit boots were electrically magnetized. They stuck fast to the hull steel. When all of the Special Tactics squad was over—the warriors ringing the suspected airlock hatch, their weapons aimed outward for security—Zrarr-Professor crossed, with Manny and Spalding in his wake. Manny felt a thrill as he left the edge of the lander's ramp, and was suspended in pure microgravity for an instant. Then his own suit boots touched down, and clamped solidly in place with their own magnets. He experimentally picked up one foot, then the other, testing to see how easily he might "walk" on the Bussard ship's hull. It would be awkward, but doable.

'Tec-Major Spalding was much more at ease, moving with the confidence of someone who'd had experience.

"Sir," the Special Tactics Sergeant said, beckoning Zrarr-Professor to the airlock hatch.

Manny joined them, and ran his gloved fingers along the hatch's edge. The metal was smoothly machined, with no messy welds.

"Without power, we'll have to hope to discover a manual way to enter."

"Here," Spalding said. She had pried open a metal panel, under which a crank interface had been installed. Both Zrarr and Spalding stared at it, judging the size of the hands which would be needed.

"You and Sci-Spec Strather," Zrarr finally said.

"Agreed," Spalding replied, and waved Manny over to join her.

Zrarr was right. The manual handle that folded out was remarkably man-sized, and built similar to what would have been found on airlocks in Known Space. Manny braced himself, and used his hands on one set of grips, while the 'Tec Major did the same, holding the opposite set of grips.

"You push, I pull, opposite hands," Manny said.

"Stet," Spalding replied.

They flexed their muscles, to no effect.

"Again," Spalding said.

Together, they flexed again. But the manual refused to move.

"Torque in the wrong direction," Manny deduced. "Reverse it."

They pushed and pulled opposite the way they'd done it the first time, and strained as hard as they could, until finally the S-shaped manual crank began to turn. Slowly, at first. No telling how long the mechanism had gone unused, even before the ship went dormant. Then, after a few revolutions, whatever lubricant was in the mechanism itself loosened, and Manny and Pryce were pushing and pulling with gusto, like four pistons stroking. Manny felt sweat begin to bead on his forehead, and his suit's temperature control kicked in, flooding the suit's capillaries close to Manny's skin with chilled fluid. The same membrane was also moisture-wicking, and spirited away the sweat as he worked.

Gradually, an inch at a time, the airlock hatch came open. Splitting cleanly down the middle, while its two halves withdrew into the hull wall.

Special Tactics Sergeant aimed his weapon—kzin-sized—down into the open hatch, while the Special Tactics squad moved again in twos, retreating from the security perimeter, and dropping through the airlock until only the Sergeant, Zrarr, Manny, and Pryce remained on the surface.

"Clear!" called the Special Tactics Corporal below.

"Sir," the Sergeant said, waving Zrarr onward.

"Mantooth," Zrarr said, waving at Manny.

He went, followed by the 'Tec-Major, and then Zrarr-Professor came in behind, with Sergeant staying above, scanning a full three hundred and sixty degrees—the muzzle of his weapon tracing his line of sight.

"Clear," called the Sergeant, who then joined them inside the airlock.

Manny gazed up through the open hatch, at the far away main artifact which circled the red dwarf. The star was halfway occluded, so that Manny could clearly see the loop's rotation. Gantries made from *scrith* rose up to either side of the Bussard ship, at the edges of the open bay where the ship had been docked for . . . tens of years? Hundreds? Thousands? Maybe more?

"No way to tell if the interior has atmosphere," the Sergeant said.

"Can we reseal the outer hatch manually?"

Lamps came on. Beams of light played around the airlock until a small access panel similar to the one on the outside was discovered.

Again, it fell to Manny and the 'Tec-Major to work the crank, since it was too small for the kzinti—with their gauntleted paws—to effectively use.

When the outer hatch was closed tightly, still another panel was discovered, with another S-shaped cranking handle. When the inner door cracked open, Manny held his breath, waiting for the rush of atmosphere which should have gusted violently through the gap. But when it didn't, he vigorously worked the cranking handle, with Spalding as his partner, until the inner door was all the way open, and the squad could examine the interior.

Like before, the Sergeant ordered his warriors forward in twos—each advancing pair covered by the pair behind them, their lamps aiming beams of light far down the corridor beyond the airlock's inner door.

"More comfortable for humans," Zrarr said, having to hunch forward lest he brush the top of his helmet against the ceiling.

Manny remembered the holographic projection of Halrloprillalar, back at the ARM museum beneath Antarctica. She'd been a "cousin" to Earth humans, according to Manny's boss. Was this one of the ships Prill's people had used? It was sized right. And most definitely had *not* been built by any shipyard in Known Space. The writing and markings on the walls—located in places familiar to anyone who'd been aboard any starship—were in a script and language unlike anything Manny was familiar with. He paused to get imagery and footage as the squad moved down the corridor, occasionally poking his head through half-open or completely open hatches as they went. In not a single instance did he see the mummified remains of either a crewman, or a passenger.

"Sinks, chairs, tables, couches, all of it adapted for zero-g use," Pryce said, as she walked around the interior of one particularly spacious cabin. "What some of the Lazy Eighters, back in their day, would have made of luxury like this!"

"A journey that takes decades demands room in which to maneuver," Manny said, experimentally taking a seat in one of the overstuffed recliners. Again, sized uncannily to human scale. The material of the chair crackled and fractured upon contact, leaving little flakes to float around the compartment. Manny quickly stood up, and went back to the hatchway, while the kzin squad peered in with their lamps on full. Making the shadows dark, and sharply bordered.

"Been a while since they had air in here," he said.

"And it's minus one hundred Celsius," the 'Tec-Major reminded him. "Just about anything becomes brittle at *that* stiff temperature."

"We have discovered no occupants," Zrarr-Professor narrated for the ship-to-ship network, which also relayed all of the imagery from their individual tactical cameras recessed into the sides of their helmets. "The vessel is clearly constructed for use by a species approaching hominid in form. But there are no bodies. And no obvious signs of damage. Nor any clear indicators of combat. Whoever inhabited this vessel left it clean."

"Any radio signals we couldn't detect before?" asked Sfisst-Captain, from the pilot's compartment in the #4 hull.

"My Corporal of Communications detects nothing," said the Special Tactics Sergeant. "He has been constantly scanning for such ever since our entry. The interior of the vessel is completely deserted."

"Urrr," Sfisst uttered. "Keep looking."

Two and a half hours passed, with the squad going up and down ladders between decks, identifying staterooms, maintenance crawlspaces, trunking for sewage, wiring, and also ducts for air circulation. Including the hydroponics plants where waste air was dumped, to be replenished with fresh oxygen. There were large auditoriums, gymnasiums with equipment for exercise as well as sport—though none for any sport men from Earth might be familiar with—and workstations tied to an internal computer network.

Which the Comms Corporal was unable to access without internal power.

"Mainframe, most probably," the Comms Corporal said, after having fairly dismantled one particular workstation, touching his probe wires from his suit computer to the wires inside the wall paneling. "If the central servers and drives aren't powered up, and the network hubs and routers are not active, these individual stations will never work."

"We should make the computer a priority for secondary reconnaissance," Zrarr-Professor said. "Our first objective is to determine if the ship is in fact deserted, then we move on to the space dock itself. The ship's mainframe can wait. What we seek may be loaded into the memory of whatever computers are running in the dock proper. There were certainly enough solar panels to provide power."

When they discovered the main gangway leading over to the dock, the Sergeant ringed his men in another security perimeter while staring down the length of the gangway, his whiskers quivering behind the clear—since exiting direct sunlight—bowl of his helmet.

"Problem?" Zrarr-Professor asked, as he stayed back with Manny and the 'Tec-Major.

"The gangway is a perfect place for an enemy to attack."

"Have you detected such an enemy?"

"No, Zrarr-Professor. But I anticipate such."

"I understand. Pilot Primary and Pilot Secondary, you have the lander. Please move to this side of the Bussard ship, and perform a fly-around on the main gangway, amidships."

A few minutes later, the squad could see—through the gangway windows—the lander maneuvering cautiously outside. The floor of the gangway itself still held their magnetic soles, so there was ferrous material under foot. Which meant it had been constructed by the same people who'd built the Bussard ship. Or, perhaps, constructed on behalf of visitors, by the creators of the space dock? Manny had to keep reminding himself that the builders of the dock—and the great ring around the red dwarf—might be significantly different from the creators of the Bussard vessel.

"We neither see nor detect any hostile threat," Pilot Secondary said on their tactical network.

"Thank you," Zrarr-Professor said. "Sci-Spec, 'Tec-Major, do either of you have anything to add to the report?"

"This was clearly an interstellar ramjet," Manny said, "constructed for journeys taking tens, maybe hundreds, of years. It's a mobile city, now emptied out. In Known Space, it would qualify as a space station in its own right, simply because of its size and independent life-support capability. If my suspicion is correct, we're looking at a cruise ship, built for tourists."

"Tourists?" the Sergeant said, his Interworld slurred with incredulity.

"Yes," Manny said. "We found an interior designed for comfort. But not a single weapon, nor anything like the sensors and equipment you have aboard the *Glaring Eye*. The crew and passengers were not concerned with threats."

"We only explored a tiny portion of the total craft," Zrarr-Professor said. "Using your city comparison, there are many districts within a city, serving different purposes. Perhaps we happened to board in the 'high-end' district, and have simply not yet discovered those parts of the ship given over to security, military operations, interstellar sensing and exploration, and so forth."

Manny nodded his head, though he knew nobody could see it through the helmet.

"Good point," he said. "But think of where we are. The main artifact is an incredible thing to see. What if the artifact itself is only partially complete?"

"I'm not following you," Spalding said.

"Think of it like a high-rise condo," Manny said. "You secure the land, get the permits, start building the thing, but in the meantime you need to advertise. Start lining up leases. Arrange tours of those portions of the condo already complete, so that you can secure contracts. The big arcologies on Earth are about the size of this ship. And new ones are being built all the time. Buildings in which a human being can live and work his entire life, and not have to go outside. The arcologies start lining up customers long before occupancy. Maybe the ring is something like that? You build it, but you begin bringing in clientele before its finished. If they're not sold before they arrive, seeing the thing—touring it, seeing the construction—seals the deal."

"You're a businessman as well as an ARM agent," Zrarr-Professor said, his Interworld toned with what Manny knew was the kzin equivalent of amusement.

"No," Manny admitted. "But ARM has to understand how the economies on many worlds work. We've expended a lot of effort trying to manage those economies—if even subtly—so as to avoid interstellar crashes like what happened when the Puppeteers vanished."

"If you're right," Zrarr-Professor said, "then we're dealing with a hub on a very, very large interstellar chain of commerce."

"Far larger than anything in Known Space," Manny said.

"And they never once came into contact with a species using Quantum I hyperdrive," Zrarr said, still sounding amused.

Manny frowned. Zrarr had him there.

"We're still guessing, until we find hard evidence," the 'Tec-Major reminded them. "Looks like the lander hasn't seen anything worth worrying about. Shall we cross?"

"Yes!" said the Sergeant, who sent his squad bounding forward in their overwatch pattern. Manny, Zrarr, and Spalding brought up the rear. It took them a long time to cross. The gangway itself was the better part of a thousand meters long. At the end, it emptied out into what Manny could only describe as the universe's most magnificent spaceport terminal. Also apparently abandoned. There was not a single living thing, nor a moving piece of machinery, in sight. Grand galleries and walkways for tens of thousands of man-sized individuals. But not a soul to reckon with. And no bodies either. Nor any apparent damage.

"Very curious," Zrarr-Professor said, aiming his lamps around the space.

Manny wandered around the terminal, marveling at the high ceiling. Microgravity still bothered his sense of balance, but he'd gotten used to walking enough that he could cover a lot of ground without discomfort. When he stumbled across the people mover, it was almost by accident. He'd been inspecting what appeared to be a live control panel—with illuminated touchscreen controls, again using script and language foreign to the human eye—when a sensor in the control panel itself seemed to detect his presence, and summoned a car. It arrived well lit, but empty, in a nearby travel tube. Two sets of doors—internal and external—opened. The interior of the car misted for a split second, then went clear.

"Atmosphere!" 'Tec-Major Spalding exclaimed.

"Indeed," Zrarr said.

"All aboard!" Manny chirruped, then proceeded to enter.

When everyone had done likewise, they stared stupidly around themselves, looking for controls of some type. Like the Bussard ship and the terminal, the people mover appeared to be made from conventional materials. Though there was nothing ferrous in the floor. They all had to grab onto the numerous hand rails which sprouted from walls, floor, and ceiling.

The doors to the people mover closed.

"I read an oxygen-nitrogen mixture filling the space," said Zrarr-Professor, no doubt observing the readings from his suit's external atmosphere gauge.

Suddenly the people mover was in motion. Manny had to hold on tight, as the people mover's acceleration was much greater than anything he would have expected from a commercial port. He grimaced, his arms straining. Everyone fell sideways, clinging by their gloved or gauntleted hands, as the people mover rocketed down the tunnel.

"No gravity thrusters, and no transfer booths either!" Manny shouted.

"Urrrr!" Zrarr-Professor replied.

Finally, the acceleration of the people mover eased off, and the occupants were able to settle themselves.

"Relative velocity," Zrarr-Professor inquired.

"We have a telemetric fix on the lander," the Sergeant said. "Gauging the distance growing between us—"

"Three hundred kilometers an hour," Spalding interrupted.

The Sergeant agreed, using kzin measurements.

"Heck of a clip for an antique form of transport," Manny said. "Programmed obviously to depart the terminal when occupants are aboard."

The Sergeant had positioned himself at the head of the car, watching through the huge, transparent window there. The sides of the tube were a blur, as they raced past. But the experience of travel was smooth. Without jostling.

"Maglev rails," Manny said, looking around the interior of the car. He could barely feel the vibration of the motors through his soles.

"Anyone dare take his helmet off?" the 'Tec-Major said, half-jesting.

"The air *is* breathable," Zrarr-Professor said. "But we have no idea how long it will last. If the—wherever it is we come to a halt—doesn't have pressure, the way the space terminal lacked pressure, it will be lethal for us when the car doors open again."

The kzin squad appeared to be gauging both Zrarr-Professor's and their Sergeant's reactions, to tell if the squad also should be screaming, or leaping, or neither. After a few minutes of calm, they gradually relaxed, and began to converse amongst themselves in the Heroes' Tongue.

Manny went back to the rear of the car—left empty—and stared at the way they had come. The tube itself had track lighting in the ceiling, which became a glowing, neon stripe at that speed. The car had not angled nor turned even once during their journey so far. At three hundred kilometers per hour, such a transport system could get from one end of the space dock to the other in half an Earth day. Or less, if the acceleration were to be dialed up again?

Manny noticed a small display at the car's rear, with alien script flowing across it. He suddenly realized that none of them had bothered to turn on their exterior microphones. He vocally ordered his suit's pickup to activate, and was greeted by a melodic, feminine, altogether undecipherable voice. It was human. Or as close to human as could be done, following paths of parallel evolution. Such a voice, had she been speaking Interworld, would have been right at home on any broadcast in Known Space.

"Remarkable," Zrarr-Professor said, catching the mic feed from Strather's suit.

"Hominid?" asked Sfisst-Captain, picking up the feed from Zrarr.

"Monkey-speech," said the Sergeant.

"And very attractive monkey-speech at that," Manny said, smiling.

The people mover went on, and on. For over an hour. Until suddenly the pleasant woman's voice—which had been repeating the same words in a recognizable sequence—changed her tone.

"Hold on tight everybody," Manny suddenly said.

"Why?" Spalding asked.

Braking caused everyone to flinch, reaching out for their closest handhold. When the car finally came to stop, everyone aboard was breathing heavily, and Pryce shook out her arms, one after the other, to loosen her knotted muscles.

The doors opened.

They waited for the air to disappear.

When it didn't, they pulled themselves through, and into what appeared to be another terminal. Only this one was lit from many different directions.

Manny was admiring the terminal's illuminated architecture, when movement caught his attention out of the corner of his eye.

"Incoming!" shouted the Special Tactics Sergeant.

🐾 CHAPTER 13 🐾

ZRARR-PROFESSOR should have known. He was a Hero, after all. But had allowed himself to be lulled by the relatively benign nature of the space dock to that point. When the attackers came, they came in force. Several dozen of them, leaping through microgravity as if born to it. Special Tactics Sergeant had been more aware, and was snapping out orders to fire. Pencils of light stabbed and sliced through several of the aliens. Followed by the concussive reports of grenade launchers. Manny had forgotten to turn off his external mic, and was almost deafened by the antipersonnel explosives.

'Tec-Major Spalding was firing her weapon as well. First the laser, then the caseless conventional rounds, followed by the laser again.

For every attacker who fell—roughly hominid, but with swollen joints, and a head that seemed too large to be healthy—two more took its place.

"Report!" said the voice of Sfisst-Captain.

"We are being overrun," Zrarr-Professor said matter-of-factly. And it was true. The squad's security circle had contracted in on itself, as the shredded and dismembered bodies of foes sailed past them, fluids spraying. But the total number of enemy was simply too great for one squad—even a kzin squad—to cope with.

"I can see your video," Sfisst-Captain said. "'Tec-Captain Benitez, can you confirm? Benitez?? *Benitez!*"

Suddenly, the audio to the #4 hull cut out.

"Sfisst-Captain," Zrarr said, wishing he had brought a weapon. "Sfisst-Captain, respond, please."

317

"This is Science-Inspector Strather, calling *Javelin*," Manny said.

There was a pause, and then a human voice—with which Zrarr was not familiar—said, "I told you not to get in our way, Strather. I said I didn't want to hurt you, and I'd have kept my word, too. But things are in motion now. Once we've dispatched with Sfisst-Captain, we'll see to *Glaring Eye*. The *Javelin* is not the pushover Sfisst seems to think. We made sure of that, to a degree even the Detective-Major is not aware. Sfisst wanted a shooting fight? Now we oblige him."

"Benitez!" Spalding shouted, then said, "'Tec-Major Spalding to *Glaring Eye*, report in, please."

"Where can we run?"

"To the people mover!" Manny said.

"Too late," Spalding reported. "It's already gone. Must have headed back down the tube when we disembarked."

Zrarr-Professor scanned about them, frantically looking for a clean route of escape. When he spotted the darkened corridor, from which no enemies were emerging—

"Follow me!" Zrarr-Professor roared, and ran as fast as his kzin legs would carry him. Not bothering to look back, Zrarr had eyes only for the creatures who'd noticed him break ranks, and were now changing direction to intercept him. When one of them came within striking distance—using hands and feet very much monkey-style, to grab onto and push off of various objects and surface—Zrarr lashed out. He didn't have weapons, but the digits of his suit gauntlets were tipped with retractable spikes every bit as lethal as a grown kzin's claws.

The foe was thrown bodily away, blood spraying in a wide arc that dissolved into little drops.

A second creature reached Zrarr-Professor. Then a third. They latched onto him with an iron grip, threatening to crush the kzin's bones through his suit. But the suit's armor reinforcement held, and Zrarr-Professor had the full force of an adult male kzin's musculature behind every blow. One foe's head was ripped clean off, while the other's back was opened up down through the ribs. For once, Zrarr-Professor didn't have to control his rage. In a red-misted glory of killing, he welcomed the creatures into his murderous embrace. Each time he destroyed one of them, he made his way closer to the darkened corridor. Bones, sinew, muscle, and tendons were gleefully ripped apart.

Once past the entrance, Zrarr stopped just long enough to see behind him. Strather and the 'Tec-Major had kept up, though the 'Tec-Major had lost her weapon, and was leaning on Strather for support. The Sergeant, one of his Corporals, and two other warriors were behind them, slaughtering the enemy as fast as they came.

Zrarr turned his eyes back to the corridor, and dialed his suit lamps on full. The path ahead seemed clear, so he moved quickly.

"How many are left?" Zrarr asked the Sergeant, between breaths.

"I know not," the Sergeant replied, also between breaths. "My senior-most Corporal elected to stand and fight, as did some of the others. They are buying us time to escape, Zrarr-Professor. Specifically, they are buying *you* time to escape."

"They have the spirit of true Heroes," Zrarr said.

"And will die the deaths of Heroes," Sergeant finished.

Suddenly the corridor branched. Zrarr-Professor took them left. When it branched a second time, he took them right. Until they were scampering out into a very large, high-ceilinged chamber which appeared to be dominated by row after row of hydroponics pods. Out of which all manner of plants, trees, and vegetation grew. Row after row of them, all daisy-chained by cable, wiring, and tubes for water and fertilizer. They were all around, suspended in an organized web that was bathed in bright light. Not light from the red dwarf star, but light almost like that of Kzin-home.

Zrarr didn't stop to look. He kept running, then began using the cables between the hydroponics pods to pull himself at a diagonal upward, into the microgravity forest. When he was satisfied he'd gone a sufficient distance, he stopped at a particularly large tree—grown comically, with no gravity to guide it—and allowed himself to think.

Strather, the injured Major, and the Sergeant—with Comms Corporal—came too.

"Did they follow us?" Strather asked, panting for breath.

"We must assume they will," Special Tactics Sergeant said. "But more important still, what has happened to Sfisst-Captain?"

"I have had no success raising that Hero on any frequency," the Comms Corporal said.

Every kzin turned to stare at 'Tec-Major Spalding. Her suit was ripped, and her helmet appeared to have been damaged. A trickle of blood had traced a crazy pattern across one cheek, than coagulated in place. Her mouth moved, trying to make sound, but nothing was heard on Zrarr's helmet speakers. Finally the 'Tec-Major ripped her helmet off in frustration, hurling it away. Whatever care she'd given about not being exposed to alien atmosphere, it had evaporated in the fight.

Zrarr-Professor and the Sergeant looked at each other, before doing the same. Strather and the Corporal did likewise, though Strather discovered his helmet would not come off.

"I think one of those things tweaked the collar when it tried to grab me," Strather said, and gave up attempting to unlatch the ring at his neck.

Each of the kzinti carefully stowed their helmets using clips on the backs of their suits.

"'Tec-Captain Benitez is a good man," Spalding said defensively. "I can't believe he's done anything to endanger the mission."

"Yet Sfisst-Captain called his name," the Sergeant said, "just prior to us losing contact."

"It could mean any number of things," Spalding replied.

Zrarr scoffed, then said, "Whoever aboard *Javelin* was prepared to act, chose to act. The minute our squad came into hostile contact. A smart decision, really. Doubtless Sfisst-Captain and anyone else aboard either *Javelin* or the Number Four hull—who was not party to the conspiracy—had his attention fixated on our voyage. Waiting until the squad met hostiles guaranteed that Sfisst and the others would be in a state of maximum distraction."

"We have to assume Sfisst-Captain is dead," Special Tactics Sergeant said.

"Maybe," Zrarr-Professor said. "But I don't think Sfisst-Captain placed himself aboard the Quantum II without having carefully thought out his plan of defense, in the event that something went wrong. Just because we're unable to reach him at this time, doesn't mean he's out of the fight. It could merely mean he's taken the fight *to* these traitors."

"And the *Glaring Eye*?" the Comms Corporal said. "I cannot reach them, nor can I reach the lander."

"Perhaps, then, it's purely a technical problem?" Zrarr speculated. "We don't know how deep into the space dock we've traveled. It's possible that there is structure between us and our initial point of entry—surely very far from here, now—sufficient to disrupt our communications equipment."

The three kzinti and two humans muttered among themselves, continuing to speculate, until 'Tec-Major Spalding asked, "Who do you think they were?"

"The bogey-things?" Strather asked in reply.

"Yes. They weren't men. Hominid, perhaps, but not men. I got a look into the eyes of one of them, right before I blew his head apart. The eyes seemed dull."

"They are strong, however," Zrarr-Professor said.

"Urrrr," Sergeant agreed. "Without this armor, I would have surely perished at least half a dozen times. Look at how much damage has been done to the plating. I am reasonably certain none of our suits is spaceworthy anymore."

"Which means we are trapped here, unless someone from the outside can effect our rescue," Strather said.

"It was surreal," 'Tec-Major Spalding said. "Those eyes were almost the eyes of a person, but the bodies? And their *faces*? No nose, and mouths like a snapping turtle, but flattened. And there were *hundreds* of them."

"Perhaps we now know the fate of the Bussard ship's crew," Zrarr-Professor said to Strather.

Mantooth merely grunted.

"Hell of a tourist trap this place turned out to be!"

Zrarr peered out from within the leaves of the tree, trying to see if any of their attackers had followed them up into the maze of the hydroponics pods.

"We seem to have eluded them for the moment."

"But what do we do now?" Strather asked. "Without communication to either *Javelin* or *Glaring Eye,* we're essentially trapped here. And who knows how many more of those things might be running around this place. They've got enough water to drink and food to eat, but they have a *severe* allergic reaction to visitors."

"Your humor escapes me," Zrarr-Professor said. "We must survive long enough to contact either Sfisst-Captain, or *Glaring Eye,* or the lander. From the looks of it, the communications unit that Corporal still carries on his back will be sufficient to the task. We just have to find out what—if anything in this place—is obstructing our signal. Or, if the *Javelin* or *Glaring Eye* have been damaged, and the lander with them. We must learn that too. Then we can form a strategy."

There was a rustling noise from far off in the daisy-chained rows of hydroponics pods.

Every head spun around, and looked to the source of the sound.

"They've come," Zrarr-Professor growled.

"Wait," 'Tec-Major Spalding said. "What's that smell?"

"Urrr?" Zrarr-Professor and Special Tactics Sergeant uttered in unison.

Without saying another word, the 'Tec-Major turned and launched herself into the maze of hydroponics pods.

"Pryce!" Strather shouted at her, trying to grab her ankle, but missed.

Then he too was following her.

Zrarr-Professor did the same, and discovered that the two other kzinti—Heroes, no one could question it now—arrayed themselves for a delaying action.

"Go!" the Special Tactics Sergeant shouted at Zrarr. "Ensure our stories are told with honor, Zrarr-Professor!"

Zrarr roared his agreement, and pelted after the two humans as quickly as his arms and legs could carry him. He wasn't as adroit in the hydroponics farm as the monkeys from Earth. They seemed to be gaining on him. Or rather, Spalding seemed to be gaining— despite her injury—while Strather lost ground. Eventually Zrarr came abreast of him, long enough for Zrarr and Strather to exchange glances, and then they were both pursuing Spalding back out of the forest of hydroponics pods, into still another corridor at a different level of the structure. This corridor was well lit, allowing them to see clearly as Spalding went on and on, as if driven.

"What's happened to her?" Zrarr bellowed.

"I have no idea," Strather replied. "One moment she seemed fine. Now it's like someone pumped her full of adrenaline."

The corridor branched, then branched again, and branched still a third time, with Spalding taking the left in each instance, until it emptied out into a much smaller grove of hydroponics pods. All of which seemed to feature the same waxy-leafed plant. Spalding leapt into the air—not bothering with a handhold—and wrapped both arms and her good leg around the pod she desired, pulling herself up to the plant at the pod's top. Her hands dug into the soil, flinging it away into the air.

When Zrarr-Professor and Strather reached her, Spalding's cheeks were incredibly puffed out with what appeared to be hunks of food. She had a large, tuber-like root clutched in both hands. Numerous bites had already been taken out of it. Her eyes stared unthinking at both Zrarr-Professor and Strather, whose own face had taken on a somewhat horrified expression.

"For Finagle's sake," Strather said, his voice muffled by his helmet. "It's like she's completely gone in the head."

He clapped his hands in front of her face several times.

"Detective-Major. Detective-Major Spalding!"

She simply stared at them for a few moments, globs of yellow-tinged saliva clinging to her chin and cheeks.

"*Pryce!*" Strather finally screamed at her.

She blinked a couple of times, almost seeming to recognize that her first name had been called, then she swallowed hungrily, and went back to shoving the tuber into her mouth.

"I do not understand," Zrarr-Professor said, watching the human woman eat with the zeal and ferocity of a kzin who's just killed fresh meat.

"I don't either," Strather admitted. "She said something about a smell."

Strather absently put a hand up to his face, to rub his nose, and bumped the bowl of his helmet.

Zrarr-Professor looked at Strather's helmet, then looked at the 'Tec-Major, then back at Strather again.

"Whatever you do," Zrarr-Professor said, "Do *not* try to take your helmet off again."

"I doubt it would budge, even if I tried," Strather said. "Assuming we get back to the ship—*any* ship—we'll probably have to cut it off me. I almost want to say one of those things left its damned fingerprints in the metal."

Zrarr-Professor examined the human's collar. The metal was indeed compressed and twisted slightly. Not so much as to break the seal, but enough so that the latches would not come undone without tools.

"Your ruined suit may have saved you from a very different fate,"

Zrarr said, watching the 'Tec-Major eating the tuber. She promptly dug another one from inside the hydroponics pod—dirt flying off into the air—and started chomping on it.

"Should we stop her?" Strather asked.

"Does she look like she would let us if we tried?" Zrarr-Professor responded. "If I saw a Hero in such an orgasmic state of feasting, I would know better than to trifle—lest I lose a limb. If the 'Tec-Major has been exposed to something harmful, I'd say the damage is already done. And since she doesn't seem to be paying any attention to anything either of us is doing, I think it now falls to you and me to decide how best we can defend ourselves in this place. When the enemy eventually finds us."

Strather's helmet dipped forward on his shoulders, and he let out a long breath. Then he reached out a hand as if to touch Spalding on the shoulder. But he stopped short, at once visibly fascinated and repulsed by the trance-like look in the 'Tec-Major's eyes. Her throat made occasional grunting noises as she moved air past her larynx, in between grateful bites.

"She'll make herself sick," Strather said.

"Again, our defense—" Zrarr reminded, before stopping cold.

Someone else had joined them. Like the other aliens, this one was roughly hominid, and with a head that seemed too large for the frame, plus swollen joints. Even the knuckles, which were knobby and pronounced. But the eyes were man-like, and the mouth was a bony, flat beak. Rather than clothing, the creature wore a load-bearing vest of curiously custom manufacture, and featuring an array of strange tools. There was a kind of backpack attached, which appeared to be made from several metal bottles. The creature also wore a kind of helmet, and when the creature moved its head, the bottles on its back made a hissing sound, pushing the creature in the direction it was looking.

Within a few seconds, the creature was just meters from where Zrarr-Professor and Mantooth Strather huddled over a dazed, groggy Pryce Spalding.

Had Zrarr-Professor been a different kind of kzin, he'd have screamed and leaped.

Instead, he merely raised a gauntlet in salutation, then said in Interworld, "Well met . . . friend?"

🐾 CHAPTER 14 🐾

MANNY STARED AT THE ALIEN. It was obviously of the same species as the innumerable kind who'd been attacking the squad since their arrival at the other end of the travel tube. But this one was sapient. The eyes—and the attached gear—made that obvious. The thing regarded its visitors with an unreadable expression. How to make a face, when one's face is frozen by bone? Except the eyes. They told much. They were like the eyes of Manny's oldest living Greatly. Eyes which had seen many years.

When the alien did not respond to Zrarr-Professor, Manny tried the same greeting, also using Interworld.

When that didn't work, Manny realized they were stupidly trying to use words which probably made as much sense to the alien as the squiggles and lines on the side of the Bussard had made to Manny during their initial entry to the ship.

He was shocked, then, when the alien said—in as clear Interworld as the thing's snapping mouth could manage, "I understand you."

"You do?" Zrarr-Professor said, continuing to use Interworld.

"I have been examining your transmissions since you came to this star. Your ships went to a great deal of trouble to make themselves known. Even more so than we did, when we first came here."

"How do you understand us?" Manny asked, fascinated.

"I listen. And when I've listened enough, it becomes clear. I don't have to work at it. It just happens. That's what it means to be one of me."

"And what *are* you?" Zrarr-Professor asked. "A horde of your kind have killed all but myself, this human woman, and her human male companion."

"Those ones will not molest you here, in this place. They know I guard it."

The alien looked at Spalding, who had assumed a fetal position, her eyes half-closed and her arms limply suspended in front of her, like a praying mantis. Manny had to keep one hand on her ankle to keep her from floating away. She'd eaten no less than three and a half of the large, yellowish tubers, and taken a few bites out of the fourth, before finally giving up.

"That one will be stupid too," the alien said, pointing a knobby index finger in Pryce's direction.

"What's happened to her?" Manny demanded, becoming angry. "Tell me what's wrong!"

"The same thing that happened to all of us," the alien said.

"We don't understand," Zrarr-Professor said. "We are visitors to this star, and are interested in the technology which created both the ring that circles the sun, and this space dock, which appears to service the ring in some way. Are you—or was someone like you— the architect of both?"

"We pretended we were, once," the alien said. "But that was a lie we told to all the others on the Arch, many, many *phalans* ago."

That last word, *phalan,* was one Manny didn't know. Though he deduced its significance, based on context. As for the Arch . . .

"You're not from this star system," Manny said, trying to use his ARM skills to piece the puzzle together.

"*Nobody* is from this star system," the alien said. "It's a red dwarf. There was no organic life here when the true builders of the Arch arrived."

"And what is the Arch?" Zrarr-Professor asked.

"My original home," the alien said. "Very far from this place. Though not so far that our commander didn't become curious, when he detected the presence of the ring which has also drawn you to this red dwarf."

"You're a visitor too?" Manny asked.

"Yes, unfortunately. And if any of us had known better, we'd have steered clear. But the commander was curious. We never thought to discover anything so like the Arch in our travels from world to world. Our people cannot abide a mystery. So we investigated. The commander liked what he saw. We set about converting the space dock for our own use. The commander thought we might host future visitors. We worked for several *phalans*, and made ourselves comfortable."

"Obviously there's more to it than that," Manny said.

"Yes. We deduced that the space dock had at one time served as a manufacturing plant for *scrith*, though none of the complex machinery was working, nor was it comprehensible to us. To build the prototype Arch around this star surely required the conversion of every planet and substantial asteroid. It was deemed vital that we discover how this was possible. The commander made us keep exploring. Until we broke through into the lair of the sleeping old ones."

"What's going to happen to this woman?" Zrarr-Professor demanded, aiming a digit at Pryce.

"In time, she will look just like me," the alien said.

Manny felt his eyes grow wide.

"How is that possible?" he asked.

"There is something in the root which changes us. It will change her too. Except the root—or whatever's in it—has grown too far out of true. It was already growing too far out of true by the time our commander docked here, and our ship emptied out. Though we hadn't discovered any of this yet. Most of the old ones—who actually made this place—had already died. A few of them remained. And made war on my people, once we woke them from their stupor. Until the old ones were at last overwhelmed, and killed. At which point those of us who survived discovered the roots being farmed by the old ones. And as you can see, once exposed to the root's aroma . . . one's destiny becomes set in stone."

"What makes the difference between ending up like you," Manny asked, "and ending up like one of *them*."

"I discovered a place where one of the old ones had kept a small sample of the original root first brought from their home, near the core of this galaxy. The smell was as overwhelming for me as any fresh root's smell. I ate it. When I came to, I was like this. Emaciated down to the bone, of course. Because there had been nothing for me to keep eating once the transformation started. But things gradually became clear to me, over time. I understood much of what I was, and also what I used to be."

"Do you have a name?" Zrarr-Professor asked.

"Deszullanlullah," the alien replied.

Manny stared at the alien for several more seconds, then blurted, "Halrloprillalar."

"What?" the alien asked, visibly startled—despite its face.

"Halrloprillalar. She came to Earth. She must have been one of you!"

"That is a name I would recognize as being City Builder," the alien said. "Though we were mighty enough in our time to spread ourselves across the entirety of the Arch, and eventually, into the heavens beyond the Arch as well. I have not seen my home in so long, I have literally lost track of the *phalans*."

"Did the City Builders build this Arch you speak of?" Zrarr-Professor asked.

"Again, that is a lie we told the other dwellers of the Arch. But only a lie. The old ones, who built this place, the ring around the red dwarf, and also the Arch, were the true builders. I have discovered that some from the Arch have also become like me, though in ways I can't be sure of. This far from home, I only know what I can sieve from the faint radio broadcasts. Things are happening at home. I can only spectate, and guess."

Manny kept his hand on Pryce Spalding's ankle.

"Help her," he pleaded.

"I can't," the alien—Deszullanlullah—said sadly.

"Why not?"

"Whatever is in the root, it's now in her too. Only, it's the kind that makes you dumb. The survivors from my ship were made dumb in this way. Dumb, as well as long-lived. I'd have killed them all out of mercy, except when you become like me—and don't take that helmet off if you don't want to be eating roots right alongside your female—you are prevented from hurting your own kind."

"Prevented?" Zrarr-Professor said.

"Your species is foreign to me," Deszullanlullah said. "But you seem to be one who understands strong instincts. Are you not?"

"Yes," the kzin Hero said.

"Then know that there is an instinct in me which prevents me from murdering what's left of my people. Though, when one of them is stupid enough to challenge me—twisted out of true!—I can kill him. Or her. Gender doesn't much matter once you're like me. I thought myself beautiful, before the change. But things like personal vanity ceased to have meaning once the change was finished. I kept myself safe, found enough to eat and drink, and began to learn. Not everything, mind you. I am smart in certain ways, but not smart in all ways. If I had been a physician, and not a pleasure-maker for the ship's crew, I might have puzzled out why the fresh roots are bad. And how to reverse the damage, too. But I am not a physician, and I only got a little bit of the old root to begin with. Enough to change—and discover that it was *not* enough to change me to my full potential!"

Suddenly, Manny was remembering something he'd stumbled across in one of the old ARM files. There had been a man—a Belter—centuries ago. He'd supposedly made contact with the first-ever alien visitor to Sol system, and then disappeared. But not before meeting an ARM officer named Luke Garner, who'd left a description of the Belter in the classified mission report. That description floated to the top of Manny's consciousness now. And seemed eerily accurate, with Deszullanlullah floating directly in front of Manny.

"Detective-Major Spalding deserves better than to wind up lobotomized," Manny said, squeezing Pryce's ankle tightly.

"I am truly sorry," Deszullanlullah said. "If I knew how to reverse it, I would. But I don't. You will have to kill her now, before she becomes like the others."

"And why didn't you kill *us*," Zrarr-Professor asked. "If these 'old ones' made war on your people upon their arrival, does that not mean you would have been compelled to make war upon us in turn?"

"I've lived a very, very long time," Deszullanlullah said. "And the hatred for strangers is not in me, like with the old ones. Another consequence of eating too little root? I realize the situation on the Arch is changing, and can feel that it's time for me to die. I had assumed one of the stupid ones might eventually murder me. But your arrival makes things simpler. I know that you bring war with you. Already, two of your ships have crippled each other. The third smaller one is hiding from one of the cripples. And the largest—the round one—is constantly circling the other three, without engaging. I don't claim to understand the larger's tactics, any more than those used by the cripples. But if you have weapons, you have the means to end all of this."

Deszullanlullah spread her—his?—arms wide, and twirled once in the air, using the jet bottles on the backpack.

"We only came for the *scrith*," Manny said, feeling a hard, hot nugget of sorrow welling up inside his chest on Pryce Spalding's behalf.

"I know that word," Deszullanlullah said. "The Arch is made of it."

"And where *is* this Arch?" Zrarr-Professor asked.

"I can point you in the right direction, but only if you promise me that you'll fulfill my request."

"To kill you?" Manny said, somewhat incredulous.

"I cannot kill myself. Again, instinct."

"And what about this space dock? The artifact circling the red dwarf? *Scrith* is only good to us if we can figure out how to make more."

"How to make new scrith was always a top City Builder research priority. We never found out how. And the machinery in this place still makes no sense to me, even after many *phalans* attempting to puzzle it out. I think once they were done building this prototype Arch, some of the old ones took essential components of the scrith machinery with them, to make the bigger, actual Arch. It's a mystery which no longer matters, if I am guessing right about what it is you yourselves bring. Had my commander lived long enough to see your vessels, and their means for traveling—clearly beyond anything City Builders used—this too would have become a top research priority. Tell me, how is it that you have voyaged to this place in vessels so small? And with engines so different?"

"Do you know what a hyperspace shunt is?" Manny asked.

"No," Deszullanlullah said.

"Then it wouldn't do any good to explain, other than to say that the shunt—and its next level improvement—are why we can get here in so few . . . so few *phalans*, to use your word for the passage of time.

Our ships don't have to be big, because we don't spend all those *phalans* traveling. We had hoped to combine *scrith* and the hyperdrive, to greatly expand the scope of our domain."

"You, and this furry behemoth?" Deszullanlullah asked.

"Yes. We work together."

"Such a creature on the Arch would make for a fearsome opponent. Some of the City Builder legends spoke of discovering people very similar, on the Arch. Why is it that you and the beast cooperate, if the others of your kind—out in space, this very moment—do not?"

Manny stopped short. He had to think about it for a moment.

"Because I am a Wunderkzin," Zrarr-Professor stated plainly. "Or at least, I am the son of one."

Manny almost choked on his own tongue.

"Your father is from Wunderland?" he asked Zrarr, shocked, but also suddenly understanding why Zrarr was what he was.

"Yes," Zrarr said. "One of the nameless dispossessed, who sought to return to the Patriarchy before my birth."

"Why?" Manny asked.

"My father thought it very important that his children understand what it truly is to be Kzin. But he was also canny enough to understand what we kzinti are now, compared to what we were then—when Wunderland was first conquered in the name of Riit— are two different things. He therefore wanted to bring some of the Wunderkzin sensibility to the Patriarchy. He is not alone in this, either. Though he cannot speak his desires openly. *I* am my father's statement. He was never prouder than when I gained a partial name."

"I can only imagine," Manny said.

Deszullanlullah appeared to spectate this sidebar with interest.

"Such novelty. Unlike anything on the Arch. Were that my commander had found your people, instead of this place. I might have been happier. Lived a much shorter life, to be sure. But much more rewarding. Versus existing in this prison. I could not even attempt to relaunch our vessel, without helpers intelligent enough to assist me."

Manny looked around him.

"If all these roots are bad, and make people into aggressive idiots, why didn't you destroy the plants?"

"That would have starved both me, and my people. I was prevented."

"Instincts, again?" Manny guessed.

"Yes."

"And if I take my helmet off, I end up like her?"

"You will be compelled to consume, so yes," Deszullanlullah replied sadly.

"Zrarr-Professor," Manny said, thinking carefully, "we have to destroy these roots. And whatever that's in them, too. All of it. A microbe. A virus. It doesn't matter. It's too dangerous. The ARM schiz in me—thanks to my Greatly Jack—sees these roots, and thinks, 'Biological weapon!' Imagine the roots pulverized, and turned into an aerosol. Unleashed through the ventilation system of a ship. Or an asteroid."

"Or into the air of an entire human colony world," Zrarr said, finishing the terrible thought.

Deszullanlullah merely shrugged, spherical shoulders bobbing up and down. "Now you see it. So, what will you do?"

🐾 EPILOGUE 🐾

MANTOOTH STRATHER, Science-Inspector of the ARM, and Zrarr-Professor, Hero of the Patriarchy, stared out the observation window. It had taken them at least a week to properly identify the actual control room of the space dock, and another two days to understand the space dock's controls—with Deszullanlullah's help. During which time Manny had kept far away from anything that even seemed like one of the plants which had enthralled Spalding. The 'Tec-Major was still aboard the space dock, with its toroid-shaped attitude ramjets aimed directly toward the red dwarf, and thrusting at full power. Manny had been hardly able to look at her, before departing—her face beginning to deform, and her joints swelling, as if from intense arthritis. She was in the care of the old City Builder now, who'd elected to die. And allowed both Strather and his companion to escape in the process.

The lander on which they rode, with Pilot Primary and Pilot Secondary in command, had managed to pluck Manny and Zrarr both from the space dock's surface, before the thrust from the ramjets had achieved full effect. Now, the space dock was on a collision course for the sun. Manny had set the coordinates to take the space dock over the edge of the ring, and directly into the star. Where the true strength of *scrith* would meet a final, ultimate test.

Sfisst-Captain had been in contact. He was parlaying with the survivors aboard *Glaring Eye* and *Javelin* alike. Being the sole Legal Entity in possession of the Quantum II drive gave Sfisst tremendous bargaining power—since he'd dispatched the few humans aboard the #4 who'd tried to kill him in the moments following hostile contact between the scout squad and Deszullanlullah's misshapen kindred.

Detective-Captain Benitez would go up on charges. Whether or not Pryce Spalding was declared a casualty of the expedition, Benitez—and his co-conspirators—would have a lot to answer for once Manny got Benitez in front of Cedara Kellerman. Assuming Sfisst-Captain could get the 'Tec-Captain to surrender his command, such as it was. *Glaring Eye* and *Javelin* had mauled each other almost to the point of unserviceability. And Benitez was being stubborn, much as the kzinti aboard their own ship were also being stubborn. If either ship had been in better shape, it would have destroyed its counterpart. But as things stood, they had co-mutinied and then co-crippled one another, leaving Sfisst-Captain to sort the mess out while Pilot Primary and Pilot Secondary wisely kept their lander far from harm's way—obeying Sfisst alone.

Benitez and his kzin counterpart now had a choice: surrender to Sfisst-Captain, or be left to fend for themselves. Sfisst would be returning to Known Space, regardless.

"We'll be coming back this way," Manny said, watching the black rectangle of the space dock visibly recede toward the blazing inferno of the red dwarf.

"Not here," Zrarr-Professor corrected him. "Further."

Zrarr had aimed a claw just off of the corona of the red dwarf, to an otherwise unremarkable patch of black sky where Deszullanlullah's Arch was said to exist.

"She never did learn the secret of *scrith*," Manny said.

"If any Legal Entity holds it, we'll find it there," Zrarr insisted, keeping his claw aimed at the same patch of sky. "Meanwhile, we have to hope that Sfisst-Captain is persuasive enough to convince the survivors of this expedition to set aside arms."

"Or he could just pick us up, and leave both *Javelin* and *Glaring Eye* to finish their business?"

"Four kzinti and one human crammed into the Number Four hull? How would you bear it? Besides, Sfisst-Captain would merely drop you at the nearest human outpost, before returning us home, and the Quantum II drive too."

"That works fine for me," Manny said, feeling tired. "ARM crawled around inside that thing for months, and didn't come up with much. As pieces of advanced technology go, it's a one-off. Spectacularly capable, to be sure, but still a one-off. It may be that Known Space eventually unlocks Quantum II for general use. But that won't happen soon. So, if either the ARM or the Patriarchy intend additional expeditions to Deszullanlullah's Arch, they'll have to take the long way."

"Urrrr! By conventional hyperdrive, it would require a journey of years." Zrarr-Professor said.

"Yup," Manny agreed, nodding his head.

"Do you believe either government will actually invest the resources?"

"Once my boss gets my final report? ARM won't hesitate. And if the ARM won't hesitate, neither will the Patriarchy, nor any other interested party in Known Space."

"The fringe could get very dangerously complicated as a result," Zrarr speculated.

"Gotten complicated," Manny corrected his companion. "Past tense."

"Urrrr," Zrarr-Professor uttered, standing corrected.

🐾 The End 🐾